Starlit Promises
Dark Sky Valley 1

Sarah Cass

Contemporary Western Romance
Romantic Suspense
Small Town Romance

A Divine Roses Ink Book
Contemporary Western Romance
Romantic Suspense
Small Town Romance

Copyright © 2025 Sarah Cass

Cover design by Sarah Cass
All cover art and logo copyright © 2025 by Sarah Cass

PUBLISHER
Divine Roses Ink
http://www.divinerosesink.com

Books by Sarah Cass

Dark Sky Valley

Starlit Promises
Sweet Sunset Serenade (Coming 2026)
Catching Fireflies (Coming 2026)

The Dominion Falls Series

Independent Brake
Changing Tracks
Derailed
Dark Territory
Green Eye
Runaway Train
Home Signal
Red Zone
Chasing the Red
Blizzard Lights
Dead Man's Switch

Coming Soon in
The Dominion Falls Series

Bird Cage
A Highball Arrangement
Blood
Grave Digger
Bad Order

The Tribe Series
The Tribe
The Wolf
The Chief
The Raven

The Lake Point Series
Santa, Maybe
Deep-Fried Sweethearts
Stalled Independence
Witch Way
A Thorough Thanksgiving
Eve's New Year
Heartstrings & Hockey Pucks
Luck of the Cowgirl
Stars, Stripes & Motorbikes
Free Falling
Love for Hire
Haunted Hearts

Stand Alone Novels
Masked Hearts
Leap

Dedication

To the nurses.
To the healthcare workers.
To the survivors.

Content Warnings:

This is a story of survival. A nurse who faced violence against healthcare workers. A man who survived domestic violence as a child, and mentions of past sexual assault. These subjects can be painful for survivors still healing. Treat yourself with love and care. You know what you can handle.

Table of Contents

Prologue

Six Months Ago – Orlando, FL

Remington

"Why on earth are you running headlong into hell?"

I rolled my eyes at my best friend, Lexi's, dramatics. She'd been harping on me in person for days. Now on the phone while I was driving to work. "It's one night in the adult ER."

"On a full moon."

I chose to ignore the interruption, no matter how accurate. "It's not the apocalypse. You know I need the overtime and bonus pay. I have a wedding to plan."

"I still can't believe you said yes."

"To the shift or the man?"

"Yes."

"Alexis Mae Oleander. You're supposed to be my best friend." I parked my car in the lot, staring at the hospital across the street. "More than my best friend. You're the only family I've got."

"I know, I know. I'm sorry." Lex blew a raspberry into the phone. "I'll hold my tongue about Kyle 'I'm better than you' McMurtry."

"Lex."

"Starting now. Did you at least get the contract since you're picking up so many shifts?"

"I signed a six-week contract for one extra shift a week for two grand. That should cover my dress." I'd gone no-contact with my parents several years ago, which meant this whole wedding would be on me. I had a decent savings account, but I didn't want to blow the whole thing on the wedding.

The wedding required more money than I wanted to drain from my savings. That meant signing any bonus contract I could, and with the added perk of being a night-shifter, I was raking it in. I worked in the pediatric ER normally, and Lex was in the labor and delivery unit. Our working nights usually coincided, but with my extra shifts, we weren't seeing each other nearly as often.

"Well, at least you were smart about that."

"Lex, I'm going to marry him. Please get on board."

"You're too good for him, but I'll get on board." Lexi sighed. "You know I'm up all night anyway. Keep me posted on the crazy train."

"I always do. Say hi to Violet for me."

"I always do."

I shut off the engine to cut off the phone call and headed into work. As expected, the ER was in utter chaos. I barely had time to breathe between patients, much less text Lex. The only thing I was grateful for is that they didn't put me with the boarding patients, of which we had quite a few. I preferred the crazy busy to maintenance care.

The whole time, Lexi's continuous disdain of my engagement to Kyle rattled around in the back of my brain. The moment I sat down for a brief five-minute charting session, it rushed to the forefront. Probably because the man in question was just leaving the nurses' station to find, supposedly, more beds, we lacked the staff to cover.

Kyle and I'd been dating for several years, and on paper we made a good match. I loved him; I was pretty sure. Pretty sure? Yeah, Lex would have a field day with that.

A scream cut through my musings. I saw a flash of movement in the room just around the corner from the nurse's station. A large form blocked the door until another scream, then the glass door shattered. I flew to my feet, charging toward the room, the charge nurse hot on my heels while we both hollered for a Code Gray.

Three Months Later

A key rattled in the lock. There was only one other soul with the key to my apartment. I didn't have the strength to keep her out any longer.

My forehead gave a familiar tingle at my distress. I ran a finger along the healed wound at my hairline. The damn thing kept bothering me. Hell, the whole event had torn my life upside down. The nightmares alone had left me with less sleep than I'd had as a full-time nurse, working copious amounts of overtime. At least I no longer had to pay for a wedding.

"Remington Sage Collier. Get your butt out of bed." Lexi slammed the door behind her, probably disturbing every neighbor around me.

"I'm right here. There's no need to yell." I turned my attention back to the window. Off in the distance, I could see the sprays of light from the fireworks at the Magic Kingdom. I hadn't gone in weeks. I had done nothing for weeks.

"What are you doing to yourself?" Lexi sat across from me on the window seat. "You've been out of the hospital for over two months. You won't go back to work."

"I'm never going back." Every bit of joy from the career I'd loved with all my heart was gone in an instant.

"Rem." Her warm hands clasped mine. "Don't give up like that."

"Did you hear it?" My lip trembled at the mere mention. The authorities released the 911 call to the public. I hadn't known what it said, or even who made it, but given that Kyle had barely shown up for me in the hospital, the engagement was already over. The bonus of his shameful disregard for the injured lives in the ER, me included, was just the final humiliating nail in the coffin.

"We all did." Tears shimmered in her eyes. "It was horrible."

"Feel free to say you told me so."

"I wouldn't dare." At my pointed look, she shrugged. "Fine, I would. If you were even close to being human again."

I pulled my knees to my chest, resting my chin on them. There was no point arguing. She was right. So many thoughts had been running through my head for weeks. None of which I'd expressed aloud. Lex was my only family left, sisters by bond rather than blood. She deserved to know where my mind was. "There's nothing left for me here. Except you and Violet. I can't do it anymore, Lex. I can't walk back into a hospital. I can barely walk outside my door."

"Have you even tried?"

"Not so much." Truth was, I didn't need to. The hospital had given me a little nest egg to shut me up. There was only one detective doing anything for the case, and he'd come up with absolute bupkis. "Why would I?"

"Me. Violet. Disney?"

For the first time in ages, an actual small chuckle escaped. "That's a pretty sad life if that's my list. I don't even have a career anymore."

"Would a change of scenery help?"

"I don't see how." I closed my eyes against the renewed tears. "Where would I even go?"

"To my patron saint of lost causes."

"What?"

"Gigi. The woman who raised me, in the town that raised me. Dominion Falls."

Chapter 1

Present Day – Dominion Falls, CO

Colton

Mountains hazy with cloud cover served as the backdrop for our family's generational ranch. My dad kept the driveway well-maintained, but I always drove slowly on my way to the house to appreciate the view. If I'd had any interest in ranching or farming, my kid brother, West, would have had to fight me for the property.

As it stood, he was the only of us four kids that had any interest in running the ranch. He'd turned it into a horse rescue. Fitting, seeing as he'd been rescuing animals since the age of eight. Dad never once stopped him from schlepping home with any number of animals until our home became a virtual menagerie.

Now it was primarily a horse rescue, as proven by the horses dotting the land leading up to the house. I knew the barns behind the home housed rescued goats, ducks, and other animals from all over the state. I admired

West for his dedication. Having to keep track of all of those animals and having a life would break my brain.

It was hard enough having a five-year-old son and a life. Of course, my brothers would point out I didn't have much of a life. Work, Brody, and home. That was about the extent of it. I couldn't remember my last date, except that it had been a blind date that proved disastrous, and added to my conviction that I would never again let Gunner pick a date for me.

Despite my slow approach to the house, no one emerged to greet me when I parked my car. The moment I disembarked, a horse whinnied. Millie, the oldest horse at the rescue, rested her chin on the fence. Her brown eyes watched me move around the car toward her. She huffed, pricking her ears forward at my approach. At around twenty-two, there'd been no dimming of her spirit. I had to admit; she was my favorite rescue.

"Hey, old girl." I rubbed her nose before pressing my forehead to hers. "How're you doing? Are you keeping all those young bucks in line?"

She flapped her lips, snorting with one stomp for emphasis.

"I'll take that as a yes."

"Dad!" The voice of my favorite person in the entire world broke through my moment with Millie. "Dad, look what I found."

I turned to find Brody practically skipping toward me with an enormous cat in his arms. The cat didn't fight the rough treatment, but also didn't look impressed. Of the half a dozen wild whiskers usually kept in the barns to help with mice and snakes, this one was unfamiliar. "Brody, what's this? I don't recognize this one."

"I found her by the pond. Unc West says she's new. She's gonna have babies. See?" Brody lifted the cat higher, exposing her broad belly. "I named her Taffy."

It was just my luck that Brody had adopted West's tendency to find strays everywhere. We lived in town, where keeping animals wasn't exactly possible. I'm pretty sure that's all that kept Brody from bringing home every creature he found at the farm.

My dad emerged from behind the house. I gestured toward the cat in Brody's arms. "Another one, Dad? You should give up the horse rescue name with all the different strays you've taken in."

"Technically, the cat was already on our land. That means she was already ours." Dad enveloped me in a big hug, as he had my entire life. He'd never been one to scrimp on affection, and after he'd rescued us from our mother's, he'd increased the strength and frequency as if he knew we needed it even more than normal. "Besides, she's pregnant. There are too many predators out there that would endanger the little ones. Brody did her and her babies a favor by bringing them to the barn."

I brushed my hand over my son's hair, drawing him closer to my side. It was a surprise that the cat hadn't made one peep of complaint despite her sourpuss. "I swear you're encouraging him and West. Even as big as this ranch is, it'll run out of room if you don't stop."

"He is encouraging them. Always has. You know he has a hard time saying no to any of you." Our dad's common-law wife stepped around him to give me a hug. She'd been his best friend for years and had stepped in to help him raise us. The support and love she'd shown us, and him, had been lifesaving. We'd all been thrilled when they'd made their marriage public knowledge six years ago. "How is the Hangman's Inn today?"

"Busy. All rooms are full, not that we have a lot of them."

"It's a niche market; that's all it takes. Here, Brody. Let me take Taffy." Paige lifted the cat from his grip. The burgeoning mama cat curled into her arms comfortably. "That's what makes the hotel so popular. Well, that and the name. Not to mention the proprietor, who looks a lot like the original owner."

I scratched my chin to avoid the subject without being rude. Sixth-generation hotel ownership in Dominion Falls' old town presented occasional irksome challenges like this. I was on the receiving end of plenty of stares once patrons saw the portraits on the wall of the lobby/restaurant. I turned my attention to my son, determined to change the subject. "You ready to head home, buddy? I've got some chili in the slow cooker for dinner."

"Aw. You didn't get nothing from Turners?" Brody's shoulders sagged. The restaurant in my hotel, Turners, was famous for delicious meals authentic to the late 19th century time period, with a few modern twists. The recipes from the original owner had carried through the generations and followed faithfully. Brody was partial to meals from there, and I knew it. Still, it was a little insulting when he'd never turned his nose up at my dinners before.

"You love my chili."

"Yeah, I guess. I like Turner's cornbread more."

"Then it's a good thing I got some to go with our chili." I winked at my boy. His immediate and enthusiastic cheering had all of us chuckling. I nodded to my dad. "Thanks for watching him. Was he good today?"

"He is every day. You worry too much. You know we love having him here as often as we can. We miss having a house full of kids. It's a little quiet with just West and us." Dad's eyes carried the sadness of the years he'd lost with us after the divorce. It was a pain I knew he'd never let go of. Paige wrapped her arm around his waist. She knew it too.

I clamped my hand onto his shoulder. "Remember, it's a mark of how well *you* raised us to have us thriving. Besides, Gunner and I aren't farmers. Prairie only likes to ride the horses and hates the care and maintenance required to keep them. This was always going to be West's thing."

"Then you should visit more often. We love having Brody around, and you, of course."

"Love that I'm an afterthought." I hugged him and Paige tight. I knew none of us were an afterthought to them. They cared for all of us with the same intensity I had for Brody. That's what took them so long to confirm what we always knew, that they were married. They wanted to be sure we were mostly grown and agreed to it. "I'm working the evening shift tomorrow, so it's possible Brody can stay the night. Would you like that?"

"*Yes.*" Brody pumped a fist in the air. "Staying at PopPop's is the best."

"We always love to have him stay over." Paige hugged Brody. "He's a joy to have around any time we can."

"Boy, the three of you are just full of ego boosts today. Come on, Brody. Let's go home and get some grub." I swung him over my shoulder.

Brody giggled the entire way to the car. His hands pressed into my back as he called out goodbye to his grandparents. He was still waving when I set him in the booster seat. Immediately, he turned to get the box with the cornbread, squirming in his attempts to reach it. The minute I pulled up the seatbelts, he settled to let me buckle him in.

As always happened on the drive home, Brody jabbered on non-stop about every second of his day. How he'd fed the goats with West and hunted for lost eggs in the brush with Paige. Dad had even let him ride the small pony they were rehabbing at the rescue, which didn't surprise me. West was determined to make the pony usable for pony rides at a petting zoo he planned to make.

I thought Brody had completely exhausted every detail of his day by the time we hit our drive. He must have, because he poked his finger at the window. "Who's that, Dad? Who is it? What are they doing? Are they a new friend?"

"Who is who, Brody?"

"That lady with Miss Gigi."

Sure enough, an unfamiliar young woman stood in the driveway with our elderly neighbor. The newcomer's short hair was bright red, almost orange in the setting sunlight. It almost didn't seem real against her tanned skin. She was dainty, yet also toned and shapely. "I'm not sure. I can't say I've ever seen her before."

"I'm gonna say hi."

"No, you aren't. What do we say about strangers?"

"But, Dad." Brody rolled his eyes; although unseen, the action showed in his tone. "She's talking to Miss Gigi. That means she's not a stranger. Right? She's a friend's friend."

"I'm not into dissecting if that's true. We have dinner waiting for us. Now, come on." I undid his seatbelt. "I'll let you carry the cornbread into the house."

"Fine." Brody scooted out of the door as soon as I opened it.

We didn't make it to the door before Gigi called out to us. "Colt. Brody. Come and meet my granddaughter."

It was a good bet that calling this woman her granddaughter was a stretch. While the right age to be one, I'd never seen her in the pictures on Gigi's walls of her many children and grandchildren. Gigi had a tendency to take in stray people like West took in stray animals. Until she'd reached her seventies, she'd rarely been without one foster kid in the house. Amazingly, she kept in touch with every single one, no matter where they lived now.

Brody took Gigi's request as all the permission he needed to race over to the next driveway. I sighed and followed him to where he was already recounting his day once again. The stranger didn't seem at all bothered by the constant stream of consciousness erupting from Brody. Instead, she clung to his every word. Her fascination with my son sparked an instant liking, pulling my attention more onto her. She wore a sundress that clung to her curves in all the right ways. It was delicate enough that the skirt swayed in the light breeze running through the valley. The pattern drew my gaze until it settled on her breasts, which were perky and round.

I couldn't recall the last time I'd bothered to pay such attention to things, but suddenly my gaze was no better than a heat-seeking missile, focused on every detail of her body; from her toned legs to the little freckle above her right eyebrow.

When she lifted her gaze to me finally, stunning hazel eyes that leaned toward green took me in. She offered a shaky smile and a small nod. "Hello."

"Colt, I'd like you to meet Remington. She's going to be staying with me for a while." Gigi clasped Remington around the shoulders. "She's never been to the mountains before. Can you believe it?"

"Plenty of people have never seen the Rockies, Gigi. Hello, Remington. It's good to meet you." I extended my hand toward her. When she took it, I found it difficult to let go; just that small connection drew me closer. I even took a step. Her appearance of daintiness was deceiving. A fire burned in her eyes, making them greener. I swallowed against my suddenly dry throat. "I'm Colt Mitchell. This is my boy, Brody. How long are you planning on staying with Gigi?"

"As long as she needs to, dear." Gigi winked my way before turning her attention to Brody. "Is that cornbread from Turner's I smell?"

"Yup. Dad made chili. Want to come over? He always makes lots and lots. We eat it for weeks after."

"Brody. Remington just arrived." I realized I was still holding Remington's hand, though we'd stopped shaking several seconds ago. Did I let it go? Was it awkward now? I blinked away the confusing thoughts, releasing her hand. "I'm sure she'd like to rest after her trip."

"Nonsense. It's a good opportunity for Remington to become acquainted with her new neighbors. We'd be happy to join you." Gigi either didn't notice or didn't care that Remington appeared no more sure about this plan than I did.

"I wouldn't want to impose on your dinner plans." Remington's voice carried like silk floating through the air. It was low and sultry, drawing me in another step. "And you can call me Remi. Remington is a mouthful."

"I can handle a mouthful," I muttered moments before my brain caught up to my lips.

A smile curved Remi's berry-colored lips. I focused on them like a moth to a flame. My stupid brain spun off into fantasies of those lips on my skin. My cock hardened in response to the mental image of her lips wrapped around it.

Fuck me. Where had this sudden influx of libido come from?

The burning heat of her gaze ramped up, the green growing deeper until it almost eclipsed any brown. It was as if she knew exactly where my thoughts went. "I bet you can. I was speaking to Brody, though."

"Okay. Are you coming, Remi?" Brody, oblivious to the inappropriately lascivious looks I couldn't stop making toward Remi, grabbed her hand. He'd truly never met a stranger and took my momentary lapse in speech to drag Remi to the house. I had to grab the box of cornbread before it spilled from his arms. He didn't even blink at its loss. "Come on, Miss Gigi. Let's go eat."

"It seems it's dinnertime." I gestured for Gigi to join us. "I hope your new granddaughter likes chili and cornbread."

Chapter 2

Remington

I'd hoped to relax, settle in, and enjoy the gorgeous views I'd been admiring since driving over the mountains into the valley. After all, I'd pulled into Gigi's driveway all of ten minutes ago. My luggage still sat in my trunk. Gigi had been looking me over and doting on me as if I really was one of her grandchildren. Lexi had warned me it would be like that, but to help the adorable little boy next door to invite us to dinner with him and his unarguably hot dad? That wasn't on the itinerary for my first night in Dominion Falls.

Gigi's agreeing to take me in without question or payment was the biggest gift after my past year of hell. That was the only reason I let young Brody drag me to the house next door. It's the only reason I didn't argue being pushed into a chair at the table across from the six-foot Adonis, whose mere presence seemed to have tied my tongue when Gigi first introduced us.

All of those thoughts were incredibly inappropriate. He had a son, which meant there was likely a mother somewhere. He wasn't wearing a wedding ring, but what did that matter? Why the hell did I care, anyway? I came here to escape my life, not to drool over a neighbor.

Brody continued his constant stream of consciousness about school, his grandparent's farm that apparently was also a horse rescue, his sheriff uncle, and his aunt whose name was apparently Prairie.

"Brody," Cole interrupted his son. "I realize it's a rare occasion to have company we aren't related to, but maybe we can let our new neighbor breathe before you take her on a virtual tour of the entire town and its inhabitants."

"A what?" Brody scarfed down several bites of dinner, ignorant of the amused glances us adults shared. "I's just telling her stuff."

A low chuckle carried across the table. The sound was enough to raise goosebumps. How in the hell was it that this man's voice alone could get my motor revving? I swear my libido barely hummed, much less roared like it was now. It didn't matter. Even without a ring, there was no way this man could be single.

"Did Lexi tell you about New Town and Old Town?" Gigi brought the conversation to me while still talking about the town. This blessed woman had raised my best friend, and was the closest thing to family I had left. That's why I was here now. She'd saved my life, if not my soul.

"She did. I won't lie, that was a big draw to coming here." The idea of the Old Town running like a full Old West town intrigued me. "The Old Town runs like it did in the nineteenth century? Really?"

"We have modern plumbing and electricity." Colt tensed as if he were defensive about the question. "Although, to be honest, the plumbing installation for the town began in eighteen seventy-three."

"Really? I thought only big cities had plumbing then." In my younger years, I'd been obsessed with the Old West, its fashion, and the way life ran. I wouldn't ever want to live where baths were a weekly ritual and women wore layers of fabric and bone or steel, but it still fascinated me.

"The plumbing was installed thanks to a generous donation to the town by Colt's ancestor, a woman considered one of the founding families of Dominion Falls. Colt is the sixth-generation owner of The Hangman's Inn." Gigi smiled brightly, even as Colt rubbed his hand over his face. His tanned cheeks darkened into a bit of a ruddy blush. Intriguing that her mention of his ancestor would do that. "His family is a big part of Dominion Falls' legacy."

"That took all of two minutes," Colt mumbled.

"What, dear?" Gigi's brows rose in an attempt at innocence. I didn't believe it for one second. "You should be proud."

"I am. I have been. That doesn't mean it needs to be the first thing people need to learn about me, or any of the descendants of those families. Sorry." Colt winced a bit sheepishly at me. "Why don't we get back to the original topic, please? Old town."

"Definitely." I grabbed his subject happily. The turn Gigi had taken clearly upset him. I was curious why. We could answer that question later. For now, we were guests in his home, and I'd let him lead. "How is the town still the same?"

"It isn't entirely the same. The mining camp, later the town of Dominion Falls, flourished for years where it stood. When the highway cut through the mountains, it was north of here, where the Settlement was back then." Colt continued when he caught sight of my expression. "The Settlement was where most of the miners and their families lived. When the highway ended there instead of Old Town, the center of commerce shifted. As businesses made plans to move, the founding families bought the old buildings to help the shop owners move, suffering no financial loss just to stay in business."

I set down my spoon, thinking about all the buildings I'd seen scattered across the wide streets of the town a few miles south of where we were. "They did? All of them? How?"

"They were vastly wealthy."

"I guess so."

"It wasn't until the fifties that they had the idea of turning it into a living museum of sorts. Many of the buildings were retrofitted to fit the theme. The Hangman's Inn was open through all stages of the town, even when many other buildings were shut down. The name has always been a big draw. It fascinates most guests."

"Why wouldn't it? The Hangman's Inn is a curious name for a hotel." I wondered why it would have such a name, but did my best to hold my tongue. Something in Gigi's comments earlier had made him uncomfortable. I wasn't sure how much he wanted to reveal about his ancestors. He clearly didn't like being compared to them. "Is it like Williamsburg? I went there once, and everyone dressed up and played out scenes for the tourists, giving little mini lectures about life then."

"Yes, and no. We dress up in period-appropriate attire. The hotel still boasts a burlesque show several times a week. As a gaming town, my casino is open and runs with many of the same games from then, although we've added a few extras, like slot machines."

Gigi nodded. "We have some of the same things. The blacksmith still sees plenty of use with the ranches around here, but he also gives little lectures to tourists while he works at the livery. Several buildings stand as displays, with guides in each. Many of the stores have found ways to function both in the modern world and keeping with the old world. The biggest element that is purely acting are the ladies of a certain element."

"How interesting. It's really quite a mix." My spoon scraped the bowl, making me realize I'd finished the whole thing. I couldn't believe I'd been that hungry. Truth be told, I hadn't felt truly hungry in over six months. Before I could lose myself in thoughts of why, I forcibly put my focus back on the topic at hand. "What about the college?"

"Another of Colt's ancestors founded the college in the early twentieth century."

"Yes. My ancestor founded it intending to create a space where women could learn alongside men." Despite his previous aversion to talking about his ancestors, he warmed to the topic quickly. Instead of begrudging admittance, his features warmed with his pride. "The medical school quickly became highly sought after, particularly by women, especially with George Young Memorial working closely to provide hands-on learning. Today, it's still sought after, even though it's been intentionally kept smaller. That keeps the cost down. It's become one reason we can staff the town so well. The students get to play dress-up and earn money doing it."

"I'm gonna be the blacksmith." Brody had polished off his own bowl, and seemed to no longer want to leave the conversation to the adults. He wore a big grin and had cornbread crumbs on his cheeks. "Or maybe help Uncle West at the rescue."

"Rescue?" I looked back to Colt for an explanation. His gaze immediately shifted away, the ruddiness returning to his cheeks. Had he been staring at me when my attention was on Brody?

"Uncle West saves horses. Lots of horses. And goats, and ducks, and chicks, and—"

"He saves a lot of animals," Cole quietly interrupted.

"Yeah, he does." Brody squirmed in his seat. "I saved a mama cat today. Her name is Taffy. She's gonna have kitties soon."

His unbridled excitement had me grinning like a fool. I loved how children saw every moment with so much life and joy. I leaned my chin on my hand to give him my full attention. "Did you really save a mama cat?"

"I did. She was at the swimming hole under the dock." Brody took a big drink of milk. He smacked his lips, which were now shadowed with a white mustache. "PopPop says the babies will be here soon and I can have one."

Colt's head dropped. His low groan filled the brief silence after Brody's declaration. He had the air of a man sure he'd lost a battle that had only just begun. I bit back a grin at his consternation, keeping my focus on Brody. "Cats can be really fickle. You have to hope you get one that loves on you and likes snuggles, or they'll turn their nose up at you most of the time. They aren't like dogs, who are so generous with affection."

"Some of the cats at PopPops hiss at me." Brody opened his arms wide enough to encircle the table. "I just wants to hug them and give them kisses."

"Then you know what I mean." I tried to offer Colt a reassuring smile. Maybe the cat business wasn't a done deal.

Colt jumped to his feet. "Did you want more, Remi?"

"Yes, please. It's delicious. Thank you for letting Gigi invite us over."

"I did no such thing." Gigi dabbed her lips with a napkin as if she were totally innocent in the whole affair. If I hadn't been there myself, I would have thought she had planted the idea in Brody's head. "Brody invited us, like the sweet boy he is."

"You're the one who accepted the offer." I would have kicked Gigi under the table to enhance my point if I'd known her better. As it stood, she was the reason I'd been able to move within three months of having the idea. Now, I just had to figure out what to do with the rest of my life. My chosen career and former fiancé were both on the big mistakes list shadowing my life. I wasn't sure I could trust myself with any other life-changing decisions.

"What do you do, Remi?" Colt set another bowl in front of me and sat with his own fresh bowl. His full attention settled on me. Those icy blue eyes drew me in like a fish on a hook. Damn, this man probably had panties melting with one look. Likely knew it, too.

"I, um. Well." Words failed me. In the past, I'd always immediately and proudly say I was a nurse. Now I wasn't sure of much, but I knew I didn't want to go back bedside. "I guess that's what I need to figure out."

Gigi patted my hand consolingly. Her kind eyes sparkled with tears.

"You don't know?" Colt's brow furrowed. Having someone my age not to have a straightforward response had to be peculiar.

"I left my previous career recently, with no plans to go back. Now I need to figure out something else to do. I haven't done anything else since fast food in high school and bartending during college."

"Weren't you saying you needed a new bartender, dear?" Gigi pushed into the conversation with that weighted suggestion. "Perhaps Remi can help you out while she gets on her feet here."

"I, uh, yeah. I guess so." Colt's eyes widened at his own agreement. "I mean, you'd have to get fitted for some dresses to wear."

"Wait." My intention to assure him he didn't have to hire me just because Gigi suggested it disappeared at this bit of news. "I get to wear period clothing while bartending?"

"Yes."

"Oh, this is going to be awesome."

Chapter 3

Colton

Three days. That's how long it had been since Remington had arrived on our neighbor's doorstep. Three days of watching her interact with Brody when we were in the backyard. There was a natural charm about her that really shone when she talked to my son.

I still didn't know how this had happened, either. Remington sat on the other side of my desk, filling out her paperwork. I don't even remember performing any sort of interview or getting a resume, or even an application, for that matter. What the hell was I doing? For all I knew, this woman had stolen from her last employer, or worse, was hiding from the law. The mere fact that she was living at Gigi's told me she was running from something.

Gigi used the past few days to get Remi over to Tayte Schaffer's dress shop to get some dresses. Tayte was the designated designer for all period clothes, and she did most of the sewing herself. She'd come by the hotel yesterday to tell me how much she liked my new hire.

It was clear Remi couldn't wait to get into character. Filling out the paperwork alone had her dancing in her seat, humming a cheerful tune. Her slight movements drew my gaze to her form again. Today, her dress was a deep blue that moved like silk with every tiny wiggle of excitement. Her enthusiastic movements had caused the skirt's edge to slip along her thigh until indecent thoughts filled my mind. Like imagining what it would be like to have her move on top of me like that.

Fuck. What was my problem? I knew I'd been celibate a long time, but how did one woman flip my mind right back into randy teenager mode so quickly? No, that wasn't right. The dreams I'd been suffering through were far more erotic than my teenage imaginings had been.

Thankfully, Remi didn't seem to notice my distraction. Her eyes were bright when she lifted her head to hand over the paperwork. "Is that all you need?"

"Yeah." I cleared my throat at the weird crack in my voice. I shoved the dirty thoughts deep into the back of my mind as best I could. As long as it had been since I'd even considered a woman, my brain and dick had clearly missed it more than I realized. I focused on the matter at hand rather than confronting my thoughts. "Is Friday good to start?"

"Friday is perfect. It'll give me time to brush up on anything new that's come along since the last time I worked behind a bar. It's been at least seven years."

"I won't feed you to the wolves right off the bat. You'll be training with Byron for your first two weeks." Her lips twitched in an adorable little smirk. "What?"

"Sorry. Byron. As in Sully?" Her smile broadened. My face must have gone as blank as my brain. "Sorry. Dr. Quinn reference. Clearly, something I need to ask him."

"Oh, right. That was set in Colorado Springs, right?"

"Yeah. I grew up with it playing on repeat. My mom was obsessed. Anyway. I'll be training for two weeks. That's helpful."

"Yes." Once again, my mouth moved before my brain. "I could show you around. Thursday, I mean. Around the bar and casino. If you're free."

With one brow lifted, amusement danced in her eyes. I must sound like an idiot, unable to form complete sentences. "A tour on Thursday? I would like that. Your hotel is gorgeous."

"Thanks, but I can't take any of the credit."

Her bright laughter danced along my skin until I leaned forward to get closer. "Well, it's beautiful anyway."

Yup, I was an idiot. Did I not have a brain in my head? I exhaled. "Good. Then why don't we say eleven in the morning on Thursday?"

"That sounds perfect. It'll help me hit the ground running. Tayte has me picking up my dresses on Wednesday. Should I be wearing period dress on Thursday?" The eager squeak in her question made me want to say just to keep that bright smile on her face.

"I'm afraid it isn't necessary at eleven in the morning. The bar and casino aren't open yet." I didn't bother trying to keep my matching smile hidden. "Friday, though, I expect you to arrive in full costume. I'll have you start at four while business is still a little slow. Things usually pick up at seven, with the burlesque starting at eight."

"The burlesque is in the bar, then?" Not knowing that detail proved I definitely needed to give her a proper tour. She resumed her excited wiggles. "I'll get to see the burlesque while I'm working?"

"The bar, casino, and stage are all in the same area. I'd prefer you actually work and serve drinks instead of staring at the stage." My attempt to be stern and boss-like was useless under the barrage of her excitement at every bit of new information she learned about the hotel. I grinned despite myself at her attempt to appear reticent.

"Sorry. I'm a little over the top, aren't I? I've been fascinated with the period my entire life. I can't wait to learn more about what it was really like. Next week, I plan to take a day or two to visit all the exhibits."

"Jane Doe's journals would be a great place to start if you want to learn what it was really like here in the past." I'd never in my life recommended the journals to a soul. Hell, I'd never considered showing anyone the originals, but Remi's excitement had me wanting to give her just about anything. "The library has multiple copies of the abridged version. Jane had an eidetic memory and recorded everything of the town's history from the time she arrived here in eighteen seventy-one."

"Really? Then I'll have to make the library my next stop. Thanks for the tip." She tugged the edge of her skirt back down, much to my disappointment. "Wait. Did you say Jane Doe? Why is her name anonymous?"

"Her full name became Jane Spencer Mitchell. When she first arrived in Dominion Falls, no one knew who she was, including herself." Warmth bloomed through me every time her eyes lit up with each bit of information

I offered. Now I really wanted to give her the full journals. They were fragile and locked away, so I probably wouldn't. Not right then, anyway. "If you come at ten on Thursday, I can give you a full tour, including the apartment where the Mitchell's lived from the time they rebuilt this hotel along with their numerous kids."

"I would *love* that." She uncrossed her legs, braced to rise. "I'll be here with bells on. Thanks so much. Was there anything else for today? I'd like to head straight to the library."

"No, nothing else here. I'll file all the paperwork and let Byron know to expect you on Friday afternoon." I walked her to the door to be polite, not to get close to her one more time today. Wasn't I just pathetic?

Remi pulled open the door, only to jump back with a squeak. She crashed right into me. It didn't take long to figure out why. My twin, Gunner, stood on the other side of the door; hand raised to knock. I had only a moment to enjoy the way Remi's body pressed against me before she spun around to face me, then my brother again. "Twins? Seriously? There's two of you?"

"I assure you, we're very different." Gunner offered Remi his most charming smile, the one he used to bed half the women visiting our town. Never had it made me want to punch it off his face like I did now. "I'm Gunner Mitchell. Sheriff."

Remi's eyes rolled in my direction. Her brow raised as she mouthed, 'Seriously?'

I chuckled with relief that Gunner's charms did not flatter her. Rivalry with my twin had always resulted in defeat for me. He's the one who had received all the cad energy of our brothel-owning ancestor. "Remi, I apologize for my brother. He likes to believe he's god's gift to women. Of course, they usually prove him right."

"Hm. Well. Personality does count for a lot, and a charming smile comes up rather, um, short." She pinched her fingers together, so they were barely a centimeter apart. "You know, overcompensation and all."

Gunner's jaw literally dropped. Not once had his charms not at least made a woman smile back. It must have been a gift that I'd met her first.

"If you'll excuse me, Sheriff. I need to go get a library card." She set her hand on my arm. "Thank you again. I look forward to Thursday."

Gunner recovered himself, stepping aside with an eloquent sweep of his arm. "Whatever the lady wishes. Good to meet you, Remi."

Her hum of acknowledgment was her only response on her way past. I couldn't avert my eyes from her departure. The dress curved around the swell of her ass, swaying enough to reveal even more of her leg than the short length covered.

Gunner didn't miss my attention to her departure. "She's a hell of a looker, I'll give you that. Where'd she come from?"

"Gigi took her in. No idea where she came from, but she's going to bartend here for a while to fill the hole from Lenore leaving. She plans to stick around for a while, which means she's not your usual type of companion."

"I get it, I get it. Hands off the merchandise."

"She's not merchandise. None of them are."

"Well, to be fair, there are *some*, but those are illegal."

"God, you're such an ass sometimes." I flopped into my seat, doing my best to ignore his laughter while I regained my equilibrium. For a few seconds, Remi's body had been flush against mine. Her round little ass pressed against me firm enough, I was afraid she'd sense my cock's reaction to the brief connection between us.

"Wow. You haven't heard a word I've said." Gunner's voice breached my meandering thoughts. He dropped into the seat Remi had vacated, propping his feet on my desk. That damn smug smile broadened. "Wait a minute. You're actually interested in her, aren't you?"

"What are you talking about?" I did my best to avoid Gunner's scrutiny. My twin had an uncanny knack of knowing what I was thinking, so he could tease me relentlessly about it.

"You really are. Huh. Never thought I'd see that again."

"See what?" I was afraid of the answer. I also wanted to know what he meant.

"You've been so focused on Brody for the past five years, you haven't so much as looked at a woman. Even those who were obviously interested. You really like this girl."

"I barely know her."

"Eh. Who cares? Sometimes the heart, or body, wants what it wants." Gunner's teasing smile flew away, replaced with an earnestness that made me uncomfortable. "You've put everything on hold to be there for Brody. You're allowed to have a life, Colt. Brody would only benefit from seeing you happy."

"Brody doesn't need to be confused by women coming in and out of my life the way they do yours. I'm not interested in a dalliance."

"Who said it had to be a dalliance?" Gunner's feet dropped to the floor as he leaned forward. "You don't have to be celibate because you have a son, you know. He's almost six. He can handle your dating. We handled worse at his age."

"Don't remind me." I blew out a gust of frustration. The conversation had turned far too serious. I didn't want to think about it. Not the past. Not dating. I shouldn't. Even though I had been dreaming of that since I first spotted Remi, I didn't need to act on it. I flipped the conversation back to Gunner. "What did you come here for? I know it wasn't to act the big brother."

"Ten minutes is ten minutes." The ass loved to remind me he'd arrived before me.

"It was six minutes."

"I rounded up." Gunner's grin broke, bringing him right back to his usual self. "Paige sent me to invite you to dinner. She wants to plan Brody's sixth birthday party. Can you get a sitter for Brody tomorrow night?"

"Brody will kill me if I go to the ranch without him, you know."

"You could bring your new friend. Tell Brody you have a date."

"Get out of here, Gunner. I'll call Paige myself and discuss the matter. The last thing I need is your brand of help."

"Fine. Call her yourself. It doesn't change the fact that you need a life. I'm serious, Colton. It won't kill you or Brody for you to date. You deserve happiness. We all do."

The scary thing was I knew he was dead serious. This wasn't a joke to him. I shook my head rather than answer. "Don't you have work to do?"

"Ah. The old brush off. I'll take the hint. Think about it, baby brother."

"Get out of here."

Chapter 4

Remington

When I'd gone to the library yesterday on Colt's recommendation, I hadn't expected to learn there were so many journals. There was actually an online challenge within the library to read them all. I couldn't imagine how, but having read the first eye-opening entries, I was hooked.

More, Colt's suggestion to read them honored me. Based on our limited interactions, I knew it bothered him to be compared to his ancestor. While at The Hangman's Inn, I'd taken a peek at the pictures hanging in the lobby. Gigi hadn't been wrong. Colt bore a strong resemblance to the Cole Mitchell mentioned within the first few entries of Jane's diaries.

"I thought you were going shopping, dear." Gigi carried a pitcher of lemonade to refill my drink. "You've been complaining about the chilly nights."

"I know, but these are fascinating. I've already read three of them. At this point, I might need to register for the online challenge." The tart lemon hit my tongue with the right amount of sweet to make it delicious. "Mmm. You make the best lemonade, Gigi."

"I appreciate the compliment, but lemonade and books won't get you sweaters and coats to wear on the cool nights."

"No, but this will." I wagged my phone in the air. The night before, I'd spent hours poring over the local store's website to find items I'd like.

"Oh, dear. You didn't order from one of those big online stores, did you?"

"No, ma'am. It turns out Jones' Junk Drawer has a website. You weren't kidding about the mix of worlds in Old Town. It's a mercantile with a website and some modern offerings." The website had been impressive. Most of the ones I'd stumbled on in the town were. "I found a few sweaters, a couple pairs of jeans, and a coat that will go well with my period dress and everyday wear."

"Well, I suppose that's alright. We do like to support our people here." Gigi picked up a journal. "Where did you hear about these?"

"Colt told me yesterday. I think I was annoying him with all my questions, so he sent me to the library to get me out of his hair." I fanned my face to dissuade the rising heat from Gigi's assessing stare. Lex had warned me that Gigi could detect a lie from a mile away. "Plus, his brother came by, interrupting my stream of babble. I didn't know he had a twin."

"Yes, twins run in the family. The Young and Mitchell lines are riddled with them. You need to be careful. It's easy to find yourself talking to the wrong one."

"I don't think there's a chance in hell I could mistake Gunner for Colt." This time, the tingling in my cheeks hit a fever pitch. I'd never admit it was because I found Colt and his personality far more attractive than his conceited jerk of a brother. Colt was humbler, and the way he was with his son warmed my heart.

"Is that so?"

"There is far more to a person than appearance. Things that you can't erase from your eyes or your face." I flipped another page for an excuse to keep my eyes averted from Gigi's. It was probably best to change the subject. "I don't think I thanked you."

"You've thanked me several times. I told you I enjoy having company. The house gets far too quiet otherwise."

"Not for taking me in, although that is wonderful in itself, but for not mentioning my previous occupation at dinner earlier this week." Having such a thing brought up within ten minutes of arriving in town would have soured the experience for me.

"It's not my place to air your laundry. Although I still stand by my belief that you'd find things different at George Young Memorial."

"The town might be different and amazing in ways I couldn't have guessed, but hospital politics are a whole different beast."

"If you say so."

"I like it here. Between the views and the two different towns, I feel like I've stumbled into a Hallmark movie. I really think I'll enjoy working at the casino. Returning to bedside nursing isn't something I'm ready to consider right now." I rubbed my finger across the scar at my temple. The damn thing always itched when I had a passing thought of my nursing career. "Besides, there are crazy people everywhere. Apparently, it always has been."

Gigi eyed the journal I waved in the air. "Of course there are and always have been. Wait, does that mean you got to the part about Linus?"

"Jane describes him as the town idiot? She says she'd seen him carrying around a rotten orange all day like it was a baby? Is that really real?"

"Yes, there are other accounts of Linus in town documents, even old newspaper articles." Gigi laughed brightly. "That part always makes me laugh. Well, what time do you need to head into town to pick up your clothes?"

"I set pick up for four. I thought I'd try the outdoor café for dinner."

"Not Turner's? It's in the hotel. You could get to know the people you'll be working with better there."

I held my breath for several seconds to hold back any embarrassment at having my attraction to her neighbor pegged. I released the breath, nice and slow. "On Thursday, I'll be having orientation and a tour of the hotel. I thought I'd try Turner's then. I'm a little nervous for both of them. Their menus appear not to have been updated since the nineteenth century."

"They haven't. It's all part of the atmosphere. I wouldn't worry too much. Food preparation has come a long way in the past hundred and fifty years. So have seasonings. You'll be fine. If you're going to the café, I'd suggest the stew. This time of year it's fresh beef instead of venison, although it's delicious either way."

"Thank you for the tip." I shooed her off. "Now leave me to these books. I'd like to exchange at least two while I'm in town, and I need to finish this one to do that."

"You're a fast reader."

"When the material is this interesting, I am." Within moments I got lost in the eighteen hundreds Colorado. Even though they were diary entries instead of a novel, Jane had a lyrical quality to her writing that I found easy to read. The stories of the people and the politics in the growing town were fascinating.

Laughter pulled me out of the deep dive into the history of the beautiful town I'd found myself in. Before I found the source, the mountains in the distance distracted me. Wisps of clouds floated over them against a perfect blue sky. For the past few nights, I'd sat on this deck for no reason except to stare at the night sky filled with more stars than I'd ever seen.

My whole life I'd been sure I was a beach girl through and through. After less than a week in this valley, everything was different. Who'd have guessed I would be a mountain girl? While I hadn't been able to get involved in town life, focused as I was on just settling in away from my previous life, I had a feeling my life here could be amazing.

Another round of laughter pulled me from my musings. The source turned out to be the backyard next door. My gaze immediately fell on my new neighbor, whom I recognized even with his back to me.

He reached back, tossing a football to another man across the yard. My libido sprang to life as I perused Colt's bare skin. Neither of the men was wearing a shirt, but Colt stole every bit of my attention. The way his muscles flexed and stretched every time he threw or caught the football had me aching and wet in all the right places. I squeezed my thighs together, sinking lower to keep my imagination and libido from making the situation worse. I could use it later alone in my room with a good vibrator, but right now I didn't need to be blatantly staring and enjoying the show.

Damn, I was in trouble with this man. I couldn't recall a time I'd been so attracted to someone. It was stupid to work for him. I had to distract myself from his back and the dirty thoughts it was causing. I forced my gaze onto his companion. The stranger's features were reminiscent of Colt in a way, though his hair was a rich brown, and he seemed to be several inches shorter. Several years younger, too.

I did my best to bury my nose back in the book. To focus back on Jane and her current frustration with Martha. Try as I might, I kept casting glances at the next yard. Colt and the stranger laughed and joked back and forth easily. Each throw of the ball increased in strength and difficulty until Colt had to jump to catch a throw.

My phone lit up beside me. Worse, the ridiculously loud strains of the song *My Humps* blared from the device. The book tumbled to the deck and, in my mad grasp for the phone to shut the damn thing off, it flew off the table, skidding across the deck.

Face on fire, I chased after it in the undignified position of my hands and knees. I glared at the name on my screen before answering. "Seriously, Lex? Did you change the set ringtone for you before I left Florida?"

"Of course I did. Why do you think I've only video called so far? I wanted to wait and surprise you with it at the right time." Lexi might be my best friend, and the only family I had, but at that moment I could have smacked the laughter right out of her. The wicked creature was enjoying this far too much. I could only imagine what she'd say if she knew what she'd interrupted me doing. I'd never hear the end of it for ogling Colt.

"What if I'd been in a job interview? Or worse, in public?"

"You already have a job, so that wouldn't have happened. If you had been in public, I would've laughed *so* hard."

"You are laughing." I dared a peek next door. Both men were watching me, still on my fucking hands and knees. The younger one was grinning broadly. "Dear Lord."

"What?" Lexi was a bloodhound for gossip. She could sense it from over a thousand miles away, apparently.

"Nothing. Nothing. What did you need?"

"Suddenly I need a reason to call you?"

"Of course you don't." I collapsed onto my lounger. "Sorry. I'm distracted."

"It's fine. Now tell me the truth. How are you doing? Really?" Lex's laughter faded easily as that. Warm concern filled her tone, bringing me to tears so easily. The level of concern always coincided with any mention of the end of my career and all the pain that came with it.

"I'm fine." I doubted she'd accept it easily.

"Nightmares?" Nope. She was going to push.

"A few. I'm not complaining. They've given me a few wonderful opportunities to come outside on the deck and see the sky in the middle of the night."

Lexi's sigh carried across the miles. "It's been six months, Rems. You aren't coping. No, you're coping. You aren't healing. Don't you think you should get some help? Therapy, maybe?"

"It's only been six months, Lex." Talk of therapy killed any rising libido, or desire to check out my neighbor again. I grabbed the journal from the deck, checking for damage. Thankfully, there didn't seem to be any. "Why didn't you tell me about this Jane Doe person?"

"We're changing the subject. Avoidance. Remi, girl. Come on. Talk to me. You were injured doing what you love."

"I wasn't the only one. I'm fine. I'm alive."

"Rem."

"No, really. You could find a heartbeat and everything. I'm alive." I pressed my fingers against the outside of my eyes, trying to stem a headache threatening to erupt thanks to the line of questioning. "Honestly?"

"Obvi."

"Being here has helped. The atmosphere is so unique. The history of this place is so amazingly rich. There are so many things you never told me about. I'm able to relax much better until my phone blares *My Humps* at inappropriate times."

"What was so inappropriate about this time?" Her voice thinned almost maniacally sly. I could hear the wicked grin in her voice. "What were you doing?"

"I can't tell you right now." Out of the corner of my eye, I could see that both men sat on Colt's deck. Colt now faced me. My skin tingled from the intensity of his stare.

"Now I *have* to know. It sounds juicy."

"Let's just say I was enjoying the local scenery," I muttered under my breath. All the while, I hoped to whatever gods listened I wouldn't be overheard.

"What scenery is that?"

"Lex."

"Is it your new boss?"

I closed my eyes to contain the exasperation. It escaped as a near-whine, anyway.

"It is! Seriously? I can't say I blame you one bit. He and Gunner have always been a pretty pair. Colt was always the more reserved one, hence why Gunner and I were best friends."

"So you agree that you're both annoying jerkfaces?"

"Well, I never. I'd have to say, though. You probably have a better chance with Gunner."

I wrinkled my nose. "No, thank you. Not interested. Unlike you, I find his personality off-putting. That smarmy charm."

"Ah, you have met our sheriff."

"I met him for all of thirty seconds. It was more than enough."

"To be fair, he's usually only a slut around the visitors."

"That's so reassuring."

"He's a good cop, and a decent guy. I promise."

"If you say so." I peeked toward Colt again. He raised his bottle in greeting. I turned away before the other man could turn around. "That really doesn't change my opinion of him. I prefer Colt."

"You do, do you?"

"Yes, way too much."

"Oh, girl. You are in trouble."

"Don't I know it?"

Chapter 5

Colton

West was saying something. Despite that, I couldn't pay him much attention. Ever since Remi's phone had blared loud enough to make West miss his catch, I'd been distracted. She'd been ass-up scrambling for her phone. It was a sight to behold. Even now, she kept sneaking peeks over here.

After a few minutes of talking to dead air, West tapped his beer bottle on the table. He even went the extra step of kicking my shin.

"Ow. Fuck, man. What?"

West quirked a brow. "Just what are you staring at? Why is it making you ignore everything I say?"

"I'm not staring." Yeah, it was a complete and total lie. I was staring. I had been this whole time. "Shut up."

"The girl?" West, who'd never had one ounce of shame, spun in his seat to get a real good look. He lifted his arm and waved wildly, even though Remi was still on the phone. "Hi there!"

Had he been within reach, I would have given the snot a whack upside the head. Then again, I couldn't complain when the delicious sight of Remi's blush creeping along her cheeks was the reward for his obnoxiousness. When her gaze cut to me, I merely shrugged. Honestly, I didn't have any control over my brother. We'd all spoiled him rotten. "Leave her alone. She's on the phone."

"Hey, she's the one who's been staring at you since we started playing."

"She has not." Had she? Could it be that I wasn't the only lecherous pig in this situation?

"Don't believe me. It's fine." He hopped out of his chair the second Remi set her phone down. "Hiya. I'm West, Colt's brother. It's great to meet you."

Remi crossed the yard, the pink light of a blush lingering. "Nice to meet you. Another brother? Just how big is your family?"

"Another? You met Gunner? Bet." West grinned broadly at Remi. I didn't miss him giving her the once-over before holding her gaze. Remi hadn't missed it either, if the deepening shades of red were any indication. "Then all that's left is me and our sister, Prairie. Oh, and Dad and Paige, of course."

"I'm Remington. You can call me Remi, though."

"Remington? Seriously?"

"Yeah." Her brows knit together. "Why?"

"Really? You're Remington. He's Colt, and his twin is Gunner? That's hilarious."

"Yeah, yeah. We're all guns. It's hilarious." I stepped into line beside my brother. It was truly impressive that I held back the urge to smack him. "I'm really sorry about him. He's a brat, always has been. Doesn't know when to shut up sometimes, really."

West protested when I ruffled his hair, making the curls stick out at all angles. In his eyes, one of the worst punishments. "Hey now. Hands off the goods."

Remi's laughter danced over me, but that didn't set me on fire as much as the heated gaze she ran over my bare chest before ducking her head. Maybe West had been right, and she'd been watching us play. I could have sworn she'd had her nose buried in a book when we'd come outside. "Sorry we disturbed your reading."

"No, not at all. You guys tossing a ball didn't disturb me at all. It was Lexi and her rotten ass changing her ringtone on my phone."

"You've been here four days and you're just now learning this?" I couldn't imagine she hadn't talked to Lexi yet, seeing as she'd been the one to send Remi to Gigi's door.

"Either I've called her, or she's video-chatted with me. This was her personal ringtone, so it only made itself known when she called." She rolled her eyes. "I'm relieved it happened here at home rather than when I was out in public."

"That's fire. I always knew I liked Lexi best." West's hand slapped across my chest. He hopped excitedly. "Hey, big bro. Where's your phone?"

"If you think I'm going to be stupid enough to give you access to my phone now, you're an idiot. Besides, wouldn't it be funnier to do something like that to Gunner? Then you could call him when you know he's at work." I actually thought it was a great idea, though I'd deny suggesting it when it came down to it.

"Oh, my God. You wouldn't?" Remi's features lit up with wicked delight. Clearly, she liked the idea of embarrassing Gunner as much as I did. "You should make it something really embarrassing, West. Like—oh, I don't know. *Fat Bottom Girls* or *Baby Got Back*."

"Or maybe even *I Wanna Sex You Up* could work, too." Their excitement had added to my enthusiasm over the idea.

Remi's eyes widened when West took off like a shot. He grabbed his shirt and ran through my back door without so much as a bye or leave. "Goodness gracious, I didn't think he'd literally take the idea and run with it."

"That's West for you. Acts first, thinks later. Except when it comes to his horses. The only time he acts without thinking is in rescuing them. He's very serious about their care and rehabilitation."

"He seems like a good guy, even if he can be a bit of a troublemaker."

"Yeah. He's a spoiled brat. We have no one to blame but ourselves for that." Behind her, I saw a stack of books on the table. "I take it you've been reading the diaries?"

"I have. They're impossible to put down. You said these are the abridged versions?"

"Some passages in the original are really graphic in their description of violence and its consequences. Not to mention incredibly explicit about sexual interludes." Her renewed blush drew me in like a moth to a flame. I wanted to find out what made this woman tick. Screw making her tick, I wanted to wipe that blush away and replace it with the flush of sexual pleasure. I wanted to be as explicit as the journals with Remi. "Jane and Cole were very enthusiastic about sex. Jane was very open about it. She even publicly encouraged women not to be ashamed of the act, and to demand what they wanted so they could see it as more than a duty."

"How progressive of her." She moved closer as well. Her hazel eyes snagged on mine, the green in them darkening as she drew nearer. "I know women weren't actually complete prudes, but they often acted like it in public for fear of being seen as immoral. Jane didn't appear to care about such things."

"No, she didn't." My skin tingled as her gaze drifted to my chest. Her fingers twitched as if to move. I drew my hand toward hers. Her phone chimed several times, startling us both.

"Oh, damn it. That's my alarm." She rushed back to her phone, sliding her finger across the screen to silence it. "I need to go to Jones'. There's an order that I need to pick up, so I have some warm clothes to wear in the evenings. I'd planned to go to the outdoor café to try the food there."

"Would you like company?" The words were out before I fully realized I would say them.

Her head popped up from her focus on re-stacking the books. "Really? Are you sure you don't mind? What about Brody?"

"It's no problem. Brody's staying with my parents tonight. He wants to take care of his mama cat as much as he can." I turned my attention to the shorts she'd worn today. While I more than appreciated the way they exposed her legs and clung to her ass, around here the sun set quickly, which led to some chilly nights. "Maybe you should change."

Her lips twitched before curving into a coy smile. "Is that so? Maybe *you* should put on a shirt. Unless your goal is to have all the women in town drooling over you. More than they already do, I mean."

"Right." I narrowed my eyes. Her surety that women were attracted to me sparked a brief glimmer of hope in my chest. Perhaps it was because she did as well. "Why are you so sure they already do?"

She gestured in a broad circle, using her whole arm. "All of that. And the fact your brother thinks he's god's gift to women. If they fawn over him, they fawn over you."

"Fair enough."

"Give me ten minutes. I need to get these away and put on some jeans. Your car or mine?"

"Mine. I'll see you in ten." My stomach did a little flip when she gathered the books in her arms. Was this a date? Were we going on a date? I hadn't been on a date in a few years. Even longer if I only thought about the dates I wanted to be on.

The door closed behind Remi. She needed ten minutes, not just time to slip on some jeans.

"Well, shit. I've got a date."

Did I? We hadn't expressly said it.

"I think."

Chapter 6

Remington

The main thoroughfare stretched before me. People in a mix of modern and period clothing wandered the street along with horses and wagons. I could imagine this was a lot what it looked like when Jane stood on the porch of the mercantile as I did now.

The Hangman's Inn at the opposite end of First Avenue was three stories tall and covered in brick now, unlike the two story wood slat brothel it was at the point of where I'd stopped reading half an hour ago. The Silver Saddle's described location is now occupied by the town's clinic, which had been named for the doctoring whore Jane mentioned as her doctor, and Cole's favorite whore. As the website described it, the Daisy Pearson clinic was both a museum and a functioning clinic. They treated minor injuries with a combination of modern Western medicine and some age-old traditional remedies.

There was so much to unpack about the town laid out before me, which was smaller when Jane first arrived. Back then, vendors had lined the streets with their carts. Now, all the businesses she mentioned in the early journals had shops of their own.

I hazarded a glance down Miner's Row to see if Colt was on his way back yet. He'd offered to take my purchases to his car so I wouldn't have to carry them around all evening. I'd been too afraid to ask him if this was a date. It had the air of one, but it was hard to tell when all we'd done was drive to town and pick up my new clothes.

My phone buzzed in my purse. The number was unfamiliar, but I recognized the area code as Orlando's. I didn't care what it was at that point. I slid my finger across the screen to ignore the call.

It immediately rang again. Annoyed now, I ignored the call. If they tried again, I'd block the number. The only person back there I wanted to talk to was Lex.

My phone pinged, but this time it was a text. The same number, though. My finger hovered over the block button, but the first few words caught my attention.

> **Unknown**: Ms. Collier. This is Detective Winder. I've been trying to contact you. It's important we meet. Some new information has come to light. Can you come to the station?

My heart stuttered to a stop at the mention of new information. Pressure built in my head, and my scar tingled again. I scratched at it, debating my response.

No. I'd left Florida to get away from it all. I didn't care anymore. All of them had failed me. The hospital, the police, all of them. It no longer mattered. I shoved the phone in my purse, but didn't block the number. Although I probably should have, I chose not to think about it further.

I took a deep breath, reveling in the crisp air tinged with just a hint of horseshit. Well, not exactly romantic, but it was at least authentic.

With a roll of my shoulders, I pushed the text to the back of my mind. I'd need to find something else to focus on. Colt wasn't a bad idea for a distraction. While I might have taken a couple of minutes to do some minimal makeup, he'd worn a nice shirt and jeans that hugged his spectacular ass. I'd been enamored by it when he walked away with my packages.

Yeah. I was as good as gone. Lex would have a field day when I told her about my inability to stop staring at Colt's ass. What would really get her, though, was that I didn't have a clue if this was a date. There'd been a definite tension in the air on our drive the few miles to the parking lot for old town. Or then again, maybe I'd been imagining it.

I shook my head against the spiral my thoughts were on. I muttered to myself, "Just enjoy tonight. Maybe you'll have it figured out by the time you get home. Maybe."

To distract myself, I made my way down the steps of the mercantile onto the cobblestone street. On the right side of First, from where I stood, was the undertaker's office. It took a moment's thought to remember; Graham Cooke had been the original undertaker. Also, a man Jane didn't seem to care for. The building sat mostly quiet, and I gathered it was more another piece of the living museum rather than a functioning business. Thank heavens.

Across the street from the undertaker's sat one of the few completely single-story buildings in Old Town. The blue paint nearly matched the azure sky above. The large sign nailed above the porch roof read *S.A.M. Detective Agency*.

That wasn't familiar to me. If my memory served, and I'd have to go back and look at the journals, this had been the church. "The Sam Detective Agency?"

"S. A. M. Sally Ann Mitchell." Colt's voice was already too familiar too soon, and so was the way it instantly eased my nerves from the text a few minutes ago. I barely knew this man, but damn if he didn't draw me in.

I pivoted on my heel to face him, finding Colt's gaze on me instead of the sign. "Mitchell."

He grimaced. "I told you, we're everywhere. The Mitchells and Youngs are from the same family tree. Thankfully, there were over five hundred people living in the settlement, or our family tree would be a bush instead."

"Care to tell me how the Mitchells and Youngs are from the same family tree? Jane has met no one with the name Young."

"If you're not there yet, I'm not telling you." His eyes flashed with a bit of wicked humor. He was enjoying keeping me in suspense.

"Well, that's just mean."

"I thought you were having fun reading them. How many have you read so far?"

"Three, no four. I've only read about three weeks' worth of entries, though. She had so much to say about what it was like living with no memory of your past or who you were. The people she met, and the words she could cite without a thought. It's fascinating and horrifying at the same time."

"You're really into them, aren't you?"

"Yes." I knew he didn't like comparison to his ancestors, but this wasn't that. "Unbelievably so. They're so interesting."

"Are they?"

"Wait. You haven't read them?"

"Bits and pieces. The lore has been passed down so heavily in our family, there's even some recordings of the family. Once the phonograph was invented, one of the Youngs immediately ordered one. The family had a lot of fun making those."

"There's recordings?" I clutched my heart. "Oh, I'll have to hear those eventually. First, I need to get through these journals. Jane was such an intriguing woman. The town itself was full of interesting people, too. The only problem is that I know eventually they'll end, and I'll cry my heart out when they do."

Colt leaned closer, pulling us out of the path of a horse. We were almost at the café, but I didn't mind stopping. It was nice to see Colt having some fun with his family's history. "It's a good bet you'll be crying your eyes out before then."

"Oh, dear. Don't tell me that." I sighed softly, falling into step when he resumed our path to the restaurant. "At least they're easy to read. Jane was skilled with a pen. They read like fiction, even though I know they're not."

"There've been several offers to the estate over the years to revise and publish them worldwide, or at least key points in time. The family did their own limited printing of them in the fifties. That's what you're reading now. We don't want anyone to change her words or her story, so it will stay with the family and Dominion Falls." He paused at the entrance of the café. A frown tugged his lips down. "Damn. I've been too distracted and forgot to mention, this is family-style eating."

Sure enough, there wasn't a single small table in the whole café. The primary seating consisted of picnic tables with red-checked tablecloths and cushions on the seats to match. There were only a handful of tables with chairs, but they were all for at least four diners. While we stood in the entrance, and I pondered suggesting somewhere else, at least two people switched their seats to another table.

He'd known this in advance and forgotten to mention it? I guess it's not a date. "I even passed by the other day, but didn't realize it then. Maybe you should pick a table. You and your brothers are the only people I know in town."

His hand touched my lower back as he wove us through the tables toward an empty four-top. Maybe it is a date? *Ugh, just ask him.*

Before I could work up the nerve, a voice interrupted my thoughts. "Colt, over here." A man with chestnut hair waved us to a picnic table with him and two women a short distance away.

Colt steered me toward the small group. "Hey Aspen. Moorely, Nova."

After the brief exchange of greetings, Aspen looked toward me expectantly.

"Everyone, this is Remi. Remi, this is Aspen. His sister, Moorely, and her best friend, who is also one of my many cousins, some number removed, Novalee."

"Ugh, please. Call me Nova." The stunning blonde half-rose to extend her hand. I couldn't place why, but she seemed familiar. "It's great to meet you, Remi. When did you get to town?"

"A few days ago. I've been settling in at Gigi's. Colt was kind enough to offer me a job bartending at the casino. Today's my first night really venturing outside of my little bubble."

Nova tugged me onto the seat beside her, leaving the seat across from me for Colt.

"Welcome to Dominion Falls." Aspen offered a warm smile. "Are you staying on permanently or just passing through?"

"I wasn't sure of that until I got here. So far, I'm enjoying everything I've discovered about the town. I don't see any reason to leave." It was an effort to keep my focus on Aspen through my answer. Colt's intense stare tingled on my skin. Clearly, he'd been intent on learning my answer as well. So, a date?

Colt gestured to Nova. "Nova runs the bakery in New Town, How Sweet. Moorely, what are you doing now? I know you were working at Tucker's until the incident, but that was a year ago, I think?"

"Yeah, people need to let it go." Moorely tapped some keys on her phone before setting it down to focus on Colt.

"After that, my illustrious sister did some bank teller work, and then it was a nanny for someone on Snob Hill, wasn't it?" Aspen tapped his chin, staring at the sky while he thought. "You did some delivery driving in between, and—"

"Leave her alone." Nova tsked at the man picking on Moorely. "She has also been building her party planning business."

Moorely's cheeks burned bright red. "I wish that were true. No, I've just been doing this and that, if you must know."

"Moorely does this and that, apparently." Colt's gaze landed on me, a wicked smirk curving across his lips. "Which is a step up from stuff and nonsense."

I did my best to keep my laughter contained. Moorely didn't seem in the mood for teasing. I still offered a wink to Colt before holding my finger to my mouth to tell him to shush.

"Where is your third musketeer?" Cole directed his question to Nova, which was smart. Moorely's glare at her drink could have exploded it in a million pieces if she had any telekinetic powers. "Is my sister up to no good?"

"Prairie? She's been too busy working late for weeks thanks to the County Fair and Founder's Day. Did you know she keeps bugging me to accept this Legacy Award thing just because I'm related to both families? It's not like I'm the only one." Nova rolled her eyes.

"You're the only one who's won a baking competition on TV, which helped spur this renewed tourist attraction she's been pushing ever since your win." Colt handed me one of the paper menus.

"Oh, that's why you seemed familiar. You were on the holiday championship, right?" I remembered seeing her win the whole kit and kaboodle with a stunning cake. Lexi was going to pay for not mentioning she knew her.

"That's me." Nova shrugged as she checked the time on her phone. "Anyhoozles, if Prairie is going to join us, I'm guessing she'll be here within thirty minutes."

"Aw, darn. I'd hate to miss her." Aspen's tone could have cut ice. After the warm greeting he'd given me, it was quite the about-face.

"Give her a break, Ass." Moorely accompanied the shortening of her brother's name into an insult with a sharp glare.

"Come on, Moose. Even you admit no one should be *that* happy all the time. It isn't natural. It's not human." Aspen's emphatic gesture sent potatoes flying off his fork right onto Nova's plate. "Oops, sorry."

Nova ignored the insult of the potatoes into the middle of her green beans. "Just because you're incapable of seeing Prairie for what she is, doesn't mean you need to spit your opinions all over everyone like a sprinkler."

These people had clearly known each other for a long time. I was a little overwhelmed by it all, the barbs, the nicknames, everything. A server relieved me from trying to keep it straight for a couple of minutes. I ordered the beef stew and a soda, and Colt ordered the same.

The other three were still bickering back and forth during it all. Colt leaned forward, raising his hand to speak behind it. Not that I think any of the three were paying too much attention. "Sorry about them. My sister isn't everyone's cup of tea, but she has her reasons for being how she is."

"I don't know. Perhaps he's protesting a bit too much." I tilted my head toward Aspen. "Such a powerful reaction is a bit extreme unless she once did something to him."

Colt glanced at his friend a minute before turning back to me. "I don't know. They've been oil and water since they met."

"If you say so." I was about to interrupt the argument, hoping to get some conversation that was easier to follow, but Nova did it for me.

"Alright, alright. Let's take a step back and move on. I heard a rumor." She grinned conspiratorially around at us. "Word on the street is Prairie got some big-name country music star to come to Founder's Day. I'm talking huge."

Aspen snorted. "Sure she did. As if she could manage a big deal like that."

Moorely pulled a notebook from the bench beside her. She thwacked her brother on the head. "Knock that shit off. We have company."

"What the hell?" Aspen rubbed his head. "Who's the older one here?"

"By age, you. By maturity, clearly it's me." Moorely plopped back onto the bench and turned her attention back to her phone.

"Fine, whatever. Go on, Novalee." Aspen performed a ridiculous sort of bow.

Nova sipped her soda, drawing out the answer as they'd made her wait to say it. "I don't know who it is, but Janet Wills was practically buzzing about it when she was in the shop today."

"The mayor's wife is buzzing about it?" Colt's brows rose and he let out a low whistle. "Then maybe it is true. I wouldn't put it past Prairie, honestly."

"I'm very good at the rumor mill, dahling." Nova fluffed her hair and batted her lashes. Then she spun toward me so fast, I jumped a little. "Now that you've seen we're a madhouse and therefore not scary at all. I want to know all about you. Where are you from? What are you doing here? Tell me *everything*."

"Oh." Every pair of eyes around the table were now on me, even Moorely. I sought Cole as the only familiar face, but all he offered was a sympathetic shrug and a mouthed, 'sorry'. I could give the broad strokes and hope it would be enough. "Well, then. I'm from Florida. Yes, before you ask, I lived right near the theme parks, and I went all the time growing up."

Nova leaned on her hand to listen intently. You'd have thought my story was the most interesting in the world. "Really? Tell me more."

"Do you want my whole life story?"

"Of course. If we're going to be friends, I must know everything."

Chapter 7

Colton

Even if the evening had been a date to begin with, it was far from it after thirty minutes around my friends. I guessed it was probably good at that point that I'd never figured it out. If it had, in fact, been a date, I'd be really annoyed about now.

Nova and Moorely completely bogarted Remi's attention. Moorely's rotten mood flipped like a switch after a text that had her grinning like a fool. Since then, she and Nova had been practically dragging Remi's life story from her. I couldn't complain too much. I was learning more about the fascinating and beautiful woman across the table from me.

Aspen nudged me in the ribs, dragging me away from a story about Remi working at Disney. "What's her story?"

"I'm pretty sure you're hearing it right now."

"I mean, is she available? Or are you claiming dibs? You know, you had an unfair advantage meeting her the night she moved in." Aspen's eyes sparkled with mischief. He'd really lay into the teasing if I admitted too much.

"I honestly haven't got the foggiest idea what the hell is going on. You know, it's been ages since I've been interested in anyone."

"Ah, so you are interested." Aspen checked to ensure the women were still chattering. "You know, I've learned it's best to lay your cards on the table."

"I don't know how to do that."

"Uh, maybe let *her* know you're interested. Ask her out. Or hell, just kiss the woman. It's not like she isn't sneaking glances at you when she can."

I glanced over to find Remi's gaze fixed on me, just as Aspen had said. Even as she continued to chat with Nova and Moorely, she gave me a smile. Aspen was right. I needed to tell her. The challenge was in figuring out how to accomplish that. Across the table, Remi's animated smile soured into a bit of a scowl.

"Hey, guys!" A hand cuffed the back of my head moments before Gunner took a seat on the other side of Aspen. He was my brother, and I loved him, but man, he was too much sometimes. My only relief now was that it seemed Remi didn't care for him, that she actually preferred me. Even better, she'd been able to tell us apart easily when we'd both been in my backyard the other day. Gunner winked at Moorely. "Did I miss anything?"

"Only most of Remi's life story." Nova didn't even give Moorely a chance to respond. She demanded Gunner's attention. Apparently, I wasn't the only one who'd noticed Gunner's interest in Moorely shifting over the past couple of months. Nova skillfully pulled all of Gunner's attention to herself. "It's not like we're only allowed to have fun when you're here, Cuz. You aren't the only life of the party."

"Ah, but it's more fun with me." Gunner turned his attention to Remi. "This ball of blinding energy isn't harassing you, is she?"

"Not at all." Remi dismissed him with a wave of her hand. Dismissing Gunner, she directed her next question at Aspen. "What is it you do?"

"I work in tech; handling the IT needs of most of the government offices. I mostly work out of my home freelancing." Aspen didn't smile as broadly as usual when talking about his job. "I created and maintain most of the websites around town."

"He's also an amazing photographer," Moorely piped in with her two cents. Even though they'd been fighting minutes before, she wasn't one to let her brother dismiss his own talents. If only she'd do the same for herself.

"Don't let him be all humble and deny it. The town uses a lot of his images for marketing. Some of his wildlife shots have even appeared in magazines."

"Really?" Remi's eyes sparked with more interest. Her gaze stayed on Aspen. She even leaned forward a little. My fist clenched in response to having her attention waver to my friend. He'd done nothing wrong, and neither had she. Hell, I didn't even know if this was a date. I seriously needed to get my shit together.

"It's a hobby." Modesty wasn't Aspen's norm, except when it came to his photography. I knew his dad frequently drilled into his head that photography wasn't a *real* career, whatever the hell that meant. He'd only gone into tech because he'd been good with computers, not because he actually liked it as a career. It was an actual stable career and kept his dad off his back.

"Published in magazines doesn't sound like a hobby." Remi offered a genuinely warm smile when Aspen looked up at her words. "To me, it sounds quite impressive."

Gunner snorted aloud. The low conversation they'd been continuing when Remi's attention had wandered must have come to some sort of head. "Nah. Baby sis couldn't have gotten a big name. At least not without telling me."

"Boy, the rumor mill works fast around here." Prairie leaned on Gunner's shoulder. She wagged her finger at him. "Whether or not it's true, why do you have so little faith in me? I could bring a big name here to our little town. After all, I can be very persuasive. Just ask Jace Cooke."

I cringed, and had a feeling Gunner did, too. He groaned loudly and added a shudder for more emphasis. "Gross. I do *not* want to hear about my sister's escapades."

A phone buzzed and rang. We all checked, but it was Remi who pulled her ringing phone from her purse. She frowned at the screen, making it dark before she shoved the phone away. She scooped the last bite of stew into her mouth and had only just swallowed when her phone rang again. The laughter she'd shared with the others had drained from her features.

With another look at the screen, she muttered apologies and wandered toward the exit with her phone. Her shoulders were tense, her fingers tight enough on the phone that her knuckles were white.

"I'm going to take Remi on a tour of the town. See you later." I followed Remi's path out of the café. She was already several buildings down, phone still in her hand. I caught up in time to hear the end of the conversation. It made me feel bad for not giving her a few minutes more.

"No. I don't want to hear it. No." She shook her head, shifting from foot to foot. "Don't bother. I don't care what you have to tell me. Don't contact me again."

I stood still a few feet away, giving her a minute. I didn't have a clue what it was about, but she wasn't happy. She paced back and forth in a small one-foot area before she leaned against the railing of the library.

A deep, frustrated groan preceded her kick backwards at the wooden railing. She pinched the bridge of her nose, tapping her phone against her elbow.

I took a step closer, taking care to slide my foot across some gravel to let her know I was close. When she looked up, I tried to smile reassuringly. "Everything okay?"

"Yes. No. I don't know. I don't want to talk about it." She pulled open her purse and dropped the phone into it again. "Sorry to leave so abruptly. They probably think I'm rude."

"Nah. You had to take a call. Everyone will understand."

"Still, I should go apologize and say goodbye properly." Her fingers still gripped her purse strap too tight. I wanted to cover her hand with mine to help ease the nervous tick of scraping her nails across the button.

I stepped aside to let her pass back into the café. By the time I got there, Nova was hugging her tightly.

"Girls' night!" Nova lifted her arms in the air in triumph. "I declare a girls' night to get to know Remi better. Saturday night. That is, if you aren't making her work on Saturday. You aren't, are you Colt?"

I'd planned on it. Still, I wanted Remi to feel comfortable here. Making friends seemed like a great start to being happy here. A valid excuse presented itself quickly enough. "No. Saturday is always crazy busy, and she's just starting. You can have her on Saturday."

Nova cheered and bounced, hugging Remi tight in her enthusiasm. "You have my number in your phone. Text me if you need anything at all. I'll send you the deets about Saturday when I've got them worked out."

"I look forward to it." As soon as Nova released her, Remi returned to my side.

I couldn't help my instinct to rest my hand on the small of her back while we wove through the tables again. A voice in the back of my head yelled a warning about the teasing I'd get from Gunner later, but a much more insistent part told me I needed to touch her. Even if it was the slightest bit.

We made it past the library again, but I paused there. "Would you like a better tour now? Or do you want to do the full tour, including the town, tomorrow?"

"I thought you had to work. You were just carving out some time for the hotel tour."

Damn, she was right. "Fine. Town tour tonight, hotel tomorrow?"

"Sounds like a plan."

I gestured across the street. "This jail was built in eighteen seventy-five. The original was on Main, down past the dress shop. As the town grew, they needed a bigger one."

She listened eagerly to every bit of information I doled out. I had to be conscious of how much I revealed, seeing as she'd already told me she wanted to learn things as she read them. It was tough to match family lore against what she'd read, especially since I hadn't read the books. At least she'd told me she was only about a month into Jane's arrival in town. That meant she barely knew anything, so it was down to basics.

When we approached the entrance to the hotel, which sat on the corner of Main and First, I guided her around the corner along the edge of the porch. "Did you see this?"

She followed my guidance toward the plaque on the corner of the porch. After a few minutes, she gasped, jumping straight up and pointing at it. "Is that what I think it is?"

"What do you think it is?"

"The original brothel."

"It is. Cole lived in that room." I pointed to the room in the upper right of the picture on the plaque.

Remi spun on her heel to face the building behind us. "So that would mean Jane woke up in that room up there."

I followed her pointing finger to the room on the upper left of the old boarding house. "Yes. Directly across from his room."

"How amazing it must be!"

"What?"

"You walk through literal history every single day." For a few moments she didn't move, her gaze fixed on the rocking chair on the balcony and the lacy curtains behind it. Her jaw hung open slightly, a shimmer in her eyes.

"More than that, it's all history that's immortalized in writing. It's incredible to think they survived over a hundred years without being destroyed."

"They were, actually."

"What?"

"I can't tell you." I grinned when she pouted. Unable to stop myself, I tapped the lip she'd puffed out. "None of that. You'll have to wait until you read about their destruction yourself. It seems like you're having much more fun learning their story on your own."

"I'm not going to lie. I really am." She held my gaze for a long minute, her eyes soft. The hazel in her eyes had turned a deep green. Her lips parted a moment, a hint of a word whispered across her lips, but she stopped it before it fully formed. Then she shook her head and turned away.

"Remi?"

She spun back around just as quickly. Brow furrowed deep, she took a step closer. "Is this a date?"

"Oh, thank god." All the tension whooshed out of me on a gust of air. Finally, she'd asked what I'd been mulling over all evening. "I was wondering the same thing."

"You were?"

"I was." We both laughed at the ridiculousness.

"Lex will have a field day when I tell her this."

"That's fine, just don't tell Gunner. I'll never hear the end of it."

"There's no reason I could think of I'd ever talk to him of my own volition."

I pulled her closer, enjoying the way she curved into me immediately. "Do you want it to be a date?"

"You know? I think I do. It's been a long time since I've had a first date, and I couldn't tell. The signals came across all mixed, especially when we got to dinner and all your friends were there."

"I was so wrapped up in wondering if this was a date, and so surprised that I'd invited myself on your errand, I totally spaced on the family-style seating. If my brain had been on straight, I might have suggested the little diner over on Fourth."

"Are you sure it was your brain that wasn't on straight, and not that something else was doing the thinking for you?"

It took a second for its meaning to sink in. When it did, I became hyperaware of how close she was, and therefore the fact that she could probably tell how aroused I was with no problem. No wonder she'd asked. "Do you have me confused with Gunner?"

"God, no."

Her simple denial, with its derision, warmed me further. If she appreciated only my appearance, she would be equally attracted to my brother. "To be honest, it's been a long time since I've been on a date myself. I guess we both need more practice."

"Are you going to ask me to go out with you again?"

"I'm guessing a date would be much better for both of us if we know it's happening. Don't you think?" I reveled in her laughter. It was as enjoyable as her blushes.

"You're probably right. The problem being that tomorrow is my tour of the hotel, and my next two nights are full of work, and apparently I'm going to a girls' night on Saturday."

"And I need advance notice of what night I need a sitter." I bit back a groan when her soft curves pressed into me. Every thought scattered on the light breeze. "I, um."

"I like it when you blush."

"The feeling's mutual."

She stepped away, much to my disappointment. Her hand rested on mine before pulling gently. "You promised a tour, so finish the tour."

"Happily, but first. There's one more thing." I tugged her back against me until her lips parted. They beckoned me closer until I hovered too close for anything but the kiss I wanted to happen. "Thank you."

"Whatever for?"

"For helping me see the joy in the history of this place again."

"Oh." Did she look disappointed that I hadn't said something else? "Well, that's easy. Is that all you wanted?"

"Not by a long shot." I closed the distance. Her lips were soft against mine, and her arms went around my neck immediately. I slipped my hand into her hair, clutching and giving a slight tug to gain better access. She opened up to me with a low moan that sent a shockwave right through me. Her taste was intoxicating, like coconuts and sunshine.

We parted reluctantly. I trailed my thumb across her swollen lower lip. Her eyes fluttered in response. "Well. I guess it is a date."

"Apparently so. I can't wait for our next one."

Chapter 8

Colton

Everything went wrong over the next two days. Instead of giving Remi the tour I'd promised on Thursday, I'd had to rush off to an emergency Town Council meeting. The disappointment she'd tried to hide bugged the hell out of me. I wanted to show her the apartment and let her do what very few people got to do — actually see the whole thing beyond the ropes.

After the emergency meeting, Brody had demanded we go to the ranch because the cat was giving birth, which turned out to be false. What was true was that West needed help to get a rescue horse from Black Forest. For the past couple of days, I'd been going non-stop. I'd even hoped to ask Remi out properly while on her tour.

Now she was working behind the bar. Pulling her from training in a rush would make me a horrible boss. I took some small comfort in the fact that she appeared to be having fun. I leaned on the railing above the casino pit to study her interaction with Byron. The man had her laughing so much that even his spouse side-eyed them from their place at the roulette wheel.

Remi, unlike many on their first day, moved in her period clothing like she was born to wear a corset and copious layers. Even though I knew next to nothing about fashion, I had to give props to Tayte. The dressmaker had done an excellent job picking an outfit for Remi. Despite her bright hair, the cream dress with bold purple accents was gorgeous. Not to mention the way the details accented her curves.

Around the clientele, Remi had no hints of shyness like she had around me or my friends on first meeting us. The bright smile she offered them, coupled with the laughter Byron continued to get out of her, brightened her until I couldn't take my eyes off her. Even though I had work of my own to do. And despite the fact that it was pretty creepy to stand here staring like I was. I really need to move along.

The biggest problem that the two days of chaos created was that doubts crept into my brain. I knew nothing about this woman, her past, or anything about her. Sure, I found her attractive and funny, and Gigi wouldn't take in a criminal. Did that mean I had to let her into my son's life?

It was one thing to have her as a friendly neighbor, but dating her was a whole other story. No matter how much I already liked her, Brody didn't need the confusion, nor did I need his questions. It was the main reason I'd avoided relationships for years. Brody and I had a good life together; we always had. That's all I'd ever needed.

None of my doubts or worries stopped me from *wanting* to know more about her. Everything I could, really. The bits and pieces I'd gotten had me wanting more. I also couldn't deny that our kiss the other night, and the kiss after that, were running on repeat through my brain, and my dreams. The way her body had pressed into mine was the stuff of fantasies. Even now, with her across the room, the mere memory of those kisses had my body reacting enough that I had to shift in place.

No doubt about it. I was an absolute mess.

Someone took up position beside me. I didn't need to look to know who it was. My twin, all too often, had an uncanny knack of knowing when he had an excellent opportunity to tease me mercilessly. My current state of confusion was fuel for the fodder.

Gunner's position on the railing almost perfectly mirrored mine. Several tourists were paying attention now. Even Remi allowed her attention to wander our way. She offered me a tentative smile. When

Gunner waved, she rolled her eyes and turned back to Byron. I turned my chuckle into a laugh.

"She doesn't like me much."

"She sure doesn't."

He turned his gaze to me, speaking low. "You really do like her a lot."

What was the point in denying it? Gunner's twin radar detector would spot the lie.

"Come on, boss." He urged me away from the railing toward the back of the hotel. It took little effort on his part to push me into the apartment. The same one I'd wanted to show Remi yesterday.

The family had converted it into a museum for the former residents, so it was no longer used as a living space. Velvet ropes blocked the occasional tour group from coming close to any furniture or 'exhibits', which were really just a part of the lives lived here. We let groups back only during the day.

While no one lived here any longer, the apartment was a family-favorite hangout. Several years ago, I'd had all the furniture reupholstered to accommodate us actually using the place without destroying fragile fabric. The result had been far more comfortable than century-old stuffing, which led to more frequent visits from us all. I'd even kept the piano in tune, and fresh liquor on the bar cart.

Gunner beelined for the liquor, pouring two glasses of whiskey. After he'd handed one to me, he flopped onto the chaise. "Drink. You're wound tighter than a drum."

"I'm supposed to be working."

He checked his watch. "False. It's eight at night. Jovie is on duty, isn't she?"

Unfortunately, he was right. My night manager had taken over an hour before. I settled onto the sofa, sipping my whiskey.

"You like Remi; everyone can see that. I can tell something else, though. You're talking yourself out of letting anything happen, just like you always do." Gunner's tone remained gentle. None of the teasing I'd expected that would have me bristling against his annoyingly keen assessment. My brother was too good at handling me, and that in itself should have been enough to rile me.

Instead, I sagged back into the cushions. He had a point, but I couldn't stop my railing thoughts. "I don't know her. I know nothing about her past. Hell, I didn't even know she was from Florida until Nova got her to talk."

"So?"

"I have to think about Brody."

"Bullshit."

"I do."

"I still call bullshit."

"You're not a dad. You don't understand." I glared at him, but he didn't react to my goading. Part of me wished he would. I would have loved to blow off some steam.

"You and I pretty much raised ourselves, and Prairie and West, before Dad and Paige finally rescued us."

"We rescued ourselves."

"True. The point is, you can't tell me I don't understand. To this day, we still can't really treat them just like siblings." Gunner left his lounging position to give me the closest thing to a glare he could ever give me. It wasn't intimidating, but it meant he was serious. "What Brody needs is his dad happy."

"I am."

"You've been happy enough since you adopted him, sure. The problem is, he became your whole life. You stopped seeking any other life or relationships once he came into our family circle."

"I don't want to confuse him." Even I recognized the excuse for what it was—weak. That didn't mean I'd let it go. It was the best defense I had against going back into the dating world. As much as I liked Remi already, the idea of dating was intimidating as hell, especially when it had been years since I'd made a genuine effort. "I'm not you."

"No, you aren't. I am one of a kind, after all." His sardonic smile at the irony of his words proved contagious.

I chuckled despite my desire to avoid encouraging him. "You're also pathetic.

"Sometimes, for sure. I'm right in this matter, though. You're allowed to have a life. Brody will understand. It's not like you're telling him every woman you meet or date is going to be his new mommy."

"I know. I know."

"Then stop being a damn idiot. Ask that woman out. If I have to watch her making eyes at you for much longer, I might be sick."

I covered my grin with a sip of whiskey. The burn down my throat didn't erase my amusement that I knew something Gunner clearly hadn't heard yet. I stared at my whiskey, swirling it around the cup. "I've already kissed her."

"What?" The cup slipped from his hands. He caught the glass before it spilled onto the carpet. Once he'd polished it off, he slid to the edge of the chaise so that only the coffee table sat between us. "Why didn't you mention this sooner? When did it happen? Is she good? She looks like she would be."

"It was the other night after we left the café. I won't insult her honor by answering that, but I will say I'm not complaining." I downed the last of my whiskey before my final answer. "And I didn't tell you because I really didn't want to go into the circumstances."

"What circumstances?"

"Neither of us knew whether we were actually on a date." Heat tingled along my face at Gunner's incredulous stare. I had to rub the back of my neck to ease the embarrassment, which didn't work.

"How could you not know?"

"I sort of invited myself on her errand into town. Neither of us said date, I didn't ask her out. Then we ended up at the café instead of a place we could have privacy. It really just snowballed until neither of us knew what was going on."

"And you call me pathetic."

I threw a pillow at him. "Shut up, asshole."

He caught the pillow easily. His laughter filled the room. Worse, he almost rolled off the chaise, his face turning red. "Jesus, Colt."

"I know. This is exactly why I didn't want to tell you."

The laughter didn't stop, but he got it down to a less obnoxious and loud guffaw. "Get a fucking grip and ask the woman out."

"I know. I should."

"Yes, you really should. You can't continue to claim you don't know her once you get to know her better."

"That's kind of what scares me."

"That's why you have to do it."

"I know." I raked my fingers through my hair.

"Oh, and Colt?"

Whatever came next couldn't be good. "What?"

"This time don't take her to the café, or to Turner's. Take her somewhere you aren't surrounded by every person you've ever known."

Chapter 9

Remington

Charming call-back name aside, Hammy's bar was raucous and crowded. A live band played on the stage across the room. The best I could say is that my companions chose a quieter portion of the bar, which was still loud. We gathered around a table near the bar, but far from the mechanical bull.

Moorely grimaced sympathetically after I'd scanned the room for the third time. She leaned closer. "I swear I tried to talk Nova out of this place. She loves it, though. It always gets her mojo going. Once she gets started, she lets us move onto a slightly less crazy location."

"It's fine." It wasn't one-hundred percent fine, but it was acceptable. I didn't think I had much room to complain. These women were extending the banner of friendship, after all. I wasn't sure if I was relieved the noise level interfered with the ability to carry on a conversation, or annoyed by it.

Girls' night was supposed to be a good way to get to know these women better. That would be difficult to do when you couldn't talk at normal levels.

"Liar." Moorely's smile softened the accusation. "Believe me, I prefer quieter girls' nights. Unfortunately, Prairie and Nova took charge of tonight's plans. Of course, Prairie is once again running late. I was too wrapped up in a book I just got to argue."

The blush that lit across Moorely's cheeks at the mention of the book piqued my curiosity. "Is that blush over the type of book?"

"I'm not blushing." Moorely touched her cheeks. "Am I?"

"Yeah, just a little." I pinched my fingers together. "What set that off? Is it a dirty book?"

"Well, yeah, actually. That isn't a big deal, though. I read those all the time." She paused, her eyes widening.

I knew why. She'd made it clear the blush wasn't about the books. "Then, what could have caused the blush?"

Her attention shifted behind me, a relieved grin lighting her features. "It's about time, girl. Give Remi one of those shots. She has to try it."

My curiosity only grew after that reaction, but I figured everyone had a right to their secrets. I certainly had a few of my own I didn't care to disclose. Even with Lex's recommendations, I didn't know these women. A disturbingly bright green shot, almost neon, landed in front of me. "Uh. What the hell is that?"

"It's an Aurora Borealis." Nova held her glass up in a toast. "Drink. It's delicious, I promise."

"If you say so." I clinked glasses with both of them and tossed the drink back. Nova hadn't lied. The sweet flavor of melon mixed with a hint of bourbon met my tongue, making me want more. Then the hit of alcohol burned down my throat, nearly wiping away the enjoyment. Nearly. I coughed and hit my chest. "Damn. Tequila? You could warn a girl."

"Of course it's tequila." Nova winked. "Now tell us all about yourself."

"I already did. There isn't much else to tell." Granted, I'd only given them the basics of my life. The parts I wanted to leave in the past remained right where I left them. If possible, I'd have fed all of those secrets to the alligators of the Everglades.

"Siblings?" Moorely sipped a blue drink, gaze intent on me. "You didn't mention."

"I didn't. That's true. I have one brother. We haven't spoken in quite a while." Heat prickled on my cheeks when that tidbit had them leaning forward for more. "Let's just say we have different values in life. I believe in human rights; he goes the other way."

Understanding dawned across the table. Nova leaned closer so she wouldn't have to shout. "Totally get that. There's an entire branch of my dad's family tree we've cut off. It's awful to realize the people you grew up with are so off the rails."

"Don't I know it?" It hurt even more when the defining people in your life, the ones that raised you, proved to have different values. I didn't even know how that had happened.

The arrival of our straggler derailed any further questions, thankfully.

Prairie had the striking good looks of her brothers, with the dark hair of the youngest Mitchell brother. Her bright blue eyes contrasted beautifully with her nearly black hair. She flopped onto a stool, immediately tossing back her shot. As soon as it was down, she launched into her excuse at lightning speed. "Oh, my goodness. I'm sorry I'm late. There are so many details involved in getting the contacts set for the fair and Founder's Day. I swear I'm going to recommend moving them further apart next year. I can hardly keep everything straight. Hi. It's Remi, right? It's good to properly meet you, seeing as we didn't exactly get any sort of introduction the other night. Nova filled me in after you left. I'm so sorry I didn't get to meet you better. You must be great if Nova and Moorely already like you."

I blinked a few times at the newcomer's rapid stream of consciousness. "Uh. Yeah. It's nice to meet you, too."

"It's going to be nice to get to know the person behind the info my girls gave." Her brow furrowed as she tilted her head. How she appeared puzzled while also smiling broadly astounded me. If I tried to pull it off, I'd look like a psycho. She maintained her beauty and cheerfulness despite the conflicting expressions. "You seem so familiar. Have we met before?"

"Just on Wednesday," I offered as a reason. With any luck, that's what she meant, although that was highly doubtful. She'd already mentioned our passing meeting. I didn't want it to be for any other reason. I'd hoped against hope that this town was small enough that the news wouldn't have reached here. Lex's assurance that it was likely true, that there was a peaceful bubble around the town, would protect me. Maybe she'd been placating me. A knot formed in my stomach when Prairie shook her head. I waved her off, grasping at another straw. "Then, no. I'm too new. I've been told before I have one of those faces, though. People often claim to have met a relative I don't have at the grocery store."

"Hm. Maybe. Anyhow. What are we doing? Has Moorely already ridden the bull?" Prairie took the dark drink, sparkling with glitter and a swirl of cream, that Nova handed her. "A Milky Way is good, but I'd really like more of those shots. I should go order more."

"Oh, no. Please don't. One tequila is more than enough for me. If I have too much, I'll regret all decisions I make for the entire night." I was damn relieved Prairie had dropped the subject so quickly. Not that I didn't want to tell my story, but I wasn't ready to talk about it yet. That's why I continued to brush off Lexi's suggestions of therapy. Out of habit, I scratched the scar on my temple. With any luck, we'd be able to keep the subject far away from me. "Is there any truth to the rumors about getting a big name for the Founder's Day thing?"

"I can neither confirm nor deny anything about the talent we've secured." Prairie's lips tilted into a secretive smile. "The rumor mill around here is plenty strong. I'm still not allowed to say whether it's accurate."

Moorely's lips pursed, her eyes narrowed at Prairie. "You are so terrible at keeping a secret, you know. It's blatantly obvious it's true. Why can't you tell us who it is? We won't tell."

"Because nothing is set in stone. I just told you there are a lot of details to these contracts, and everything takes time. I'll tell you when I can tell you."

Nova waved her arm through the middle of the table. "Okay, okay. Clearly, Prairie is going to stand firm on this for now. We'll continue to pester, but just a little at a time."

Prairie preened, sipping her drink again. Her blue eyes focused on me again. Though she said nothing, my skin tingled at her attention. I cleared my throat. "So, why did Prairie ask if you'd ridden the bull yet, Moorely? Is that something you do a lot?"

"When she's had a bad day," Nova confirmed before Moorely could speak. "Or sometimes just because she's read a really good book."

Moorely gasped, slapping her friend's arm. "That isn't why. I have toys for that, you pig."

"Sure. Because toys are all you need."

Prairie let out a squeak, pointing at me. My entire body tensed. *Shit.*

"I know where I know you from." Prairie's eyes lit up along with the stage lights. Damn, I'd really hoped that the short shelf-life of social media notoriety would work in my favor. "It was all over social media for a few weeks. You're that nurse, aren't you? The red hair threw me, because you were blond."

Every bit of blood drained from my head to my feet. Denials stumbled from my lips over coherent argument.

"Yeah, you're not blond anymore, but it's totally you." Prairie hopped in triumph. Her pride in her skills of deduction surpassed her ability to notice how she'd popped my bubble of peace and anonymity.

Nova's brows pursed as she studied me. She finally shrugged, turning to Moorely. "Do you have any clue what she's talking about?"

"Not at all." Moorely's expression was soft. "What's she talking about, Remi? You're a nurse? Why didn't you tell us that?"

"I, um. I need another drink." My voice pitched into a hysterical laugh as I all but ran the ten feet to the bar. I requested a Milky Way from the bartender before I dropped my forehead to my hands. I scratched the tingling scar again. "Damn it."

"Hey there." A shoulder bumped into mine. The voice was close, but not quite right to be who I might have initially thought.

I lifted my gaze, reaffirming my belief that he was the wrong twin. "Great. Lucky me. Hello, Gunner. Leave me alone, please."

All humor flew from his features. His brow puckered as his blue eyes searched my face. In the moment of kindness, he actually looked more like his brother. "Is something wrong?"

"No. Yes. I don't know." I scratched the scar again. When the bartender set the drink in front of me, I grabbed it to take a huge sip.

"I know Prairie can be a lot sometimes. Is she bugging you? I can talk to her if you'd like." The teasing, smug smile he'd worn at every one of our previous meetings was nowhere to be found. Could he be serious?

"No, she's a lot, but no. She isn't bothering me. Exactly." I risked a glance over my shoulder only to find the trio huddled close together. Great. The whole sordid story would be all over town in no time at this rate. "I just thought I'd have more time, is all."

"More time for what?" In our normal, everyday meetings, I wouldn't have given him the time of day. His current attitude led me to keep talking.

"Peace." I slurped the drink. There wasn't any way I could go back to face all the questions yet. "Is your sister a gossip?"

He snorted. Any hope I'd had faltered with the derisive noise. He raised a brow, his features growing serious again. Curiosity sparkled in his icy blues. "Why?"

"Are you a gossip?"

"I'm all about law and order, ma'am." He tipped an imaginary hat.

It was my turn to snort. Somehow, his dry teasing made it easier to believe him. "There was an—incident—at my last job. The ordeal made headlines, and I barely survived both physically and otherwise. That's the basics of it. Apparently, your sister saw the story even from thousands of miles away."

"Her entire life and career are based around social media. Of course, she did. Look, I'll talk to her for you. I'll let her know she needs to keep her trap shut."

I couldn't understand the sudden burst of helpfulness. "What's in it for you?"

"Nothing. Why?"

"Because you're being nice."

"Hey, if Colt likes you, you must be worth treating well. It's probably not a great idea to scare you off too quickly." He raised his glass before crossing to the table.

I did my best not to stare when he slung his arm around Prairie's shoulders. All three women glanced my way when he leaned in, and I ducked my head back to my drink, turning my back on the whole affair. As the lone survivor, I'd had to face way too much scrutiny and pitying looks.

After I'd heard the administrator, also known as my fiancé Kyle, on the 911 recordings, I knew I'd never return. To the hospital. Or my career. I'd walked away and had no plans to look back. Ever.

Gunner's tall form returned to my side. "I wouldn't worry."

"Easy for you to say."

"They won't say anything. I don't think they planned to." He tapped my arm to get me to look at him. "They're worried about you. It'd probably be best to go back before they come to retrieve you."

"I need another minute. The last thing I want to do is talk about it."

"Tell them that. They'll honor your wishes, I think."

"Curiosity is an ugly monster."

"Then remind them it killed the cat."

"The only problem is, if they know the full phrase, they'll know satisfaction brought it back."

Chapter 10

Colton

As expected, the hotel had been swarmed all day and night. Even at ten, the casino continued to buzz with activity and life. The lobby at least sat mostly quiet. A few people at the tables were having a late-night snack or Turner's semi-famous cocoa.

As soon as the burlesque began a couple of hours ago, I'd made my way into the lobby for some peace and quiet. I had plenty of staff to handle the crowd, and with the show going, I didn't need to be a constant face of the hotel. It was good timing, seeing as I expected West to return with Brody any time now. I'd hoped they'd be here soon so I could go home.

I flipped through the reservation book so look for any openings that needed filled. Not that it mattered much in my distraction. Between wondering what was taking West so long, and how Remi was doing with the girls, I couldn't focus.

Brody tore through the lobby without noticing me behind the desk. It was way too late in the evening for him to be so hyper. Unless there'd been sugar involved. I cast an accusatory glance toward my approaching brother.

West lifted his hands in surrender, or maybe defense. "We went to the drive-in. I told you we'd be going there. You know it's impossible to go to the movies without popcorn and candy."

"Popcorn, yes. Candy, though? At this time of night?" I did my best not to cringe at the squealing giggle from Brody when he raced back into the lobby.

"Hiya." Brody slid to a stop in front of me. "Did Unc West tell you? We turned his truck into a bed. It was so cool. And there was a cooler with pop and cupcakes from How Sweet. We should always take the truck to the movies. Why don't we have a truck? Is Trudy here?"

I didn't get an answer out before he was already racing to the kitchen. "No cookies or cocoa. No more sugar at all."

The kitchen door swung back and forth in response to my last words. That didn't bode well for his listening to my orders. If he'd even heard them in his hyper state. "Cupcakes, West? On top of candy and pop?"

West leaned on the counter. A curl of dark hair flopped across his forehead. "I'll camp on your couch and handle him tonight. I accept full responsibility for him being hopped up on so much sugar."

"You don't have to do that." The protest was automatic. Honestly, it sounded like a great idea. Brody could be more of a handful than usual when he had too much sugar. Plus, I'd have more time to get some work done.

"I know I don't. How much longer do you have to work here tonight?" He flipped through the pages of the reservation book mindlessly. "Isn't this on the computer in your office?"

"Seriously?" I flicked his forehead. "Hello, McFly."

"Oh, right. Old town. Duh. Brain short-circuited. Did you just call me McFly?"

"Yeah."

"We should watch that movie again. I'm going to text Dad and let him know I'll be at your place tonight, but should be back to take care of the horses in the morning." West's thoughts switched with lightning speed, almost as quick as Brody and Prairie's did. "Done. Let me go grab Brody and get him home. You'll be back soon, yeah?"

"I'll be just a few minutes behind you. Trudy's closing the kitchen, Bryon's closing the casino, and my night manager has been here for over an hour. I've just been waiting for you to bring Brody back."

"Sorry. I should have texted when we decided on the double feature."

"It would've been nice, but it's fine. Since you're offering to stay, I'll use your babysitting time to finish some of this paperwork. As long as you both calm down, maybe I'll finally get caught up on my ordering and taxes for the month."

"Bo-ring," West singsonged.

"You'd have to do the same for the rescue if Dad wasn't saving your ass." I kept my tone light. I didn't blame West. He could handle just about anything with horses. Business was his weak point. "You'll be in trouble when Dad decides he wants a real retirement."

"Don't you dare speak of it." He turned when the kitchen doors swung open, expelling Brody. He held his arms out to catch his nephew when Brody launched himself at him. "Oh, boy. You're going to be a laugh riot until you crash, aren't you?"

"I'm not going to crash. Are we going to crash? Maybe I should drive with Dad. Are you coming home, Dad?"

"Nobody's crashing. It's a thing people say about when the sugar wears off because you'll be fast asleep super-fast." I grinned at my son. His excitable energy never failed to fill my heart. I'd give my life for this kid. "Since I'd bet the casino that Trudy gave you one of her chocolate delights, I'm going to say you'll be sound asleep by eleven at the latest."

Brody's eyes widened to saucers. "How'd you know?"

"You've got chocolate on your teeth, silly." I ruffled his hair. "West's going to stay over at our house tonight. Do you want to ride home with him or me?"

"Truck, please." Brody bounced in West's arms. "Can I go for a ride tomorrow?"

"We'll see. Let's get home." I followed them from the hotel. All the way to the parking lot behind Fourth Street, Brody chattered on about the movies they'd seen, and the new horses at the rescue. It didn't matter that I'd been the one to go with West to Black Forest to get those horses and therefore knew all about them. Nope, Brody had his own fantastical take on their arrival at the ranch. Something told me I wouldn't get anything done until Brody finally had his sugar crash.

Brody didn't disappoint. The steady stream of conversation carried on through changing into his pajamas and even brushing his teeth. I helped him get settled on the couch, where West had created a next of blankets and pillows for them, the TV already on and ready for a movie.

"Hey, Dad?" Brody snuggled closer to his uncle.

"Yeah, Brody?"

"Do you think Remi and Gigi could come ride horses with us tomorrow?"

"I don't know if Remi rides, but I'm sure Gigi would love it." As he yawned wide, I smoothed down his hair. At least he was settling down. It probably wouldn't be long until both he and West were out for the count. "I'll text Remi and ask if they'd like to go to the ranch tomorrow. For now, you get some sleep."

"I'm not tired." Brody hadn't closed his eyes, but they were mere slits. He was so close to sleep, but he'd fight it as long as he could.

"Of course you're not." I winked at West when Brody snuggled closer to him. "Thanks for staying over to help."

"Are you kidding? He's my favorite nephew."

"He's your only nephew." I chuckled, standing to full height. "Please choose something that won't get him going again, would you? I'd like him to get sleep tonight."

"You got it, boss." West gave me a thumbs up before he resumed flipping through the channels.

I had a mountain of paperwork to do, but I couldn't sit still. In the kitchen first, I worked for about ten minutes. Too restless out there where I could hear the TV, I moved to the desk in my bedroom. That didn't help me one bit, either. I moved back to the kitchen again.

No matter what I did or where I went, my brain wouldn't focus. Brody and West crashed out on the couch before I made it back to the kitchen after my brief foray to my desk. I hovered for a few minutes, contemplating moving Brody to his bedroom.

In the end, I didn't have the heart to move Brody to his bedroom. I let him and West be, although I stopped to pull Brody's thumb gently from his mouth. In waking hours we'd mostly broken the habit. Apparently, in sleep he still needed some help.

I dug through the fridge in search of some caffeine and a snack. While I scooped the yogurt into a bowl and began cutting some fruit, I thought about texting Remi with Brody's question. It was a good bet she was still plenty awake. Maybe a little drunk, but awake.

I didn't want to interrupt her fun, though. I'd write the text, but schedule it to be sent in the morning. That would get it off my mind, and then maybe I'd be able to focus.

As soon as I cleaned up the cutting board, I grabbed my phone to get the text ready. For all I knew, Remi probably had plans for tomorrow. She'd mentioned multiple times wanting to enjoy the living museum part of town. She'd probably already planned for it. I just didn't want to disappoint Brody. That's the only reason I sent the text immediately instead of scheduling it. It had nothing to do with wanting to check on Remi.

For the next half hour I could pretend I wasn't waiting for my phone to ding with a reply, or to see headlights turning into the driveway next door. I hoped she'd let Moorely drive her home. Moorely was the resident designated driver as she'd never cared for drinking, and no one had seen her drink since after the night of her twenty-first birthday.

"I'm such a loser." My head dropped to the table.

"I wouldn't say that." West's quiet voice made me jump a mile. He held a finger to his lips. "Shh. I got out from under him, but barely. He could wake up at any time if I don't get back soon."

"You scared the shit out of me. I thought you were as asleep as Brody."

"I was." He rubbed his eyes, then ran his hand through the curls that stuck up everywhere after his brief sleep. "Got thirsty. So why are you calling yourself a loser?"

"No reason."

"Ah. Is it the girl?"

"Try my lack of experience in dating."

"You'll figure it out." West yawned again. "You like her. She likes you. It's not difficult."

Oh, to have the carefree belief of the young. West might be in his twenties, but he had the bright-eyed optimism of Brody. Probably because he'd been so young during hell, and once we got him out, all of us spoiled him in hopes he'd never know some of the harsh truths we'd learned. "If only life were so easy."

"It can be if you let it." West downed half the bottle of water he'd grabbed in no time. He smacked his lips. "Aaaah. What?"

"Did you even breathe? That's a liter bottle, and you just downed half of it."

"I told you I was thirsty. I had a lot of sugar, so I have to clean it out somehow."

"Just go back to bed, you little weirdo."

He shrugged. "Fine, but I'm telling you. Stop overthinking everything. You're getting wrinkles right here. I'm going to have to send you to my girl for some Botox. Unfortunately for you, you didn't start with skin care as early as I did. Look at me, smooth as silk."

"You're twenty."

"And no wrinkles will come either. I know what I'm doing. Plus, I'm not an overthinker like you. I barely think at all."

"Liar." I waved him off. "Get out of here. I told you I have work to do."

"Sure you did; that's why you were beating your head on the table and bitching at yourself." He raised his hands in mock defense. "I'm going, I'm going. Sheesh."

I rolled my eyes at his departing back. After five minutes, I went to check on him and Brody. West was already dozing on his stomach, with Brody sprawled out on his back like a starfish. They both snored at the same time.

It took some effort to cover my laughter. I hauled out my phone and snapped a pic before either of them could move. This was going on the family's Christmas reel, for sure. Every year, we collected pictures of some of the best moments of the year and projected them like an old slideshow on the wall. It always proved a hilarious way to end a good day.

The phone chimed before I could return it to my pocket. My heart leaped at the idea Remi might have answered. Damn it. I needed to stop acting like I had a schoolboy crush.

> **Gunner**: Your girl is upset.
> **Me**: Not my girl.
> **Gunner**: Yet.
> **Gunner**: Prairie made a faux pas that got her upset. I think
>   I defused it alright, but I'd check on her
>   tomorrow.
> **Me**: How did Prairie upset her? They just met.
> **Gunner**: You'd have to ask your girl. I'm not a gossip.
> **Me**: Still not my girl.
> **Gunner**: Yet.

About a million questions formed in my head. The entire goal of tonight had been for Remi to have fun and start making friends. How had it gone sideways?

The reason could have been just about anything. I didn't dare guess. However, I had one burning question.

> **Me:** How did you get involved? I mean, if you aren't a gossip.
>
> **Gunner:** Because they didn't go to the super-secret bar where no one would ever see them. How the hell do you think I got involved?
>
> **Me:** Did you interrupt girls' night? And why?
>
> **Gunner:** Look, Mother Hen. I was at Hammy's with friends. Probably fifty percent of the population over twenty-one was there. It's a Saturday night. I know you're a stick-in-the-mud who stays home all the time, but most of us have actual lives.
>
> **Me:** Gunner.
>
> **Gunner:** I ran into her at the bar. She was upset. I talked to her.
>
> **Me:** Did *you* upset her?
>
> **Gunner:** She didn't throat punch me. Didn't even look like she wanted to for the first time ever.
>
> **Me:** That's saying something.
>
> **Gunner:** I can be nice. From time to time.

I shut down my phone screen, wondering what had happened at Hammy's. That's probably why she hadn't responded. I considered texting again, just to check on her. It wasn't my place, though.

Not yet, anyway.

Chapter 11

Remington

I could barely hear from the shouts echoing through the small room. My head spun enough my arms almost gave out on me. Why my head hurt, I couldn't remember. The vision in my right eye blurred. I tried to blink away the blurriness, to no avail. I wiped at it, and the blood on my hand confused me.

What was happening?

I squinted through the dim light to where someone lay on the floor.

Casey. It was Casey, our CNA. Blood seeped out from under her in an ever-growing pool of scarlet. The tang of iron mixed in with the overwhelming sounds of the argument raging feet away. The charge nurse, Cyndi, had given up on therapeutic listening and de-escalation. She had no escape, so she fought.

A flash of metal caught my attention. Where had the knife come from? Had he had it all along? His arm raised in an arc, rushing down toward Cyndi brutally fast.

A scream wrenched out of me so abruptly my throat instantly closed.

I sat up quickly. Sweaty with my heart pounding in my chest double time. Where was I? I tried to regain my bearings. The plush bed beneath me was a perfect juxtaposition to the cold floor I'd been lying on in my dream. Silence met my ringing ears, replacing the endless screams and shouts of my nightmare.

"Fucking hell."

I didn't doubt that Prairie exposing my past to the others had made that dream more real than it had been in a while. Anyone talking about it always did.

After Gunner had talked to them, I'd returned to the table. I apologized for leaving so abruptly and allowed the briefest admittance of my involvement. After saying I didn't want to talk about it, they dropped the matter immediately.

The whole thing had put a big damper on my evening. I didn't blame Prairie. Her surprise made her blurt it out. It wasn't like I'd never done the same thing. I put on the best show I could for the next two bars, then excused myself. I texted Lexi as soon as I got home. She was working, so I'd only received texts in reply. I thought it had helped.

Apparently not.

I glared at the bottle of Xanax on the nightstand. "You weren't any help. Jerk."

Throwing off the covers, I padded to the kitchen. I'd lean on my standby of tea and stargazing to settle my mind and heart. Maybe tonight I wouldn't fall asleep on the deck chair. Or maybe I would. If it meant I slept, I'd be okay with that.

I didn't know whether Gigi heard my nightmares or nighttime wanderings. We never spoke of it. A chamomile blend of tea had appeared in the cabinet alongside her black tea after the first nightmare, though. It wasn't the best at helping me find sleep after a nightmare, but it had a lovely calming effect. It was better than nothing.

I got together some supplies to take outside while the tea steeped. I couldn't explain what it was about staring at the millions of stars that helped get me out of my head. Honestly, I didn't need to. If it helped, that was good enough for me. Very little had helped back in Florida, not even revisiting the theme park on Lexi's insistence. I'd take anything that didn't make me want to pull my hair out after a nightmare.

I grabbed my e-reader in case I needed more distraction or if the mood struck. Otherwise, I planned to leave it to the tea and the stars. They hadn't failed me yet.

I carried my fresh brewed cup of tea out to the deck and settled into a lounge chair. There was a bit of a chill in the air despite the supposed approaching summer. Fortunately, I'd brought a blanket out with me to get nice and cozy.

The town had become a Dark Sky community years ago. That meant the towns kept light pollution to an absolute minimum. That in itself made it an excellent way to see the stars, but it was the surrounding mountains that helped protect from light from other cities that took it over the top. Even in the Everglades, I hadn't seen this many stars.

On some of my trips outside after a nightmare, I'd taken to counting the stars instead of sheep. For tonight, I was content to trace the swirling fabric of the Milky Way across the darkness. It felt like a privilege to see this view as often as I wanted, and I didn't want to waste it or ever take it for granted.

"Remi?"

Colt's voice startled me out of my reverie. What on earth was he doing up and outside at this hour? I didn't think anyone was awake at this time unless they worked at the hospital. Of course, he was probably wondering the same thing about me. "Colt?"

"Yeah." There was no creak or yawn of tiredness in his voice at all. Maybe I wasn't the only one who had trouble sleeping. "What are you doing out here at three in the morning?"

"I could ask you the same." My eyes had adjusted to the dark enough to see him leaning on the fence between the yards.

"Couldn't sleep. You?"

Never mind that I hadn't slept well for over six months. Maybe longer, if I was honest. Some days it seemed like every inch of me was just exhausted. "Same."

"Are you okay?"

It was a simple question. It still sent a ratchet of tension through her. Had he heard already? Did the rumor mill fly that fast around here? No, it couldn't be. Right? They'd promised they'd keep things quiet.

"Remington?"

"Hm? Oh, right. Sorry."

"It's okay. I'm just concerned because you're out here in the middle of the night. Are you doing okay?"

"I guess that depends."

"On?"

"What do you know?"

The gate clicked open and shut a second later. His footsteps drew closer. I closed my eyes to avoid getting any preview of what he might think about me if he'd heard everything. The chair beside me creaked. "What do I know about what?"

"Did Prairie say something?"

"Prairie? No, I haven't talked to her since yesterday."

"Oh."

"Gunner texted me earlier, though."

I'd only given him a broad-strokes sketch of what happened, completely vague and non-specific. Still, the fact he'd told Colt riled me. It wasn't his business to tell him. He'd said he wasn't a gossip. Guess he lied.

"All he said is that you were upset. It seems like you are."

"It's not something I like to talk about. To anyone, really."

"I get that."

Something in his tone gave me the courage to open my eyes. He wasn't even looking at me. Instead, he focused on the sky as I had been before he spoke. Maybe he understood. "You do?"

"Sure. There's plenty of things that are tough to talk about, period. Even with the people who went through it with you. Forming the words can be tough with those closest to you, much less a virtual stranger."

"Exactly."

"We don't have to talk unless you want to."

"We can just enjoy the view?"

"This view is one of the best parts of living here."

"It really is." I settled into the lounger, drawing my tea close again. "Would you like some chamomile tea? I can go get some for you."

"No, thank you. That'll knock me right out. Even though West is in the house with Brody now, I need to get back before daybreak. He has to go back to tend to the horses."

"If you're sure." I sank back into my comfy position, the tea keeping the chill away from my fingers.

Comfortable silence descended between us, filled only by the quiet sounds of nature. A wolf howled somewhere in the distance. Or maybe it was close. It was hard to tell with the way the sound carried through the valley.

His being there, not asking questions even if he knew I was upset, soothed my nerves. The tea might have something to do with it, but a lot of it was having the freedom to exist without explanations. My crazy was as it was.

It was so much more than what had happened six months before. It was how Lex had become my family instead of my flesh and blood. It was how I'd nearly died twice because of my career. It was how the second one had broken me.

Lex was right. I seriously needed to consider therapy.

I brushed away a tear that slipped down my cheek, clearing my throat. He noticed, but didn't ask questions. Instead, his hand settled on top of mine, adding his warmth to the chill that settled over me.

I released an inaudible sigh, letting my gaze fall back to the sky. An owl hooted in a tree at the edge of the yard. Moments later, a vast shadow flew right over our heads. We both ducked, me going so low I almost fell out of the lounger.

He laughed when we righted ourselves. "Those damn things can move way too silently for my liking. That scared the shit out of me."

"Me too. What was it?"

"An owl. Probably joining its friend we just heard."

"That was huge." I released a shaky breath, trying to calm my racing heart. "I wasn't that scared when the bear crossed through the backyard yesterday."

"Yeah, the owls come out of nowhere and move like nothing more than shadows."

"The shadow knows," I muttered.

"Did you just reference *The Shadow*?"

"Yeah. What of it?" I pulled the blanket closer. In my circle growing up, I had a long-standing rank of being a total geek. Not just about Disney, either.

"I don't know many people who know that reference, is all."

"How do you know it?"

"I watched a lot of TV growing up. It was on repeat late nights for a couple of years on one of the cable channels. Gunner and I watched it ad nauseam."

"Huh." A little tidbit about him. I appreciated it, so I offered a bit of my own. "I'm a total nerd about quite a few things. Went to ComicCon a few times growing up. My dad often had business trips that took him to California, so he let me tag along to attend and go to Disney while he worked, even scored free tickets through work."

"Wow."

"That came off as braggy, didn't it?"

"A little bit." He chuckled. "I'd brag too if that was my childhood."

Heat flooded my cheeks, leaving me grateful for the dark to cover it. "Still. I didn't mean it that way. I meant only that I love a lot of classically nerdy things. Ah, hell."

He patted my hand, still laughing softly. "You're kind of cute when you're embarrassed."

"Just kind of?"

"I, um."

It was my turn to laugh, which unfortunately turned into a snort. "I'm not the only one who's cute when they're embarrassed."

The amusement lasted for several minutes, but eventually settled back down into quiet calm. I traced the path of a satellite moving steadily across the sky. He pointed with the hand not resting on me. "Shooting star."

I caught the tail end of the streak. "I never realized how many there were on any given night. Living in the city, I thought they were rare. I've seen so many sitting out here at night."

"Do you come out here often?"

"More than I'd like to. Mostly because of the reason I come out here." I took a shaky breath, bracing for the inevitable question. It never came; he simply squeezed my hand. "Thank you."

"What for?"

"Not prying."

"It isn't healing to tell a story under duress."

"No. It really isn't."

Chapter 12

Colton

Brody skipped about the barn eagerly. Remi willingly let him drag her behind as he named every horse fit for human riders. She asked many questions on his haphazard tour about each animal, petting the nose of a few when Brody gave her a second to breathe.

Gigi stood at the edge of the stall I'd just removed Millie from to saddle her for the older woman. Her kind smile followed the pair through the barn. When we'd arrived that morning, my dad and Paige weren't home, unfortunately. I'd wanted to introduce them to Remi. West told me they'd gone north to Buena Vista to conquer a couple more of the 14ers.

Remi'd been full of questions over what the 14ers were. Much to my chagrin, West had taken it upon himself to tell her about the mountains over fourteen-thousand feet, and how Dad and Paige had scaled about twenty of them so far.

Then Brody took over and started a tour for Remi. They'd started in the small barn with the birds and goats and one ornery donkey, then moved onto the barn they now stood in. All morning it seemed every time I had a chance to get close to Remi, someone else took the reins.

Speaking of which, I finished saddling Millie, then nodded to Gigi. "She's ready for you."

"When everyone else is ready, I'll get her to the steps." She kept her attention on Brody and Remi. "Would you like me to distract him for you? Give you some time with Remington?"

"What?" I swear my ears were on fire at being pegged so quickly.

"You haven't stopped staring at her since she came into the barn. I'm surprised you managed to saddle Millie at all." Gigi approached the old mare, rubbing her nose. "Go help her with the horse she chooses. Me and the old girl here will be fine."

I would have argued that I needed to help Brody with his, but West reappeared. In his hand he carried a Stetson small enough for an almost-six-year-old. Brody squealed and raced over to West. West plopped the hat on his nephew's head. "There. Now you're a real cowboy like me."

I bit my lip over the objections racing through my head. We lived in the middle of a neighborhood where the yards were barely big enough for a dog and lined with a thick treeline that wildlife regularly wandered through. Most days I barely had time to parent, much less raise any animals.

Wholly incapable of disappointing Brody, I bit my tongue. West grinned at me as I passed him on my way to Remi. My attempt at a glare toward my brother never manifested as Brody shouted *yeehaw* and galloped around his uncle waving an imaginary lasso.

Remi remained at the stall where Brody had abandoned her. She didn't seem at all bothered by his leaving her alone. Her forehead pressed to the horses, her hands running along his jowls. The closer I got, the more I realized she was talking to him as well.

"Damn. Look at you, Remi." West paused beside me with Brody right beside him. I knew they were heading to the last stall with the gentlest horse on the ranch for Brody to ride. West hadn't yet let Brody ride by himself, so the two of them always took out a large mare that wouldn't hurt a fly, Sillabub.

Remi lifted her head. Rather than look at my brother, she smiled at the beast in front of her. "What about me, West?"

"Well, not to worry you, but he's a nasty sort." West's features creased in something I rarely saw on him-concern. "Every time I try to deal with Fiyero, he nips at me."

"I don't know what you're talking about." Remi stroked her hand down his nose. "He's the sweetest boy, aren't you?"

West's mild concern blossomed into genuine worry for me. It drew me closer. When I got just a couple of feet away, Fiyero snorted and lifted his head. He swung around, teeth bared.

"Oh, now, now. There'll be none of that." Remi wrapped her hand under his head to draw him back to her. There hadn't been a moment of panic in her. "It seems like maybe you don't like men too much, do you? I don't blame you. A lot of them can be awful. I think West and Colt are exceptions to that rule, though. You should be nice to them."

West and I exchanged glances.

"If you wanted to bite Gunner, on the other hand. I wouldn't complain."

West's laugh brayed out, causing a few horses to snort and stomp in their stalls. "I really do like you. I'd still recommend another horse for the ride. He hasn't been broken to saddle yet."

"Because you're a man." Remi sighed. "I don't want to risk his biting Brody, though. Do you mind if I come back and work with him sometimes?"

"I didn't know you knew about horses." I wanted to move closer, but Fiyero continued to give me the side-eye.

"My grandparents raised thoroughbreds in Ocala. I spent a lot of weekends there." She continued to run her hand along Fiyero's nose. "They passed away one right after the other in my early twenties. The will forced us to sell the farm, so we wouldn't fight over it."

"Do you have any experience with rescues or saddle-training them?" West's smile warmed at her admittance. "If you can get this jerk to listen, I'm all for it. I can't tell you how many times I've threatened to pull out the Grimmerie and turn him into Scarecrow."

Remi narrowed her eyes at my brother.

"What's a grimry?" Brody tugged his uncle's hand. "Why do you need it for a horse?"

Remi's glare twitched into a smile. "It has nothing to do with horses and everything to do with your uncle believing only magic will help a horse."

Brody's eyes widened. "PopPop says Unc West has a magic touch. Are you magic?"

Remi's laughter flittered through the barn. "Well, if I wasn't just called out by a very astute young man."

"Come on, bud. Let's go get Sillabub ready." West winked at Remi. "Come by any day we're free and we'll see how Fiyero responds."

"Tuesday." Remi kissed the horse on the nose. "Alright, young man. I'll see you in a couple of days, and we'll show him what you're made of."

I grinned when she turned toward me. Fiyero used her distraction to nibble at her hair. "I think you've got a new friend."

"Horses are the best."

"I was going to offer to saddle your horse for you, but I'm guessing you don't need the help."

"Not really. I probably should have told you that when you asked. I was too excited to see horses again." She followed me to a stall. "And who's this?"

"Dolly."

"Don't skimp on the name, Colt." How West had heard me over the help he was getting from Brody was beyond me.

I pursed my lips in frustration. "Dolly Gallagher Levi."

Remi's lips twitched as she ran her hand along the mare's nose. "Well, then. Hello, Dolly."

I groaned under West's braying laughter. "In case you couldn't tell, my brother has a theme going here."

"I'm surprised he hasn't renamed the ranch the West End." Remi giggled softly. "Let's get ourselves ready to go, Dolly. I'm looking forward to a nice bit of wind in my face."

We both went to grab a saddle. By the time we got out of the barn, the rest of our party were ready to go. Remi didn't wait for them, instead spurring Dolly into a full run toward the mountains.

West's eyebrow lifted as she disappeared from view. He held Brody steady when he cheered Remi on. "You go on ahead. We'll keep Gigi company. Sillabub doesn't like to run like that."

I glanced at Brody. "You good with Uncle West?"

"Yeah. He's got the food." Brody grinned, squirming in his seat. "Miss Gigi brought something from How Sweet."

"In that case, I'll make extra sure Remi remembers to join." Hopefully, Remi would slow down once she got to the trails through the woods; otherwise, it would be tough to catch up.

We had to run over several hills before I spotted Remi in the distance. The only reason I caught up to her is that she'd stopped right near the edge of the ranch lands. Her head tilted back toward the sun as the wind stirred her hair to life behind her. I slowed to admire the soft smile gracing her features, and how relaxed she seemed in that moment.

Princeton snorted, pulling the attention of Dolly and her rider. Remi's smile grew when she saw me, and she urged Dolly into a gentle lope toward me. "Sorry. I can't tell you the last time I had a good ride. I didn't realize how much I missed it until Dolly and I started."

"You missed the trailhead."

"I saw it, but I wanted to run. Sorry, I abandoned you all. I promise I was looking forward to riding with Brody and Gigi and you." Pink sparked across her tan cheeks before she turned her face back toward the wind. "Your ranch is so beautiful."

"My dad's ranch, and eventually West's. I've never been interested in running a full ranch." I followed her gaze across the rolling hills. "Remind me to tell West you need to go see the wild horses next time he goes out."

"What?" She spun in her saddle, eyes wide. "What do you mean?"

"West is part of a group that helps monitor the wild horses in the state. Every couple of months he goes to one of the sites to collect data." The excited hop she gave as I explained had me chuckling. "I take it that means you'd like to see a herd?"

"If he's allowed to bring me, hell yeah." She turned Dolly back toward the ranch. "Should we go join the others now?"

"We could. Or we could let these two run until we have to meet them for lunch."

"How long do we have?"

"A couple of hours." I pulled out my phone to double-check the time. "We'll be meeting them at the swimming hole around one, so that gives us two and a half hours."

"I wouldn't mind running." A whisper of a frown was almost immediately replaced with a wicked grin. Her eyes flashed with mischief. "Well, then again. That depends on one thing."

"Is that so?"

"You say you're not much of a rancher."

"Yeah." I gripped my reins, suspicious of the way she turned Dolly.

"Then the real question is..."

With every step Princeton, she danced away. "What is it, Remington?"

"Do you think you can keep up?"

Chapter 13

Colton

Every fiber of my being fought to get up and pull Brody down from the metal dome climber. He had no clue about my internal struggle. Unworried about any danger, he made it to the top, cheering into the sky. I knew he'd never learn and grow without doing things on his own. I'd climbed way more dangerous equipment than this growing up on tougher turf. That didn't mean I didn't worry about every single time he came within range of the lightest whisper of danger.

It did Brody a world of good for his confidence to do this on his own. Plus, my interfering would be an embarrassment. That's what helped me bite my tongue.

Brody didn't know the meaning of fear. I didn't think he ever had. To that end, he flipped upside down and hung on the bar by his knees. His shirt slid up his belly as he swung back and forth a little bit. A broad smile lit his features. His chubby cheeks dimpled in his glee. "Dad! Look! Look! Dad! I'm upside down!"

"I see that." Not even my worries could keep my smile away. His antics always did that to me. At his age, I hadn't had half of his free-spiritedness. For that matter, I had little of it now. I'd been called a stick-in-the-mud occasionally by my siblings and friends alike. Brody was my daily reminder that life could be light and fun if I let it be for once in my life.

Unfortunately, I couldn't figure out how to do that. Every time I let a moment of easy joy into my life, all of my old fears and terrors broke through. Sometimes I wondered if all those years put into therapy had been a waste. Prairie and Gunner had each learned to live life to its fullest. Why couldn't I?

"It's killing you; I can tell." Speak of the devil. Prairie flopped onto the bench beside me. Her lunchbox thumped onto the bench beside her. She already had the sandwich in her hand with a few bites gone. I wonder where she'd been eating before she came over. I don't remember seeing her on our walk through the park. "Letting him climb that thing. You want to protect him from falling."

"Of course I do; I'm his dad."

"I'm proud of you for letting him do it, anyway. You've gotten a lot better at letting him be a kid. Heaven knows you never let me or West take risks."

"That was a completely different situation."

"Blah blah."

"I don't have to worry about him hitting a self-destruct like I did with you. Then again, you went the opposite way in the end. You became Miss Sunshine for the entire world."

"I wouldn't say the whole world. Sunshine always casts a shadow, after all."

I didn't miss the flash of storm clouds darkening her eyes. Before I could say anything, she waved off the thought.

"Besides, thanks to you and Gunner, I figured out how much easier it is to get what I want when I use honey instead of vinegar."

"You always buried everything under a smile."

Her smile faltered for a split second. As if she knew it, she took a bite of her sandwich rather than reply right away. It wasn't a secret that Prairie was the one Gunner and I worried about most after we escaped our mom's house. Even with what happened to me, her abuse had been far more prolonged and of a different nature than ours. Because of it, Gunner became a cop and swore he'd never miss the signs again. At least the town knew he would take domestic abuse cases seriously. It had been his biggest platform when running for sheriff, even though no one but his family knew the real reason.

Prairie focused on eating her sandwich to the point of completely avoiding me. Guilt rose in an ugly wave. She didn't deserve for me to pick apart how she'd chosen to adjust to life after coming to Dad's. "I'm sorry. That wasn't fair. You took a lot of steps on the way to where you are now. You're as strong, no stronger, than anyone I know. Most people just don't realize how much strength is in that cheeky smile of yours."

Red ghosted along her cheeks, but that very smile returned for a few seconds before fading again. Her lips twisted in a flash of remorse as she set aside her sandwich. She dusted crumbs from her hands, avoiding my gaze again. "I'm really sorry about blabbing."

"Huh?" The subject change was too abrupt to keep track of.

"Blabbing. At girl's night. You know Remi's situation."

"Stop right there." It had been a little over a week since that girls' night that led to me finding Remi on Gigi's back porch at three in the morning. Outside of our ride on the ranch on Sunday, I hadn't seen her as much as I'd have liked. She'd been working most of the week training with Byron until he'd said she was ready to work on her own.

On her one day off, she'd been at the ranch with West, working with Fiyero. West gleefully told me all about their day and how much she'd helped his grump of a rescue.

During the entire week, on the few occasions I'd had to see her, I'd done everything I could to follow through on my promise not to pry into what upset her. On the one hand, I was dying to know. On the other hand, I knew all too well that sometimes there were things too difficult to talk about. No one outside the four of us kids and our parents knew the whole truth about our past. I exhaled slowly, ignoring Prairie's hard stare to focus on Brody's continuing climb around the dome. "I don't know what any of that was about last weekend beyond that she'd been upset by something. Don't tell me any details."

"Oh. I thought for sure she'd told you." Her blush deepened as she ducked her head. She picked imaginary crumbs from her skirt. "I've told no one else. I told her as much when I apologized. When my brain made the connection, I was so surprised I blabbed it out loud without thinking. I know not everyone likes to remember bad things. She really didn't tell you?"

"No, I won't push the matter either. We both know what happens when you push someone to talk before they're ready."

A bright laugh bubbled out of Prairie. It caught the attention of a few of the parents dotted around the play park. The joyous sound reminded me again of how far she'd come. "I don't think Paige or Dad has recovered from what I did when they forced me into that therapist's office."

"I don't think any of us have."

"It wasn't so bad."

"Wasn't so bad? Seriously?"

She fluttered her eyelashes in mock innocence. "It wasn't, was it?"

"You pierced your septum with a safety pin, which you didn't bother to replace with a ring. No, you left the safety pin in place, and then decorated it with a pink ribbon you tied to the earring in your ear from another new hole you'd made."

"Hey, don't mock. I was pastel goth before it was cool." She added flair to her words with a twirling bow. "Maybe I'm the one that made it cool. You don't know."

"I wouldn't be the least bit surprised if you were. For months on end, you wore that pink leather jacket you'd bedazzled with a turquoise skull and purple roses on the back. Ripped white jeans, and you staunchly refuse to remove the safety pin. To this day I don't know how on earth that didn't get infected."

"I know how to take care of myself. Lots and lots of antibiotic ointment was involved. Mostly I left it alone and applied the ointment every night." She fluffed her short, dark hair with her palm, preening as if she were the biggest genius in the world. "I traded out ribbons depending on my outfit, of course."

"Oh, I remember. I swear Gunner nearly had an aneurysm on the daily. It was my job to reassure him we didn't have to worry until you stopped with the Barbie pink."

"Please. He worried anyway. Still does." Her nose wrinkled, and she glared across the playground. "He's so overprotective he shows up wherever I'm hanging out, especially if I dare to go on a date."

"It's probably just a coincidence. We do live in a small town, after all."

"Correction. We live in *two* small towns. There's no reason on earth to find me every single time I'm trying to have a good time. I'm not a fragile little girl. I won't break at the first stiff wind. That's something I made clear years ago."

"You did, and in spades. Maybe you should stop posting everything you do on social media. He won't be able to track you that way."

"That's not the only way he does it, because I don't air every single thing I do. Yet, he shows up wherever I'm at. I'm thinking he's tracking me. He seriously needs to get a life. Those random hookups aren't occupying enough of his time. He needs a legitimate hobby that isn't keeping an eye on me."

"Right. Telling Gunner not to worry about you or West would be akin to telling the sun not to shine. You do realize that." Much to my relief, Brody tired of the climbing dome. He rushed over to the slides, climbing them with a friend from day camp. Now that my heart wasn't in my throat, I relaxed against the bench. "I can talk to him if you'd like. Not that I think it'll help."

"No, it's fine. I know it won't make him stop. Nothing will." She gestured to Brody. "Has he convinced you to take in a kitten yet?"

"Not yet. That's not to say he didn't make a concerted effort when we went to the ranch. The little fiend even roped Remi into helping him butter me up."

"Then I'm truly surprised you haven't caved."

"How's that?"

"Oh, come on." She stared at me in utter silence for several long minutes. When I said nothing, her eyebrows raised in disbelief. "Are you really going to tell me you don't like that girl?"

"I'm not denying it." Too many people had called me out on it, so I clearly wasn't hiding it from anyone. I rubbed my hand along the back of my neck to ease the prickle of heat rising to my face. "She's skittish and dealing with something big. Hell, I'm skittish, too. I've got someone else to think about here."

"Have you two gone out on an actual date yet? You know, one you both know you're on."

I clamped my lips shut against a sharp retort. Damn it, did everyone know about our non-date-date? I scrambled for an excuse, and didn't have to look far for a genuine one. "She's been busy training at the hotel, and she's been helping West with Fiyero."

"Colton Lee Mitchell."

"What?"

"Ask that poor woman out. You like her; she likes you. Just get off your ass and do it already."

"I plan on it." A sharp pain pulled through my arm when she punched me hard. "Damn it, Prairie."

A few glares came from a nearby bench because of our cursing. The biggest glare of all burned from right beside me. Prairie narrowed her eyes. "Stop using Brody as an excuse. That boy loves it when you're happy. And I know she likes you. She blushed every time one of us mentioned you."

"I guessed she liked me thanks to our kiss."

"You kissed?"

"Yes."

"And you haven't asked her out yet? You stupid, stupid, stupid man." She punctuated each 'stupid' with a punch to my arm. The repeated sharp, hard hits had me convinced I'd have a bruise from the abuse. "Oh, you're so lucky I have to go back to work right now. Ask her out, Colt. Before she thinks you might not like her after all."

I definitely didn't want that. Prairie stormed off before I could ask her anything about exactly how to ask Remi out, or what to do on the date if she said yes. I was drawing a blank on a good idea for a date. It had been years since I'd even asked someone out, if that hadn't been clear from our first non-date date. Would she really give up on me if I didn't ask soon?

Did I want to risk it?

Chapter 14

Remington

My heart lay shattered in a million pieces. I'd spent half the night crying—no, sobbing—over the damn Doe Diaries. In my head, I knew it to be illogical, but damn it. Everything I'd been told about this town, everything I'd seen, I'd never once expected this brutal end to the story. It didn't make sense. How could it have happened like that?

I might kill Colt for recommending I read these. He knew they'd end this way, and he might've even known it would shatter me so cruelly. For weeks he'd happily asked where I was in Jane and Cole's stories. I'd foolishly been so eager to tell him, to exclaim over my latest discovery and how it connected to the streets I now walked.

Now it was over? How would I ever learn about the rest of the town's history?

With the last few books clutched to my chest, I approached the desk to the right of the main entrance to return them. The librarian, whose nametag identified her as Margot, eyed me quietly. I must have looked like a mess, because her brows knitted together in concern. "Are you alright?"

"No." I set the diaries down as quietly as I could, even though I really wanted to slam them down. "I can't believe they're done, and so brutally. I'm never going to recover."

Margot lifted the books to peruse the spines. "Oh, heavens no. You're nowhere near done."

"What?" That didn't make any sense. I thought about the online challenge I'd joined. I hadn't added these books yet. The website only showed more books once you input what you'd read. I'd obviously assumed these were the last. There wasn't any way for them to continue. "But Jane's in jail. They're about to hang her for murder and fraud."

A secretive smile crossed Margot's lips as she scanned the books back into the library. "I won't argue with you on that. She did go to jail and face the noose. That doesn't mean the story is over now, does it?"

"But how?"

Margot gave me no clue at all, no help in my misery.

My mind raced over the possibilities, a million questions forming. "Did someone else start writing? Was she not hanged? How was she spared if not? Was she spared? What do you mean?"

Margot's bright laughter carried through the lobby. Her gray eyes sparkled with her amusement. "I can't tell you any of that. It would ruin the opportunity for you to read the rest of the story."

"Then I have to know the rest. How many more are there?"

"I'm still not telling. There's a reason we keep them out of public view. It's the worst to have the surprise ruined. Most people get more emotionally involved when they never know when it's going to end. My word, you've been reading these fast." She hit a few keys. "You've gone through over thirty journals in just two weeks."

"I've spent most of my free time reading them." Granted, I'd had the girl's night, horseback riding, helping West with Fiyero, and most of my nights working at the casino. In between, I'd been devouring the journals as fast as I could. It wasn't a productive use of my time, but it was wholly absorbing.

"Let me get you the next few journals. Do you read often? I mean outside of these? We have a book club here if you're interested. I'd be happy to get you the information."

"That would be great. I'm new to town and always looking for ways to meet people and get out more. Not that reading encourages the second part of that."

"You should also check out the farmer's market on Saturdays in New Town. There's a building for it so we can hold it year-round." Margot's voice faded when she disappeared into a small room tucked behind the office. She reappeared a few minutes later with a few more volumes in her arms. "The local authors have a group table together if you're looking to read something unique."

"Thank you so much. You're quite the fount of knowledge."

"It comes with living here your whole life. Here's a copy of the book we're reading for book club as well." She pulled a book out from under the counter, scanning it in with the diaries she'd brought out.

Bright pink lettering accented the shimmering silver of the cover. I recognized it before I even read the title, *Local Woman Missing*. The book had been highly visible during my searches for a new read and had shown up in a few of my social media feeds. "I've heard of this one. It's a thriller, isn't it?"

"It is. Is that not your cup of tea?"

"Just about anything is my cup of tea, except outright horror. Although *This Delicious Death* was a fun read, even with the gore and zombies."

"That was a good one. Here," she handed me a booklet with weekly calendar schedules filled with information on each day, "is a schedule of activities both here in the library and in town. The information is on our website as well, but around here many people like to keep things classic with a physical copy."

"I like a physical copy myself. Thank you. I'll see you at book club if I can get the day off from work." I'd been enjoying the conversation, but now that I had the next books in the diaries in hand, I had to read. Immediately.

More than anything else, I had to know how there could be more books. What had transpired after that last entry where she'd sat with Reverend Greene? After she drank the tea provided by David? She'd talked about the brutally cold December day, about the texture of her simple wool dress, about the wind cutting through town. About how she'd tried to convince Cole not to go to her hanging, to remember her as she was.

The tears were already blurring my vision. Answers were needed before I lost my hold on sanity. I didn't bother going anywhere beyond the front porch of the library. I settled onto the bench right outside in the shade to settle in and get some answers so I could resume some semblance of normalcy. My traumatized heart needed to heal as quickly as I could gobble up the words.

The first page of the next diary noted that Cole Mitchell's verbatim quotes comprised the first quarter of the entries, which spanned several weeks.

Any hope I might have had with Margot's teasing shattered into a million pieces when Cole spoke of watching the woman he loved hanged in front of him. Tears clouded my vision too much to read any further. The tragedy of what happened to this incredible woman was overwhelming. Not to mention this man, who'd only begun to show his true feelings, who'd already lost one love only to lose another?

"It's not fair. None of it."

A hand settled on my shoulder. "What isn't fair?"

The scream that wrenched from me, accompanied by my tossing the book in the air, and the rest of the books tumbling to the floor, was far too extreme a reaction for the surprise. I'd been far too engrossed in the story. Heat flooded my cheeks as I scrambled to grab the books. "Shit. Shit."

Damaged library books, any damaged books, were a sin. Thankfully, the couple I'd dropped escaped serious damage. I desperately searched for the book I'd thrown, worried it had suffered a terrible fate. When I turned, I found the book clasped in the hand of a familiar face. Colt's brow pursed as he took me in from head to toe. "Sorry I scared you. What's wrong? Are you okay?"

It took his brushing a thumb across my cheek to realize I'd actually shed several tears while I read. "Oh. I'm, um. How could you do this to me?"

"Do what to you? You mean scare you? I didn't know you were that caught up in the book. I also said your name a few times before I came over."

"No. Not that. This." I took the book from his hand and waved it in front of his face. "Recommending I read these books. How could you? Knowing this happened? Jane didn't deserve what happened to her. She didn't deserve to hang for Clara's crimes."

"Ah." His confusion smoothed into a warm, slightly secretive smile. One far too similar to the librarian's. Why did everyone here enjoy the secret so much? "I take it you got to her sham of a trial?"

I shoved the book right under his nose. "They hanged her. I just read Cole's description of it. It wasn't just a sham trial. They hanged her. Right in front of Cole. Right in front of the whole town. David pulled the lever? He actually agreed to do it? How could he? What in the world? Why would you tell me to read these?"

The infuriating man's lips twitched to hide a grin. He clearly hoped to appear sympathetic, but it came off more like he might laugh at me. "You really need to keep reading."

I scowled. How rude of him to find this all funny. "Excuse me? How in the world is any of this funny? I've been crying all night."

"I'm sorry about that, but you really need to keep reading. The reward is worth the risk, I promise. After all, I'm here, aren't I?"

"That's true."

"I know. Look, I'm real." He poked my arm. "You can feel me and everything."

"Being a smartass doesn't help. It doesn't make much sense." I flipped the book over in my hand, sighing deeply. "I should get home where I'm not reading this tragedy in public so the whole world can see me openly sobbing over a story they can laugh at me for being so upset over."

"No, sit down." He guided me back to the bench. "I'll sit with you until you get through to where you're mad at me for a different reason."

"What reason would that be?"

"For not telling you in advance what happens."

"Why would I be mad about that?"

"You're mad at me now."

"But it ruins a story to skip ahead and peek at the ending before you get there naturally."

"Most times, yes." He leaned back on the bench, eyeing me quietly. Daring me to continue. His smug smile hadn't moved. It was tempting to smack it off his face, as Jane had once done to Cole. He'd deserve it for picking on me so much.

"Stop picking on me."

"I promise that's not what I'm doing. I'm actually excited to see you get through this part."

"If you say so."

"Read. It's worth it. I'll protect you from any other unwanted surprises."

"Who said you're unwanted?" My cheeks flamed. I turned my focus to the book to cover it. Even so, I couldn't miss the way he'd turned his full attention back to me.

"Would you like to go out on a proper date?"

"What?" That was about the only thing that could've distracted me from reading more of Cole's torment. I turned to face the man who'd been infuriating me only moments ago. His wide eyes proved he was as surprised by his question as I was.

"Well, last time neither of us was sure if we were on a date. We agreed we should try it again when we knew. I'd like to try again now. Well, not right now, but sometime this week."

"I don't know. It could be a trick. My boss is working me like crazy this week."

"Ah, but I happen to know your schedule?"

"Are you stalking me? I'm into dark romance, but not stalker romance." To hide my amusement, I had to bite my cheeks at his blush.

"I, um. No?"

"Is that a question or an answer?"

"I mean, I'm not. Although it could seem like it since we live next door to each other and work at the same place."

"You're actually my boss, you know. Oh, that's another trope."

He waved his hands in the air. "No. Shit. I am your boss. You don't have to do this. I won't fire you or anything. I didn't mean to."

"Relax." I clasped his hands, relieved that his panicked backpedaling stopped immediately. "I was joking. You don't strike me as that kind of person. You wouldn't hold it over my head if I said no."

His shoulders dropped, as did his head. He pulled a hand free to rake through his hair as he expelled a big breath. "Man, I suck at this."

"Oh, I don't know. I don't think you're nearly as bad as you think. Or maybe I just like you too much to care. I'd love to go on an actual date."

"Are you sure? I'm probably going to be this bad on a date, maybe worse."

"I'm counting on it. For entertainment purposes mostly."

Chapter 15

Colton

Between Brody, my work schedule and Remi's schedule now that she had work, a group of friends, West's rescue, and had apparently joined the library's book club, finding time for us to go on a date was proving difficult.

In fact, tonight should have been prime time for a date. I didn't have work, and neither did Remi. Instead, my supposed friends had absconded with her for another girls' night. If I weren't happy that she had found such a full life for herself here, I'd be more upset.

The greedy part of me would much rather be getting to know her better. The horny man who had been locked away for a long time, kept flashing back to our kiss, and the way her body pressed against me. To the things we could do if we just had a little time to ourselves.

I shifted in my seat, trying to push those thoughts and ideas away before I needed a cold shower. I needed to focus on my task at hand. It was mundane and frustrating. A combination that would hopefully keep my mind off the fact that I wasn't on a date right now. That, in fact, the woman I'd like to be getting to know better, was getting to know my cousin and sister better.

The jerks.

Prairie was the one who told me to ask her out, then went and stole her right out from under my stupid, awkward nose. When I'd complained to her, she said I should have picked a day when I asked Remi instead of just suggesting we figure it out. She had a point, but I hadn't planned on asking her right then. I hadn't even known I'd see her that day.

I glared at the computer screen in front of me. It wasn't the only reason for my current level of frustration, but it was part of it. The hotel's schedule was a mess. My seasonal workers were usually enough to cover any gaps while the college students were on break, but this year it wasn't cutting it.

Two people were on vacation; another had gotten injured on a training exercise with search and rescue. On top of that, Bryon and Rune were off for an undisclosed amount of time so they could be in Denver with their surrogate, who was due to give birth anytime.

There wasn't any way to resolve these gaps in the schedule unless I worked them myself. I'd barely have any time off to spend with Brody, much less do anything else. That wouldn't help my attempt to listen to my family and get a life for once.

I'd have to hire some more people. That's all there was to it. That, and asking my part-timers if any of them wanted some extra hours to round out the workload.

A door clicked open, the faint sound only reaching me because of the utter silence thanks to the late hour. It could only be one person, but it was awfully late for Brody to be up and about. He was normally a sound sleeper; once he finally went down, he stayed that way.

His small footsteps padded down the hall, disappeared when he hit carpet, then started again when he reached the kitchen. He stopped in the doorway, rubbing his eyes sleepily.

"What's going on, Buddy? It's late."

Brody shambled toward me, still rubbing one eye while he slipped the thumb of the other hand in his mouth. A small whimper squeaked out when he flopped against me. He stopped rubbing his eye, instead squeezing his fist into my shirt.

"Was it a bad dream? Come here." I pulled him onto my lap. His small body curled into a ball against me. "Bad dreams are rough."

"Scary man." The words were a little garbled around his thumb, not that it mattered. I understood all too well what such nightmares were like. "Chaseded me into the mountains."

"That is scary."

"Then a big bear. Big teeth, big claws." The rest of his statement was lost when he buried his face in my chest.

"Poor guy. Do you want to know when I have bad dreams?"

"You have bad dreams?"

"I sure do." It turned out that years of therapy wasn't enough to keep a real-life nightmare from invading your dreams. Especially when it left you with terrible scars, both emotional and physical. Several therapists down the line I'd learned to live with it all, but nothing could rid me completely of the nightmares.

"But you're Dad."

"I am. That doesn't mean I don't have bad dreams."

"But, Daddy's don't get scared."

"Sure we do. Dad's have nightmares. The world can be a big and scary place for anyone. Dad's, grandpa's, hockey players, and even police officers."

"Does Unc G have nightmares?"

"It's a good bet he does." We didn't talk about them anymore, Gunner and I. Over time we'd found dissolving into an argument about a past we couldn't change was easier than facing the consequences in the form of our dreams.

"Gigi, too?"

"Probably."

"Remi?"

I didn't have a second of doubt that Remi did. The previous week when I'd found her on the deck behind Gigi's, I could have sworn I'd heard a loud scream from inside that cut off too quickly to have been anything else. I didn't want to embarrass her or upset her, so I'd never mentioned it. "I have a feeling she does. You could ask her when you see her next."

"Huh." His fist squeezed and released my shirt as it used to when he was a baby. Those long lashes fluttered as he fought returning to sleep. "What do you do?"

"Me? When I have a nightmare?"

"Yeah."

"When the world is big and scary, I make it smaller."

He sat straighter to face me. "How?"

"Come on. I'll show you." I didn't put him down; I just picked him up to walk back down the hall. We went right past his bedroom to the third bedroom I'd converted from my office into his playroom when his toy supply got way too big for his bedroom.

"Are we gonna play?"

"No, sir. It's too late for that." I set him down in front of the play tent in the corner of the room. "But you are going to camp in here. We'll turn the starlight on."

"I like the starlight."

"Me too."

Brody immediately dropped to crawl into the tent. "There's no bed."

"Hold on." I grabbed a couple of cushions off the couch to slide through the opening. While Brody giggled, moving them around, I retrieved the blanket from the back of the couch and the starlight from the credenza. The light projected the night sky onto the ceiling in a pretty good replica of what we'd see if we went outside. It probably wouldn't shine as brightly on the tent, but it would provide light and a little comfort.

I hoped.

"Thanks." Brody pulled the blanket in with him. Crowded against the back of the tent, he was little more than a pile of cushions and blankets now.

"Here you go." As soon as I settled it in the corner of the tent, I switched on the starlight. Stars and the Milky Way burst across the fabric. I'd been wrong. The canvas of the tent was apparently heavy enough to give a good, bright display of the night sky.

"Wow." Brody curled up into the blanket, his gaze on the tent above him. "It's better than on the ceiling."

"Less surface area, but yeah."

"Huh?"

"Nothing buddy. Are you good? Or do you need me to stay?"

"Stay. Sing a song."

I couldn't carry a tune in a bucket and didn't think it would help soothe Brody at all. "How about I put on some music instead? My screeching would keep you up."

Brody giggled, nestling further into his nest. "Okay."

With a few quick taps on my phone, I got some soft lullaby type of music to play on the Bluetooth speaker in the room. It didn't take long at all for his eyelids to get heavy. He drifted asleep, easy as anything.

If only I could sleep so well.

Chapter 16

Colton

After half an hour, I was satisfied that Brody was finally sound asleep. I turned off the music so the speaker wouldn't blare if I got a notification. After I'd backed out of the room, I shut the door almost all the way. I lingered for a few more minutes to see if he woke up now that the music was off.

Silence.

I breathed a sigh of relief, heading back to the kitchen. Every kid had nightmares. I had to keep reminding myself of that. My burning need to protect Brody from anything bad aside, it was a simple fact of life. It didn't mean I'd done anything wrong. Since it was past ten, I resisted texting Paige for reassurance. It wasn't all that serious.

A loud, rapid knock on the front door stopped me short. It was too late at night for anyone to come calling, definitely to be knocking that loud.

Everyone knew I had a kid. I rushed down the hall to check on Brody. He was still asleep, thank goodness.

I pulled the door almost all the way closed again and ran to the door when the next set of knocks began. "What the hell do you think you're doing?"

Aspen's grin didn't falter at my sharp tone. "It's about time you answered."

"Brody just went to sleep after a nightmare. You're lucky you didn't wake him."

To his credit, Aspen winced. "Sorry. I wasn't thinking about him being asleep already. It's only nine."

"It's ten."

"It is? Damn. Sorry."

"What do you want, Aspen?"

"Look who's in town." He stepped aside to wave in the general direction of the shadows beyond the reach of my porch light. I couldn't really see much, but it seemed to be two people who jumped apart when Aspen pointed them out.

The larger of the figures stepped forward into the light. The familiar face of our old friend Briggs grinned up at me. "Hey, Colt. Good to see you."

"Briggs. What the hell are you doing in town?" I stepped onto the porch, closing the screen door behind me so I wouldn't disturb Brody.

Briggs shrugged. "I had a couple of weeks between training sessions. Thought I'd pay a visit. I had a promise to keep."

"A promise? To your folks?"

"Not really. To myself, I guess." We clasped hands and clapped each other's backs. "It's not like I never come home. Everyone acts like it's crazy that I'd want to."

A loud scoff came out of the darkness. Moorely stepped into the light, casting a sideways glare at Briggs. I thought she'd been out with Remi, Nova, and Prairie. Did that mean Remi was home? I couldn't help myself. I glanced over to see if her car was in the driveway. It wasn't. Damn.

Moorely glared at Briggs on her way past him. "We all think you don't like it here. Before this past year, you never came home. Now when you do, you don't bother to visit anyone but Aspen."

"That's not entirely true." Briggs grinned at her. For a moment, I could have sworn I saw him wink. Weird.

Moorely's cheeks pinked, but she turned away from him to storm into my house. "I've got Brody for you. You boys have fun."

"Wait, what?" I turned to Moorely in confusion. She was already halfway to the couch. "What do you mean?"

"Aspen's being all caveman with Briggs here. He's declared you men need a night to get Briggs some vacation tail. That's not really anything I want to witness, so I offered to watch Brody."

"But I thought you'd be out with Nova, Prairie, and Remi."

"I originally had other plans." She glared at her phone. In the light from the screen, I could have sworn I saw her blush darken. "But that changed. And since I've never exactly been welcome to join you guys, I'll stay here."

"I *did* tell Aspen I wasn't interested in hooking up with any strange. That doesn't interest me anymore. I just want to see my friends and have a few drinks." Briggs shrugged, leaning sideways to peer into the house. "Mo's being a little melodramatic."

Moorely stuck her tongue out at him.

"I can't go, guys. Brody had a nightmare. I don't feel right leaving. What if he has another one?"

Moorely set her hand on my arm. The warmth of her smile replaced every bit of annoyance. "Don't worry, Colt. I can handle Brody and any nightmares he might have. We like hanging out. It'll be fine. Go have fun. Tell Randy about Remington."

Briggs groaned. "Don't fucking call me Randy, Mo." He'd always hated his given name.

"Earn the name Briggs. Then maybe I'll use it." Moorely moved deeper into the house.

Aspen grabbed my sleeve, giving it a tug. "Let's go."

"Hold on. Let me check on Brody one more time."

Aspen frowned. "If you're not out in five minutes, we're coming in after you, and we won't be quiet."

"We're not in a college frat, Aspen." Briggs nudged Aspen. "Relax. We can give him a couple of minutes to check on his kid. He did just have a nightmare."

"You're right. Sorry."

I tugged my sleeve free. "I'll be right back."

On my way back to the room, I noticed Moorely following. I crept in to check the tent. Despite all the chaos at the front door, Brody still slept. His thumb had slipped into his mouth again. As much progress as he'd made curbing the habit awake, it was much harder to break in sleep.

Moorely crouched beside me to peer into the tent. All the annoyance with the men at the door had softened. "He looks pretty well settled. I'll call you if there's any problem. It's not the first time I've watched him."

"I know. I'll pay you."

"Good. I need the income."

I pulled the door mostly shut behind us. "Why would you? I thought you were working at the law firm."

Moorely grimaced, fiddling with the phone in her hand. "It turns out I hate being a legal assistant as much as I hated working at the bank. I think I've tried almost every job in town. I just can't find anything that works for me."

"What about your party planning?"

Moorely frowned, tucking her phone in her back pocket. "It's hard to run a business when you have no funds for startup costs. Every once in a while a friend throws me a bone with a shower or something, but that's it. Don't worry. I'll find something. I always do."

"Even though you hate working in Old Town, I could really use some help covering vacations at the hotel, if you want a few shifts."

"Really? That would be great." She let out a gust of relief. "I have a couple of things planned coming up, and a shower for Trudy. I'll leave the dates on your table."

"You said yes pretty fast for someone who hates wearing period costumes."

"I left the law firm over a month ago. I need the cash." Her cheeks darkened, and she hesitated. She glanced toward the door, biting her lip.

"Let me guess. Aspen doesn't know."

"No, he doesn't. Don't you dare tell him. At least not until I'm officially on your schedule. You can tell him you desperately needed the help, and I agreed after some begging."

"It's not entirely a lie. I really do desperately need help if I want to do anything other than work and sleep." I nudged her shoulder. "Thanks for watching Brody. I'll try not to be too late."

"No rush. It's not like I have a job to get up for. I can crash on your couch."

"Thanks." I hugged her tight. It worried me she'd been job hopping for so long. Unless she was at her little home on her big plot of land, she so rarely seemed entirely happy anymore. "If you need anything else, let me know. References, anything."

"See? This is why I like you more than Aspen."

I chuckled, releasing her to go join my friends. Aspen and Briggs used the whole ride into town to rib each other back and forth. With them it was never-ending, but they'd go to the mat for each other. Most of us would, actually.

Thankfully, Briggs insisted we go to one of the smaller bars in New Town. The quiet atmosphere meant we could really talk instead of being in dark, loud chaos.

We settled in with a couple of drinks at a table in the corner. Briggs positioned himself with his back to the center of the bar. He grimaced my way. "I don't want any untoward attention."

"What's up with that, man?" Aspen tilted his beer back. "For the past year you've been avoiding hooking up when you came home. When I visit you at games, too. You used to love the puck bunny life."

"Used to. A while ago. It got old."

I sipped my beer. "Sounds like you grew up."

"Maybe that's it. I stopped enjoying the whole thing a couple of years ago. I'm more interested in something real now. That's hard to get when you're on the road all the time." Briggs took another swig of beer before fishing his phone out of his pocket. He frowned at the screen before opening it and typing.

"Come on, Briggs. In the conversation. We finally got Colt to look at a girl." Aspen seemed to delight in taking credit for something he had nothing to do with. Or like the whole town was in some conspiracy when really it was only Gigi who'd introduced us. "A literal girl next door, if you can believe it."

"First of all, you had nothing to do with it. Second, we haven't been on an actual date yet, so don't put the cart before the horse."

Briggs' brows rose as he tucked his phone away again. "Really? You like someone? I thought you'd sworn off women after Kelsey in college."

It was my turn to grimace at the mention of my disastrous relationship. Things had ended pretty ugly when she'd displayed some disturbing behaviors like gaslighting. Thankfully, I'd been in therapy at the time and had recognized the narcissism pretty quickly. She didn't like my calling it off and stalked me for a while. "That wasn't a good time for me, admittedly. I've had other girlfriends since her. One or two serious ones. It's been since I told Rhodes I'd take Brody. He's been my focus, and I don't regret it one bit."

"I bet that's nice." Briggs fiddled with the label on his bottle. He didn't notice when Aspen and I exchanged confused looks. Honestly, his entire mood was off tonight. It was as if he didn't really want to be there, either. "Having something that completes your life like that."

"His life isn't complete."

"It is. I've been happy." There wasn't a doubt about that. I'd never felt like my life was incomplete, or like I was missing anything. "I wasn't looking for a relationship, and still don't have one. However, I do like her. She's cute, funny, and smart."

"Margot said she's devouring the Doe Diaries." Aspen knew I usually avoided anyone too fascinated with my history like the plague. For Gunner's and my entire life in Dominion Falls, all we'd ever heard was how similar we were to Cole. Gunner lapped up the attention while I grew tired of it after a while. "That doesn't bug you?"

"Not with her."

Chapter 17

Remington

It took forever to get my bustle in place. The damn thing wouldn't lay straight for anything. A quick glance at the clock told me I only had five minutes left to finish getting dressed and fix my hair before I was supposed to be on the floor. I was going to be so late.

It had been a comedy of errors leading up to this frustrating conclusion. After weeks of using my card in Colorado, the bank chose today to flag my usage as fraud. Only the cash tips I had on hand had saved my butt there.

Even though I'd been careful to ask how the risotto was made, it turned out the server didn't know what he was talking about. The fish stock they'd used set off an allergic reaction. Thankfully, I'd caught it at the first bite and hadn't needed to resort to using my EpiPen, but it meant I'd ended up napping after a dose of Benadryl.

To put the cherry on the turdcake of a day, my car battery died. I had to have Gigi drive me into town, assuring her I'd find a ride home. Moorely had told me she was working tonight. Hopefully, our clock-out times would be close. Or even Colt, since he lived next door.

My phone buzzed with a call. The last thing I needed was further delay, but Lexi's name made me pause. I'd have to apologize to Colt for my lateness, because I couldn't ignore her call. "Lex. What's wrong?"

"I could ask the same of you. What's going on?"

"Bad day. What did you need?"

"Um." Her hesitation made me stop halfway through lacing my boot. "I hate to add to it."

"Lex. I don't have time for this."

"Fine. Didn't you tell the police you were moving out of state?"

Anything but that. Anything at all. I closed my eyes against the immediate headache blooming. I just knew my blood pressure was too high after the day I'd had. "No. Why would I? I left for a reason, Lex."

"Detective Winder was still looking into it. You could have told him."

"Drop it. I'm sick of talking about it. I don't want to do this right now."

"He came to my work. Said you've been ignoring his phone calls?"

I sank onto the bench, still with only one shoe on. Rather than answer, I took several deep breaths to quell the flutter of panic. "Why would he visit you at work? You had nothing to do with it."

"When you kept ignoring his calls, he went to your apartment, which isn't your apartment anymore. He came to me, as your emergency contact he talked to in the hospital, and asked where you'd gone."

"You didn't fucking tell him, did you?"

"Rems. Don't be an idiot. He says it's really important. Just talk to him."

"I don't want to know." I sniffed against the tears at the edge of falling. "Please, just stop. I don't want to go back to where I was."

"You will if you don't deal with it."

"I need to get to work. I'm already late. After the shit day I've had, the last thing I needed was your judgment."

"It's not judgment. It's worry." Lexi sighed softly. "Call me tomorrow. We need to talk about this. Please."

"Maybe. After I've had a good night's sleep. If that's even possible after you dumped this on me." My head dropped, guilt over snapping adding to my rotten mood. "I'm sorry. You know I don't believe they'll ever do anything. It's over, and I just want to move on with my life."

"I know, but I still think you should take his call."

"I'll take yours." The locker room door opening caused me to jump. I spoke low to Lex. "I really need to go. I'm so late, and we're short-staffed."

"Fine. LYL."

"Love ya lots, too." It took me several minutes to feel steady enough to return to my task. Considering my lateness, I didn't bother with my hair at all. I rushed the rest of the way through dressing and rushed onto the far.

Colt was my fellow bartender for the evening. We were too busy for much talking after my apology. I knew I wasn't in the right headspace for work. My poor tips reflected my mood and lack of usual candor.

At least the night passed quickly enough. I brushed off Colt's checks on my mood during every lull. It wasn't until the casino's last customer left around two-thirty that I had a moment to breathe or think.

I scrubbed glasses on autopilot while my mind raced. Logically, I knew it would be said and done quicker if I just listened to the detective. Since the attack, nothing brought to me was good. The footage didn't show his face. He'd disappeared into the concert crowd. My description couldn't help their sketch artist because I hadn't seen his face.

"Remington?" Colt took the glass from my hand. "Are you okay? You've been washing this glass for five minutes."

"I—what? Oh. Sorry."

"You've been off all night. Is something wrong?"

"Yes. No. It's just been a horrible day. Speaking of, can you drive me home? My battery died, and I didn't have time to replace it before I came in."

"Yeah, of course." He studied me for a few minutes.

"What?"

"I'd like to show you something. I think it'll help your mood."

"What could it hurt?" I winced. "Sorry."

"Nothing to apologize for. Come with me." He took my hand, leading me across the pit to the stairs in the back. Instead of going to the front of the hotel, he led me toward the back stairs.

We went right past the back stairs and down a dark hall. "Um. No offense, but this is sort of looking serial killer-ish."

His warm laughter soothed my nerves. "Sorry. I don't like to turn on the hall lights. It would encourage curious people to see what's back here."

"Still serial killer-ish."

"Fair. Let me know if it still is now." He opened the door into a dimly lit room. Soft light from faux oil lamps and candles lit the large room. Velvet ropes encircled the area in front of the door we'd entered.

In the corner of the room sat a small wood stove with a teakettle. An antique couch and chaise created a sitting area focused on the large window on the back wall and a baby grand piano. Between the chaise and back door sat a tall desk, with a book open on it that looked suspiciously like a journal.

"It's Jane and Cole's apartment."

"It is? Oh." I drank in the details eagerly. The steps to my right, and the doors to other rooms both to my right and left. There was a small table in the corner, with a checkers board between it and the stove. "Really?"

"I've been wanting to show you this. Come on." He unclipped the rope. I hesitated. "What?"

"I'll let you in on a little secret." When I didn't enter, he pulled me in. "The ropes are just up for guests. We still use it regularly as a hangout, or in bad winters if we aren't sure we'll be able to get into Old Town."

"You still use it?" I was afraid to touch anything. The couch and chaise appeared in pristine condition, but also as old as the apartment.

"Have a seat."

"I couldn't."

"I reupholstered them a couple of years ago. The fabric only appears vintage. I promise you won't hurt anything. My idiot brother puts his feet on the furniture on a regular basis."

"That doesn't surprise me." I carefully sat on the couch, trying not to fangirl over the fact that Jane had probably sat right where I was. It was a safe bet Colt wouldn't appreciate that. After all, to him this was apparently just another place. "I can't believe this is all still here."

"After Jane and Cole were gone, none of those that took over the hotel stayed here. By the time any of us have taken over, we've had our own places. Jane's robe is even still on the bed." Glasses clinked when he moved the bar cart. "Prairie was here recently; there's wine if you'd like some. Or whiskey, bourbon, and gin. Apparently, Gunner's been here, too. He either drank all the scotch or took the bottle."

"Wine if it isn't red. I don't want to spill and stain." I couldn't help myself any longer. Knowing this was Jane's apartment, I had to go to the desk where she likely wrote many of the diary entries I had yet to read, especially seeing as this hotel wasn't even a reality where I was in the diaries. A plastic protector lay on top of the desk, with papers arranged underneath.

One of them was a letter addressed to Cole. I traced the letters, admiring her handwriting. Colt handed me a glass of wine. "Did this help?"

"Are you kidding?" After the day I'd had, the last thing I expected was to be smiling. "This place is incredible. You really just hang out here?"

"Yeah. It's normal for us."

"That makes sense. Even if I'm squealing inside, this is your every day."

"It makes it easy to take it for granted, I guess. I don't remember the last time I got excited about much around the history until you got here." He set his whiskey on the coffee table before taking a seat on the couch. "I've got to say, it's fun seeing these things through your eyes."

"I thought it would annoy you." Carefully, I set my wineglass on a table card as I sat beside him.

"It doesn't bother me with you." He moved a little closer. "You know, this is the first time we've had a minute alone in days."

"I'm aware." It seemed like one of us always had something going on.

"How about Monday?"

"What about Monday?"

"For our date."

Butterflies danced in my stomach at the word, and the way his eyes darkened as he said it. "Monday sounds great. Dress code?"

"Casual. Comfortable."

"So, not period clothing."

"No." His genuine smile drew me closer like a magnet.

"Thank you."

"For what?"

"Making my day this much better." I scooted closer. His gaze dropped to my lips.

"Happy to help." His arm went around my waist. We closed the distance at the same time into a kiss that burned through me to my toes.

I didn't hesitate to take the mile from his inch. The minute I swung my leg around to straddle him, he pulled me as close as possible. Which wasn't anywhere near close enough. The voluminous skirts I wore puffed between us, separating us by several inches.

His crooked grin when I met his gaze sent me laughing.

I fussed with the fabric. "It makes you wonder how they managed."

"Word on the street is Cole was pretty creative." His warm hands found the bare flesh of my calves. He slid them up slow as molasses toward my thighs.

"According to what I could gather from the abridged versions, so was she." I took a shuddering breath when his fingers trailed along my inner thighs. A low groan at the lack of contact carried between us. I needed so much more than these teasing touches.

He reached up, and I met the kiss willingly. With every sweep of his tongue, I tried to move closer. His fingers clamped onto my thighs, urging a moan out of me. In a move so swift I thought I'd fall, he flipped me onto my back. The moment he raised his body, my skirts puffed into his face.

My squeak of a giggle grew louder when he fought with the petticoats before getting them pushed back down. His attempt to glare at the offending layers of cotton dissolved into a smirk. "This is going great."

"It's not so bad." I hooked my leg around his hips to pull him tight against me. His eyes shuttered closed at his moan.

The skirts no longer seemed an issue with another steaming kiss. His fingers moved along my thighs again, while his erection pressed into my heat. Fuck, he felt so good. I curled my fingers in his shirt. "Please, Colton."

"Tell me what you need."

"I need you to touch me. Please." My whole body hummed with the need for his touch. I trembled as his fingers moved toward my center again. I whimpered when his weight lifted, only to moan when his fingers swept under my panties along my pussy.

"Fuck. You're so wet." He slid one deliciously long digit in deep.

"More. I need more." Ripples of pleasure accompanied his following my request. His fingers pumped in me. The moment his thumb pressed into my clit, I arched toward him.

He bit along my neck, moaning my name.

It wasn't enough contact... I tugged at his shirt, pulling it free to run my fingers along his bare skin. When he rewarded me with a forceful thrust, my breath caught in my throat. I reached his waistband, desperate to give him as much pleasure.

He bit my shoulder when I ran my fingers along his hard length.

"Colt? Where the hell are you?" A familiar voice echoed down the hall from somewhere in the hotel.

"Damn it." Cole met my gaze, his pupils still dilated. His breath was as ragged as mine.

I whimpered when he pulled his fingers free quickly. The tremors of pleasure were already subsiding thanks to the bucket of ice water.

"The door's open," he whispered. Quickly, he helped me to sit.

I straightened my skirts while he handed me my wine. "Um, Colt."

He followed my gaze to where his erection was still damn prominent in his period clothes. "Fuck."

"Colt?" Footsteps echoed down the hall.

Colt moved close enough to pull my skirt partially across his lap. He glared at the door. "What are you doing here so late, Gunner?"

"I wanted to—oh, hello." Gunner's voice was way too mischievous. "What do we have here? Have I interrupted?"

It took a lot of effort to keep the heat from my cheeks. I didn't dare look at Colt, which would likely give Gunner more fuel for his teasing. "Go to hell, Gunner."

"Remi had a bad day. I thought seeing the apartment would cheer her up. We're just having a drink." Colt's voice was strained. Poor guy probably had blue balls. I know I was frustrated as hell we'd been interrupted. "I repeat. It's late. Three in the morning late, actually. What did you need?"

"West is at the ER. Got his hand caught between a new rescue and the trailer. Might be broken." Gunner flopped onto the chaise, propping his feet on it much like Colt said he did all the time. His gaze flicked between me and Colt. "So, how are you two?"

"We're fine. I really don't think you're doing a damn thing to help Remi's mood."

I ignored the argument as my brain locked onto Gunner's news. Sounded potentially like a crush injury. That could lead to compartment syndrome. "Maybe you guys should go see your brother. It sounds serious."

Gunner raised an eyebrow at my interruption. "He said he's fine."

"All ranchers do. Did he decide himself to go to the ER or did Paige tell him to?"

"He decided."

Alarm bells rang in my head. "You guys should go. I'll finish cleaning the casino."

"How are you going to get home?" Colt frowned. "You don't have a car."

Damn, I'd forgotten. "Don't worry about it."

Colt pulled keys from his pocket. "Take my car. Gunner can bring me home. You really think we need to go?"

"Haven't you ever heard the adage that if a rancher or farmer takes himself to the emergency room, you know it's serious?"

Chapter 18

Colton

I still didn't know how Remi had known we needed to get to the hospital. When we got there, it was to learn West had somehow driven himself. I called Dad and Paige while Gunner got the scoop from our friend, Keely, on how West was.

He'd needed surgery and was facing a long recovery. If he took it. Fortunately, when the Coleman ranch heard of the incident, they offered a couple of ranch hands to help us with our current stock of horses.

West spent every minute complaining about the animals that would suffer because he couldn't go save them. I felt bad, but we weren't going to hire more hands so we could keep rescuing. It would take too long to vet people who would meet West's standards for working with his horses.

Remi called a few times to see how he was, and even offered to cancel our date if I needed to be with my family. When West heard about it, he'd adamantly refused to let me miss out on the date. I was infinitely grateful for his staunch refusal. After the other night at the hotel, I wanted nothing more than to get some more alone time with Remi.

Plus, it would be nice to actually be dating. I couldn't think of a time I'd come so close to being with someone before we'd been on a date. This woman had my head spinning in so many directions, I couldn't think straight. I was pretty sure that was a good thing.

The problem came when trying to figure out something to do for the date. I'd had to rely on my friends and brother for suggestions. There was plenty to do around town; I knew that. However, I had had no reason to think of romantic opportunities in a long time.

As it turned out, not much had changed since the last time I had dated. The drive-in. I only hoped Remi liked the idea. West let me borrow his truck for our excursion, and it looked like the weather would be nice and mild for the evening with a cool down after sunset.

The whole day I'd run on nervous energy alone. I kept checking and rechecking the snacks, what time I needed to pick up our dinners, the snacks and drinks, and figuring out what shirt to wear. Brody had been bound and determined to stay at the ranch to help, since West was out for the count and there was a foaling mare. He didn't seem to care one bit about what I would do without him at home.

I stepped outside to head next door for Remi, but she was already coming out of Gigi's front door. She looked amazing in a pair of jeans that hugged her figure and a bright blue shirt that dipped low at her chest. I couldn't stop myself from tracing the curve of her breasts. As much as she might enjoy wearing period clothes, there was something to be said for having fewer layers and more exposed skin.

When I met her gaze, one corner of her lip quirked in a smirk. She knew exactly what I'd been doing. "How's West doing?"

I was grateful she didn't call me out on my lechery. "The surgery went great, but he's miserable that he's not out there saving equine lives right now, or for a long time."

"That's a rough recovery. He'd better take it seriously if he wants full function back." Her eyes widened, and a flush filled her cheeks.

"Do you mind if I ask how you know?"

"Um. Well. I'm friends with Lexi. She's a nurse. Yup." A blush colored her cheeks. Before I could ask more, she went for a complete subject change. "Do I get to know what we're doing now? Why do you have West's truck?"

"He's not using it, and my car wouldn't work for where we're going tonight. Well, it could have, but it wouldn't have been as comfortable."

"Color me intrigued." She accepted my help into the passenger side. I said a silent thanks West had a retractable truck bed when she tried to peek in the back. Seeing what I had back there would have either clued her in or offended her. It could go either way.

Once on the road, my nerves kicked into high gear. What would be the best way to start a conversation? She'd been guarded about her past. I didn't want to cross that line. If I did, would she call an end to the night?

What the hell was wrong with me? I could practically fuck this woman at the apartment with the door wide open, but I couldn't start a conversation? Maybe I was a lech.

"I can't imagine what it must have been like growing up here. It must have been so much fun. Of course, people say that to me all the time, and it wasn't always fun, so I could be wrong."

"I actually haven't lived here all my life." I reflexively gripped the steering wheel at the admittance. It could be a slippery slope talking about the past. She probably felt the same way. "We lived in Texas for about seven years before we could come home again."

"Really? Huh. I'd never have guessed. You fit in here so well. It seems like you've always been here."

"I wish I had been." I tried to release the tension in my jaw. She didn't need any of that sordid mess ruining our first date.

"I'm sorry."

"For what?"

"Whatever kept you from here."

A red light made me slow the truck to a stop. I took my eyes off the road to meet hers. Her hazel eyes were soft brown in the evening sunlight. My tense muscles relaxed; it didn't seem like she was going to ask a ton of questions. I scooped her hand into mine before turning back to the road. "Thank you. What about you? You said you're from Orlando, so you really worked at the parks? I caught only bits and pieces of Nova's interrogation."

"It was chaotic at that table." Her delicate laugh filled the cab. "As for working at the parks, I did. The House of Mouse gave me my first job, actually. I worked there through school and stayed part-time when I was at college. Free entry to the parks was a great perk."

"That must have been an interesting job." Even with the heavy social media campaigns Prairie put out to boost tourism to the sky lodge, the casino, the college, and the chance to pan for gold, we didn't see nearly the amount of tourism they had in Orlando.

"It could be at times. You know how customer-facing jobs are sometimes a nightmare. Especially when people spend so much money for their picture-perfect vacation. They get frantic over one little issue."

"I can see that. Dad and Paige took us when were in high school. It was a lot of fun, but there were a lot of annoyed parents yelling at their kids. Thankfully, we were old enough that we could give Dad and Paige some space, not that they were admitting they were in love back then."

Remi sat forward, still holding my hand as I turned into the drive-in theater. I couldn't see her face to see whether she liked this idea.

"Is this alright?"

"Are you kidding?"

"No. I could turn around and we can go somewhere else if you'd like."

"Don't you dare. I *love* the drive-in." She bounced in her seat, her hand leaving mine as she pulled herself forward to read the listed moves.

Her excitement eased more of the tension out of me. "I'm glad you're happy with the date so far."

"Definitely. Although a truck bed at a drive-in on a first date could be considered forward."

I fumbled the card I'd extended to the attendant. He glared at me on his way down to pick it up off the ground. "Right. I didn't think."

"Relax. After the other night? I think this is small potatoes comparatively. It's blatantly in public."

I was sure my face was on fire. "I'm not—I mean—we don't have to."

"I'm teasing. You're nervous, aren't you?"

"Honestly?"

"Please."

"This is my first date in about four years, and that was a disastrous blind date. As for me asking a woman out, it's been about six years, give or take six months."

"Really? That means since Brody was born?"

"Before, actually." I steered the truck through the maze of poles. The speakers on them were purely aesthetic nowadays. The theater used wireless sound projection, and West's speaker was already set up for it.

"Do you mind if I ask what happened to his mom? Did you guys split?"

"No. It wasn't anything like that." I got the truck into position. Once in park, I hit the button to retract the bed cover. "His mom was my cousin."

"I—what?"

My word choice hit me like a ton of bricks. "Well, that sounded hella incestuous."

She pinched her fingers together. "Little bit."

"It wasn't like that. She asked if I'd adopt Brody. I was happy to."

"Really?" Remi circled behind the truck before she spoke again. "That seems like a story I'd like to hear, if you're comfortable sharing."

"I'm always happy to tell the story of Brody. Let's get ourselves situated first." Even though my reason for taking Brody had its own sadness, I didn't mind telling it as much as some other stories. Plus, I wanted to share with Remi. I helped her into the truck and followed behind. We got settled on the mattress. I did my best to hide my grin as I curled a blanket into the space between us. "There, so you don't think I'm going to get fresh with you."

She laugh-snorted. It was so adorable, I wanted to kiss her right then. She lightly punched my arm. "Punk ass."

"Hey, you started it with that forward comment."

"Fair."

"Before I go into the tale, let's go over what we've got here. I have drinks in the cooler. I didn't know what you'd like, so I have a little bit of everything in there. Wine, pop, and water." I extracted a pop for myself and waited until she did the same before gesturing at the bag in the corner. "Snacks are in there. Candy and popcorn. West informs me that those are both essential to going to the movies. At least that's what he said when he brought Brody home hopped up on sugar."

"Ah. So he's the *fun* uncle."

"Yeah. He lives for the title." I shifted to bring a basket out from the corner. "If you were wondering why we got here so early, this is it."

Remi glanced around the theater at the vehicles dotting the spaces. We weren't the only ones taking advantage, even on a Monday night. "It seems to be the trend, but do tell me more."

"I brought proper food for a decent meal before the sugar rush. There's about half an hour before the sun sets, and I'm contractually obligated as a dad to say that a meal consisting solely of sugar is not dinner."

"Was that in the owner's manual?"

"Yup, tucked into the diaper bag between the binkies and diapers."

That won me the delight of another giggle-snort. She leaned closer, inhaling deeply. "That smells heavenly. What did you bring?"

"I brought some dove pie and venison stew. You can have your pick."

She paused with her hand halfway in the basket. "I'm sorry. Did I hear you correctly? You said dove pie? Dove?"

"Yeah. You do know they're basically pigeons with a prettier backstory, right?"

"I do, but I've never eaten pigeon or dove. Snake, alligator, sure.."

"Tastes like chicken." The smack on my arm got me chuckling right along with her. "I'm sorry. I had to say it."

"Is it really dove?"

"Yes, it's the one bird around here that's in season year-round. That means the restaurants have come up with some creative recipes for it. Did you want to try? If you don't like it, I'm happy to take it."

"I'm willing to try anything once. That's the reason I've had crickets."

"Crickets?"

"Yeah. It was pre-pandemic. I went to Thailand. It's a real delicacy there." She helped me set up our dinner on the flat top of the picnic basket.

I couldn't imagine willingly putting a bug in my mouth. Just the thought had me shuddering.

"Oh, come on. It tastes like chicken." Her eyes sparkled with her laughter. When I reached out to get her, she squealed and ducked out of my reach. "You started it."

"I did."

She divided the two entrees between the plates. "I trust you. Now, you were going to tell me about Brody."

"For that, I need to start a little further back than that. Rhodes was his mom. She was my cousin, born two days after Gunner and me. When we were little, the three of us were inseparable. After we moved back, things were...different. For us. She was still one of my favorite people, and stuck by us until we were better."

She searched my face for a long minute. I swear I could almost see the wheels turning as she processed what I'd said. I was worried about which point she'd land on, and prayed it wasn't us getting better. Her brows pinched together. "Was? Past tense?"

"Yes. She passed away six months after Brody was born from cancer." I pushed a piece of venison around my plate while I tried to think of a short version. "She got married young, at nineteen. It was her pregnancy that led them to find the cancer. She had a choice between chemo and probably killing the baby or keeping the baby and losing months to fight the cancer.

Her husband didn't like her choice. He left her while she was still in the hospital bed. Sent divorce papers within a couple of months."

"Damn. She had an impossible decision, and he lost his mind?"

"Yeah. After that, she came to stay at Dad's. After talking about all the options, she didn't change her mind. Bringing Brody into the world was more important to her. We wanted her to fight like hell, but it was her choice. She pointed out that even if she got an abortion, there was only a forty percent chance she'd make it."

"I don't know how she made that choice. I'm glad she had the support of you guys, but I have no idea what I'd choose."

"Before all of this, Rhodes was always so full of life, a lot like Prairie is." My throat tightened. "Right up until the third trimester, she kept going as she always had. Once she hit the third trimester, she got so weak."

Remi's hand covered mine. Her warmth was like a balm. "Fetuses take everything they need from their moms. Even the healthy ones can get run-down near the end. I can only imagine how much worse it was for her."

"By month eight, she was pretty weak. She was sure she wouldn't make it long after he was born. That's when we started the arrangements for the adoption. I offered to take Brody. She'd already had me take her to all her appointments. I was already attached. I also made a lot more sense than Gunner."

"No argument here."

I chuckled, grateful for the distraction from the sorrow. "I felt ready to be a dad, too. It turns out I love it. I've found a lot of joy in parenting."

"I can see that. Brody absolutely adores you. If you hadn't mentioned it, I would never have guessed he was adopted. He's very much your son."

"He is."

"You said Rhodes lived for six months?"

"She did. We all stayed at the ranch because it was big enough for all of us and her hospice care. During those six months, Brody never stopped being her priority. She was a great mom. He sometimes talks about her like he remembers her."

"Kids are mysterious that way. I believe it."

"That was a bummer of a story. Sorry if I put a damper on the evening."

She scooted a little closer, pushing the basket out of the way. Her eyes met mine. "It's not a damper if I'm getting to know you. It's a sad story, but it also shows the kind of man you are."

Chapter 19

Remington

The last thing I'd expected out of this date had been a trip to the drive-in. I could barely remember the last time I'd gone to one. If tonight was any indication, I'd been missing out.

The fact Colt brought an actual dinner and a ton of snacks based on the size of the bag? That made tonight even better. I no longer even cared what move would be playing.

It was no secret that I was physically attracted to Colt. I mean, just one look at him shirtless during my first week here had fueled my fantasies until one of the most intense make-out sessions a couple of days ago took over my entire brain and body. I'd been so close to orgasm before his brother ruined it all. And that was just with his fingers. For a man who claimed not to have been with a woman in a long time, it sure hadn't ruined his skills.

It made me realize how right Lex had been all along about Kurt. Things with him had been fine, but nothing like what had happened in that apartment.

What was worse is that the more I got to know this man, the more I fell for him. The way his son adored him had been enough. Learning what had led to Brody's adoption? My heart melted into a pile of goo at my feet.

If we weren't in public, I easily could have jumped his bones right there. Even though that was tremendously inappropriate and I really needed to start thinking with my brain instead of my clit. I snorted, almost choking on the bite of dove pie I'd just taken.

Cole clapped my back, concern pinching his brow. "Are you okay? Did you not like it?"

"No, that's not it." I swallowed down the food and followed with a few gulps of soda. My throat still twinged a bit. I cleared it a couple of times. "Wrong pipe."

"You know you're supposed to chew and swallow your food, not inhale it, don't you?"

"Ha ha." I cleared my throat one more time, taking another swig of my soda. "Anyway. Before it tried to kill me, I was going to say the pie is delicious." It really was with the rich brown gravy and warm spices. The dove had a richer flavor, like duck that the spices enhanced without making it too gamey.

"And you were skeptical."

"Not gonna lie. I was. I shouldn't have been. Everything I've had at Turner's has been excellent. Not that I have any intention of ever trying the liver plate." I shuddered. "My grandma used to make us liver. Just the idea makes me ill to this day."

"Can't say I blame you there. I know it's supposed to be good for you, but blech."

I helped him clean our mess. While he tucked away the basket, I pulled the big bag of sweets out of the corner where it would be within reach. It took us a few minutes to get settled, but eventually we got comfortable with the bag beside me while we leaned against the cooler.

He raised a brow when I grabbed a candy bar the second the pre-show started. "Was dinner not enough?"

"It's not about dinner not being enough. Movies require snacks, you know. Snacks are life. Sugar really is a food group in itself. You shouldn't say otherwise."

His low chuckle carried under the pre-show song emitting from the Bluetooth speaker. "I'll have to keep that in mind. You seem pretty adamant about it."

"Oh, I am. There isn't a nurse alive who wouldn't agree. Especially us night shift nurses..." My heart sank into my stomach when I realized what I had said. Damn it, that was the second time in thirty minutes I'd messed up. At least knowing about West's recovery could have been blown off as anything, even watching too many medical TV shows.

This time the words rolled off my tongue so naturally, as they had before the incident. It wasn't even a conscious thought to say them. My heart went from being a giant lump in my belly to pounding in my throat. I put down the candy bar I'd crushed.

I could feel Colt's gaze intent on me, but I couldn't talk about it. I released a gust of air, focusing on the screen. Maybe he'd just drop it. "What are we watching? There were a few movies on the sign out front."

"Remington." The rich timbre of his voice curved over my name in a way that made me shiver. I tried to ignore the soft kindness in his tone. It was too close to pity. No, that couldn't be right. Colt wasn't that kind of person. "You're a nurse? Why didn't you say so? You shouldn't be bartending when there's a great hospital here."

"No, I'm not a nurse." Tears burned at the back of my eyes and nose. The image on the screen blurred. "Not anymore."

"Okay." He didn't press for more information, which I was infinitely grateful for. That was the sort of man he was. He'd already proven it to me when he'd found me after my nightmare. It wasn't fair to shut him out when he'd revealed something of himself. His hand settled warm on mine. There were no questions, nothing but silence and the comfort of his hand on mine.

My shoulders sagged. I turned my hand over in his until our fingers laced together. He wouldn't push for me to tell my story, he'd said as much before. That alone made me want to tell it, or an abbreviated version. "There was an incident at work."

"You don't have to explain."

"I know. You aren't pushing or asking even one question. I guess that's what makes me want to tell you." Leaning into his shoulder, I stared at our interlocked fingers. "I don't know how much you've heard about the rise in violence against healthcare workers in recent years."

"Bits and pieces here and there. Not too much, though."

"Well, it's become a real problem. If you pay attention, there's at least a story a day about a healthcare worker being attacked." I let out a long breath, willing my fingers to relax and stop squeezing his. "The short of it was I was part of one of those incidents. Two of my coworkers died, and I was injured. The hospital did nothing to help me. A few months back, the tape of the call to emergency services was released, and it was a real gut punch. Insult to injury. I'd already been unable to return to my old job. That made me want to leave the profession altogether. I didn't want to do it anymore."

He released my hand to pull me against him. I curled into his arms willingly. His warmth and calm reaction soothed my racing heart a little. When he spoke, his voice was gravelly with an emotion I couldn't decipher. "What a horrible thing to live through."

I closed my eyes to relax in his arms. There'd been no pity in his voice. Maybe Lex was right, that I needed to talk about it. Nope, I'd never tell her that. I'd never hear the end of it. I blew a raspberry. "There's something else."

"More?"

"The hospital administrator on the 911 call was my fiancé. He essentially said that the staff didn't matter, that he wanted the attacker caught and not to worry about the injured or dead staff until the other matter was resolved. I was in an ER, so it wouldn't have mattered so much, but they refused to let any staff into the room to help us because it was a crime scene. I'm pretty sure he guessed I might be dead, but didn't bother to check."

"What a bastard."

"You can say that again. Lex warned me. I hate when she's right." When his hand rested atop mine on his chest, I relaxed more. "I should have listened to her when she said he was a jerk."

"Would it have stopped what happened?"

"No, but it wouldn't be adding insult to injury."

"Literally."

"Exactly." If the pattern repeated, I'd be a hot mess soon. I didn't move for two reasons. The first being that I was afraid moving would pop the bubble that seemed to keep out the usual gut-wrenching fear that came up when I talked about it.

The other was just because I was so very comfortable right where I was. Colt's fingers trailed up and down my arm until my eyes drifted closed.

I forced them open to look at the screen. We were at the movies. I don't know if my calm was because I'd told it, or because Colt's reaction wasn't what I usually got. Pity and deflection were the norm. Kyle was the prime example of that tactic on me and my coworkers. He'd tried to gaslight me while I was still in the hospital bed. He was excellent at hospital politics, but a terrible fiancé. I sighed softly. "Well, didn't we both put a damper on the evening? To top it off, it looks like we missed the start of the movie."

"It was two depressing stories. I think there's some good in it."

"What's that?"

"You're lying in my arms. I'm rather enjoying that. Wait. Does that make me a pig?"

"Maybe. Just a little." I grinned, relieved to have the weighty conversation replaced with some light teasing. It wasn't deflection; it was acceptance. "It's pretty forgivable considering I wasn't about to complain about being here."

"Good. There's one more thing."

"Yeah?"

"We both told each other something important. We're getting to know each other better. Isn't that what dates are for? To get to know a person beyond initial attraction, which I think we can agree we both felt."

"Uh, yeah."

He chuckled. "So we were able to learn more about each other. That's good for a date. Or did I totally forget the point of dates?"

"No, that's the point. First dates aren't usually trauma dumps, though."

His thumb ran up and down along my shoulder in a gesture that both comforted and raised goosebumps in its wake. His breath stirred across my hair. "There's one little problem."

"What?"

"The candy is all the way over there."

Chapter 20

Remington

Soft piano music drifted from the nearby Bluetooth speaker. There wasn't a sound in the house to disturb my quiet. I actually had the day off and not a plan for a change. It felt like I'd been going non-stop since arriving here.

I couldn't complain. The time I got to spend with Colt was among my favorites. After our first date, we'd had another in the middle of the week. We hadn't yet gone anywhere near where we'd gone at the Mitchell's apartment that night, but something told me it would be soon.

If it wasn't Colt by himself, there was also Brody. Every minute around that kid was like sunshine on a cloudy day. There were times I went out onto the deck hoping to see him playing in the backyard, just to hear all about his day or any recent adventures. If there was one thing I missed about my career, it was the kids. Connecting with each one that came through the pediatric ER.

Then there was my new group of friends, who were bound and determined to make sure I didn't miss a minute of having fun or being occupied. They were all so nice, and I was enjoying my time here so much that I'd started looking for a home to rent.

In between all the things to keep me busy, I was sharing a home with Gigi. I adored Gigi, but I'd lived by myself for seven years. It was an adjustment. Plus, I really liked it here. I understood why Lex missed it so much. Even though I had a good idea of why she couldn't move back, I hated that for her.

I, however, didn't have that problem. It was time to find a place so I could really settle in here. But first, I was going to enjoy a day with no work and a quiet house. I'd purposely picked soothing music to fill the quiet. A piano-only version of Taylor Swift music had won in the end. I wanted soft, but classical music wasn't my thing.

The small canvas before had only the bare bones of the image I wanted to create. The piece I'd finished earlier sat beside me drying. A turtle in vibrant colored dots with swirls of purple ocean around it had been an experiment to do something besides simple mandalas. I liked it so much I was trying again with a flamingo.

I held the dot tool above the dark canvas, contemplating the position of the dots and drags I'd use for the wings. Although I'd had a lot of creative endeavors, these dot paintings had been my go-to since nursing school. I found the monotonous nature of painting one dot at a time a Zen experience. The rhythm of placing the dots in a pattern soothed whatever made my head swirl with overthinking, creating a deliciously blank mind of any worries or panicked thoughts.

Right now, I needed my mind deliciously blank. Yet another nightmare had plagued me no matter how many times I'd fallen asleep last night. Even texting on and off with Lexi hadn't helped soothe anything.

Working on the turtle this morning had let me calm down enough to nap. By the time I started my current piece, my hand no longer trembled as it had for the turtle.

The nap hadn't really helped. I was still damn exhausted. I'd spend the rest of the day painting dots if it meant I'd sleep through the night. Even if it didn't actually happen that way, it would be nice enough to have the calming distraction for a while.

Independence Day was in a few days. I'd automatically volunteered to work that night. I was used to working holidays; it didn't bother me. Gigi would be in Denver through the next week on her visit, and with my hours I could still have burgers with Colt and Brody before I went to work. Brody had been upset that I wasn't going to the ranch to watch the fireworks from their front porch, and that was my only disappointment in working that night.

I dabbed my dot tool into the paint, bringing it back to the canvas. Right before I could touch the paint to the surface, a knock echoed through the house. I glanced toward my bedroom door, contemplating. I wasn't expecting anyone and was enjoying my quiet time.

I turned my attention back to the painting. The only person I could imagine visiting would be Cole, but he mentioned something about Brody and a playdate. That meant it probably wasn't him.

Another knock caused me to twitch enough to smear the dot I'd placed. I groaned, glaring at the bright pink smear across the black. That would be a pain in the ass to fix. I used another tool to scrape away as much of the pain as I could.

Whoever was at the door clearly had no plans to stop as the knocking continued through my attempt to clean away the mistake. Once I thought I might be able to salvage the piece, I made my way toward the door. "I'm coming."

"It's about time." A familiar voice called back, sweet as pie. "We've been trying to reach you all day about your extended warranty."

A grin twitched across my lips despite my annoyance at the interruption to my day. "If that's true, I can keep this door closed happily and put on headphones to ignore you."

"You wouldn't dare." Novalee's stunning visage grinned at me when I swung the door open. She flicked a lock of hair over her shoulder. "Come on. We really have been trying to reach you for hours. We're having a cookout at Moorely's since not everyone can do July fourth. Why haven't you been answering your phone?"

"I put it on 'do not disturb' because I didn't want to be disturbed."

"Oh, that worked like gangbusters, didn't it? Are you coming or not? You'll love it. I promise times a thousand. The views on the Conway lands are incredible."

"I don't know." I'd been enjoying having a day all to myself for a change. Then again, Moorely had told me about her five acres attached to her brother's ten acres of untouched land. I'd like to see it for myself.

"Please?" Nova's expressive features morphed into a doe-eyed pleading, complete with clasped hands. "Pretty please? With a cherry on top?"

"Oh, you're pitiful."

"Never claimed I wasn't. Is that a yes?" She batted her eyelashes at me. My reserves were weak enough, but the fact they wanted to include me so much, Nova would come to get me out of my isolation, warmed my heart.

"Fine. I'll need to change." Even though a cookout was plenty casual, my ratty old llama pajamas and their matching tank weren't appropriate for public consumption. For that matter, it wasn't thrilling that Nova was seeing them now. They were worn thin. "Come on in."

"I think you look cute." Nova's earnest tone was the only thing that kept me from rolling my eyes. The woman was wearing crisp white denim shorts and a bright pink blouse that were stunning. Completely the opposite of my current clothing choice designed for the Netflix and chill days.

"For what I was doing, sure. To go out in public? I don't think so. I'd like to put on real clothes, and I'd really like not to be wearing something practically see-through."

"The guys'll love it if you do." She kept right on my tail. "What were you doing that had you too wrapped up to answer the door?"

"I was having a loafing day. Seeing as I didn't have to work and Gigi was out of town, I put on my comfies and was relaxing."

"Loafing days are important. I can't argue there."

"Yes, they are. You're interrupting mine." I knew I didn't sound mad. I really wasn't.

"Please. Colt told me how many of the diaries you've read. If you've read that many of those books, you've had loafing time." She followed me into my closet. "Today it's all about dogs, burgers, beer, and s'mores."

"You should have led with the s'mores. I might've left in what I was wearing." I riffled through the closet, trying to decide what to wear. "Who is going to this cookout, anyway?"

"Moorely and me, obviously, do you need more?"

"I don't need more; I was curious. Goofball." I held up two different shirts, trying to decide between them. My clothing choices were so much more limited since I'd dyed away my blond. Maybe it was time to reconsider that option.

"Fine. Aspen and Briggs started this idea because they caught Moorely and me chatting in the super-private produce department at the store. Aspen has a new grill he wanted to try out. From there, it's grown. Keely and her daughter Kaia, Prairie, West, Gunner, and of course Colt and Brody will be there."

I did my best not to react to that news, but I immediately chose the lower cut of the two shirts. He hadn't minded the view on our date, after all. "I'm probably going to need a jacket for when the sun sets, won't I?"

Nova disappeared from the doorway, her voice growing only fainter. "The temp could get down into the fifties, but we'll have the fire. What's this?"

"That's nothing." I didn't doubt she'd seen my desk; it wasn't like my room was huge. It would be pointless to hide what I was doing, even if my first instinct was to do just that. It was a hobby I did for myself; I rarely shared it. "I use it to clear my brain when it gets too full."

"These are great." Nova examined the turtle. "Do you sell these?"

"No. I do it for myself. These are the closest I can get to meditation, which I suck at." I hopped into a pair of shorts before grabbing my shirt.

"You should sell them at the farmer's market. I bet they'd sell like hotcakes."

"Not my jam. I like going to the market, not selling at one." I gently pulled her away from the desk.

"Don't be so modest."

"It's not modesty. I told you, this is how I clear my brain. They're my form of meditation. Good or not, I don't care to sell them."

"Too bad. I'd love to get a much bigger one for my shop."

"I've never tried anything bigger than this. It would take forever and a day."

"If they're your meditation, who cares?" Nova linked her arm with mine. "Let's get moving. I want a cold drink and good food."

My stomach rumbled at the mention of food. "Apparently, I want food, too."

"Good. We've got plenty."

Chapter 21

Colton

Brody and Kaia raced full tilt across the field that comprised Moorely's yard. Prairie had started a game of tag with them a few minutes ago. It had taken no time for Kaia's mom, Keely, to join in. West, who was stuck sitting in a chair watching the fun, had encouraged his best friend Wick into the game as well. He cheered on Brody and Kaia the whole time. Moorely joined him in a chair of her own so he wouldn't feel lonely.

Paige had tried to encourage West to stay home. He'd only been out of the hospital for a couple of days. West was tired of being cooped up, and who could blame him? He spent his entire life outdoors. I bet he could sleep in a barn or in a single-room cabin under the stars and be perfectly content. He'd begged me to help talk Paige down, and I had, with promises to keep him from doing too much.

Wick was a lot like West in some ways, but different in others. Wick didn't rescue animals, but he bred and trained dogs for both search and rescue and protection. In fact, the giant German Shepherd on Moorely's porch watching the activities was one of his. Curiously, Scully had raced to greet Briggs earlier, wagging her tail like a puppy waiting for a treat. Not even Moorely's brother got such familiar treatment from the dog, who took her task as guard dog seriously.

A squeal pulled my attention back to the game of tag. Keely and Kaia were tumbling across the grass. Keely flopped onto her back, staring at the sky as she caught her breath. I had a feeling that of the group playing tag, she'd wear out first. As a fellow single parent, I knew she worked insane overtime at the ER and still volunteered at the school at least once a week.

Thankfully, she had a great support system between her parents and the small town. The hospital even had its own childcare center, which had been a lifesaver for Keely when Kaia was a baby. None of that meant Keely wasn't tired. Hell, I was tired half the time, and I was in the same boat. Then again, I think it had gotten worse in the past couple of weeks that I'd been fitting Remi into my schedule more.

Briggs was supposed to be manning the grill with me, but his mind and gaze kept wandering. It kept drifting toward the group playing with the kids. I nudged his arm to bring his focus back to our task. We were expecting even more people to arrive within ten minutes. I hoped to have the food ready so we could relax for the rest of the afternoon. "Earth to Briggs."

"Huh? What?" He shook his head as if to clear away cobwebs. He lifted the tongs he'd been using to stare at them like they were some ancient alien artifact. "Sorry. What did you want?"

"Seriously? You're standing in front of a grill with tongs."

"Right. Right."

"I've got the burgers. You're supposed to be taking care of the dogs and Brats, remember?"

"Yeah. Of course I do." He finally turned his attention back to the grill. Even though it had been Aspen's idea, and Aspen's grill, somehow I got roped into grilling duty.

Before Nova had left, she, Aspen, and Moorely had set up five six-foot folding tables and piled food on a couple, while adding chairs to others. I didn't know where Moorely had come up with these supplies. Her tiny house had no storage. It wasn't even the holiday, which was a few days away, but Moorely had outdone herself with this completely impromptu cookout.

"Okay, Briggs. Spill. What's going on with you." Even after my nudging, he kept turning his attention to the group. At least the dogs weren't burning now; he was giving them some attention. I checked to see where Brody was before flipping some burgers. Briggs still stared off toward the tag game. "Are you watching someone in particular?"

"No. No, of course not." Briggs blew a raspberry at the mere suggestion. Even so, all his focus and attention were suddenly on the grill in front of him.

"Come on. Is it Prairie? You know I don't care."

Briggs snorted, giving me a sideways glance. "Do you really think I'd go near that girl with a ten-foot pole when we both know that Aspen's denied he likes her for years? He'd rip my balls off and feed them to Geordi and still deny why he did it."

"He swears up and down that he can't stand her."

"Yeah, and I didn't make MVP two years in a row."

"I know better than to argue with him, either way." That left only two possibilities. "I doubt it's Keely. Is it Moorely?"

"My best friend's sister? I wouldn't. Again, balls gone, his giant pit bull fed." This time he pointedly avoided looking at me during his protest. Huh. Interesting.

A couple of car doors slammed, effectively pulling me out of my musings. Because, like it had a radar just for her, my body immediately tingled in anticipation of seeing Remi. I knew Nova had left to go get her since she had answered none of our texts or calls. Somehow I knew it was they who had just arrived.

I glanced over my shoulder to check and found Remi staring right at me, with a warm smile on her face. That smile faltered into a yelp when Nova dragged her toward the cooler of drinks. I tilted backward to follow them when Briggs blocked my view. Remi wore a pair of shorts that were almost indecently short and a tight, low-cut shirt today. I studied the length of her legs right to the curve of her ass when she bent over the cooler.

A sharp nudge to my ribs brought me back to the grill. "Speaking of being distracted."

"Yeah. One little difference."

"What's that?"

"I'm not denying I liked her." I gave him a pointed look before flipping some burgers. "We've been on a date or two; we're still trying to decide if our first date was a date."

"How could you not know?"

"It was situational confusion."

"Sure, sure. That makes absolutely no sense, but sure." Briggs' normal demeanor had returned with the turn of conversation. He was about to tease me again, but I immediately noticed the figure that appeared beside him.

I grinned at her, giving a nod. "Glad Nova found you."

Briggs turned at my greeting. He extended his hand. "Hi. Remington, I presume. I've heard a bit about you."

"Please, it's Remi." Her warm voice coasted over my skin, both relaxing me and working me up. I could still remember what it sounded like pleading for more. "You're Briggs, right? From what I've heard, you play hockey."

A broad smile cracked Briggs' face. He tugged her against him into a hug that smushed her face into his chest. "I already love her. She doesn't know who I am."

Red rushed to Remi's cheeks, and she wobbled a bit when he released her. She blinked a few times, staring at him. "What?"

"You had to ask who I was and confirm what I did. You didn't know or gush. I am Briggs, and you are right about my playing hockey. Thank you so much for not gushing over me."

"Is that required or something?"

"Not required, but it happens a lot." Briggs still hadn't let go of her arm. It wasn't clear whether he even knew it.

I took her hand to pull her free of Brigg's enthusiasm. It had absolutely nothing to do with Briggs still touching her. I wasn't jealous. Nope. Great, now I was lying to myself. I was relieved when she leaned into me a little. "You'll have to excuse Briggs. He's every bit the Neanderthal you'd expect out of a hockey player."

"Honestly, I wouldn't know what to expect. I'm not big on sportsball of any kind." Remi shrugged. "I've never known a hockey player. Is this a sport I'm going to have to get some familiarity with around here?"

"Considering we have our own homegrown hockey player on the Chicago Tsunami team, it wouldn't hurt." I wrapped my arm around her shoulders, all jealousy fading when her thumb hooked into the waist of my jeans. "Then again, Briggs sometimes has a big enough head that he doesn't need another fan. Maybe you can continue to plead ignorance."

Briggs winced at the assessment. "That used to be me. I've gotten better over the past couple of years. The player life got old. That's why I enjoy hanging out back home now. This lot of miscreants doesn't let me be anything but humble."

"We've all noticed how much more often you've been home this past year." I looked over toward the tag game, pondering Briggs' earlier distraction. "Anyone we need to thank for your renewed love of home?"

"No. I told you that already. I'm just tired of the life." Briggs piled the dogs and brats onto the platter, all of his easy humor gone. "Dogs are ready. Get those burgers wrapped up so we can eat."

Remi's brow furrowed when he walked away. "What was that about?"

"I can only guess." I had a good guess what it was, but Briggs clearly didn't want pushed on the subject. "It doesn't matter. Want to help me get cheese on these so we can eat?"

"Gladly. I'm starving. I forgot to eat lunch."

"How can a person forget to eat?"

"A healthy helping of ADHD, a dash of hyper-focus on a task, and add in a tincture of exhaustion and you get me missing more than a meal a day."

"Exhaustion?" I didn't like the sound of that. "Did you have trouble sleeping again?"

She slowed in her task of separating the cheese slices. After she'd handed me the next one, she shrugged. "It happens more often than not."

"Maybe if—"

A loud engine revved. Gravel scattered loudly behind us. I spun around to find a familiar truck pulling in beside Prairie's car. I didn't know where Aspen had gone after dropping off the grill, but he was red in the face with anger. He hollered across the yard, "Moorely Sky Conway, you son of a bitch."

"Language," chided Nova.

"Shut up, Nova."

Chapter 22

Remington

All activity ceased at Aspen's yell. From what I could tell, no one had a clue what he was so up in arms about. Not even the current focus of his fury, Moorely. Her face went completely blank before her brows pursed.

Aspen's nostrils flared, his face almost turning purple with every step he got closer to his sister. I was seriously worried about his blood pressure at this point.

I drew closer to the gathering group, aware of the man following close behind me. My first guess for his following was to remove Brody from the situation, but a woman I didn't know was redirecting the attention of Brody and another child elsewhere. Maybe Colt was as curious as me, and the rest of the group, about what had Aspen up in arms.

Moorely didn't back down from her approaching sibling. She took a Wonder Woman pose, hands on hips, chest out. Her confusion had morphed into determination not to back down from Aspen's anger. "Who pissed in your Cheerios?"

"I know it was you." Aspen was close enough that he wasn't shouting as loud anymore, thankfully. "Don't pretend it wasn't."

"Considering I have no clue what you're talking about, I can confidently say it probably wasn't me." She held out a hand when he got close enough, bracing him an arm's length away. "What has you so damn pissed off?"

"You *know* what." He dug into his pocket before raising his fist above them both. Some brightly colored objects sprinkled through the air to the ground. A rainbow of what, I couldn't tell at first. Aspen's lips drew back in a sneer. "Your own special brand of humor."

It clicked then. The ground between them lay littered with miniature penises in every color of the rainbow. A lot of them. My laugh came out as a cross between a cough and a bark. "Oh. My god. It's the mini-penes."

A ripple of laughter went through the gathered group. Nova's bright giggles being the loudest of all. On our girls' night, my new trio of friends had shared the story of Moorely planting approximately a hundred 3D printed mini penises in the office of her former boss last year. The guy was a misogynist, and Moorely was seeking revenge for her firing. According to legend, he was still finding the damn things to this day.

Moorely's nose wrinkled. She shoved him away, openly gagging. "Ew, gross. Like I'd revenge penis my own brother. That's the total ick and a little incestuous."

"You're the one getting these printed somewhere." He held a tiny green penis up for us to see. "Who else?"

"Uh, plenty of women have those nowadays, not just me. Besides." Moorely stepped closer, brushing the penis away. She cocked her hip, a brow raised as she stood face to face with her brother. "I can't think of a single thing you've done that would piss me off badly enough to warrant such revenge. The question is, why would you think it was me? Did you do something that you expected to piss me off that bad?"

"I thought you were trying to be funny."

"Mini penes are not meant for humor; they're meant for revenge."

"Who the hell did this, then?" Aspen scanned the group. Honestly, we were all still at various levels of laughter. He landed on Nova, whose giggles were still coming hard and fast as she pointed at him. "Nova? Was it you?"

She waved her hands in the air in a sort of surrender. Admittedly, even I was wondering if she'd done it. She shook her head, sucking in air to gain enough composure to speak. "It wasn't me. Fuck, I wish it were, though."

"Excuse me?"

"Seriously. The look on your face?" She swiped at tears. "What's your problem? Are you afraid of a few little penises? Hitting too close to home, maybe?"

For a minute, I didn't think Aspen knew how to react. Too many emotions flashed across for me to catalog. He lunged forward, pulling Nova into a headlock. At her shriek, he started rubbing his knuckles on her forehead. "Punk ass."

The crowd broke apart then, with Moorely pointing at the ground and telling her brother to clean up his mess before the kids saw it.

I turned to see Cole's take on the whole scene, but he was back at the grill. He all but flung the burgers onto the platter. As I drew close, I saw a few were dark and understood the rush. "Oh, dear. I hope someone likes their burgers well done."

"I don't know who might, but I know who's eating them." His lips twisted in a smirk. "After that show of dramatics, Aspen can have them. He's the reason they're overcooked."

"What *was* that about?" Across the yard, the group clustered around the ground where the mini penises had been dropped. They were all laughing together, all signs of animosity gone in the whisper of a breeze through the valley.

"I'm not sure. Someone's mad at him." Colt gestured with the tongs. "Moorely's right. Once she pene'd Tucker, the whole thing snowballed through town. I'm pretty sure there's a secret underground club where they're exchanged."

"Are you saying there's a dark, seedy underbelly of penises in this town? You should have told me sooner; there would've been no hesitation about my staying."

"Behave." He nudged me with his elbow. "As for Aspen, it could've been just about anyone in this group. Most of us have his garage code because we've all been pegged to watch his dog. The man goes on vacation a lot."

"He has a dog, too?" I gestured toward the porch of the tiny house where Moorely lived. An enormous German Shepherd watched the events of the party with rapt attention, seemingly always poised for a command. "Like that one?"

"Aspen's dog isn't quite like Scully. Then again, Geordi is a gigantic dog. He's a pit bull, though. And unlike Scully, he's more likely to drown you with kisses than bite your face off at a simple command."

"Wait. Hold on. Her dog's name is Scully, and his is Geordi?"

"Yeah, Aspen and Moorely are both huge nerds. Their parents are scientists and nerds in their own right. Like you, those two have been to ComicCon a few times."

"Wow. I'd make fun, but I'm clearly a nerd as well. Mostly about Disney if it comes down to it." To allow him to set the platter on the crowded table, I moved things around. "I even had a cat named Stitch."

"I thought Stitch was supposed to be a dog." His hand settled on his hip, pulling me into his orbit. A delicious shiver ran up my spine; tingles ran along my nerves from that one touch point.

"I rather enjoyed the irony of that." When I turned, our bodies were even closer than I'd realized. Those blue eyes drew me in like a magnet. Fuck, I was so screwed. This man was winning me over, body and soul.

His gaze dropped to my lips. He drew me closer until my body pressed into his. My mouth went dry. I licked my lips to bring moisture back, but that only made his eyes dilate wider.

"Should we tell everyone the food is ready?" Why the fuck did I say that? That was the farthest thing from what I wanted.

"In a minute." He trailed his fingers along my jaw. His thumb brushed along my lower lip. I clenched my thighs against the sudden rush of heat. Fuck me. Was he really going to do this out here in front of everyone? Including his son? A child screamed, shocking a little space between us. Not enough, because he was still zeroed in on my lips. "I. Um."

"Yeah. It's probably best. After all, we're still figuring this out, and Brody is right over there."

His features softened, and he caught my hand before I could back away any further. "What if I told you that wasn't why I stopped? Or at least only a small part of it?"

"Is it because you'd find it difficult to stop if you started?" I sure hoped so, because that's how I felt.

"That's definitely a big factor. You understand."

"Well, I'm generally pretty on top of things."

"I can think of somewhere you could be on top." His lips twitched as my cheeks flamed. Of all the responses I could have expected, that wasn't one of them.

"Look at you being all vulgar when I can't fight back."

"Is that a no?"

"No. But I also can't take you up on such offers with a crowd around."

"I thought you liked Cole and his vulgarness with Jane." His phone chimed, breaking his intense gaze.

"Trust me, I do. I like it better coming from you." I noticed Gunner had arrived during our exchange. He was striding toward us with a smug grin. That grin faltered when Colt stepped away from me without another word.

He stormed past his brother toward his car. Gunner's brow twisted in confusion, but he spun to jog after his brother.

What the hell?

West jogged past me toward his brothers. Gunner called for Prairie, which had everyone turning their attention to the gathered Mitchells. Colt's shoulders were tense as he glared at his phone. Gunner's jaw ticked with his tension.

Moorely leaned against the table next to me. "What was that about?"

"Damned if I know."

Chapter 23

Colton

If Gunner hadn't taken my phone from my grip, I might have thrown it. Or run it over with West's truck. Anything to erase the existence of the four words on my screen from an unknown number. Hell, my reaction is probably why he'd taken it from me. I'm surprised it didn't crack with how tightly I'd gripped it.

Years of therapy and peace did nothing when my bubble broke. I couldn't think straight. My hands shook as I raked them through my hair. Neither Gunner nor West said a word to me as I paced in front of my car.

I didn't understand why this had to happen now. Except that things were going well. Even better with Remi in my life. Fuck, Remi. I'd just walked away.

Well, fuck. Now, I wanted to hit something. Hard. My punching bag was at home. I rubbed at my chest; my heart pounded a mile a minute.

Gunner stepped into my path to stop me when Prairie finally arrived. "Stop, Colton. Stop."

His hand sat on my chest, right where my scar sat. He'd probably guessed the scar burned like fire right now. I clenched my fists so I wouldn't take my urge to hit something out on him.

"Breathe, please." He didn't let me go when he glanced at our sister. "Did you get a text?"

"A what? Why do you care?" Prairie's brow furrowed. "What's up with Grumpy?"

Gunner pushed back against me at my snarled step. "Not now, Prairie. Just tell us."

She rolled her eyes, pulling her phone from her pocket. "Nope. Not one notification. It's not surprising. Everyone's here."

"Work phone?" Damn Gunner for being so thorough.

"I left it at home. What does it matter? Who would text?"

"Our." My jaw ached as I tried to force the words through my clenched teeth. "Mother."

"What?" I'd expected her to be loud, but she went the opposite way. A harsh whisper, husky with tension, drew the words out. Her body had stilled, her hands clenching at her side. "You're kidding, right?"

"I wish he were." Gunner showed the phone screen to her. He and West had already read those four words. Neither of them appeared as shaken as I did. Hell, West had been the least affected of us. For me, the mere existence of the text itself, and that she knew my number, was more than enough cause for alarm. Knowing that her husband was locked up kept me from totally losing it.

"Okay. So?" Prairie glanced between us. Her nose wrinkled. "Gods, Colt. Get a hold of yourself. She's basically saying hi. What's the big deal?"

"I'd like to know why she's reaching out after all this time? I mean, it's been five years since she last tried to get in our good graces." West took my phone from Gunner. "Isn't this how she started last time? Except she texted all of us then."

"She's testing the waters. That's all. I'd block the number. Ignore her." Gunner took my phone back, then tossed it my way. He wasn't outwardly showing any signs of stress, but I saw it in his darkened eyes. I had a feeling mine looked similar.

I glared down at the text. If wishes were horses, she'd feel my anger and know not to attempt it again. I knew better. It was a cycle I hated. At first, it had been every year, then every couple. I'd let myself get comfortable in the five years without hearing from her. "What good would blocking her do? It's not like she knows nothing about Dominion Falls. If she wants to find us, it doesn't take a genius."

"Which she isn't. She's just craving attention. She must have sobered up enough to make nice again." Gunner's lip curled at my phone before he tamed the reaction.

"The restraining order will keep her away. Seriously, what the hell? All of this drama over one stupid little text." Prairie flounced away without another word. She'd gone so fast, I couldn't tell how much of it was false bravado.

"There's no problem until there is, right?" West shrugged. "That's her style, anyway. I'm with Gunner—deleted it, block the number. Be done with it. Hopefully, for even longer this time."

That wasn't good enough. She wouldn't get the message that way. We had to make sure she knew she wasn't welcome back in our lives. Not for anything. Blocking her and ignoring any attempts at communication wouldn't do anything. Then again, telling her to fuck off hadn't ever worked, either. There wasn't a right way to handle this. No way out I could see.

"I don't want her anywhere near Brody. He's never seen her; he doesn't know she exists. He doesn't need that exposure. Blocking her won't keep her away. You know it won't."

"We all know it. It's our first defense. If she goes further, we'll take another step. If we talk to her now, even to tell her to leave us alone, it'll just encourage her to reach out more. She lives for the attention and to play the victim." West clapped me on the shoulder. I know he meant the best, but he didn't have a son to protect from that woman. I didn't object when he headed back to the party as well.

Gunner didn't leave my side. With our siblings gone, some of my anger reflected in Gunner's tense jaw. He glared at my phone as if he could still see the screen. "They were too young. They don't really remember what happened every time she popped up. West was a baby when we got out. Prairie had it, in many ways, rougher than us. She's worked too hard to erase that part of her life to even let in a crumb, I think."

"That isn't exactly true. She dealt with it in therapy. I can't say I blame her for not wanting to think about it. I sure as hell don't, especially now. For the past five years, I've been happy to put it behind me. I just don't understand. Why now?"

"We've all been happy to put it behind us." Gunner tapped his thumb on his thigh, looking east toward the mountains in the distance. I couldn't help but follow his gaze. Forty miles past those mountains was where our nightmare had begun. "There's something else."

I'd guessed as much by that thumb tap. It was his biggest tell. My jaw clamped together. I couldn't even speak to ask what it was.

"He got out."

My body went numb. It wasn't possible. The judge sentenced him to decades. How had I not known? Maybe I'd taken a lesson from Prairie's playbook if I was that out of touch. "Why the fuck didn't you tell us?"

"Because he left Texas heading east. I figured if it became an actual problem, I'd say something. I've got Hagen keeping an eye on it every couple of weeks. There's been some chatter out east about someone possibly having the same tattoo, but the images are too blurry to know for sure."

"Jesus, Gunner. Do you think he and our mother are back together? If he got his hooks in again, I don't want to think of the consequences."

"I doubt it. Like I said, I haven't heard anything." His gaze wandered back to the party. "I'm honestly surprised she didn't reach out to West first. He's the most soft-hearted of us all."

"And the only one not Dad's."

"He is in every way that counts. That doesn't mean he isn't a soft touch."

"How would she know that? He was too young when we got out."

"True. He's still a good place to test the waters. Placating him with a sob story? Works every time, just look at the ranch."

"We'd see through it, though." I dropped my head back to stare at the sky. I wish the clouds held the answers. My life would be so much easier. I could go on as content as I had been that we were free of the suffocating weight of our past.

"What are you going to do?"

I closed my eyes, biting back a sharp retort. "I'll ignore it. She won't get any shred of acknowledgment from me, but I'm not blocking. I need to know how persistent she's going to be. The last thing I need is for her to get here and around Brody."

"Nobody wants that."

"I know they don't. We'll have to tell Dad." He and Paige were finally happy and content. I didn't want to ruin it for them. Even so, the bitch blamed him for the divorce, even though she's been the crazy one. "Will you let me know if you hear anything about either of them being in the area? My priority is Brody."

"If I thought either of them were near the Valley, or even in the state, I'd tell everyone. I'm not an idiot." Gunner folded his arms across his chest, nodding toward the party. "Your girl was pretty confused when you stormed off. What are you going to tell her?"

"For now, nothing. This isn't exactly the time or place to share that story. It's too dark."

"And twisted."

"As fuck." I rubbed my hand across the back of my neck to ease the lingering tension. It didn't help. "I'll tell her it was some bad news, which isn't a lie."

"You know, it's more than a dark and twisted story. It's a fucking horror show."

"And I've got the scars to prove it."

Chapter 24

Remington

Moorely nudged me gently. "Let's get this crowd eating. Stop staring at him."

"I'm not staring at him. Exactly." Honestly, I was worried. Based on body language alone, I could tell Colt was really upset. Prairie and West each left the confab. Neither of them appeared as troubled as the twins did. "Just hoping he's okay."

"Prairie and West don't seem any the worse for wear. I'm sure he's fine. Come on. Food." Moorely tugged gently on my arm. She grabbed a plate, which she promptly loaded with some pasta salad.

I tore my attention away from the conversation. It wasn't my business, and I wasn't the prying type, but my concern kept me glancing over to the brothers.

A small body barreled into me hard enough that I took two steps back. "Remi!"

"Hey there, Brody." And just like that, my worries burned away under the force of his grin. I crouched down to wrap him in a tight hug. "It looks like you've been having a lot of fun out there with your friend."

"Her name's Kaia. Where's Dad? It's time to eat. I'm hungry. Do you smell that? Hot dogs, yum. There's cookies, too. Nova brought them."

I fought my laughter down into a smile at Brody's train of thought running off the tracks. "Your dad is talking with your Uncle Gunner. If you're hungry, we can try to get some food in that crowd."

Everyone had swarmed the food table once Moorely started filling her plate. I thought distracting Brody with food would be a good way to keep him from intruding on whatever the twins were discussing. Brody eyed the crowd, his grin growing. "Do you think I could push one and they'd topple like dominoes?"

"I don't think humans work like that." As I stood back up, I took his hand. "I'll help you make a plate so when your dad gets back he can join you without having to make two plates. And you won't have to wait for him to eat."

"Sure. Can I get a hot dog?"

"If there's any left. We might have to bully our way in to get one."

"Dad says bullying is bad."

"Good point." I kept his hand tucked in mine as we got to the table. "Then how about we sneak our way in?"

"Okay. I like chips, too."

"Good to know. I think they have every flavor on the table here." Thankfully, Prairie stood right by the plates. I leaned in close. "Any allergies I need to know about?"

"Not a one we've seen. Especially not in food." Prairie crouched at her nephew's level. "Not too much. You don't want a stomachache because your eyes were bigger than your stomach."

"My eyes aren't bigger than my stomach!" Brody made his hands into goggles. He peered at his aunt, then me, then back again. "See? They're so small."

"Do you want to know how big your stomach is?" I kneeled down at his level. "I can show you if you'd like."

He took his hand-goggles off, nearly whacking me with his enthusiastic "*Yeah*."

"Okay, then." I chuckled as I wrangled his waving limbs in front of him.

"Wait." He braced his hands in front of him, palms toward me. His wide denim-blue eyes stared at me seriously. "Are you gonna take out my stomach? It's inside."

Prairie's giggles had her nearly doubling over. "Oh, Brody. She won't take out your stomach."

"No, I won't. It's on the inside, like you said. Here's a trick, though. Make a fist, like this." I closed my hand in front of me. When Brody did the same, I wrapped my hands around it. Sure, it was a partial misconception that the stomach is the size of a fist, but it was always a hit with my pediatric patients. I told this old wives' tale too many times to count over the past eight years. "Right there. It's the size of your fist when it's empty. When you eat, it gets bigger."

He didn't miss a movement as I expanded my hands around his. "Wow. How big does it get?"

"That depends on how much you eat, but it really can only expand a certain amount. That's why you get a stomachache when you eat too much."

Brody puffed out his stomach and clapped his hands on it. "What if it's bigger like this? Like Mayor Wills' belly?"

Both Prairie and I had to clamp our hands over our mouths to keep outright laughter at bay. It took a few minutes, but I collected myself enough to respond with very little amusement in my tone. "Think of your stomach like a balloon. If you blow it up, then release it, what happens?"

"It makes a funny noise." He pushed his lower lip against his teeth and made farting noises.

Prairie did lose it that time. "Oh, he's got you there."

"Okay, okay. I meant it shrinks back small, right?" I waited for him to nod. "Well, if you do that all the time, eventually the balloon stretches, and the size it shrinks to gets bigger and bigger. The bigger it gets, the more it wants filled, so it's hard to stop."

Prairie collected herself. "I bet you can show all your friends that at summer camp and they'll love it. In the meantime, I'm pretty sure we're holding up the line for food."

Brody and I took our places in line, but I grabbed both plates. My appetite wasn't huge, so I wasn't too worried about being weighed down by both plates. I grabbed a little of everything Brody pointed at, from mac and cheese to pasta salad to corn and, of course, the hot dog.

Prairie remained in line behind us. "Is that true? About the stomach?"

"Sort of. It can actually get as small as a walnut depending on how much you eat regularly, or be as big as a grapefruit. And yes, kids are smaller."

"Huh. Then the old wives' tale is kinda true?"

"Yup." With my hands full, Brody couldn't drag me along behind him. Instead, he took on a role like an aircraft marshaler. Waving me in the right direction. At the table with his friend and her mom, he plopped onto the bench. I set down his plate and my own before extending my hand. "Hi. It's nice to meet you. I'm Remi."

"It's great to finally meet you, too. I've heard plenty of chatter about you; this town loves some good gossip. I'm Keely. This is my daughter Kaia." Keely's affection for her daughter shone through her features. The young girl mirrored her mother in their bronze skin and black hair. She ran her fingers along her daughter's braid before turning back to me. "It's been utter chaos for me."

"I think it's been like that for everyone I've met so far. It seems like life is constantly bustling around here. I'd never expect it from a small town."

"Oh, it can get worse. Wait for the fair and Founder's Day." Keely let out a breath. "Between summer camp, summer dance camp, and picking up extra shifts for the bonuses, I'm worn out."

My hand clenched on my plastic fork at the mention of extra shifts for the bonus. Memories flashed through my head. The glint of metal, the screams, the metallic tang of blood. The air thinned as my lungs closed. I closed my eyes to get myself back together. I wasn't there anymore. It wasn't happening.

"—vacation at the end of summer, and I'd like all the bonus pay I can to make it fun." Keely's voice came back to me as I collected myself. I'd missed part of what she'd said, but it didn't seem like she'd noticed. She was grinning at her daughter. "We're planning to go to Disney."

"Oh, you know what, Kaia?" I snatched at the subject change like a drowning woman grabbing a life preserver. My hands still shook, so I dropped them into my lap. "I used to work at Disney."

"You *did*?" Both Kaia and Brody spoke over each other with rapid-fire questions about everything from what Mickey did on his off hours to if there were really alligators in the lake. How these two young ones had heard about the alligators, I didn't know.

"I'll answer all the questions I can, but one at a time." I shared a grin with Keely. "And as for you, before you even feel the need to ask, yes. I'm more than happy to give you all my tips and tricks to getting through the parks with your sanity intact?"

"That's possible?" She wasn't even there yet, but Keely already seemed frazzled.

"It really is."

"That would be the best." Keely's shoulders dropped with her gust of relief. "It's been so overwhelming trying to narrow down all those tips and tricks on the internet and deciding what we want to do, how many days to spend at which park. It's a lot."

"I'm happy to help. I've seen enough vacations ruined because the parents are miserable, the kids are running rampant, and they don't get to do the things they actually wanted to." A hand touched my shoulder, pulling me from the conversation. I found those shocking ice-blue eyes turned down in worry. Colt mouthed 'sorry'. I shook my head, patting his hand to show it wasn't a problem.

"What are we talking about?" Colt took the seat on the opposite side of his son, a full plate already in hand. "Look at your plate, Brody. It looks like you controlled yourself for a change."

"Remi told me my stomach is this big, and she made the plate, so I guess it's so my stomach doesn't get too big and stretched out like the Mayor's. Right, Remi?" Brody shoved more mac and cheese in his mouth as soon as he finished the question.

"That's right." I ruffled his hair, winking at Colt over his head. "We didn't want a tummy ache when there's still plenty of fun to be had, after all."

"Good point. Also, this way you can go back for seconds if there's something you missed the first time around. Or you can save all that room for dessert." Colt returned my wink. When his hand caught mine behind Brody, butterflies danced in my stomach.

"Dessert!" Brody danced in his seat. "Remi worked at Disney. She was gonna tell us all the stuff. We have lots of questions."

"I did promise. Let's start, shall we? One question at a time."

Chapter 25

Colton

Near the fire pit, an argument was brewing. Aspen and Briggs were bickering over the proper way to build a fire. They were battling over the positioning of the wood and what to use for kindling. The nail in the coffin of continuing peace in the matter was my twin heading toward them to add his two cents.

I wasn't going near that mess with a ten-foot pole. Wick didn't have the same idea, as he jogged toward the fire pit as well. Things were going to get a lot more chaotic before they calmed down.

Brody and Kaia's laughter carried easily across Moorely's wide-open land. They both flopped onto the grass, rolling down the hill until they bumped into each other or hit the bottom. Then they'd run back up the hill to do it all over again. It reminded me so much of Prairie and West when we'd first come back to Dominion Falls and they'd been able to be kids, my heart twinged a little.

As they rolled again, my dad brain kicked in, urging me to warn them about ticks. I held my tongue and let him play. The only thing I'd ever wanted for him was to have a happy childhood free of the things that had plagued mine. I wasn't about to interrupt a good time for a tick check. We'd do that later. Of course, I also knew that Moorely kept a broad area around her small home sprayed for ticks because of her dog, Scully.

The same large German Shepherd currently nuzzling under Remi's arm. Her laughter rang over the initial raised voices from the fire argument. She slipped Scully what looked like an ice cube. Scully lifted her muzzle, the gleam of the ice cube peeking out of her mouth, and trotted back to the deck.

My silent apology seemed to be accepted over dinner, but that wasn't good enough. I wanted to clarity that I hadn't meant to be rude. My brain had switched over too quickly for any bit of politeness. No, I couldn't tell her that without telling her more.

She'd been so great with Kaia and Brody at dinner, fielding all their questions about Disney. Along with those, she'd told some stories that had them clamoring for more. It was a wonder anyone got them away from her to play some more.

I crossed the yard toward her, calling out so I wouldn't surprise her, "Hey."

"Hey there." Remi stood with two beers. She handed one off to me before popping the cap off hers. "Sorry for dominating the dinner conversation. Once I get on a roll, it's hard to shut me up."

"I'm pretty sure that wasn't you."

Her nose wrinkled delicately. "It kinda was."

"No, I'd say it was more Brody and Kaia dominating the conversation, peppering you with questions and begging for more stories. I'm impressed you could field both of their excitement so well. Keely and I were both a little overwhelmed, and they're our kids."

She smiled warmly. "Sometimes kids are so much easier to deal with than adults. They have such wonder about so many things. Their questions are simpler and more straightforward, although greater in number."

"Truer words were never spoken." I opened my mouth to apologize, but she spoke before I could.

"I've always loved kids. That's the thing I miss about my job."

My apologies died in my throat at this small admittance. Her gaze drifted toward the sky, a shimmer catching in the fading sunlight. I hated to break the spell. When I tried, my mouth was too dry to utter a sound.

"Hospitals are so scary for them, especially the ER. Even if it is a children's ER. There was magic in helping them find their bravery and joy again." She blinked a few times, her cheeks darkening as she took another swig. "Well. That was dramatic."

"You worked with kids?"

She looked around to see if anyone would overhear her. "Pediatric ER nurse. The night it happened, I'd picked up an extra shift in the adult ER."

I rubbed her arms at the shivers I knew didn't come from cold. She took a step, and I folded her in my arms. "You want to stop talking about it?"

"Very much. What about that fire? Do you think they'll get it started?"

"At this rate, no. Brody will be mad if we don't get s'mores."

"Brody? Hell, I'll throat punch a dickhead that keeps me from getting my s'mores." Her grin spread wider at my outright laughter. "If they don't start it themselves in the next ten minutes, I'll do it myself."

"I don't doubt you would."

"Good for you." She polished off her beer.

"I'm really sorry about storming off like that earlier." If I didn't say it, I'd regret it later. There wasn't a clear opening, so I'd forced a path through.

"You don't owe me an explanation."

My heart twisted. Why would she think that? "I think I do."

"You really don't." She set her hand on my chest at my protest. "Listen."

"Okay."

"I'd have to be blind not to see something upset you. You received a text and went with your family to deal with it. I don't need details, and you don't owe me any explanation. I only have one question."

The tension seeped out of my shoulders at her reassurance. A bit of returned when she said she had a question. "That seems fair after I ghosted you in person."

She chuckled softly. "Not quite. You came back."

"That's true. What's your question?"

She set her hand on my forearm. Her amusement settled into soft concern. She searched my eyes so intently, I noticed little flex of gold in hers. "Are you okay?"

"Oh. Yes. No. I'm not sure yet?"

"I'm so glad we cleared that up." Her eyes danced with laughter.

I didn't bother to cover my amusement. Her understanding helped push away much of my anger. "I made that clear as mud, didn't I?"

"Maybe not mud. Maybe a puddle in the mud."

"Is that supposed to be better?"

"Sort of." Her gaze landed on the guys still battling over the firepit. Even though she looked exasperated at their antics, her voice was kind. "If you ever need an ear, or to sit in silence and stare at the Milky Way. I'm available. There's no pressure for you to tell me all your secrets, just as you've given me no pressure to do the same."

The last remnants of tension gusted out of me. Warmth flooded my cheeks when she turned a bright smile on me. "You are one hell of a woman."

She actually ducked her head. "I wouldn't say that."

"I would." A rowdy cheer went up near the fire pit, drawing my attention and hers. "I'm really beginning to think we won't have a fire."

"No s'mores would be the true tragedy. Should I go help?"

"Maybe if we threaten there'll beno s'mores, they'll make progress."

"You've got a lot more faith in them than I do." Her brow furrowed. "Did I just hear Briggs claim he was in the Boy Scouts? And they still don't have a fire lit?"

"Pathetic, isn't it?"

Her musical laugh danced across me. "Should we step in?"

"I'm not about to get in the middle. Let them suffer. Moorely will set them straight soon enough. She finds the lot of them highly annoying."

"That's fitting. Especially seeing as the loudest mouth is her brother. I'm pretty sure it's a given you're always thoroughly annoyed by a sibling."

"It's an unspoken rule."

"What would you like to do while we wait?" I leaned against the house next to her. "We could join the kids."

"I can't remember the last time I rolled down a hill. It's been ages. I'm not entirely opposed." She fanned herself. "First, I need to cool down. I've been in the sun all afternoon. It's warm today."

"Aren't you from Florida?"

"Isn't it eighty-five degrees?"

"Yeah, but it's a dry heat." I hadn't been able to keep the dad humor out. I clamped my lips together to suppress my laughter. The look Remi shot me made it even more difficult. The moment she laughed, I let loose every bit of my amusement.

"That is such a dad thing to say." She shoved my shoulder, then bumped her hip with mine. "You're terrible."

"Probably. Am I wrong?"

"Actually, no. I have to admit it's better than eighty-five in ninety percent humidity, but that doesn't mean it's not hot. Smartass."

"Being a corny smartass was worth it if it made you laugh that hard."

"Does that mean you plan to make it a habit?"

"If you ask my brother, he'll tell you I've always been like this."

"Maybe I picked the wrong brother to like."

Even with her teasing tone, tension crawled back along my limbs. I gripped my beer to redirect the tension somewhere. With some effort, I forced neutrality into my tone. "If that's what you prefer."

Her delicate snort let me know I'd failed miserably at nonchalance. "Oh, you are terrible at hiding jealousy."

"Am not."

"Please. Your face is an open book. I guess you're pretty different from your ancestor."

"Is that a compliment? Or an insult?"

"I guess it depends on which parts are different and which are the same." Her face flamed when her words hit home.

"I can't account for *all* our similarities. Unless Jane left actual measurements in her journals. We'd have to check the originals to be sure." My lips twitched when her jaw dropped.

"Maybe you're more alike than I realized. You're a bit of a cad."

I pinched my fingers together. "A little bit. I could say you bring it out in me."

"It's my turn to wonder if that's a compliment."

I tugged her closer, happy to have her lean willingly against me. "It is."

"Good to know." She laced her fingers with mine. "Tell me the truth. Are there measurements in the full journals?"

"I told you I didn't read them."

"According to family lore, then."

"That's a secret I won't reveal. I'll just let you know when the time comes."

"Or when I do?"

I swear a tingle of energy passed between us. My cock twitched when she licked her lips. Her hazel eyes had deepened to green as she gazed through her lashes. "Oh, you're dangerous."

"Am I really? I've never been told that before."

"You are to me."

"That's very good to know."

Chapter 26

Remington

"Remington."

I stirred a little at my name.

A warm hand squeezed my knee. "Remington. Wake up. We're home."

Colt's words sank into my hazy, half-asleep brain. Home. I blinked my eyes open, taking in the garage we sat in. A yawn stretched my mouth as I stretched my body. "I fell asleep?"

"You did. You have an adorable little snore, too."

My jaw dropped, and I smacked him. "I do not. Do I?"

"No, I'm teasing." He leaned forward to brush a lock of hair off my face. The familiar heat from his touch blossomed as he trailed his finger down along my jaw, then the curve of my neck.

I leaned closer, my eyes fluttering closed as his hand embraced my neck. His breath brushed along my ear, sending a shiver down my spine.

"Would you like to come in?"

Boy, howdy, did I ever.

A snort from the back seat jolted us apart. We both chuckled at the interruption. I turned to find Brody sprawled as much as a child could be in a booster seat. His mouth hung open, arms above his head. "Wow, he's out."

"Fun in the sun will do that. If I hadn't had to drive, I might have fallen asleep, too. I almost did by the fire a couple of times." Colt laced his hand with mine. "I need to get Sleeping Beauty into bed. You're welcome to come in if you aren't too tired."

After a long day, the idea of my soft bed had its temptations. Nothing could be the draw of the man sitting across the console from me, though. "If you think it would be alright for me to come in."

He followed the jerk of my head toward Brody. I didn't begrudge him the momentary hesitation. There was a lot to think about when there was a child involved. Colt nodded slightly. "It'll be fine."

"Then I'd love to come in."

His eyes darkened as he scanned me from head to toe. A shiver followed his eyes, heat flaring. Those lips curved in a wicked smile. "Glad to hear it."

"I'm glad you're glad." The breathy note of my voice drew his gaze back to my lips. "Shall we?"

"I'll get Brody. Will you unlock the door for me?"

"Of course." I took the keys he offered and unlocked the door. He carried the still-dozing Brody inside, leaving me to shut the garage door.

"There's some beer and wine in the kitchen. Make yourself comfortable."

"Thank you. What would you like?"

"Whatever you get is fine." He disappeared down the darkened hallway with Brody clinging to him like a dozing spider monkey. I smiled at the visual before making my way into the kitchen.

After the beer and soda at the party, wine sounded pretty good. There was a surprising variety in the small wine cooler to choose from. I selected a good red before starting the hunt for wine glasses and a corkscrew. Both were right above the wine cooler as I'd hoped, so I finished in a few minutes.

I didn't want to make the living room too bright. Brody had earned his sleep after a long day of sleep and didn't need anymore disturbance than what it would take for Colt to get him in bed.

A small lamp on a side table seemed safest. The light was minimal enough that I was pretty sure it didn't carry down the hall to Brody's room. I could hear murmurings and a small whining note from Brody. The poor kid was too tired to argue too strongly, though. It wasn't long before Colt emerged back into the living room.

I'd already freed the cork and poured us each a glass. As he sank onto the couch, I handed him a glass. "Did he put up a fight?"

"He wanted a story, even though he was pretty much asleep."

"I used to do that to my parents after a day in the parks. I wasn't ready for my fun day to end. I'd tell them I was pretending to sleep. They never believed me."

"That seems pretty close to what Brody was trying to pull." His low chuckle warmed my heart. We clinked our glasses before taking a sip. He hummed after his swallow, lifting the glass to examine the red drink. "You picked the tawny. Delicious, but I have something that'll probably pair nicely with this. That is, if you aren't completely sick of food."

"Um, never."

"Then give me a minute." On his way to standing, he gave me a gentle kiss. It seemed to surprise him as much as it surprised me as he paused before moving on toward the kitchen.

I touched my lips, settling back on the couch while he rattled around in the kitchen. The kiss hadn't been filled with heat, but had been almost unconscious in a way that made the butterflies return to their fluttering. He emerged with two plates, setting one in front of me. I leaned forward, eyeing the slice of cake in front of me. Caramel dripped over the top, making my mouth water. "What is this?"

"A caramel-soaked, salted almond cake from Turner's."

"That sounds, and looks, delicious." One bite was enough to prove me right. The smooth caramel had a smoky note to it, and the almond cake was moist. Paired with a sip of wine, the whole thing was incredible. The moan that rose out of pure deliciousness alone wasn't to be stopped. Cole's eyes flicked to me, but whatever he'd planned to say disappeared at his first bite.

His eyes closed as he moaned as well. A slow grin crossed his features. "I thought you were teasing me with all that moaning. I had no idea. This is the first time Trudy's made this."

"I wouldn't play with you like that. It's just so fricking delicious. I wouldn't be quite so cruel with your son in the next room."

"You wouldn't, hm?"

"Well. Maybe a little wicked, but not cruel."

"Now I'm curious what qualifies as a little wicked." He continued to work on the cake, taking a sip between each rich bite of cake.

With food in front of us, I ignored his curiosity for the time being. We ate in companionable silence for a while. Once his plate was empty, he refreshed our drinks. I settled back on the couch, still taking bites of my slice. "You'll have to tell Trudy she needs to make that cake more often."

"I sure as hell plan on it. She sent it home with me to test. Cora Turner's estate just released some unknown recipes to the restaurant on the condition that we never share them or sell them for profit. This was the first one she tried."

"It's a shame; you could make a killing selling recipes like this."

"I leave the convincing of those ideas to my sister." He took another sip of wine, his gaze heavy on me. "I don't want to ruin the mood."

"That's a hell of a non sequitur."

"I know. Bad way to start a conversation. I've been wondering something, though. It might upset you to ask."

Enough time around Colt had shown me he was kind to a fault. Despite the flutter of nerves in my belly, I nodded. "I know you don't. Go ahead."

"What happened to him?"

"Him?" I tried to figure out what he meant with that vague question. If he was worried about upsetting me, it logically meant what happened to me in Florida. That didn't make sense, though. I'd told him what had happened. The rest could be found with a simple online search. "Which 'him' would you be referring to?"

"The man who attacked you."

It took a few minutes for that to sink in. I sat straighter to look at him.

Whatever my face projected, he winced in response. "I'm sorry. I shouldn't have asked. It's a difficult subject."

"No. I mean, yes. It is, but no. I don't understand."

"What don't you understand?"

"How you don't know. All it would take is a simple online search to find out."

"I didn't search."

"You didn't search." My heart rate sped up. Everyone always searched. People like Prairie knew my story before I could tell them. The minute they heard the smallest tidbit, they went online and looked for more. "Really?"

"Remington. It's your story to tell. Not some online news article, or any article that probably didn't get the authentic story from you."

My breath caught in my throat. I pushed around the last few bites of cake with my fork. "You're a good man, Colton Mitchell."

His cheeks darkened. "I don't know about that. It's just common courtesy."

"Most people wouldn't care. They'd let their curiosity take them wherever they needed it to so they could get the story. I forgot. You aren't most people."

"I try not to be." His thumb trailed along my arm, leaving goosebumps in its wake. "You don't have to tell me."

"He got away. They still haven't caught him."

"How?"

"Circumstance. Security at the hospital is a joke—slow and unable to use anything but tasers when they do finally show up to an emergency. He'd run out of the ambulance doors before they even arrived. No one tried to stop him, not that I blame my coworkers; he had a weapon." I shivered, closing my eyes. Most of what I knew was what I'd been told, as I'd been pretty out of it by the time he ran. Brain fog marred the details I could remember.

His fingers laced with mine in gentle support. He didn't push for more information. He granted me the peace to keep working through it.

"To his fortune, rather than ours, there was a concert that night; which not only delayed the cops, but helped him disappear. Even with CCTV, he got lost in the crowd. They never found him. We didn't have his name since he'd come in emergent from an overdose. Which means he's just gone. Somewhere. At least until he finds someone else to attack."

"That's horrible. It's terrifying knowing the person who did this to you is still out there somewhere in the world."

Something in his tone had me searching his features. He wasn't looking at me anymore, and his jaw ticked with tension. I ran a finger along his tense jawline. "Hey. I'm okay. I'm thousands of miles away now."

He jolted at my touch, but after a few blinks, shook his head. "Right. Yes, of course. You're safe now."

"So are you." Maybe it was the haunted look in his eyes that made me say it. Maybe just instinct. Or a little of both.

"I...what?"

"I don't know what happened to you, and I don't need to; but it's clear that something haunts you, too."

Chapter 27

Colton

Not once since escaping my past had I wanted to give anyone all my secrets. Hell, not even our friends knew the story of what we'd gone through; they just knew it was an ugly divorce, and we were content to let them think that was it. My siblings and I had always had some sort of unspoken pact never to reveal that dark part of our history. It was better that way.

Most of the time.

The way Remi was looking at me now made me *want* to give her every single one of my secrets. The way she was understanding before I told her a word. She didn't need to know to accept that I had something happen to me I couldn't talk about.

I opened my mouth to tell her. The words tangled in my throat until I thought I'd choke on them. The second I closed my mouth, Remi gently placed her finger on my lips. A gentle smile softened her features. "I never said you had to tell me. The point was to let you know I knew you were struggling. Knowing every bit of your history isn't necessary to offer support."

"Thank you." I scrubbed my hand over my face to cover my annoyance that I couldn't tell her. Every minute around her showed me how incredible she was, and she'd shared so much with me already.

"You know, it's funny."

"Huh?" I had no idea what could be funny in all of this. She chuckled at my sideways look. While I remained silent, she took another bite of her cake, the caramel dripping a little on her chin.

"I honestly can't tell if we're incredibly enlightened or totally pathetic." Her tone grew lighter with laughter. "All of this understanding each other's trauma without dumping the trauma. Are we avoiding or helping?"

"Both?"

The warmth of her laughter soothed every taut nerve. She polished off the last of the cake, setting it on the table. "Fair enough. Maybe one trauma dump per deep conversation is enough. We can confront your demons another time."

"To be fair, the only demons that have been exposed are yours."

"Most of my demons are public knowledge and splashed all over the interwebs for anyone with a notion and an internet connection." She stared at the dark TV for a moment. "Plus, you told me about your cousin. Even with the happy ending, it's a heavy story."

"There you go with that delusional enlightenment again."

Much to my immense pleasure, that comment made her snort with laughter. "Oh. My. God. Delusional enlightenment. That's perfect."

"Hey, you're the one that's been wondering if we're enlightened or pathetic."

Another adorable snort. God, she was cute. "Sorry. I can't help with the snorting."

"I think it's charming." The disparaging look she sent my way made me raise my hands in defense. "Honest. I'm not lying. I think it's adorable."

"Sure, sure. You're just saying that to stay on my good side. I know just how annoying it can be when I'm always snorting when I laugh."

"No, it's adorable." I moved closer quickly enough for her to startle a little. The laughter softened into a gentle heat when she held my gaze. That little drop of caramel still sat on her chin, drawing my gaze there. "Just like that is."

"What?"

"You've got caramel." I set my thumb on her chin, right near it. Her throat bobbed in a heavy swallow. "Right there."

"I—I do?" She took a deep, quivering breath that drew my gaze to her breasts for a minute.

"You do." I lifted my gaze to hers. Her eyes were almost fully green in the thin line that showed around her dilated pupils. Fuck, she was gorgeous. Her hands settled on my knees, and my cock hardened at her wispy whine of an exhale. "Would you like me to get it for you?"

Her husky voice ghosted across my lips with how close we'd gotten. "That depends."

"On?"

"Just how much caramel dripped. Should we get more?"

"Fuck, Remington." My mouth slanted over hers, drawing her tight against me. This time, there were no excessive layers keeping me from touching her soft skin again. I slid my hands under her shirt, cupping her breasts.

She clawed at my shirt, tugging it until we parted to get it over my head. Within moments she straddled me again, her heat pressing against my erection until I thought it wasn't possible to get harder.

"That's not fair." I ran my thumb along the lace of her bra until it rubbed across her taut nipple. "I need to see these pretty nipples."

There wasn't any hesitation when she whipped off her shirt. Her head tilted back with a moan when I took her nipple into my mouth right through the lace of her bra. The scratch of her nails along my neck caused a rumble deep in my chest.

Her hands slipped over my shoulders to my chest. We both paused when she reached the scar there. Her delicate fingers danced along the line for a moment. She met my gaze quietly; the rushed heat of moments ago faded into something else. Something deeper that made my heart twinge.

She took my hand in hers, lifting it to her temple. The ridge of a small fresh scar I'd noticed before stretched further back into her hairline. My heart pounded in my chest while we both explored the physical reminders of our pasts.

Her forehead pressed to mine when I buried my hand in the silky strands of her hair. Our mouths were a breath apart. This time when our lips met, we moved slower, more deliberate in our exploration of each other.

The rushed heat faded into something so intense I could barely breathe. This woman was proving to be much more than I expected. It made every brush of her fingers intensify. Her hips shifted against me, and I groaned.

When she lifted off me, I reached for her. She held me back with her fingers to my chest. I watched her, unclear of what she was doing until she pushed my knees apart and kneeled in front of me. I moved to pull her back. I didn't think I'd last long if she touched me, and I wanted to savor this moment.

She shook her head. "I want to."

My hips bucked against my will when she unbuttoned my jeans. "Fuck."

"Not yet."

I let out a choked laugh. "Not funny."

"A little." Then her fingers brushed along my cock, and all sense left me. My head fell back against the couch. She teased my length for a few minutes before she moved to my waist. I automatically lifted my hips to give her space to pull my jeans down.

When my dick came free, she whimpered a little, her tongue tracing along her lips. I didn't think it was possible to get any harder until she did that. She wrapped her hand around my length. The gentle squeeze sent a shockwave through me.

Her eyes snapped to mine, locking on without wavering as she leaned forward and ran her tongue all the way along my length. Holy fuck, it was hot. She flicked her tongue across the tip, her eyes flashing with heat.

Warm heat surrounded the sensitive flesh as she took me in deeper and deeper, not breaking eye contact. I shuddered, my eyes shuttering closed. A sharp sting on my stomach brought me back. With her nails still in my stomach giving me a bit of pain, she sucked hard as she pulled back up my length.

"Remington." I buried my fingers in her hair, gripping tight.

My urging didn't get her to move faster. She took her time, that delicious tongue swirling and massaging with every trip. The sting of her nails didn't disappear for a second, adding an intensity.

Every muscle in my body trembled when she started moving faster until I was begging her with every stroke to finish me. My balls tightened, and I clamped my mouth shut to keep from shouting. Her eyes held mine until I couldn't keep mine open anymore. She took me in the deepest yet when I came with a muffled grunt.

Her tongue stroked my pulsing cock, sucking every last bit of come out of me. She slowly released me, sliding up my body until her lips found mine. I tugged her close, desperate to give her the same pleasure. "Remington."

"Yes?"

"That was the hottest fucking thing ever."

She giggled softly against my ear. "You're telling me."

"Your turn." I half lifted her to lay her down. She stretched like a cat when I stood to remove my jeans, but pulled my boxers back up. Her hair remained mussed from my rough handling, and one breast was still out of her bra.

When I didn't move right away, she eyed me curiously. "Is something wrong?"

"No, you're just damn gorgeous."

She flushed, a pleased smile warming her lips. "I could say the same, cowboy."

"I'm not the cowboy. That's my brother."

"Well, I can't call you sailor. That's just weird." She grabbed my wrist and gave it a tug. "Besides, you ride. So you're a cowboy. And right now, I feel like saving a horse."

I chuckled as I hovered over her. "You really are bad sometimes."

"I know. I excel at terrible humor. You should know, you excel at dad jokes."

"We're getting off the subject here."

"We are? How's that?"

I leaned down to suck her taut nipple back into my mouth. Her soft gasp and the arch of her back were all I needed to turn me on again. Not that it would've taken much after that blowjob. I flicked my tongue across her nipple and gave a gentle bite, which stirred her further, her leg hitching around my waist to pull me close.

A scream shattered the heat and bliss of the moment, startling my scattered brain. "*Daddy!*"

What was that? Then it clicked into place. "Brody."

Remi sat as fast as I stood, her eyes wide. "What's wrong?"

"Probably another nightmare." I rushed toward the hall only to trip on my own pants.

Remi was at my side, helping me to my feet. Her gaze fell behind me, and she clutched my jeans to her chest. "Go on."

"Daddy!"

I didn't wait to figure out her distraction, rushing to Brody's bedroom as quickly as I could. Terror streaked my son's face in a way I'd never seen, nor hoped to. "What is it, buddy? What's wrong? Was it another nightmare?"

"Scary man." Just like the last nightmare. He sniffled and buried his nose in my shoulder. The rest of his sentence was muffled. "Outside my window."

"Another dream."

"No, he was really there. Right there." He didn't look, but pointed to the window along the back of the house.

I peered outside, but saw nothing in the yard. The trees that lined the backyard rustled, and I thought I saw movement, but that could have been a breeze. The play of our backyard light on the trees often made shadows where there was nothing. "It was a dream, Brody. There isn't anyone outside."

"No. He was there."

"Okay. I believe you. I'll make sure your windows are locked, and maybe we'll close the curtains tonight. Okay?"

Brody sniffled through his nod. "O—kay." He hiccupped between syllables.

I checked the locks and drew the curtains across the window. "There. Better?"

He rubbed his eyes, tears still shining on his cheeks. "I guess. Who was it?"

"I don't know." It had to have been a nightmare, but his conviction that it was a real person made me question. "Do you want me to stick around until you fall asleep again?"

He nodded against my arm. His thumb drifted to his mouth again. I didn't want to chide him when he was so scared, so I let him resume the habit for the moment. "Stay, Daddy."

"Any time you need me, you know I'll be here."

Chapter 28

Remington

Movement outside distracted me from running to Brody along with Colt. I gathered his jeans to my chest as I crossed into the dining room to look out the window.

Motion pulled my gaze toward the trees. I peered into the darkness beyond the reach of the bright backyard lights. Was that something moving? I thought it might be, but it was probably just an animal.

I'd seen many wild creatures make their way through town, and these yards, since I'd been here. From raccoons and squirrels to monsters like bears and elk. There was no shortage of wildlife to keep life interesting.

I released my tension in a gust of air, but kept the jeans tucked against my chest. I needed to cover up. What if Brody came out here?

I rushed back to the couch and scrambled for my shirt. My earlier flush had faded in the confusion and distraction, but my mind still raced over what just happened. I had no idea what came over me. For the first time in my life, I'd initiated a blow job, and fucking enjoyed the hell out of it.

My skin tingled as I thought of Colt's reaction, and the sense of power it gave me. I closed my eyes to gather myself back together. Now wasn't the time. Something had scared Brody enough for that scream. I didn't need to reflect on my libido right then. It was something I could examine later.

I flipped my shirt over my head and straightened it out. My fingers snagged in my tangled hair when I tried to brush them through. I regretted cutting it so I couldn't just shove it back in a ponytail. After a few more passes with my fingers, I thought it might be acceptable.

I crept down the hall to check on the boys. Brody still sniffled and whimpered, asking questions of his dad. One peek into his room showed his eyes were wide open as he clung to his dad. Whatever had woken him would make it tough to get back to sleep. I thought I knew a way to help with that.

If it worked, Colt probably wouldn't be upset about my going through his kitchen. The milk was where you'd expect, and the vanilla right next to the stove with the spices. It took a few tries to find first the sugar and then a small saucepan. Once I had everything I needed, I set about making the drink my mom used to make us anytime we struggled to get to sleep.

I waited until the milk was warm without being too hot and transferred it to a small mug I guessed to be Brody's. Fortunately, I made the exact right amount without a drop left over. Just like Mom used to.

Out of nowhere, a wave of melancholy hit me hard. Happy memories always did that to me. Knowing what life was once like compared to what it became over the past decade ripped my heart to shreds every time.

I shook that off as best I could. "Well, fuck. If Brody's scream didn't kill my libido, that sure did."

I leaned against the counter to focus on pushing those thoughts back into their compartment, where they lived ninety-nine percent of the time. Finally settled, I gathered Brody's drink to carry down the hall.

As I'd suspected, Brody was still talking, eyes wide open. His thumb tucked firmly in his mouth, which I knew he'd worked hard to stop doing. The poor little guy was really scared. "Hey, Brody. I brought you something I thought might help."

Brody eyed the mug. His thumb pulled from his mouth. "What is it?"

"It's something my mom called a hot angel. It helps you sleep."

"Angel? Does it bring the angels too?"

"It sure does. All of your guardian angels come to watch over you while you sleep." I kneeled by the bed, holding out the mug. "Do you want to try? If you don't like it, I won't be offended. Promise."

Brody hesitated before reaching for the mug. He gave it a big sniff. The mug turned in his hand, his brow furrowed. "It looks like milk."

"It sure does. I think it's called a hot angel because it's white." I could feel Colt's gaze on me, but kept my focus on Brody.

After another sniff, Brody took a tentative sip. His lips pursed after he swallowed. He took another sip. Finally, he smiled. "It's yummy."

"I think so, too. It was always one of my favorite drinks. Sometimes I pretended I couldn't sleep so I could have some. Drink up." I clasped the hand Colt held out. While Brody finished his drink, I turned my attention to him. There was a sort of fire in his gaze. Somehow even more intense than earlier. I wasn't sure of its meaning, but it made my heart flutter.

'Thank you,' he mouthed.

I squeezed his hand in response. Brody drew my attention back to him with a particularly loud slurp. "My goodness. Does that mean you're done?"

"Thank you, Remi." Brody held out the mug. "Does it really work?"

"Oh yeah. I always conked out pretty quickly when my mom gave it to me. Sometimes against my wishes." I ruffled his hair. "But you have to lie down and get comfy if you want it to work. I'll let your dad take care of that."

"Okay, Remi. Night, night."

"Night, night. Sleep Tight. Don't let the bedbugs bite." I left them to re-situate Brody in his bed. Their murmurs carried down the hall with me, but I didn't listen in. Restless energy kicked in, carrying me through the living room to clean up the mess Colt and I had left.

The last thing I wanted to do was rush them, but it felt awkward to sit in the dimly lit room alone while I waited. Despite my assurance, it might take some time for the sweet, warm milk to work. Or Colt would want to stay close out of concern. I didn't want to leave without saying goodbye, but it might come down to it. I'd give it ten or fifteen minutes. If Colt didn't come out, I'd go wave goodbye and leave him to his son.

Since I was feeling restless, it seemed a good idea to wash the dishes. I'd handwash everything, even the things that normally went into the dishwasher. I had caused half of the mess; it was only fair to help clean up.

Once again, Colt proved what an amazing dad he was. In the middle of our rounding the bases, he'd dropped everything to tend to his son. It meant so much to me to see. Those privileged might think it was a totally normal thing. After years in the ER, I'd come to see it wasn't. There were a lot of messed-up families out there. Families you couldn't help until it was too late.

My parents were amazing when I was growing up. We traveled all the time, visited the beach at least once a month, and were annual passholders at the parks in the area, so we were always at Disney or Universal on the weekends and sometimes the weeknights. They'd been mostly supportive, although there'd been disappointment at my lack of interest in sports.

Total lack of interest. I couldn't have cared less, and seeing as my dad was a big sports guy, he didn't hide his wish I'd take up something 'practical' like a sport. Not that I could say what was so practical about a sport when half of them meant a high risk of injury.

Instead, I chose dance and theater.

When I went to school for a 'real' job like nursing, they'd been thrilled. After spending my high school years trying to discourage me from pursuing the activities I loved because they held no future, nursing made them happy.

Never mind the fact that my talents got me into my roles at Disney. To this day, I hadn't told anyone what roles I'd played outside of being a dancer in the parades. I kept mum about what princess parts I portrayed in the parks. My secrecy had little to do with our being told over and over not to give away proprietary secrets. I actually enjoyed the mystery of it. It was always fun to hear someone guess which princess I'd appeared as.

"You didn't have to do that," Colt's voice was a low whisper. He stared at the dishes drying on the rack.

"I helped make the mess, and you had a bigger priority."

"I'm really sorry."

"Uh-uh. None of that." I stepped closer, cupping his face in my hands. "I love how Brody is your priority. It's part of the reason you're so hot."

His lips twitched with a hint of a smile.

"I didn't mind cleaning while you helped him feel comforted enough to sleep. Is he okay now? What happened? A nightmare, like you said?"

"I think so. He swears he saw someone outside his window and even made me close the curtains. He never does that."

I smoothed my fingers over the furrow of his brow. This didn't seem like the time to tell him what I'd seen, not that I even knew what it was. He was already so worried. Still, it might not be a bad idea in case he wanted Gunner to look into it. "This might be nothing."

"What?"

"I thought I saw—something."

"Something?"

"I don't know. It was outside when you went to get Brody. I saw movement in the backyard by the trees."

"Do you know what it was?"

"I couldn't say. For all I know, it was a bear or elk walking through the woods." I ran my hands along his back to soothe his rising tension. "I caught movement, but by the time I got to the window, it was just a flash of brown."

"It could have been an animal. That seems more likely. Gunner's been telling me to get a camera on the back of the house forever. It never seemed necessary. Our town's pretty safe."

"It might be, but your town also has a lot of tourists. As much as it pains me greatly to say it, Gunner might be right."

His nose wrinkled. "Did that hurt to admit?"

"Greatly." I clutched my heart for emphasis. "If nothing else, a backyard camera could get you some fun footage of the wildlife passing through the yard. I know Brody was having a lot of fun looking through the binoculars at Moorely's to see the elk near the foothills and the hawks flying overhead."

"Please never tell Gunner you thought he was right."

"I'd rather die." The humor didn't breach the tension he still carried, even with his participation. His gaze kept drifting toward the hall as though he could see Brody from where we stood. I refused to take any more of his time or focus away from his son. Especially after this. I was just glad I could say good night properly. "I should go."

"You don't have to." His warm hands clasped mine, pulling them to his chest. "You could stay."

"Any other night, I'd take you up on that in a hot second. Tonight, you're worried about Brody. As you should be." I brushed a gentle kiss across his lips. "I already told you, it's super-hot you worry about him so much."

His full attention returned to me at those words. A sexy smirk curved his lips. "Super-hot?"

"Oh yeah. Definitely. We'll have another chance to finish what we started tonight. For now, focus on Brody. I have a mess to clean up back in my room. Nova interrupted me in the middle of something."

"What did she interrupt?"

"Painting. I was trying to still my mind."

"Does that actually work?"

"Not even a little."

Chapter 29

Colton

The last thing I'd expected to be doing was spending two hours at the home improvement store. Thanks to Dad and Paige offering to take Brody to Canon City to ride the Royal Gorge Railway and fly-fishing, I had to take advantage of a few days without him there to get ready for the surprise.

He'd had a bee in his bonnet to make our own garden ever since he tried Paige's fresh tomatoes from her garden. I'd thought the obsession would pass with time. Instead, Brody stubbornly held onto the idea, mentioning it every few days. For his birthday next week, I planned to have us build our own little greenhouse together. It wouldn't be anywhere near as grand as Paige's, but it would suffice for us.

While I planned for us to build it together, I wanted to have everything prepared ahead of time so it was more assembly than power tools. I planned to spend my mornings over the weekend cutting the wood to size.

With any luck, I'd have my evenings free. I knew Remington had the next couple of days off as well. Since she'd offered to work the holiday, I'd given her the days after it off. I hoped to take advantage of us both having time off with Brody gone to spend time with her. Hell, who was I kidding? What I really wanted was to finish what we'd started the other night.

I'd spent more time than could be called decent over the past week remembering the feel of her soft skin under my fingers. The way her lips wrapped around my cock and took all of me. I wanted to have my taste of her. I wanted to hear what sounds she'd make as I made her come. The little tastes I'd had weren't enough. I needed so much more.

If I had any say in what happened this week, Remi would be at my place. Without the danger of any interruptions. I could have the amazing sensation of her beneath me again. Her body arched toward me with need, want. The peek of her tongue when she licked her lips in anticipation, something I wasn't even sure she knew she did.

After the pleasure she'd given me the other night, I'd been the closest I'd ever been to snapping at my son. The amount of fear in his scream had quickly pushed away that impulse.

Remi stepped in to help by giving us space and by making Brody that magical drink that actually helped him get back to sleep quicker than I expected. I'd have to ask her how she'd made it so I had it in my arsenal. I could use that as an excuse to have her come over. Not that I truly thought I'd need an excuse. All it would take was asking her.

My biggest concern is that someone else had tried to take advantage of her days off. Namely, my sister and her friends. They had radar for when Remi had days off so they could go out to the bars. Maybe this time I could beat them to it.

I dragged my phone out of my back pocket to text her when a car door slammed. Hoping to spot the woman at the center of my thoughts, I stepped out of the garage to check the driveway next door.

Empty.

Remi's car wasn't there as I'd hoped. Damn it. I scanned the area and spotted a strange car on the street at the end of my driveway.

A woman walked around the car. Something about her tugged at my memory enough to send my heart into a brutal pace before I understood why. My mouth went dry when she continued up the drive. Her head remained lowered, but my mind was scrambling into a panic. My hand clenched around my phone, and I took a step back. When she lifted her head, I swear my brain shattered into a million pieces. "Ma."

"Colton." The youthful, smooth features and calm smile from our youth had been ravaged by addiction. The source of the start of our pain, and her every excuse every minute since. "It's so good to see you again."

I backed another step away when she reached toward me. This wasn't happening. My eyes darted around in search of an escape. Gunner had been sure that if I ignored her, she'd give up. She had before. She gave up on us long before we could take care of ourselves. Why would it be any different now? My tongue felt thick when I found my voice. "What do you want, Darlene?"

She flinched at her name. "To talk. That's all."

"I'm not interested in anything you have to say." All I wanted was to beat a hasty retreat to my house. I was halfway there when she spoke again.

"I want to apologize."

That drew me up short. My betraying heart, which still longed for the life we'd had before the divorce, reached out. A sharp pain in my hand made realize I still had my phone clenched there. It took some effort to release the tight hold and slide it back in my pocket. I closed my eyes, every betrayal and minute of neglect flashing before my eyes stilled any bit of longing and turned it back into anger. "You're joking, right?"

"No, I'm not. I promise I mean it this time. I want to apologize for everything I did—and didn't do—to you and your siblings."

"Not good enough." It wasn't and never could be. There wasn't a damn thing in the world she could say to make anything better. I spun on her. Something nagged me about the whole thing. "Why start with me? Because I was always the easy target?"

"No. No." Her voice wavered. She glanced behind me toward the house, then back at her hands. My heart seized at the thought that she might know about Brody. She wouldn't have any place in his life. In my life. Never again.

"There's not a goddamn thing you can say or do to erase what you did. You did nothing to protect me or Prairie. A real mother would protect her children."

"I know. I'm so sorry."

"I'm not interested in your apology. This apology has nothing to do with me or Prairie, or Gunner, or West. It's all about you. That's all it was ever about."

"That's not—"

"Honestly, I'm glad you didn't start with Prairie. She doesn't deserve your selfish begging for forgiveness. You won't find it here." All the years I'd spent trying to heal from this. All the things finally going right. One visit from her and it all caved in around me. "Go away, Darlene."

"Look, I'm in therapy." How the hell was she being so stubborn now? She'd always been weak, backing off at the first sign of anger from anyone. A simpering mess, turning to her damn drugs to hide from the truth.

"Yeah, I believe that. I also still believe in Santa Claus and the Easter Bunny."

"I'm serious."

"Fifteen years, Darlene. Fifteen years since we got the hell away from that nightmare. Why the *fuck* would you suddenly start therapy now?"

"It was two years ago, actually." She wrung her hands together. Her body was still so thin and skeletal. I found it hard to believe she'd stopped using.

"Really? Are you going to tell me you stopped using drugs, too? I'm way too old to believe in fairy tales."

"I did. I'm clean."

"Fuck off. I'm sick of your lies."

"I'm finding it difficult to eat right. I'm craving, but I've been clean for a year." She curled back in on herself during my yelling. That was a familiar sight, although it had always been the asshole Bryce doing all the yelling when we were little. He'd do more than yell, actually. "I'm really trying. I even have a job now."

"Darlene, go." I took a pause. "You didn't answer my question. What made you start therapy so suddenly? You were always content in your ignorance."

"I started when he got out of jail."

That didn't compute. Gunner told me he was out, but not that he'd been out for two whole years. Even then, it still didn't make sense. He'd also said there'd been no sign since Bryce went east. None of that mattered. I needed her gone. "Maybe you should've started when he went to jail. It's too late. Stay the fuck away from us."

"Colton, please." Her bony fingers grasped my arm. "I came for a reason."

"Make it fast."

"He knows about the boy."

Chapter 30

Remington

I released my disgruntled groan as I slumped into the chair across from Moorely. She grimaced sympathetically right before I dropped my forehead to the table.

"What a waste of time." The past few hours were a bust. Thankfully, I'd had Moorely along for the ride, which meant I'd had company in my misery. We still didn't meet my end-goal. "It shouldn't be this hard."

"That's most definitely *not* what she said." Moorely giggled at my responding grunt.

"What's wrong with her?" The clink of plates on the table told me Nova had brought something to eat. I didn't know if I had the energy to get excited over what it might be. "Remi, girl. You're in a bakery with cakes and sweets all around. *No one* should be unhappy here."

"Except maybe the type one diabetic who can't thoroughly enjoy her own creations?" Moorely hadn't stopped chuckling since she had told her terrible joke.

"Oh, stop that. I get by just fine and still get a taste of my creations."

"Fine, but go easy on her. We've spent the morning looking for a place for her to rent. You know what the rental situation is like around here." Moorely's laughter stopped a moment before she gave an indecent moan. "Novalee June, what is this decadence?"

"It's a new recipe. You like?"

"I love. Remi." A hard tap landed on my head. "Remington Sage, get up."

"Ow." I rubbed the spot on the back of my head. She'd hit harder than I thought necessary. I wanted to remain pouting where I was, but the offense was enough to make me sit up and face my attacker. "What was that for?"

"Try this. Seriously." Moorely waved her fork dramatically over the plate in front of her.

I took in the plate Nova had set beside my head. A tower of sweets sat atop it. A tower might've been dramatic, but somehow it didn't quite feel like it. The whole thing looked like two desserts in one, at the very least. "What on earth is this?"

"A salted caramel cookie butter cheesecake with mini molten lava chocolate cake on top." Nova licked some chocolate from her spoon. At my look, she shook her head. "I manually checked to make sure my pump was reading right."

"You know that isn't the way to treat yourself properly." I shook my head, but at least Nova's helping was a lot smaller than ours.

"Yes, but I must at least try my new recipes. Either way, I don't know what to call it." She scooped a little of the cheesecake, along with the caramel and melted chocolate, onto her spoon. "Except maybe sinful."

"I'm not going to lie. It sounds incredibly rich, and delicious." Chocolate oozed from the cake onto the cheesecake, mixing with the caramel as I drew my spoon through the dessert. The moment the sweet and salty combo hit my tongue, I closed my eyes. My own indecent moan rivaled Moorely's. "Oh. My. God."

"Right?" Moorely scooped another bite into her mouth. "You'd think it would be too rich, but it's so good, you just don't care."

"I don't even care about not being able to find a place to rent anymore." Maybe that was a stretch, but I was grateful for the delicious distraction. The next bite I scooped into my mouth made it too full to speak.

Nova chuckled at my continued moans of appreciation. "You'd better save sounds like those for Colt."

I nearly choked on what remained of the bite I'd taken. After several coughs and some generous pats on the back from Nova, I cleared my throat. "That was rude. You can't say that when someone has a mouthful of food."

Moorely's face was red with laughter, her gasps for air and slaps to the table exacerbating the effect. She pointed at me, then Nova, then back. It reached a point where she wasn't even making a sound except for the occasional strong gasp for air. It was almost like a baby in a breath-holding spell.

"Moorely, breathe." My own barely controlled laughter strained against my throat. "I'm seriously concerned about your brain with this lack of oxygen."

She took a deep, gasping breath before exhaling a bray of laughter. After a swipe of tears, she got some control of her laughter. The occasional hiccup of laughter still came through as she wiped the chocolate from the corners of her mouth. "There you go. Call it afternoon delight."

Nova's cheeks darkened, but her denim blues sparked with amusement. "Children come in here. I couldn't do that."

"Too bad. It's the perfect name." I savored the flavor of my next bite, letting the sweet and salty mix into the perfect bite. I managed not to moan this time, but it was a close call.

"Back to the original subject. Why exactly are you so impatient? You know Gigi would let you stay forever if necessary. She loves having someone in the house. If you go, she'll probably take in someone else." Nova patted my hand. "There isn't a rush."

"I know all that, but I'd really like a place of my own to call home. I agreed to stay at Gigi's because I didn't know if I'd like it here. My whole life I lived in a big city, never a small town like this, and also, I've never lived through a winter. Turns out I love the small-town thing. If winter changes my opinion, I'll deal with it then."

Every single place I'd see that day wasn't right. There was always something missing from what I'd pictured, or it didn't have the right feel or location. It was likely I was being way too picky, but if I was going to stay here, I wanted to be comfortable.

Moorely pushed aside the plate she'd practically licked clean. "I don't know if you'll find what you want unless you're willing to buy land and build. This girl is picky as hell, Nova."

"I know what I want. There's a difference."

Nova waited until I'd cleaned my plate before stacking all three together. Her features were soft in contemplation. "There's nothing wrong with knowing what you want. I'm wondering if there's another reason for the trouble, though? Like, maybe you're not eager to move away from where you're right next door to that man you couldn't stop staring at with googly eyes the other day?"

"I didn't have googly eyes." My cheeks flamed at the insinuation. True or not. I certainly didn't care for being called out on it. "Not exactly."

"Ri-ight." Moorely grinned my way. "We all saw you."

"Can you blame me?"

"Not one bit," Moorely asserted.

"He's a relative, I can't comment without ick." Nova smirked. "But objectively, I can see your point."

"That's what I thought. Now, on that note, I need to get back. Gigi comes home in a couple of days, and I plan to make sure the house is in good order for her." Sure, it was only a half-truth, but thanks to their most recent bout of teasing, I wasn't going to tell them I wanted to stop at the grocery store because I was supposed to have dinner with the very man they'd been teasing me about. Of course, I hadn't heard from Colt about where he wanted to eat. I planned on making dinner for us, but wasn't sure either of us wanted a quiet evening in Gigi's house.

I sent off another text to him to see what time he wanted to meet as I walked into the grocery store. There wasn't a shred of doubt that I liked Colt. It wasn't just how sexy he looked pretty much every minute in everything he did. If it were looks alone, Gunner would have been as attractive to me. No, it was the whole package that was Colt.

The other night had been so amazing, it was all I could think about. The warmth of him above me, the tug of his hands in my hair. I wanted to feel him everywhere, to bathe in his intensity, his kindness, and his strength.

Heat pooled between my legs so that I had to clench my thighs. I tried to brush the thoughts away. Fortunately, no one was too close to me at the store as my imagination wandered continuously toward what might have happened if not for Brody's nightmare.

As quickly as I could, I got the rest of the supplies for our dinner. The local butcher had recommended a local fish to me and suggested the best way to cook it. From there, I got my usual supplies for a family favorite. I already knew Colt had an excellent wine to pair with it.

When I pulled into Gigi's driveway, I noticed Colt's garage door wide open. Good. If he were outside, I could confirm our plans for tonight. I hopped out of the car, crossing the small strip of grass between the houses.

A sound made me pause. Considering the pile of lumber in the driveway, I'd expected to hear a saw. Colt had mentioned he planned to build a greenhouse with Brody for his birthday, and hoped to have everything ready to start when Brody got home.

A grunt, a thump, another thump. I peered into the shadowed garage, but the bright sun made it impossible to figure out what was going on. "Colt?"

When I got close to the garage, I shielded my eyes to see inside better. The man I had fantasized about for weeks was tucked into the back corner of his garage, where his gym equipment was. Shirtless and sweating.

I bit my lip, stepping just inside the garage. His back was to me, and I didn't want to startle him. I also didn't mind the view. His focus was on the punching bag, the grunts and thumps coming from each hit. I lost my ability to speak for a minute as I admired the flex and twist of his muscles that came with each swing of his muscles.

As the pace became increasingly frenzied, concern took over admiration. "Colton?"

Something was wrong. I couldn't see his face, but it was clear in the way he brutalized the bag. He twisted to kick it before resuming the punches.

"Colton!"

He froze, his chest heaving in ragged breaths. Without turning around, he yanked an earbud from his ear.

"Are you okay?"

"Go the fuck away, Remi."

The rapid beat of my heart stilled. "I, okay. Can I—"

"Go away!" He punched the bag again.

I wanted to do as he asked, but I didn't understand. When he spun on me, the darkness in his glare made me take a step back. He stalked toward the door inside. "Colton?"

Negativity poured off him in waves that pushed me back another step. His glower remained fixed in place as he slammed his hand against the garage door opener. The door rattled down right in front of me. I couldn't move, even when it blocked him from view.

I blinked back tears when I heard the door to his house slam. The garage door hit the ground with a slam that sounded much louder to my ears.

What just happened? Had I done something?

It wasn't my place to cry over this. I swiped at the salty trails on my cheeks as I backed away. One official date, two undoubtedly hot sexual encounters weren't enough for me to get this upset about.

Sure, I thought we'd been open with each other, as much as we could be, about our own brokenness. Then again, maybe it was I who upset him somehow. But if I had, and he didn't bother to tell me or talk about it, that wasn't my problem. It was his.

I squared my shoulders, hitting the key fob to open my trunk. "It was probably all in your head, Rem. Or just pure physical attraction. There's no need to worry about it." I reached into the trunk, gathering up as many bags as I could. If I could make one trip and not have to come back outside for the rest of the night, that would be just fine with me.

"Can I help you with that?"

I spun around in surprise at the voice. When I saw who it was, I let out a screech, dropping the grocery bag. Vegetables rolled down the driveway, but I couldn't stop staring at the man who'd approached in my distraction. My mouth was dry as a bone when I croaked, "Detective Winder."

"Miss Collier."

"What-what the hell are you doing here?"

"You were refusing all my phone calls, and I'd guess deleting my voicemails. I told you, I have some information I think you should know." His gaze fell on the bags and vegetables scattered on the ground. "I didn't mean to startle you."

"It's fine. I'll clean it up later." I slammed the trunk, heading to the front door. This was too much. My emotions were already in turmoil thanks to the confusion of the past few minutes; this would send me over the edge. My hands shook as I tried to put the key in the lock. "I really don't want to hear what you say, but you won't fucking leave me alone, so make it quick."

"Agent Mercer wanted to come in my place, but I thought you'd prefer a familiar face."

I paused with one foot in the door, turning to face him. "Agent?"

"The FBI is involved in your case now. It appears your attacker has crossed state lines."

"That's not—how could you know?"

"A man fitting your description of him has been involved in several crimes. From robbery, to kidnapping, to murder, across several states. Georgia, Kentucky, Missouri."

The world faded into one tunnel of light. Buzzing overtook the sounds of nature I'd come to love. "He's moving west."

"He is."

Chapter 31

Colton

THUMP.

With any luck, that would be the last time Gunner attempted to get me to answer the door. For the past two days, he'd come knocking every couple of hours. I wasn't about to answer for him, or anyone. Hell, I hadn't even gone outside for two days.

There'd been one moment right after I'd shut out Remi that I almost had. That moment that I'd heard her scream. She'd sounded horrified, and it had shaken me out of my mood for the briefest of moments. It didn't matter, she deserved something better than my fucked-up self.

Throughout the entire day, Gunner'd been far more insistent in his attempts to get me to respond. I don't think he'd stopped knocking at every entrance all day, save for one hour earlier.

I didn't want to be bothered. Definitely not by him.

Another round of rapid-fire knocks sounded. Gunner's voice carried through the door. "That's it, Colt. I've tried to do this nicely, but you've left me no choice."

If I had one lick of energy left, I'd have run to the door at the sound of the key in the lock, but I didn't. I stared at the TV without even flinching when the door slammed open. I no longer even knew what movie was on, nor did I care. About anything.

"Ugh." Gunner's nose wrinkled. He looked around my living room at the mess I'd left. "It smells like a fucking frat house in here. What the hell is wrong with you?"

"Get the fuck out of my house."

"Not going to happen. Brody's coming home tomorrow. Is this how you plan to have this place when Dad drops him off?"

"You acted like it was no big deal. You're a fucking ass. You lie to make your incompetence look good."

"What the hell are you talking about?" He stepped over some beer bottles. "What happened? Why are you drunk as a skunk in the middle of the day and watching kung fu movies?"

So, that's what was on. I couldn't remember what I'd originally put on. I'd just let it auto-play since I started. "You knew it wouldn't work. You just didn't give a fuck because it wasn't you. Worse, you didn't tell us. Everything is fucked up because of you."

"What wouldn't work?" Gunner picked some trash off the floor. Gunner. He must have been worried. The jackass never cleaned. Good. He needed to worry. He needed to be held accountable for what he'd done. "What did I keep from you?"

"Darlene didn't stay away, and you fucking knew Bryce was having a parole hearing two years ago and didn't bother to tell us."

He froze in place, three beer bottles tinkling ominously as his grip tightened.

"You knew they were going to release him and didn't give us a chance to fight." It wasn't a question. I knew he knew. "You didn't bother to tell us. Any of us."

"I let the lawyer deal with it. I never thought they'd release him. Afterward, he left the state. Skipped his parole and skipped right out of Texas. Last I heard, he hasn't been back." Gunner set the bottles on the table before he collapsed into a chair.

"How would you know? If he skipped his parole, no one's keeping table on him. He could be right here in town and not a fucking person would know. They don't know a goddamn thing about him or his existence." The mere idea of Bryce being anywhere near my siblings or, God forbid, my kid? My jaw clenched, my heart racing so hard I thought it might beat out of my chest. "I've got a son to protect. You should have told me."

"And let you live in fear for years? For all we know, he's dead. It wouldn't surprise me."

"Darlene was here. Here at my house. She had my phone number and address. Who's to say he isn't able to get the same information? Or that she gave it to him. She admitted he fucking *knows*."

"Knows?"

"About Brody."

"Fuck." He ran his hand through his hair. "I thought I was helping. We spent so long living in fight-or-flight mode, I didn't want to stop the peace we'd found."

"You thought wrong." The bastard that was our stepfather had done more than enough to be in jail for much longer than fifteen years. According to Darlene, not that she could be trusted, overcrowding and supposed good behavior had pushed through his parole. His original sentence hadn't been near long enough to be enough, especially when the prosecutor combined the attempted murder and sexual assault charges to shorten the trial, resulting in a mere twenty-five-year sentence.

Dad may have paid for a top-notch lawyer, but we'd had a judge who was just fine with combining the sentences. Supposedly to protect us from any further harm. That worked out so well when the joke of a prison system deemed him ready to return to society? What a fucking joke.

"I'll check with Hagen again. Especially since Darlene's come out of the woodwork, it might give Hagen more to work on since he's been in touch with her." It was a pitiful attempt at an apology, but even in my drunken haze I appreciated the effort.

"He's clearly good at evading the law. Fuck, he did it for eight years when we were forced to live with him. And some grainy pictures won't do shit."

"Hey, you know Walker. You've met her. She knows our case and will put in the work. You just have to give her time because she's not assigned to it and is working on other things."

"What if we don't have time?"

"I think we do." He didn't sound as confident as in our previous conversation. Based on Darlene's arrival and her news, it was damn good he didn't. "She'd be thrilled to get him back in custody after what he did to Prairie and you."

Prairie and I had gotten the worst of the situation. Even though Gunner and I both tried to stop him every time, it was me he'd almost killed. "We have to tell them."

"You saw how Prairie reacted when you told her about Darlene reaching out. She ignored the whole thing and acted like it didn't matter."

"Exactly. *Acted* like. It did matter, and you know it."

"Fine. We tell them."

"Damn straight." I rubbed my hand over my face, trying to clear my head.

"You could have spent the past two days being a human instead of wallowing if you'd let me in sooner."

"I didn't let you in."

"I went to Dad's and got the key. If I hadn't known you would make me pay for the door, I might've used a battering ram."

A smile twitched on my lips despite myself. He wasn't wrong. The amusement didn't last long, and I immediately tumbled back into the dark spiral of thoughts. "Fuck, I hate this."

"You and me both."

"She claims she's in therapy, believe it or not."

"You're fucking kidding."

"I wish."

He snorted, pushing himself to his feet. "Come on. Let's get you cleaned up. You go shower and scrub the personal frat party off of yourself. I'll clean this shithole while you do."

"You must be worried if you're going to clean."

"Go to hell, Colton."

"Back at ya."

Chapter 32

Remington

The past week was a total blur. Between Colt's continuing cold shoulder and the news Detective Winder had thrown my way, my heart and head were a total mess. Winder introduced me to the FBI agent in charge of the case, Mercer. It turned out they didn't have any actual news. No identity, they weren't even sure it was the same guy.

Whoever he was, was smart enough to elude good camera footage. It was customer descriptions and the dark swirl on his forearm that tied any of the images or videos together. Between hats and hoodies, there wasn't a clear shot of his face to be found.

I was sort of embarrassed over the visceral reaction I'd had when Winder pointed out the crimes were moving west. Lex and I talked for hours and hours on the phone that night. Surprisingly, not at all about Colt. It was several nights later that we hashed that out. I still didn't have any insight about what had happened, or what I'd done.

I'd seen West in town a few days ago, and he'd said that the planned birthday party for today had been changed. It was going to be his parents and Brody only. I thought of the lumber piled in his driveway that disappeared the next day. I thought of Brody's excitement over West letting his friends ride the ponies, which I knew were going to be part of a petting zoo he'd planned. All of those birthday plans gone. Clearly, it wasn't me he was mad at, or I simply would have been uninvited from the party. Despite everything, I'd left Brody's present on Colt's porch in hopes he'd get it.

No matter what was going on, all Colt would've had to do was say he needed space. Instead, he'd shouted and then completely shut me out. Barely anyone saw or spoke to him, even at work. He'd stopped doing anything customer-facing. He'd become a totally different person.

Gigi had returned home on Monday as expected, and I'd been avoiding her almost as much as Colt was avoiding me. Almost as much, because Gigi wasn't one to be ignored. Thankfully, I'd been able to beg off many talks thanks to work and house hunting.

The worst part about the past week was that I wasn't even enjoying my stargazing as much as I had. I still loved it here, but I was struggling.

Movement at the entrance to the café caught my eye. I did my best not to groan as Nova and Moorely practically skipped my way arm in arm. They both wore similar huge grins as they stepped over the bench across from me.

"We found it." Moorely wiggled in her seat. "It's perfect. I swear it."

"Really, Moorely found it. I appreciate receiving some credit, though." Nova flipped her hair over her shoulders like Galinda of Oz. "I do *always* deserve credit for anything good that happens, after all."

"And you're so modest, too." Moorely bumped Nova's shoulder. "Wait. What is it, Remi? What's wrong?"

I fought off a grimace. All week I'd been trying to put on a good face. It was getting harder and harder. It seemed like I couldn't hide the grumpiness anymore. "Nothing. I'm fine. What are you two on about?"

Nova hummed from pursed lips. "I don't believe you."

"Please just tell me what you're talking about?" I sagged under the scrutiny. "Please. I'd give my right arm for something happy right now, and the way you two just flounced in here, I think you might have it."

"Fine, but we're circling back to this." Nova swirled her finger in a circle in my direction. Then she gestured to Moorely. "Go on, show her."

Moorely tapped her phone a few times before flipping it my way. On her screen sat the most picture-perfect gingerbread house. The mountains stretched to the heavens behind it, the sun streaked with the cotton candy colors of a sunset. It even had a white picket fence. Every inch screamed perfection. It looked infinitely familiar.

"Oh. My."

"I told you she'd adore it." Nova leaned toward me, her smile growing. "You'll like this even more. It was originally Nick Young's house."

"Wait, what?" If anything could blast my melancholy away, it was that exciting tidbit. It was too good to be true. The house originally belonged to one of Jane's brothers? "You aren't serious? An actual Young home?"

"Yup. I double-checked with my granny and everything. The listing isn't lying. The house is still in the family, but that branch of the tree went back to Buffalo. While they still own the house, I guess in case they move back, they rent it out constantly. Over the past two years, they've been working on repairs and upgrades."

"Two years?"

"It takes a lot to get any improvements past the town council, especially in a house this close to old town. Either way, the house was just listed yesterday."

"I asked Jasper to let you have the first look." Moorely practically preened. Her dark ponytail swung as she wiggled in her seat again. "He owed me a favor, so he agreed."

"You're both absolutely the best." I studied the picture on the screen again, not quite believing it could be true. "This is the house on Tanner Road, right? A little way outside of town?"

"That's the one." Nova beamed my way right alongside Moorely. They were both so excited for me, I couldn't help but be touched. "It's actually the house next to the Schaffer house."

"The one Jane Doe initially used before she moved into the saloon? Too bad that one isn't available. I'd lose my actual mind." Not that I was far from it these days.

"Ah yes, but the Schaffers still own and use it. The town even tried to buy it to turn into a museum. They refused, sort of like the Youngs with this house." Nova tapped the phone to emphasize. "But they're good caretakers of the homes and haven't really done anything that the town wouldn't like."

"This town cares a lot about its history." I offered Moorely her phone back after one more look at the pretty house. "When can I see it?"

"This afternoon, if you want. I'll text Jasper now to tell him you're definitely interested." Moorely didn't even look up from her phone as she fired off the text. "Does two work?"

"Two sounds great." I didn't want to tell them I had a job interview scheduled at four. That would lead to more questions. Seeing the house at two gave me two hours to see the inside and hopefully sign the lease. The sooner I could do that, the sooner I could move. If I could get a new place and even a new job, maybe I could stop wondering every time I saw him.

"Now back to you." Nova tapped the table in front of me to regain my attention. "What's wrong? Don't you dare tell us it's nothing."

"It's silly."

"Doubt that." Moorely leaned her elbows on the table as she studied me. "You've been radio silent for a week. Ever since we had that sinful afternoon delight the day you were frustrated about the house search. Even with that, you were in quite a good mood."

"Okay, okay." I had a feeling they wouldn't let me be if I didn't talk.

"Go on, spill." Nova waved me on encouragingly.

"I don't know what happened. I don't know if I did something, but Colt hasn't spoken to me in a week. When I went home that day, he was in his garage. I tried to talk to him, and he yelled at me to go the fuck away and closed the garage door in my face. Since then." I jerked my hand across my neck with a click of my tongue. "Nothing. Even when we're both working at the hotel, he barely acknowledges me. Or anyone, really."

"That's weird." Moorely cocked her head. "Everyone saw the way you two were flirting at my place. It was mutual. He's got it bad."

"Based on what happened that night when we got back to his place, I thought so too. We were busy the next couple of days with work and the holiday, but we had plans to have dinner together when his parents took Brody to Canon City. That never happened." I stabbed my fork repeatedly into the remains of my potatoes. Telling these two wasn't making anything clearer than when Lex and I had talked. Pain bloomed as I thought of what I'd given him that night, how much more I'd planned to give him. "Instead, he shut me out."

"Do you know what you need?" Moorely rushed to my side of the table. She burrowed around in her backpack for a minute. "Come on, where is it? I always carry one with me."

"Moorely." Nova dropped her head with a groan. "Don't tell me you're going to give her what I think you are."

"Ah-ha. Here it is." Moorely whipped a mesh bag from the depths of her backpack.

I eyed it curiously, even more so at the tinkling rattle it made when she slid it across the table. "What's this?"

"Shhh. It's a secret." Her voice dropped to a whisper. "Revenge penises."

"It's what?" The party came flooding back, and Aspen's red-faced arrival. "Wait. You mean Aspen?"

"Oh, ew. I already said I didn't revenge-pene my brother. That's disturbing." Moorely shuddered.

"Moorely started the trend, as you know. She's even begun supplying women with penises on a regular basis." Nova's cheeks pinked at the admittance, even though she wasn't the one doing it. "I have a bag at the shop. *Just in case*, as Moorely told me. Even though I don't have any men in my life that would inspire such tactics."

"You know you're insane for starting this trend, don't you?" I still hadn't picked up the bag.

"Or genius." Moorely winked.

"I'm pretty sure Tucker's still finding the penises she left in his office." Nova's embarrassment subsided into laughter. "Once word got out, it's been happening all over town. I'm pretty sure Moorely used Aspen's 3D printer when he was out of town to print a ton of them."

"You're diabolical, you know that?" I balanced the bag in my hand. As intriguing as the idea was, I wasn't exactly mad at Colt. I was hurt, confused, embarrassed, and a little broken-hearted, but not mad. I'd seen the torment in his features, and after hearing from West, I had a feeling I wasn't the only target. That didn't lessen the hurt, but it helped soothe my temper. "No. I don't want to do that to Colt. I'm not really angry."

"Understandable." Moorely sighed. "Well, keep them anyway. You never know."

"Has anyone pene'd Gunner yet?"

Both Moorely and Nova eyed me before breaking into simultaneous grins. Nova shook her head. "No."

"Now that's surprising. He's a cocksure pig most of the time." I slid the bag into my purse. "Maybe the opportunity will present itself."

"And you call me diabolical."

Chapter 33

Colton

Darlene's reappearance had turned my pleasant life into utter turmoil. I had no one to blame but myself, except maybe her. My mood had been absolute trash, even after Gunner tried to snap me out of it. It was seeping into every aspect of my life. As was the worst part of it all—the creeping tendrils of fear that snaked around every one of my nerve endings.

I couldn't shake it no matter how hard I tried. Around every corner, I just knew one of them would be there. Whether her or him, I didn't know. I hadn't left the house with Brody in days, and then it was just to go to the ranch.

After I'd convinced him the man he'd seen outside his window was a dream, I'd turned around and drilled him over and over about the person he'd seen. He'd again become convinced it was real. He was afraid to sleep in his room now, preferring the tent in his playroom.

Everything I was doing was wrong in every way. I knew it with every fiber of my being, but I couldn't let it go. My fingers curled with the need to hit something. It was neither the time nor the place, especially as I was cooking dinner.

Brody sat at the kitchen table somberly coloring. None of his usual pep lingered in his expression or movements. His legs hung perfectly still under him instead of swinging happily. The constant chatter I was used to was nonexistent.

I hated myself for what my temperament was doing to him. It wasn't fair, and it wasn't right. Every time I tried to bring myself back to normal, the curse of thinking someone was out to get me reared its head. I'd thought for sure I'd left that feeling in the past.

The constant, recurring texts from Darlene didn't help. Even though I'd sent her away without the least bit of sympathy or forgiveness, she wasn't giving up. Each ding of my phone twisted my stomach in knots. I was popping Tums like I'd been eating nothing but curry.

Of course, Darlene wasn't the only one I'd sent away. My actions meant that none of those texts were from Remington. She didn't check on me once. I was angry she didn't even try, even as I simultaneously knew why.

One more thing to blame myself for. God, I hated myself right then.

A knock on the back door jolted through me. The wooden spoon I'd been using to stir the mac and cheese noodles flew across the room. "Shit. Damn it."

Brody stared at me with wide eyes before turning his attention to the back door. For the first time in days, a broad smile broke across his face. He skipped to the door without asking permission.

"Brody. Wait."

"It's Gigi. Gigi!" He pulled open the door and rushed across the threshold to throw his arms around the older woman's legs. It took all my restraint not to peek and see if Gigi was the only person outside. A minute later, Brody dragged our neighbor into the house. "She brought cookies. Chocolate chip."

"You didn't have to," I started.

"Nobody forced me to. I love baking, and Brody loves cookies. It's the perfect combination." She set the plate of cookies on the counter. Without asking whether I needed help, she pushed me away from the stove. She moved about my kitchen as easily as if it were her own. With a replacement spoon and colander in hand, she tended to the noodles. "I haven't seen you around lately, and my granddaughter is in a mood. Of course, that won't matter much longer seeing as she's moving out soon."

The words were a gut punch. I pushed the reaction down as far as I could. Remi had been through enough in the past year. My shitstorm didn't need to involve her in any way. I'd prefer it didn't involve Brody, either. The misery was bad enough for me to tolerate, but it was too much for him. Misery didn't, in fact, always love company. I swallowed against my dry throat. "Where's she going?"

"She rented the old Young house on Tanner. Signed the lease before it was listed for a day. I suspect a conspiracy, but she won't confirm it." Gigi's head disappeared behind my fridge door. "She's pretty excited to live in a piece of history. I know she'll honor its memory well. It's too bad, though. I enjoy having company around."

I could only manage a grunt of response. In no time at all, Gigi would have someone else using one or more of her spare rooms. She collected stray people like West collected stray animals.

"I know Brody will miss her. I also know she promised they'd talk more about Disney any time she saw him around town."

"She *knows* Mickey, did you know that, Gigi?" Brody danced in his chair. His legs kicked back and forth with happy abandon again. "And Stitch. And *all* the princess. She even danced in the street with Peter Pan once. Oh, and she said the best ride is the one that doesn't even go fast, it goes slow. She knows *everything.*"

"Well, not everything." Gigi chuckled, stirring the butter into the noodles. "But everything about Disney? That might be right."

"That's what I meant." Brody rolled his eyes as if that was obviously the only subject in the world that mattered. Two weeks ago, the only subjects that mattered were the horses and kittens at the farm. He grew so damn fast. I was losing too many moments in this dark pit.

"I'm so sorry." Gigi pointed her spoon at him. "You'd best get those crayons away and wash your hands. Your dinner will land on that placemat soon."

I sank into a seat across from Brody. He scurried to do as he was told, returning minutes later with still-damp hands. He and Gigi continued to converse happy as clams around me. I couldn't bring myself to join. She set a plate in front of me before joining the two of us at the table. I prodded the mac and cheese with my fork a few times before taking a bite.

For at least a week now, I'd been debating taking Brody away. An extended vacation in an RV seemed like a good idea. It was the middle of summer, which would be ideal for a trip around the country like that. It would get us away until whatever was happening with Darlene blew over.

Traversing the country with no schedule could be fun. I could ask my cousin to watch the hotel for a few months. He managed it already at night, so it wouldn't be a huge transition. Maybe then I could get out of this funk that had real potential to destroy my relationship with my son.

The question was, would that be enough to keep me from looking over my shoulder and around every corner? Probably not.

Gigi's hand settled on my shoulder.

I startled, looking around the kitchen when I noticed the chair in front of me was empty. "What? Where's Brody?"

"He's getting ready for bed." She settled into the chair beside me. "You're a million miles away, and in one hell of a rotten mood to boot."

"I'm aware." I knew she was trying to be kind, and that's all that kept me from yanking my arm away from her gentle pats.

"Are you?" She held my attention with her fierce gaze. Gone was the laughter of her conversation with Brody. It was a stark reminder of how she'd kept so many foster kids in line. "Your mood is infecting everything. Including your business. Byron told me business at the casino was down when he returned this week. He said it's the slowest he's ever seen it."

If there'd been any point, I would've argued. Unfortunately, she was right.

"The one thing your ancestors and you have in common is a way with people, a way that draws people in. When you lose that, you lose a lot. Including a good woman."

My jaw tightened at the insinuation. There wasn't anything I could say. I wouldn't apologize. Remi would be better off far away from it all. Even if I knew I'd been better around her. And Brody adored her. My eyelids fluttered closed while I tried to forget that thought.

"Fine. Be that way. I'll put the boy to sleep so he can have pleasant dreams tonight. Maybe you should try to pull your head out of your ass tonight so he can wake in a good mood, too."

It was a losing battle. I didn't have the strength to fight right then. I only nodded.

"I don't know what happened to you when I was in Kansas visiting Cheyenne, and it's none of my business. That girl *is* my business, though. If nothing else, don't you think she deserves an explanation for why you dumped a bucket of ice over her?"

I knew she did. Every bit as much as Brody deserved a dad who was present.

"Think about it. You, Brody, and Remi all deserve better."

Chapter 34

Remington

The weather was ideal. After several days of arranging for movers and getting my things shipped from Lex's storage space, not to mention shopping for the perfect furniture for my new living room, I'd earned a break.

In one week, I'd be in my new place. It had an adorable front porch that would just fit a small table and two rocking chairs where I could people watch or read. I was thrilled the house included its own back deck and a detached garage at the back of the generous yard.

Even more, there was a small, well-maintained stable that had been there for over a century. I'd always imagined having a horse of my own one day. Maybe with the stable there, I'd get my wish. I didn't plan to get enough horses to fill all four stalls, but I wouldn't mind having one. Maybe I'd even get chickens.

I chuckled to myself. When did I become interested in a country, homesteader life like this? Either way, I was excited to see what would come next. Mostly. There was still the matter of the man next door. Of course, that seemed beyond hope at this point.

So did my search for a new job. Although I had to admit that my attempts were lackluster at best. Despite Colt flat-out avoiding me at every turn, I really enjoyed working in the casino more than I thought I would. The clientele always made for an interesting evening of conversation, and the tips were pretty amazing in a gambling room. Now that Byron had returned to work with plenty of pictures of the new baby, we had a lot of fun. When both of us and Moorely all worked together, it was a guaranteed fun shift.

I gathered my latest stack of Doe Diaries and a pitcher of Gigi's lemonade to help keep me cool. Once I got settled into the lounge chair with a nice glass of lemonade, I opened the next volume of the diaries. After some dramatic years of adventure and suspense, life seemed to have settled down for Jane and Cole. Except for Cole's business partner, Graham, their days were filled with love and life, even if the guy couldn't say those three words to her.

Even with their daily life calming down, the story still had my attention whole-heartedly. Margot had hinted that there were quite a few more diaries to go, and I had a long way to go to complete the challenge of reading them all. For now, I was savoring the quiet peace in everyday life Jane and Cole shared during this time in their life. I was curious when it would all blow up in their faces again, but not enough to rush through my current stack of books.

A squeal preceded Brody sprinting off his deck so fast he was several feet away when he landed. I buried my nose in my book so I wouldn't see Colt outside of work right now. It was easy enough to be ignored at work, much harder when outside of work. It wasn't Colt that spoke, it was Prairie.

"Slow down, you little cretin. I have to put the sunscreen on you or your dad is going to kill me." Laughter warmed her words into something far from truly scolding. The ensuing chase between aunt and nephew was adorable and hilarious. Prairie finally caught Brody, and they both tumbled to the ground still laughing.

Brody's pure, unadulterated laughter lightened my heart. He was the most adorable little kid. I'd miss our talks when I moved away. Sure, I'd still see him at work sometimes, and in town as well. It wouldn't be nearly every day like now. Even with Colt being an unfeeling bastard at the moment, I could always count on Brody for a smile.

Prairie marched her nephew onto the deck, where a can of sunscreen perched on the table. She commanded him to stand with his arms out, then turn. As soon as the bottle landed back on the table, Brody was off like a shot.

That's when she noticed me. With an enthusiastic wave, she headed toward the fence separating the yards. I joined her there, nodding to Brody. "He's in a mood."

"I don't think he's been able to come outside much in the past couple of weeks." A rare and troubled frown darkened Prairie's features. She watched him running around the yard for a minute. "Colt's in a mood."

"I noticed." It wasn't a subject I really cared to broach. Even though I could feel Prairie's eyes boring into my skull. Heat rose to my cheeks, but I shook my head against questions. "Moorely gave me one of her bags of dicks for dickbags."

Prairie laughed much louder than I expected. "Oh, those are classic. You know it's a trend around town now. No man is safe."

"Apparently not even her own brother." I chuckled as Brody attempted a cartwheel. "He definitely has a lot of energy to burn and needs to learn how to do a cartwheel."

"That's something I can show him. First, that child needs to let off some of the excess energy he's built up over the past couple of weeks. Even his birthday was a drag."

"That's too bad. No one's birthday should be a drag. Especially when you're six."

"Agreed." She rested her chin on her hand with a hefty sigh. "Paige did all she could to make it fun for him, but without any of his friends there, it wasn't the same."

I didn't miss the way Prairie's expression darkened again. "Is everything okay? I don't want to pry, but you seem upset, too."

This time, it took a physical shake to rid herself of the dark look. "It'll pass. For now, we've all been offering to watch him as much as we can to give him and Colt a break."

In all the time I'd known Colt, which was admittedly not a lot, he'd never once needed, or wanted, a break from his own son. The whole thing was too much. It hurt my heart, and not just for myself. For Brody. And for Colt and whatever he was going through.

"Anyway. I heard you got the Young place. I've always loved it, but I'm home so little I could hardly enjoy it, so I stick with my apartment. Plus, it has the bonus of a free pool I don't have to maintain."

"Definitely a bonus." I eyed Brody as he rolled down the small hill that comprised the backyard before darting back to the top to throw himself down in another roll. "My goodness, you weren't kidding about him being wild today."

"I know. He's nonstop."

Brody scrambled back up the hill again. This time he spotted me and waved. "Remi! Hi! Watch this!" He threw himself back down the hill. Halfway down, he let out a shriek and hopped to his feet. Tears streaked down his face as he ran over to us, his arm outstretched.

"What happened?" Prairie kneeled to meet him when he got to us. She searched his arm, pouting at the red bump on his forearm. "Looks like a bee sting. I think the stinger's still in there."

Instinctively, I turned my attention to Brody's features. For the moment he seemed okay, just a little puffy from crying. "Has he ever been stung before?"

"I don't think so. Why?" She brushed the tears from his cheeks. "Paige used to make a paste that would draw out the stingers. I think it was just baking soda and water. I'll have to text."

While she did that, I kept my eye on Brody. Although bee venom allergies are less common than, for example, peanut allergies, a first sting should always be a concern.

Brody hiccupped a few times, sucking in his lower lip with each one. The stuttered breath of his cries grew deeper. "It. Hurts."

"Brody. Come here." I checked his arm to find that the site had swollen even more. With his chin, I tilted his head toward me. His eyes were glassy, and his lips looked swollen.

"R-R-Remi." He sniffled.

"Shit." I launched myself over the chain-link fence to examine him closer. His breathing was rapid and shallow. I tugged on his chin to open his mouth to check his tongue. It wasn't swelling yet. "Prairie."

"What is it? What's wrong?" She lowered her phone to stare at me.

This was one of those rare occasions I was grateful for that pesky shellfish allergy. "I need you to do a favor for me and do it fast."

"What?" Panic ticked her voice higher.

"Go into the house and get my purse. Now. Then call 911."

Prairie did as I asked without question, thankfully. I helped Brody to sit, keeping my eyes on him. This time when he tried to speak, it was muffled. "What."

"Shhh. Don't you worry. Look at me. I need you to nod yes or no. Are you having trouble taking a breath?" His nod twisted my heart. "I thought so. Focus on me and try to follow my breathing. In two, three out two, three. Slow and steady, as deep as you can."

The high wheeze I could hear without a stethoscope told me all I needed to know. I needed that EpiPen fast. No amount of controlled breaths could help you in anaphylaxis. The best I could do was keep him calm. I'd have him breathing in no time.

Prairie practically fell over the fence getting my purse to me. Her phone skittered away in the fall. She scrambled to grab it. "I've got them on the line. What's happening?"

"Tell them he's having an anaphylactic reaction to bee venom. I'm administering epinephrine now." I pulled the pen out of my purse where I always kept it. Brody gripped my arm, gasping for air. I kept my focus on him while I prepped the EpiPen. "You're going to be fine in a few seconds, Brody. This might hurt a little, but it's going to help you breathe, okay?"

He nodded weakly.

I jammed the pen into his thigh, expelling the dose of epi. After it was done, I pulled him close so I could keep an ear on his breathing. "There. You're going to be fine in no time. We're going to go to the hospital, though. We need to make sure you don't have trouble again. Are they on their way, Prairie?"

"Yeah. I'll call Colt and let him know."

"Good idea." I let out a relieved breath when Brody took a big gasp of air. He curled against me, his small hand gripping my arm hard. I didn't argue, relieved to have him on the mend. "That's better."

His thumb went into his mouth. Considering his ordeal, I didn't think Prairie or I would object to the reaction.

"You're going to ride in an ambulance, Brody. How about that?"

He gave a weak smile. His eyelids were heavy.

"You're going to be fine. They'll take good care of you."

"You take care of me."

Chapter 35

Colton

This wasn't happening. This couldn't be happening.

I slammed my fist into my horn, barreling down the suicide land on a path to the hospital and through every red light in my path. Prairie's tale had lacked detail, but burgeoned with panic.

A bee.

Not breathing.

Brody had stopped breathing? An ambulance took him to the hospital, straight to the ER. My heart raced in my chest. I got dizzy for a minute.

The hospital wasn't far, but the distance felt like a thousand miles. I'd never honked my horn so much in my life. All I wanted was to get to Brody. To see him. Breathing. Alive. Prairie said he was, but I had to see it for myself.

How could I have forgotten for one second he was all that mattered? For the past two weeks, I'd been such a mess. I'd been distant, snappy. Nothing like the man or father I'd been for years. To think that's how I'd been for Brody right before he had a life-threatening emergency was more than I could bear.

I'd be better from now on if he'd just be okay.

I needed him to be okay.

In front of the ER entrance, I slammed to a stop. I left the car there to tear inside. "Where is he? Brody? I need to see my son."

"Colt." Keely waved at me from the door. "He's in here. I've been keeping an eye out for you. Brody is doing well. Remi's EpiPen saved the day. She treated him the minute she knew what was going on."

That didn't make sense. Remi had been there? I'd only caught brief glimpses of her for over a week. Most of those were at work. I shook off my confusion to follow Keely back. I stopped short outside the glass doors.

Brody perched on the bed playing with a stuffed giraffe, laughing it up with Remi. He didn't seem fazed by the monitors hooked up to him. Remi had him thoroughly distracted. In fact, as I watched, Remi stuck a small needle in his arm without a whimper of complaint. With quick efficiency, she attached tubing to a bag hanging on a pole. When she was done, she poked him three times up the same arm before ruffling his hair.

His laughter filled the room, catching like wildfire among the staff inside. My throat was dry as a bone. "What?"

"Remi's been great with him. Suze tried to get that IV in several times. He kept freaking out whenever she got near. I don't know how, but Remi got him to be cooperative in no time. I didn't know she was a nurse."

"She's not." My voice caught. She was still helping Brody despite everything. "Anymore. That's what she said, anyway."

"That's too bad. She's had that room running smooth as anything. We don't have a dedicated pediatric ER team, so when we get them, it's a different ball game."

"Yeah." I furrowed my brow. "She doesn't work here. She doesn't work as a nurse anymore. Why are you letting her?"

"I'm not, the director of nursing is. There's only a couple of pediatric nurses on staff. The pediatric unit is small and understaffed. The most critical cases are usually flown up to Colorado Springs. Remi had a multi-state license on hand, and apparently tons of experience in peds as an ER nurse. The DON gave her special permission."

The party at Moorely's right before everything went to shit ran through my head. When she talked about creating magic for patients in a crisis, her eyes had shone with the light of the very joy she'd spoken of. I'd thought I understood. I hadn't. Watching her with Brody now, I got it.

I shook away the distraction, but couldn't tear my eyes from Brody as he played happily with Remi. "What about Brody? What happened? Prairie wasn't clear." My sister sat behind Remi, chewing her nails to the stubs like she'd done as a teen filled with anxiety.

"Anaphylactic reaction to bee venom. He's not the first with a bee allergy. You'll have to keep an EpiPen on hand at all times. Goodness knows you won't be able to keep him from playing outside. Nor should you."

That stuck the knife of shame deeper in my heart. For the past couple of weeks, we'd been inside more often than not. I could see him wilting during my foray into misery. No, I couldn't keep him inside for his whole life.

Prairie approached the bed when Remi waved her over. My sister spotted me through the glass. After whispering something to Remi, which had her stiffen in her seat, Prairie headed his way instead. Tears streaked her face. Her eyes were puffy from crying. "I'm so sorry. I didn't know. He always rolls down the hill. I wouldn't have let him if I'd known. He could have—"

A large hiccupping sob interrupted her sentence, thank God. I pulled her into a hug. "It's not your fault. I didn't know. How could you?"

She sobbed into my chest. Keely touched my arm before slipping back into the room. Prairie sniffled. "I didn't know what to do. I didn't even know it was happening. Remi knew, though. She said she's allergic to shellfish; that's why she had the pen."

"I'm not mad, Prairie. This scared the shit out of me is all." It scared sense into me, too. From where I stood, Brody appeared perfectly fine and as animated as usual. It was time to see for myself how he was. "I'm going in."

"Okay. I'm going to call Dad to update him on how he's doing."

"Sure, thanks." The minute I slid open the doors, the beeping of monitors and quiet discussion hit me. Even Brody and Remi spoke in hushed tones, though their conversation was animated. I cleared my throat to clear the absolute lump blocking my speech. My voice creaked through the two syllables. "Brody."

He stilled at my voice, his hands tightened on the giraffe a little. He looked to Remi, who patted his leg before he looked my way. That hesitation in his response gutted me. Fuck, I'd been a complete and total ass for the past couple of weeks. He didn't deserve that. I never wanted him to live any part of his life afraid to do something, or afraid of me.

Remi patted his leg again, Brody offered a weak smile. "A bee stung me, and I couldn't breathe. It was scary."

"I've heard." I rushed forward to pull Brody into my arms. It might have been too tight a hold, but he didn't try to get away, he curled into me. "Thank goodness you're alright. I was so scared I ran every red light."

"Really?" Brody peeked at me. "Did Unc Gunner help you?"

"Nope. I did it without his help." His giggle cracked through the clamp around my heart. "I'm pretty sure I made all the tourists mad racing past them on the suicide lane."

"Cool." Brody held out his arm to show me the IV like it was a badge of honor. "Look. Remi did it. I barely felt it. It hurt less than the bee did. I told her she'd take care of me, and she *did*."

"That's impressive." I tried to get Remi's attention to give her genuine thanks, but she avoided me. I couldn't blame her after how I'd treated her.

No, it was more. While I felt like I was shaking all over, Remi actually was. I could see her hands shaking when she drew them into her lap. Her hair even trembled. After a few slow blinks, her eyes darted around the room. The color drained from her features, her hands curling into fists in her lap. She cleared her throat. "I'm gonna—I've got to—go."

"No." Brody caught the edge of her sleeve. "Don't go. Stay. You said."

"I did." Remi collected herself for him, giving him a strong hug. When she settled back into her seat, her hands still shook.

"Thank you, Remington. For saving him." Maybe by talking to her directly, she could put her focus on something other than what was happening in her head. "I mean it. There's nothing I could ever do to thank you enough."

Her nose twitched, her lips thinned into a tight line. Still freaking out? Or just still royally pissed? Either was probably legit."

"She stabbed me." Brody slammed his fist into his leg.

A genuine, bright laugh destroyed every bit of tension. Everything about her softened when she set her hand on Brody's. "I thought we agreed to stop saying that to everyone. I gave you medicine as fast as I could."

"By stabbing me."

Her shoulders sagged in defeat. "I suppose that's as true as it can be."

The affection between them melted the ice I'd built around my heart even further. This woman treated my son like he was the best person in the world, which he was. She'd even left a birthday gift for him after I canceled all plans.

"It hurt, but then I could breathe again. Like this." Brody took a huge breath through his nose until his chest puffed out.

I chuckled, as did just about everyone in the room. With the heaviness lightened a little, I took in my son. He had some circles under his eyes and his hair was askew, but otherwise he seemed well enough. "Why did he have to come to the ER if the shot saved him?"

I'd directed the question at Keely, but Remi answered. "Because of the possibility of a biphasic reaction."

"Huh?"

"It's possible that the epinephrine will help his systems for a while, but then he could rebound back into them worse than they were. It's safest to have him here." She still didn't look at me once. Her focus remained solely on Brody.

"Oh. How long will he have to stay?"

"Your pediatrician wants him here overnight, and for you to make an appointment to test for any other allergies so you aren't surprised like this again." Keely tapped keys on the computer in front of her while she spoke. "The doctor already put in the orders for overnight observation. He'll be on the pediatric unit, room 347."

Remi's eyes shuddered closed. She took some deep breaths, her leg bouncing like mad. When she finally opened her eyes, she was looking at me, likely by accident. There were tears in her eyes, and not one bit of the anger I'd expected. She looked scared as shit.

"He's okay," I whispered.

"I'm. Aware." She clenched her jaw so tight that she could only grind the words out through her teeth. "I need to..."

I nodded. She should go if this was too much for her. I had no idea if she'd been in a hospital since her attack. When she stood, her movements were jerky and a little uncoordinated. It reminded me of something I couldn't place right then.

Remi said nothing about leaving this time. She backed away from the bed slowly. When she raced out the door right past Prairie as she returned, it hit me why her behavior seemed familiar.

Prairie's wide eyes turned to me. "What happened?"

"Shit."

Chapter 36

Remington

Air.

I needed air.

My lungs squeezed tighter until I nearly wheezed as Brody had. My vision narrowed to pinpricks. I stumbled through the doors to the waiting room, then followed the brightness of the sun.

The second the doors whooshed open, I gasped deeply. My whole body shook, my limbs growing weaker. The shaking went deeper, down to my bones. I slumped against the brick wall and sank to the concrete, pulling my limbs in toward myself.

I gulped for air that didn't want to fill my lungs. My mouth hung open like a fish out of water. The rapid beat of my heart swooshed in my ears until. The light breeze felt like fire across my raw nerves.

A sting of pain in my palms from my nails did little to bring my brain back into focus.

"Remington."

A touch to my arm sent me flailing against the intruder. Flashes of my nightmares and reality flashed across my narrowed vision. I tried to scream, but couldn't get enough air to.

"Remington." My fight didn't stop them from pulling me tight against them. The encompassing pressure of the bear hug slowed my trembling. My nerves eased their crackling heat. "That's it. Tell me five things you see."

"I. Um." My voice shook as much as my body had moments ago.

"Tell me, Remington. Five things you see. Focus."

I forced my eyes open, trying to see past the narrow vision still plaguing me. "Bricks."

"What else?"

"A car. Stop sign." The forceful focus on solid objects eased the tremor in my voice. My vision widened enough to take in more of my environment. "Wheelchair. Tree."

"Good. Now four things you can touch or feel."

"Bear hug." The warm chuckle in my ear eased my nerves further. I touched everything as I focused on it. "Concrete. Shoelace. Sock."

"Three things you can hear."

"You." My eyes drifted closed again. I relaxed into the hug. Air passed more smoothly into my lungs, easier with each breath. "Traffic. A starling."

"Two things you can smell."

"Asphalt. Some kind of flower."

"One thing you can taste."

"My own blood." I must have bitten my cheek in my panic. I probed the area with my tongue. Yeah, that would hurt for days.

"What?"

"I bit my cheek."

I didn't move from my position against him, even though the brutal wave of terror had passed. When I opened my eyes again, a pair of black work boots under brown pants were in front of me.

"What's going on?" Gunner's tone held a bit of laughter. I imagined we looked a sight with him wrapped around me in a bear hug.

"Panic attack," Colt supplied.

Gunner's smile faltered before it dropped completely. He crouched in front of me, studying my features intently. "Looks like you're out of it now. You good, Remi?"

"I think so." I patted Colt's arm where he still had it wrapped across my chest. "You should get back to Brody. I'll be fine."

Gunner's gaze shifted over my shoulder to his brother. The pair seemed to have a silent conversation before Gunner nodded. "I'll go say hi to him. I heard on the radio what happened. Thought I'd swing by when I had a minute. Take your time."

"Prairie's in there." Colt's hold on me didn't ease until the doors hissed open, then closed. He set his hands on my shoulders, rubbing them slightly. "Are you really okay?"

"Brody." It wasn't right that he was out here with me when his son was in the ER. I know they hadn't had the best couple of weeks, and he should be with his son.

"I know. I'll go back in once I'm sure you're feeling better. Brody will want to know. You made sure Brody was okay, it's only fair you are, too. Was that your first time in an ER since it happened?"

"Yeah." My mouth had gone bone dry again. I'd promised Brody I'd stay with him, but I wasn't sure I could go back inside. A small shudder passed through me.

"You're okay. You're safe." He didn't bear-hug me this time, but he pulled me close again.

In the back of my mind, there was a voice telling me this should be completely awkward sitting here wrapped in his arms when we hadn't talked for two weeks, where he'd been cold as ice. The tincture of adrenaline still coursing through me kept me right where I was. "Everything was fine. I was fine during it all. Right until you walked in the door. Then it all came crashing down."

"You were shaking like a leaf. I'm surprised you stayed as long as you did." He rubbed my arms vigorously. "You should go home and try to relax."

"I promised." Even though I knew it wouldn't be a problem with all the family that would likely show up, I'd promised Brody I'd stay and take care of him.

"How can you help when you're too terrified to be in the room?"

I scooted away from him like I was the one that had been stung. Once on my feet, I brushed off my shorts. My jaw clenched to keep tears at bay. "I made a promise. That means something to me. I needed a minute, and I took it."

Colt set his hands on my shoulders. The warm concern that shone from his eyes reminded me of the man I'd met and had been falling in love with. "Are you sure? It isn't fair to you to put yourself through that. Brody will understand."

"Maybe he would, but I wouldn't. I don't break promises."

His features fell at my sharp tone. Instead of tensing in anger or raising his voice in protest, his shoulders sagged. He offered a small nod. "Yeah. I've been a total ass for the past couple of weeks."

"Yes. You have." I couldn't keep the hurt tone at bay. A few tears sprang forward. I wanted to have it out with him right there and then, to express everything I felt. This wasn't the time or place. I had a promise to keep. "I'm going back in."

"Remington."

"How did you know what to do?" I couldn't go down whatever road he was trying to go. I had to get my wits about me. "For that matter, how did you know what was happening?"

"You mean your panic attack?" Colt moved aside to let me pass through the doors.

"Yes."

"Prairie had them a lot after everything. Gunner and I had them too, sometimes. Paige helped us learn how to manage them. She's a psychologist."

The closer we got to the ER, the harder my heart pounded. Colt put a steadying hand on my arm. I hated it helped keep the rising panic at bay. I was mad at him, hurt by him. He shouldn't be confusing me by helping. To keep those thoughts, and my dread, on the back burner, I focused on the conversation again. "I didn't know that."

"Yeah. She retired a few years ago. We put her through the wringer for a long time. I think we exhausted her enough to make her retire."

Amusement bubbled against my better judgment. "I would think Gunner would be enough to do that on his own."

"Would be enough to do what on my own?" Gunner emerged from the room. He looked me over with an assessing gaze. His sharp gaze didn't miss Colt's hand on my arm, but he snapped back to me quickly.

"She thinks you and your sparkling personality were enough to make Paige retire early."

Gunner shrugged with both his hands raised. He pursed his lips, then nodded. "I can't say she's wrong."

"Are you heading out already?" Colt had his free hand on the door.

"Yeah. I'm still on shift. I'll move your car before I leave. Keely said he'd be staying for observation." Gunner stepped closer, clasping my hand in his. It was the first time I'd seen him completely earnest, not even the night in the bar when he'd helped had he seemed so serious. "Thank you for your help. Keely says you're one hell of a nurse."

"Was. I *was* a hell of a nurse." The panic crawled up my esophagus, burning my throat. A tight squeeze of my elbow brought me back.

"You were again today." Colt met my gaze with solid strength. "And I'm grateful."

Damn that man, sparking my hope with one look.

Chapter 37

Colton

Light cut through the darkness. I groaned my way back to consciousness. It didn't matter that I'd been told repeatedly I didn't have to wake up every time they came to check Brody's vitals, but my nerves had me too on edge to sleep

The nurse whispered an apology before tending to Brody. The poor kid was so tired he barely stirred at her ministrations. If only I were that tired. Unfortunately, adrenaline still rattled me every time light shone in the room.

I swiped my hand over my face. It was time to give up the ghost. Dawn would be along soon enough, and I didn't think I'd be able to get back to sleep. While the nurse was in the room, I headed to the public kitchen to make myself a coffee.

After his shift, Gunner went to my house to get me some things to bide my time. While I waited for daytime, I'd get some work done. I planned to spend the next few days at home, making up for my rotten mood to Brody.

All evening he'd been happy when everyone else was around, but became subdued when it was just him and me.

I would do everything in my power to make sure it would never be like that again. I didn't want my mere presence to make Brody think he had to be any less than what he was, which was incredible on its own.

The first step to righting my wrongs would be to spend time with him like we always had. I'd always treasured my relationship with Brody, and it was time to do it again. I was ashamed that I'd let it come to that.

It might take a few conversations with Paige about how to get out of my head. I'd been in a panic and fear spiral for two weeks. That was a hard cycle to get out of.

My phone pinged, pulling me out of my thoughts. It was a surprise to see Remi's name. Of course, the text only asked about Brody. It would take a lot more than helping her out of a panic attack for her to forgive me for my treatment. I'd probably have to eat crow and admit I was a total and complete idiot.

From the minute I met her, Remi'd been nothing but an understanding and kind soul. It was one of the things I admired most about her. She'd never pushed me for information about my past. She'd understood and accepted that some things were too painful to deal with. The whole time she'd been infinitely patient with my reticence to share.

Then I had to go and push her away. Why?

Because I was an idiot. An absolute ass, to boot.

It was that simple. All I had to do was open my mouth and talk. Instead, I'd yelled at her to get the fuck out. I might have been annoyed that she listened so easily, but I couldn't blame her. When I took a hard look at the man I'd turned into since Darlene's arrival, I'd earned it.

I sent a quick text giving her an update on where we were. If I had to guess, I think she already knew what was going on. She'd only left when visiting hours ended, after all. Once we'd left the ER and made it to his room, her continual struggle had eased a little.

With my family, she'd had amiable smiles and funny stories. Some of them had even involved her acting out portions, much to Brody's absolute delight. He'd been enamored of her every second she was there. That was another thing I'd robbed him of in my desolation.

For me, there'd been a well-earned chill to our exchanges on her end. It wasn't a surprise, but I didn't like it. It was my intention to change it. After I made amends with Brody, of course.

To my surprise, Remi responded almost immediately. This time she asked how I was holding up. My shoulders lost some of their tension at her concern. I wouldn't get my hopes up. I shouldn't. Remi was a kind woman, and that's likely all this was. Kindness. Despite her anger, she could still share some with me.

I told her the truth. That I was exhausted after all the vitals checks during the night. Not to mention my own worries keeping me awake.

> **Remington:** The hospital is the last place to go if you want to rest.
> **Me:** I've noticed. Between calls over the PA and them coming in to check his vitals and administer meds, I think I've slept maybe 10 minutes.
> **Remington:** Earplugs would have been smart.
> **Me:** I wish I'd thought of that. I could have had Gunner get me some when he got my things from the house.
> **Remington:** Would it really help? I think it's your nerves more than the noise.
> **Me:** No doubt. I wasn't kidding about the red lights yesterday. I've never known panic like that.
> **Remington:** I've seen it a lot.
> **Me:** I don't know how you could witness that every day.
> **Remington:** Because there are happy endings.
> **Me:** I hope there is this time. I have a lot to make up for.
> **Remington:** ●●●

I stared at those three dots that came and went several times. It didn't take me long to screw up. I couldn't help myself. I just had to let her know I realized I had work ahead of me. The dots appeared before I could write more, this time resulting in a message.

> **Remington:** It's good you know that. Don't forget. He adores you, and it won't take long.

This time it was me typing and deleting messages. I wanted to tell her I knew I had to make things up to her, too. I didn't want to push. Especially since it would be days before I had a chance to really talk to her about it.

Not willing to scare her off before I'd started making up for being an asshole, I resorted to focusing on the reason she'd texted me. Then again, was it really Brody?

> **Me**: I never want something like this to happen again.
> **Remington**: Allergies happen. Get him tested, and there won't be any surprises.
> **Me**: Not the allergies. This rift I caused in my life. I don't know how to begin fixing all of it.
> **Remington**: Just remember what it felt like to realize he was ok. The rest of your troubles will seem so small compared to what they could have been.
> **Me**: Does that work?
> **Remington**: Probably not. It's a mouthpiece they told us to say.
> **Me**: What do you say?
> **Remington**: Love him. That's all either of you needs.

My heart squeezed tight. I looked toward the bed where Brody still slept. The interruptions hadn't disturbed his sleep much at all. After the excitement of the ambulance ride and the ER, and then basically everyone we knew showing up to check in on him, bringing games and snacks, it was too much excitement to last.

I went to my texting homepage and selected Paige. She wouldn't be awake, but I needed to take the initial leap while I had the courage and the fortification of Remi's words. Talking about everything had never been our family's strong suit. Paige might have made a big impact on our openness with each other over time, but that didn't mean we were comfortable talking about the past. Ever.

> **Me**: Paige, when you're up and have a minute, I think I need to talk. I'm in a spiral. I'm struggling to stop.

I set my phone aside to open my laptop. Before it finished booting, another text alert sounded. Considering the hour, I didn't know who it could be besides Remi, who'd already proven she was awake.

> **Paige**: I was wondering when you'd come around.

> **Me:** What are you doing awake?
>
> **Paige:** West has a mare foaling. Since he's out of commission, Tom and I are taking turns watching her.
>
> **Me:** That's right. It was chaotic last night. I forgot you mentioned that was why you and Dad took turns visiting.
>
> **Paige:** There isn't a soul or creature on this farm that has slept all night. The mare is already sick, and labor isn't being kind.
>
> **Me:** Oof. Get some sleep. We can talk tomorrow. I want to spend time with Brody at home tonight, anyway. I had to text before I lost the nerve.
>
> **Paige:** I'm always here. You don't have to ask.
>
> **Me:** Thanks.
>
> **Paige:** Love you, TonTon.
>
> **Me:** Love you back, Dosie.

The nicknames lightened my mood enough to help me smile. They were special between us. With everyone calling me Colt over Colton, and my childhood obsession with Star Wars, Paige had taken to calling me TonTon. I'd wanted to return the favor of a nickname, and she'd left it up to me. I don't know that I ever told her the reason I called her Dosie. Maybe I should. She'd probably like it.

Brody twitched in his bed. I waited to see if he'd settle back into sleep.

He didn't. It got worse with a whimper and a thrash. I crossed the room immediately. Hopefully, he wouldn't push me away after the past couple of weeks. With the IV still in and the unfamiliar bed, I didn't want him to wake in a panicked state.

I slipped into the bed and pulled him against me. He settled against me as easily as he always had, gripping my shirt. Within moments his mouth hung open, and his childish snore danced on the air.

I situated myself until I was as comfortable as I could be, Brody's head resting on my chest.

Work could wait. This was more important.

Chapter 38

Remington

O ver the week leading up to move-in day, I'd been too busy to worry much over the events of the previous week and the hospital stay for Brody. I'd seen him a couple of times during the week, and he seemed to be doing well. Once again he was glued to his dad's side, and Colt appeared the better for it.

It was good to see Colt spending so much time with Brody. I knew the whole thing had scared Colt half to death. I think it scared him out of whatever had darkened his personality.

It was impossible to get subtext from text messages, but Colt had made several further attempts at text conversations under the guise of checking in on me after my panic attack. He'd even used Brody as an excuse for several of them.

I would have doubted the sincerity if Brody hadn't been so excited to see me and share with me some stories of his week whenever I saw him in town. As it was, I thought perhaps Colt was trying to make up for his previous behavior as best he could. It wasn't enough, but I wasn't about to begrudge him time with his son. That was far more important than my hurt feelings.

Fortunately, I was far too busy to examine any of those thoughts or wonderings in much detail. Every time I turned around, I thought of another thing I needed to get for my new home. Repeated texts with Lex reminded me just how much of my stuff I'd sold instead of storing. It made for cheaper transport for the boxes, but it meant I had to buy more.

I'd had almost too much, and definitely way too enthusiastic, assistance from my new girlfriends. Nova, Moorely, and occasionally Prairie, were all along for the ride of getting my new home prepped how I wanted it.

We'd spent several hours together poring over the catalog at Jones' Junk Drawer to pick out furniture that was both functional and period appropriate. It wouldn't ever be a museum, it was my home after all, but I wanted it to feel like I did when I stepped into old town. Most importantly, I wanted to be comfortable living there.

After taking a considerable chunk out of my savings, we made a dent in all the essentials, and a few other details I'd wanted to add in tribute to the original owners.

Now that I was set to move in that very day, I couldn't seem to pass the threshold. I had only two hours before the truck arrived to deliver all my carefully thought out purchases, but I couldn't stop staring at the house. If I'd had a dream house, this might just be it.

It was absolutely perfect.

White siding and dark green trim made it stand out against the mountains in the background. Delicate scrolled wood decorated the corners of the porch and wove in front of the railing posts. Flower baskets hung from the beams between the columns, filled with a colorful mix of petunias, calibrachoa, lobelia, pansies, and white alyssum. I hadn't even known what half of them were before I'd let Ren at the Mountain Palette flower farm help me pick them out. She shared her knowledge enthusiastically. I was glad of it, because the baskets looked beautiful on my porch.

My garage was in the back, and there was no parking allowed on the street in front. That was a bit of a shame, because I loved this view. Not that the back of the house wasn't cute, but there was something special about the front of the home.

A window sat on either side of the door, and one above the porch for the large upstairs room. On the left side of the house, the original owner built a large expansion for a joint home office and printing press.

The story of Nick Young and his wife was one I'd be interested in hearing. In the Doe Diaries so far, Nick had proven a unique person, and very lonely. Haunted. I knew that feeling well. Margot had promised me that the library had information on them as well when she'd heard I was renting the house.

I took in the tall trees in the yard that provided a lovely shade over the front of the house. I could picture one day having a swing hanging from the branches of those trees. If I lived there long enough. There wasn't a single detail I'd change in the entire house.

"It's perfect."

"Doesn't moving in involve you actually going inside the house?"

I yelped, spinning so fast my coffee splashed out of my cup right onto Colt's shirt. "Oh. Damn. Sorry."

He stared down at it for a minute. A grimace crossed his features as he raised an eyebrow at me. "I guess you're still mad, then."

"I'm not mad. You startled me. I wasn't ever mad. I was, well, hurt."

His features crumpled. "I know. I was an absolute asshole."

"Well, you take all the fun out of it when you say it yourself." I had to turn away when heat rose to my cheeks. "I'm sorry I spilled my coffee on you. If you'll excuse me, the truck will be here soon with my furniture, and I need to figure out where it's all going to go before they arrive."

"Remington." His fingers curled around my wrist in a gentle hold. Just enough to keep me in place. "I'm here to help. Apparently Prairie, Moorely, and Nova have all decided today would be a surprise move-in party for you. I came early to give you some warning."

"Oh." It was a sweet gesture on their parts, but it wasn't how I'd pictured move-in day. I'd been looking forward to having the home to myself immediately. I planned to have everyone over in a few days to add life to it.

"Do you want me to get Gunner to help me hold them off?"

"No." I pursed my lips while I pondered. It would be nice to have help with some of the more tedious parts of unpacking. "They've been so helpful with this. It seems rude to say no."

"Are you sure? They are sort of imposing themselves on it."

"No, it's fine. Wait." I froze as an additional concern rose. "They aren't planning to make this a sleepover or anything, are they?"

His warm chuckle coasted over my skin, easing my nerves. I'd missed his easy humor more than I liked to admit. He shook his head. "Not to my knowledge. I can't say it'll be a calm evening, but I think it'll end before you go to bed."

"Then I guess I don't mind. When should I expect them?"

He checked his watch. "Hour, hour and a half? The text thread was very noncommittal about an exact time."

"No wonder Nova wanted to know what time my furniture was being delivered. Here I thought she was being nice. I should have expected shenanigans." I fidgeted with the keys in my hand, now looking forward to what peace I could get in my new home before it was overrun.

"I'll let you go inside. I know you've been excited about this." He squeezed my shoulder. "Go on."

"Thanks." I paused halfway up the walk to turn to face him. He wasn't even watching me. His focus was on the home. A wistful softness to his features. "What?"

"This place is perfect for you."

"Why do you say that?"

"It is you."

Heat rushed to my cheeks again. "Care to be more specific?"

"It's historic, and you go crazy about the history of the town. I haven't seen someone so invested in it for a while."

"Probably because you usually avoid anyone who will compare you to Cole."

"Ouch. Accurate, but ouch." His smile was warm when he faced me. "Then there's the house itself."

"Meaning?"

"It's warm, adorable, and welcoming. Just like you."

"Oh, you are trying to make me forgive you."

"Is it working?"

"Maybe. A little."

Chapter 39

Colton

Despite my stopping by a couple of hours before our arrival, Remi gave every appearance of being surprised by the large crowd of friends gathered on her porch. More than that, she put us all to work without hesitation. Maybe my warning had only helped give her ideas on how best to use our help.

Over several hours we were arranging and rearranging furniture, hanging TVs, rearranging the furniture, putting away dishes, and rearranging furniture. Then a second, smaller delivery truck she'd failed to warn us about arrived with more boxes that she'd had sent from Florida for us to get into rooms.

As part of the whole conspiracy, Moorely and Aspen arranged for a full spread of food for dinner. I still didn't know how I'd gotten roped into setting up the buffet on the reclaimed wood dining table Remi bought for the dining area.

Remi sat on the sofa with Nova and Moorely going through boxes from the second delivery. She went through every piece with a critical eye to decide if it fit in her new aesthetic. She was a harsh judge, and they were all laughing together. Moorely and Nova were placing bets on whether she'd keep or toss each item. Probably half of the items got put in a box for charity, while the others she contemplated good ways to incorporate them into the home.

Gunner's hand dropped heavily on my shoulder. He gave a quick squeeze that expressed more than his words. "It's good to have you back."

"I'm not a hundred percent, but I'm working on it. I've spent this week making amends to Brody. We've made good headway, but now it's time to make amends to others." I didn't bother trying to hide my glance back at Remi. She was looking my way herself. A delightful blush pinked her cheeks before she turned her full attention back to her task.

"It seems like you're well on your way to that." He took in the open living room and dining area. "Auntie Juju did a great job with this place. No wonder it took her over a year. Did you see that master bath? And the kitchen?"

The bathroom off the master bedroom had been added on by their grandparents. Their aunt took the past year of no renters to expand it further. It was now a luxury bathroom with an incredible view of the Sangre de Cristo mountains behind the home through an enormous picture window we'd determined had a mirrored reflection on the outside so no one could see in. The bedroom now had a similar picture window that hadn't been there before the remodel.

The portion of the open space they stood in had always been the kitchen. A small wood-burning stove still stood in the corner of the room that would easily heat the entire home in winter. That, and a few shelves, were all that remained of the original kitchen, besides the large pantry off the north end of the house.

Juju had turned the bedroom on the north side into an airy kitchen full of windows. She'd clearly expanded the room until it was almost the same size as the master bedroom, adding slate blue cabinets and bright white subway tiles. One counter was completely butcher block, and the other one, and the island were granite. I honestly was surprised Juju hadn't planned to move back in based on the kitchen alone. She'd even added a huge six-burner gas stove with a double oven. It was one hell of a kitchen.

Across the living space from the kitchen was what had been Nick and Amelia's dual office. The original printing press he'd given her as a wedding present still resided in the room. Remi had turned it into a guest bedroom, decorating the wall with framed articles by Amelia True, as well as a copy of the first edition of her women in business magazine. I knew she hadn't reached the point of the diaries with Amelia in them, but she'd clearly received some intel into the matter.

The upstairs room, added on by the original owners, was now an office. A desk faced the large peaked windows, and a comfy chair tucked in the corner near them. Bookshelves lined the walls where they'd built them for one of my grand-aunts.

"Juju made it modern while keeping the history. I'm impressed she did all of this from sixteen-hundred-hundred miles away." Our aunt moved away years ago. She'd never sold the home back to anyone in the family, or anyone else for that matter, so no one complained as long as the renters were respectful of the history.

"She could make a killing selling this place if she wanted. I wonder why she rented it again, to a newcomer at that."

The same thought occurred to me. I'd have to ask Remington when I had a chance. For now, I was content to leave her to her task. She laughed brightly when Nova pulled a jar out of a box. Nova's nose wrinkled, and she squealed, shoving it at Remington. I wondered just what was in the jar to cause that reaction.

"Your girl is in her element here."

"Not my girl." Even if she'd been so close to it a few weeks ago.

Gunner scoffed. "Yeah, right."

"No, seriously. I haven't earned the right to say that. I'd barely earned it before I went and shit all over it."

"You really mucked that up. It doesn't seem to me like all is lost. She's been checking you out a lot, just like you have her."

This time I restrained my compulsion to look back at the couch, even as the next round of laughter filled the room. I didn't want to do anything to fuel Gunner's fire. He might be pleasant right now, but he could turn teasing in mere seconds.

"You heard from her again?" He leaned closer to mutter the next word. "Darlene."

My jaw clenched at the simple mention of the name. With a lot of effort, I forced back my urge to react so strongly. "Why the fuck would you bring that up now? I was having a good day."

"Don't let it ruin this for you. I was curious, is all."

"Yes. Okay? At least three times before I blocked the number." I downed the rest of the beer I'd been trying to enjoy. "Drop it now."

"Will do." He gestured toward the kitchen, wiggling his bottle like he needed more. I really didn't want to follow, convinced he wasn't about to drop it as asked. I needed another beer myself, though. Gunner tossed me one before I made it halfway across the room. "Are you going to tell her?"

"Which her?"

"Don't be stupid. You know who." He pointed the bottle toward the next room. "Remi. Are you going to tell her about everything?"

"Eventually. First, she needs to be willing to listen." I wasn't sure how long this unpacking party was going to last. I'd really hoped to talk to her tonight. If we could make up, we could get to that awful conversation. "For that to happen, I have to apologize properly."

"Hard to do with that gaggle out there, and the noise upstairs." He gestured to the ceiling where we could hear Aspen, Wick, and Ryker joking around instead of doing whatever Remi had asked of them.

"Eventually dinner will be finished and the crowd will break up. Right?"

"A man can hope."

Chapter 40

Remington

Nova lingered in my doorway. She glanced over my shoulder toward the kitchen. The gentle clink of plates being washed carried through the now nearly empty house. She twisted her lips, then knitted her brows as she studied me. "Are you absolutely sure? I will happily stay and kick him out for you."

"I appreciate the gesture, truly." Honestly, I was half-tempted to take her up on it.

"It wouldn't be a problem. It's been years since I've bullied this cousin instead of Gunner. I know just how to annoy them, you know."

"I don't doubt it one bit. It's been a week since what happened with Brody, and he's been better since then. I'm willing to give him a chance to apologize. If he flubs it up, I'll kick him out myself." The look of doubt she gave me brought a chuckle. "Really. I'm perfectly capable of kicking him out."

"Sure you are. I'll bet you kick handsome men to the curb every day."

"No, I don't. That's what makes this a very special opportunity." I gently pushed her out the door. "Stop worrying. I'll text you later and let you know what happened."

"You damn well better." She hugged me tight before heading down the front walk. I waited until she'd rounded the corner toward the old town parking lot to get her car before shutting the door.

Now it was time to see what Colt had to say for himself. I wasn't fooled into thinking he'd stuck around just to be nice and help with the dishes. He'd clearly hoped for the chance to get me alone. I swear it was Gunner's idea to pretty much shove everyone out the door after dinner. The pair of them had been conspiring before we ate.

I would be mad if I weren't relieved I hadn't had to push them out myself, save for Nova. I'd been looking forward to a quiet night in my new place. There was still plenty to be done to decorate, but the biggest pieces were in place and we'd gone through at least half of my Florida boxes. I'd even got Ryker to install the TV. Considering I'd just met him tonight, I was glad he helped. He was the first genuine cowboy I'd met in my group of friends. West was, sort of, but Ryker Coleman was a genuine cowboy as the foreman of his family's ranch up at the north end of the valley.

Thanks to his efforts, my TV hung on my wall just as I'd imagined it. The screen was framed, and Aspen had rigged the screensaver to scroll through paintings and photos that I'd selected, each with significance to the town. Right then, Jane and Cole stared back at me through side-by-side portraits. After about thirty seconds, they scrolled away to a painting of the mountains under a cotton candy sky.

"I think that's the last of it." Cole emerged from the kitchen, still drying his hands on a towel. His brow furrowed as he looked around the room. "Where'd everyone go?"

"As if you don't know."

"I don't."

"Your brother ushered everyone out as soon as you started on the dishes. Nova escaped and stuck around a little longer because she'd been in the bathroom. He was less than subtle."

Red darkened his cheeks. "I swear I didn't tell him to do that."

I hummed rather than state my disbelief. It was sus, considering he and his brother had been in conversation and then disappeared into the kitchen.

"Fine. I get it. That's hard to believe after the past few weeks. I don't blame you." His shoulders dropped. "Do you want me to leave?"

It was good of him to offer. Based on everything I knew about him before he'd turned complete asshole, he wouldn't push this on me. If he'd truly returned to the man he'd been, that was. "It's not necessary. I have to admit, I'm curious what your defense could be."

"No defense. A heartfelt apology and an explanation. If you'll accept them."

"The evening is young. I suppose anything is possible. Would you like coffee? Nova left plenty of her cookies to enjoy."

"Coffee sounds good, and I'll never say no one any of Nova's sweets."

I bypassed him to the kitchen. Nerves about the conversation ahead made me jittery. Coffee might be a bad idea, but I had to keep busy through this rush of nerves. Colt followed me into the kitchen, but didn't interrupt my progress. I gestured to the barstools on the opposite side of the island. "Have a seat. This shouldn't take long."

He took a seat as suggested. While I bustled about the kitchen, he picked at a cuticle. "First of all, I'm sorry I treated you that way. You didn't deserve it."

"No, I didn't."

"So sorry." His voice faltered. "None of what happened had anything to do with you. It was all me reacting to something else. Something that had everything to do with the shitstorm that preceded my life in Dominion Falls."

That got my attention. He'd struggled to broach the subject too often to count. I didn't want to push, but he'd piqued my curiosity. If it had anything, or everything, to do with his recent behavior, I wanted to know how. "Texas, right? You said you lived there before you moved back with your dad."

"Yeah. Our parents divorced when Gunner and I were five. Prairie wasn't quite a year old. Mom cheated on Dad with his brother, which resulted in West." His lips pulled back in a weak semblance of a smile. "He's still a Mitchell and is as good as Dad's son. He's just from another branch of the immense family tree."

"Huh. I never would have guessed. Except for your coloring, he looks a lot like you. His coloring is like Prairie's, so I never guessed."

"The Mitchell genes are strong."

"You can say that again." My lips twitched against a brewing smile. The man didn't appear to know whether or not to laugh. I took pity on him and chuckled. "All four of you look alike. It's the nose, I think. And the eyes."

"Typically, the Mitchells are all pale blue, the Youngs' deep blue. Except for Juju, the one you're renting this place from. Her eyes are brown. A weird quirk of genetics."

It didn't escape my notice how quickly his focus faltered back to his cuticle. Part of me wanted to reach out to stop him messing with the cuticle, and to comfort him. Only the lingering pain kept my hands where they were. "Every family has its genetic quirks. I'm the only one with blond hair. Under this dye job, anyway. Everyone else has brown hair, almost mahogany like Moorely and Aspen."

Silence descended between us. Muscles twitched along his jaw. Slight movements and the rustle of fabric led me to believe his leg bounced a mile a minute. His brow furrowed into deep lines, then smoothed again. His internal struggle to have this conversation remained clearly written on his features, and with every pick of his cuticle.

I set a coffee in front of him before starting my own. Whatever he had to say had to be done in its own time, not under duress. He'd given me that grace with my story. I could do the same for him.

He blew out a long breath. "I guess I should start somewhat at the beginning."

The tail end of the word ticked up more like a question than a statement. I nodded. "They say it's a very good place to start."

"Dad and Darlene divorced after she got caught cheating. She got custody. Dad fought for us the whole time, but the law almost always favors the mother first. So, she moved us to Pueblo."

The fact he'd called his mother by her name raised red flags across the board. I set the plate of cookies on the counter, along with some sugar and creamer for coffee. Once I sat next to him, I kept my focus on making coffee. I feared too much direct attention would stall the story. "Pueblo isn't too far."

"Dad still visited when we lived there. Darlene was still generally okay, complaining about her pregnancy mostly. She wasn't the warmest mother, never had been. Including flat out saying it, she made it clear she took us to get back at Dad for kicking her out." He plucked a cookie from the plate. It spun in his fingers a few times before he nibbled off the edge. "West's deliver wasn't easy for her. She needed a C-section, which in turn got infected. Another surgery, lots of antibiotics, and plenty of pain pills, which is where it started."

"It's a slippery slope." All nurses received annual training on addiction. In my shifts in the adult ER, I'd seen addicts of all kinds. Even in the peds ER, there were parents clearly struggling with signs of it.

"She slid right down quickly. Within a year she met—"

The shudder that went through him cracked his cookie in half. Crumbs tumbled from his hand as he clenched it around the cookie. I set my hand on his arm, hoping to help him find some calm. "You don't have to do this."

"I know. I want you to know. It's difficult to tell, is all." His throat bobbed in a heavy swallow. "Bryce. Her second husband. They got married and moved us to Texas without telling Dad where we went. She never told him or us, a thing about it. We just up and moved one day. After that, life became hell."

Chapter 41

Colton

The warmth of Remi's touch to my arm helped with the worst of my internal panic. A little. She offered a reassuring squeeze without interrupting, passing judgment, or even encouraging me to go on.

"Bryce was abusive." Talk about playing something down. "To put it mildly. We didn't realize how abusive until we were teens, but it was there. Always. The screaming. Hitting. Emotional abuse. He started with Darlene. When she became too wasted to be any fun for him, he turned to those of us that could fight back."

I rolled the cookie I still held through my fingers. If I looked over at Remi, I knew I'd see pity. I couldn't stand pity. It would weaken my resolve and end my willingness to tell the story. The last thing I ever wanted was to be pitied.

"He was a truck driver for a while. It was always better when he was gone." I picked the icing off the cookie with my nail, sprinkling her shiny counter with green sugar. "It helped to have him gone for a week or two at a time during long hauls. When he was home, Gunner and I were the primary targets, being the oldest and most likely to fight back. Or so we thought. "

She plucked the ruined cookie from my hands and dropped it on the plate. Her fingers intertwined with mine, holding on strong despite what I was telling her. She sighed softly as her thumb ran along mine. "You're alluding to more abuse, Prairie?"

The words tangled until I could only nod. It took several minutes to force the words out. "She was barely three when we moved to Texas."

"Practically still a baby. What a sick bastard." The venom in her tone gave me the strength and hope to face her. I might have expected pity before, but I found ferocity. "You were too young to understand what was happening. What about other adults?"

"We weren't in school. Once we went to Texas, they kept Gunner and me out of school, then Prairie and West when they grew more. Texas is very homeschool friendly, so no one questioned why we weren't in school."

"There's still laws against it, aren't there? They have to register or something."

"As long as neighbors didn't ask questions, that didn't matter. We'd go to the library whenever we could. We'd had a couple of years of school in Pueblo, and the library was a good escape. We taught ourselves as much as we could, improved our reading on our own with a book in one hand, a dictionary in the other. It was tough to bring West or Prairie along, but we tried to as often as we could."

"You homeschooled yourself is what you're saying."

"Basically. We didn't understand the homeschool thing, or that other kids were, so we planned our trips around when school was out during the school year. It was Gunner's idea. He'd know when it was school by the buses down the block."

Her nose wrinkled. "Don't make me actually like the guy."

Against all odds, I laughed. "Sorry. Should have warned you. He's the hero of this story."

"I doubt that." A smile tugged the corners of her lips. "And don't be sorry. I'm glad it got you out of that dark spiral of a headspace for a moment."

"It's easy to spiral. Much easier than it should be." I closed my eyes against the renewed rush of panic closing my throat down. The story had to be over sooner rather than later. If I spiraled again, I couldn't guarantee she'd be able to make me laugh my way out of it. "When we got older, Gunner and I caught on to the fact that we might be the only ones getting abused. We faced physical abuse. Prairie suffered worse."

"No. Not worse. Different." The words were soft, but the hold she had on my hand never wavered in its strength.

"Darlene didn't do a damn thing to stop any of it. If he was abusing us, he wasn't abusing her. If she ever got a mind to do anything, a shot of heroin or meth or whatever the fuck she was using was enough to wipe away all her concerns."

My jaw ached with the tension ratcheting through it. A small whisper of noise from beside me made me realize I'd nearly crushed Remi's hand in mine. I released the hold immediately, pulling my hand free. I didn't get far, she slipped her hand right back into mine.

"Gunner and I, we would plan and plot. We thought we'd go to the cops, but we couldn't say with one-hundred percent certainty that he was abusing Prairie. We didn't realize that just about everything about our life in that shitty little apartment was illegal." I rubbed my thumb along the back of her hand to keep from squeezing it again. "Until one night. We knew for sure what he was doing."

Words disappeared completely. My voice disappeared in a whisper. A tremor started in my stomach and raced along my limbs until I was stiff as a board. My stomach churned until I thought I'd lose every bit of the food we'd had earlier. After a few deep breaths, I got control of my stomach.

The whole time, Remi's hand brushed along my arm in a soothing pattern. I hadn't realized it before, but a soothing hum carried through the air. Had she been doing that all along? I blinked a few times, trying to focus on where I was instead of what was coming next.

"What do you need?" The humming stopped long enough for that, only to resume at the same pace as the brush of her hand to my arm.

"To get this story finished."

"What do you need to accomplish that? You're overwhelmed. Maybe close to a panic attack like the one you got me out of."

I met her gaze desperately. Her features didn't move from their gentle concern, although I'm sure I looked half-wild. Her words made me realize that those deep, controlled breaths I was taking were nothing of the sort. I sucked air in short, ragged gasps. "Fuck."

"Come here." She pulled me off the stool. Abandoning the untouched coffee and food on the counter, she pulled me into the living room. Despite my stumbling steps, she expertly guided me through the maze of boxes to her couch. She tugged me down beside her.

With the simple suggestion of a push to my shoulder, she had me lying down with my head in her lap. I stared up at her for a few minutes until her fingers trailed through my hair. As her nails scratched gently along my scalp, my tension lessened with each tingle of my nerves. She laced her free hand back into mine, letting them both settle on my chest. "Squeeze if you need to. I'm tougher than I look."

"You're plenty tough."

"Thanks for noticing."

My breath shuddered free from the confines of my tense muscles. I closed my eyes, letting her gentle touch work on soothing the tension still holding me in its grasp. "We caught him at it, hurting Prairie. Both of us together went after him. The whole ordeal seemed to last forever, but I don't know how long it was. By then we were thirteen and getting some strength to us, so we could fight back for real. We rarely did when he went after us because it made him more wild, but seeing him go after Prairie lit a fire in us like nothing before."

"She's your baby sister. You tried to protect her all along."

"And that night we learned we'd failed. The fight, it kept going and going, through the apartment. I don't remember much, but at some point he hit me hard enough to stun me, and it was just Gunner. By the time I got to my feet, ready to join again, he had a knife." My eyes flew open when her hand clenched in mine.

Something dark crossed her features before the calm mask returned. I wanted to ask her why, to say anything to avoid the next part. She noticed my hesitation and offered an encouraging nod.

"Gunner got a cut. Me, he drove the knife into my chest."

Her soft gasp cut through the quiet after my statement. Those gentle hazel eyes drifted to my chest as if she could see the scar again.

"The fucking bastard ran. Darlene wasn't there, off on a bender somewhere. Gunner got Prairie and had her grab West. He dragged me out of the apartment and down the hall, pounding on every door until someone called the cops. The knife nicked an artery, but we got out. I lived. Dad got custody of us after that, and he and Paige raised us from then on. The asshole went to jail."

"Ash he should. For a long time."

"It was supposed to be." I frowned at the ceiling, trying to keep the tension from returning full force. Her fingers resumed their calming trail along my scalp as if she knew. "Three weeks ago, Darlene showed up at my house. Said she's been in therapy and sober. It looked to me like she was still using. She told me he'd been released almost two years ago for overcrowding and supposed good behavior."

A bit of my horror reflected in her features. "She just showed up out of the blue?"

"There were a few texts beforehand, but yeah."

"Fucking hell. How did she know your number? Or where you lived?"

"Exactly."

"And why you?"

I grimaced against the illogical shame that remained. "I was always the soft heart. For years I tried to show her sympathy. When he was first abusing her, I tried to protect her. That's when the beatings turned to Gunner and me. Ever since, she's always tried to find a way in through me during her bouts of sobriety."

"Shit. I never would have guessed anything like this prior to the last couple of weeks."

"Paige and Dad are the entire reason we ended up even close to well-adjusted. He loves West as if he's his own son, and they really took care of us in every way afterwards. They got us the help we needed, guided us through all our ups and downs and managed the fits of rebellion we all had."

"Understandably so. I imagine it was much worse than my pitiful rebellion of not telling my parents where I was sleeping over one night and that it was a boy-girl sleepover, not just a sleepover at my friend's."

I bit back a laugh. "That was your whole rebellion?"

"What can I say? It wasn't until I grew up liberal that I really became the black sheep. Before that, I was the perfect princess with perfect grades."

"I think it's safe to say we were definitely worse. Although Prairie was the worst of all."

"Worse than Gunner?"

"Yup."

"I don't believe it."

Chapter 42

Colton

Sunlight flashed across my eyes, stirring me toward consciousness. It went away only to return a moment later. After three or flashes of light, I gave up on trying to sleep. The smell of bacon drew my eyes open. I looked around to find the source of the flashing. The wind chime on the porch wasn't a wind chime; it was a sun catcher. Every time the breeze caught it, sunlight arced across the couch.

I was still at Remi's. Still on the sofa. That would probably hurt tomorrow. I was too small to fit on the small surface. Every muscle complained as I sat slowly. I stretched the kinks out of my back, each one straining against me. Yup, I was going to be sore as hell.

I tilted my head back and forth to stretch out the kinks there. Music caught my ear. The swinging door to the kitchen was closed, but sounds still carried out. Music and the sounds of cooking drifted out.

If I was still at Remi's, when had I passed out? So much had transpired, yet nothing at all.

The emotions I'd lived off and fed during those first weeks after Darlene's arrival had grown dimmer after telling Remi everything. The crushing weight pressing on my chest eased into a dull ache. As a family, we'd never shared what happened to us with anyone outside of our household, except our therapists, of course.

I hadn't realized how much it could help to share it with someone else. The fact that she hadn't shown me any pity at all made it even better. There'd been concern and anger, and that was it. The last thing I remember before drifting off was her fingers still running along my scalp, her soft humming easing what her touch didn't.

My stomach rumbled loudly at the smell of breakfast. I wove through the boxes on the floor to get to the kitchen. The music kept playing, and now I could tell that Remi was singing along with it. I was pretty sure it was a Taylor Swift song. Her voice pitched higher as she really got into the lyrics. Then, probably realizing her rise in volume, it dropped again.

I chuckled, pushing open the door. "I didn't know you sang."

She yelped, jumping a mile. Worse, the fried egg on her spatula went flying across the room where it splattered against a cabinet and slid to the counter with a gross squelch. "Oh shit. You scared me."

"Sorry." It was a struggle to keep my laughter contained. A struggle I was losing fast. Red seeped into her cheeks, and her brow furrowed. I thought for sure she was aiming for mad and I was in trouble. Instead, her laughter burst free.

"First time cooking in this house and I made a disgusting mess." She became a flurry of activity as she rushed to clean the egg from the blue cabinet. "I was hoping to have breakfast done before you woke. You crashed pretty hard last night."

"Emotional upheaval will do that to a person."

"Been there." She stepped back, leaning this way and that to check the cabinet. "I think I got it all. Since you're awake, how do you like your eggs?"

"You don't have to cook for me. I can cook my own eggs."

"I'm already cooking. Well, when I'm not flinging eggs across the room, that is. If you want to help, you can get the toast ready."

Before she could get back to the stove, I caught her arm. She turned in surprise, practically crashing into me. "Sorry. I just—I have a question to ask."

"What's that?"

"Am I forgiven?" We might have gone over everything from my past, but that had worn me out. Not once did we get back to my attempted apology. The last thing I wanted to do was impose on her if she wasn't ready to forgive me. My past wasn't an excuse, it was only an explanation. I still had to make up for my behavior.

Her lips twitched, hinting at amusement for too brief a moment before she straightened them. Her hazel eyes peered at me through her lashes. "What if I haven't decided yet?"

"Then I can leave. This was your first night in your new home, and I've already imposed enough on your kindness."

"Don't be silly. If you were imposing, I would have kicked you out last night. As it is, I merely let you sleep on that tiny sofa instead of sending you to the spare bedroom with an actual, comfortable bed."

"Oh, I see. That was intentional."

Her smile broke free. Amusement set her features alight, warmed by her mood and the early morning light. She drew me in like a siren, and she wasn't even singing anymore. It was just her and her light and kindness. "I'll never tell. Now, toaster. Do you remember where you guys put it yesterday?"

"Yes. Right where you told us."

"Eggs?"

"Pretty much how the one you splattered on the cabinet was."

She narrowed her eyes at me. "Smashed?"

"Over-medium." We fell into an easy rhythm after that, getting breakfast prepared. She carried the plates out to the table while I waited for the last batch of toast to pop up. Since she hadn't confirmed if she'd forgiven me, it was her turn to lead the conversation. That meant keeping my mouth shut, even if our breakfast was silent. "Here we go."

"Thanks." She added a piece of toast to her plate, then dug into her food.

It didn't take long for me to question whether I really should remain quiet. Was it right to place it on her? Maybe I should try to apologize again. I might've felt better after releasing everything last night, she'd left me to sleep on the cramped sofa. I'd scraped my plate half clean before I worked up the courage to break the silence. "How can I make it up to you?"

Her nostrils flared, her eyelids shuttering before closing. She dabbed her mouth with her napkin. A heavy swallow bobbed along her throat. "Okay. We're doing this now."

"The silence was kind of killing me."

"I'd tell you to suffer, but I did leave you on the sofa."

"I'm going to be sore for days."

She straightened her shoulders, finally meeting my gaze. With the front windows behind her and the rising sun, I couldn't read anything in her eyes. She took a sip of milk and cleared her throat. "Last night you revealed so much more than you ever needed to. I appreciate the gravity of all you shared. It tells me a lot about the man you are and what you overcame. I understand why you reacted like you did to Darlene's arrival."

"I sense a but in there." I gave her a moment. She rearranged her napkin on her lap, taking another sip of milk. I think I knew what she meant before she had to say it. "You didn't deserve to be shut out in that way, or yelled at. I left you feeling like you'd done something."

"Or given you too much." Pink dotted her cheeks again. She wiggled in her seat as if remembering what we'd done a few days before I turned asshole, or what we'd done in the Mitchell apartment. Then there was the fact she'd told me everything, and I'd shut her out instead of saying anything.

"I'm an ass. One hundred percent." I rubbed my hand over my face. My appetite was gone just like that. "Maybe I don't deserve your forgiveness."

"I wouldn't say that. There *were* other factors involved, and I can appreciate that in its context." She pushed her hash browns around her plate with her fork. "It was the complete, and brutally nasty, shutout. If you'd just said you needed time to deal with something. You didn't even have to tell me to my face. A text would've worked. If you'd said *anything* except yelling at me to get the fuck out and then turning ice cold."

"I hurt you."

"I know it probably wasn't done intentionally. You were having a visceral reaction. That doesn't mean I wasn't hurt. I thought we were getting closer. I thought that night meant something to you, too."

"It did. Both of the nights that won't leave my brain meant a lot." I grimaced. "But then I went and cut you off with nothing."

"Not to mention how angrily you did it."

"It made you think it meant nothing to me. That *you* meant nothing to me."

"Pretty much. Yeah."

I reached across the table to set my hand on hers. "Nothing is going to fix this but time. A thousand apologies won't help. Only my behavior can."

"Your trauma dump might've helped a little."

"Delusional enlightenment for the win?"

"Seems to be the way for us."

Chapter 43

Remington

Brody dragged me along behind him. Colt's protests that we had to greet Brody's grandparents fell on deaf ears. The boy had one singular focus, and it appeared to be the barn. It didn't matter that I'd been coming out here every week to work with Fiyero. It didn't matter that I'd seen every animal on the farm, because West had turned tour guide since his injury. I'd come by more often to help because even with their loaned hands from the Coleman ranch, I knew West was miserable not being able to care for the horses.

No, Brody was determined to get me where he wanted, to show me what he wanted to. "You gotta see, Remi. You just gotta."

I shrugged at the couple coming out of the home before Brody got me into the barn. Dust motes floated through the sunlight streaming in. The familiar earthy smells of dust, dirt, and grain mingled with old barn wood and new wood chips, and fragrant manure filled the space. Horses huffed and moved in their stalls. Fiyero nickered to get my attention, but Brody dragged me behind a hay bale in the corner.

The tiny mewls of kittens reached my ears before I saw the litter. They were bigger than the last time I'd seen them. Their mama rested nearby. The kitten's eyes were now wide open, and they were really active.

Brody dropped to the floor next to them. "I saved them."

"You did?" I knew the story already, although every time Brody told it, the tale expanded like an old fisherman with his monster catch. Sometimes there was a villain, like a hawk or a mountain lion, nearby.

I didn't mind letting him repeat it again, which he did while I looked over the kittens. There were six, each in varying degrees of gray; from one kitten completely gray head to tail to one all white with the barest bit of gray at her ear tips and tail. Brody picked up the whitest one to hand to me while he finished his story. "Then Unc West said he'd help them."

"You did a good thing, and so did your uncle." I scratched the mewling creature under the chin, and a tiny but strong purr vibrated through her. "They're very cute."

"Mama was scared until I saved her." Brody tapped the mom cat's head gently. "I want to keep one. Dad says no."

"I said we'd wait and see." Cole crouched behind us. "You could've said hi to your grandparents. I'm sure Remi would like to meet them properly."

"Cute kittens always win, didn't you know?" I winked at Colt. Over the past week, we'd made some progress. We'd had a few dates, both with and without Brody. When he'd received another text message from his mother after he'd blocked her previous number, he'd been open about it. The man was really trying.

He'd brought me today to meet his parents, since I'd only seen them in passing. At the hospital, they'd been there one at a time with a crowd of others. And despite my numerous trips to work with Fiyero, we'd only had the briefest of introductions as West kept me busy while I was there.

Colt's lips pursed. "Kittens win over everything?"

"Yes!" Brody bounced on his knees. His hands clasped together to plead with his dad. "Please, please, can I have a kitten?"

"They're still too young, Brody. A few more weeks and we'll talk about it." Colt ruffled his son's hair. "Now can we go say hi to Dad and Paige?"

"Okay." Brody pet the head of the darkest kitten. "I want him."

"Really? I like this one." The kitten in my arms still purred, curled into my chest. It took some effort on my part to put her back with her siblings.

"You want him?" Brody danced in his excitement. "PopPops says they can't all stay as mousers. We have to give three away."

"We'll see what happens when they're old enough." I accepted Colt's help to my feet, brushing the hay and dirt from my legs. "Maybe I should have worn my jeans from the start instead of packing them for a ride later."

"I warned you." Colt's hand settled on the small of my back as he led us out of the barn. Brody raced ahead of us to tell his grandparents I wanted a kitten, even though I'd only said I liked her. "I think you accidentally committed to a kitten."

"That's what it sounds like. So did you."

"I think that was a given the minute he dragged that mama cat back to the farm. He's as bad as West, wanting to keep every lost animal."

"Some people collect lost souls. Whether people or animals. I think it shows they have a lot of compassion, even if they go overboard sometimes."

Colt leaned in close to speak low in my ear. I should have been paying more attention, but the warmth of his breath along the shell of my ear sent a shiver through my spine. He paused our progress to eye me, amusement ticking at the corners of his lips.

"What?"

"Did you hear what I said?"

"Um." I scrambled to think over the past few minutes. The last thing I needed to do was embarrass myself moments before formally meeting his parents. I pushed past the sensations I'd felt to recall his words. "Something about not telling West. It'll go to his head?"

"Was that a question or a statement?"

I narrowed my eyes, hoping to chastise him. He only laughed in response. I smacked his arm lightly. "Oh, you stop it."

"For now." He led me the last few feet. "Dad. Paige. I think you've met Remington."

"In passing." His dad nodded, actually tipping his finger to his hat. "This young lady has been helping with that stubborn mule of a horse, Fiyero. West can't stop talking about his progress."

"He's a sweet horse. Please call me Remi. It's nice to actually meet you properly, Mr. Mitchell, Mrs. Mitchell." I shook each of their hands.

"Call me Tom. You saved our Brody, you've earned the right." Tom's smile was every bit as warm and welcoming as his son's. Colt hadn't been lying when he said Mitchell genes were strong. Even though Tom's hair was almost black, his eyes were the same shocking blue.

"And call me Paige. If the kids do, you certainly can." Paige had a warm, comforting air about her with warm brown eyes and a few smile lines that arose at her bright smile. I could instantly see how easy it would have been to accept her care and love after what the siblings had lived through. "We don't stand on ceremony around here."

"That's for sure." Tom pulled her close against him. He kissed her temple as her hand settled on his chest. The strength of their affection was obvious in action, if not in the length of their marriage. These two were infinitely comfortable with each other. I'd once wondered if I'd have a love like that. Now I had some hope I could. Tom grinned with a bit of wickedness that reminded me of Gunner. "It'll be nice getting to know you better. Brody can't stop talking about the lady with the orange hair."

"Is that so?" I tried to contain my laughter. I'd aimed for red every time, but it faded so fast, it inevitably appeared orange. I'd have to do something soon to fix it. "You didn't use my name in your stories, Brody?"

Brody rolled his eyes so dramatically that his whole body took part in the motion. "I used your name. Jeez."

My laughter broke free. "That's good to know."

"Yes, you did, but your PopPops will always remember you describing her as the lady with the orange hair." Paige grinned at Brody.

Through our brief meetings, I knew the Mitchells were nice, warm people. Colt had told me a little more during our week of repairing our fledgling relationship. "Paige, Colt tells me you're a quilter."

"Oh, mentions that, did he? Yes. I've dabbled a bit."

Both Colt and Tom snorted at that. Tom shook his head. "Dabbled? Dear, you've won three of the county fairs with your quilts. Not to mention the quilts you've made for every person we know on big occasions. That's a little more than dabbled."

"And they're all gorgeous and well-loved," Colt added. "You've seen mine and Brody's."

I had. Brody's was on his bed, and I assumed Colt meant the quilt across the back of his couch since I hadn't seen his room. "I have. They're gorgeous."

"They are, and they're a lot of work." Colt tapped his stepmother's elbow. "You shouldn't minimize your skill."

Pink dotted Paige's cheeks, making her even prettier. Her honey-colored hair swayed with the shake of her head. "Now, that's more than enough flattery. I'll think you're both up to something."

"I would love to see some more of your quilts. My grandma used to quilt, both by hand and then with a Bernina once they came about." I glanced between the men, settling on Colt. "If that's alright, of course. I don't know what all you have planned."

"That's fine. I have nothing planned but our ride later. Go on, have fun." Colt pressed a kiss to my temple on my way past. The move was so casual, so natural, my heart gave an appreciative little flip.

Warmth tingled through me even as Paige laced our arms together to pull me toward the large home. She leaned close. "Brody thinks you're quite the woman. So does Colt, it seems."

Heat flooded my cheeks, but I managed a shrug that I hoped made me appear cool and collected. "I think Brody's just impressed I worked at Disney. Plus, he's a sweet little boy. I doubt there's a soul he can't make friends with."

"That much is true. That boy has never met a stranger." Paige glanced over her shoulder as she held open the door for me. "Colt, on the other hand, is very particular. He's kind to everyone, but has spent no special time with anyone since Brody was born."

Colt had told me the same. I took a shaky breath at the additional confirmation. "Right. No pressure there."

"Actually, there isn't. That means you've passed whatever unconscious test he has to deem someone worthy of spending time with him and his boy. That means you're good enough for us. We've been hoping to have a proper meal and conversation with you for a few weeks, but I know there were some issues recently."

"We're working on them."

"I'd say so, based on the way you look at each other."

"I guess you'd know, after seeing you and Tom together."

"That's something I never meant to happen." Her features softened wistfully.

"I get that. Same here."

She smiled affectionately, squeezing my hand. "I only meant to comfort a friend, and then help him with his children when he got them back. Love was unexpected, but not unwelcome."

"Isn't it always?"

Chapter 44

Colton

The afternoon flew by quicker than I'd expected. Between the ride through the ranch, its trails, and showing her Brody's favorite place–the swimming hole–half the afternoon was gone just like that. Brody spent the rest of the time reintroducing Remi to every single rescued animal in the place, as if she'd never seen them before. There'd barely been time to breathe, much less make it to dinner on time.

The only dark spot in the day so far was when Remi got a phone call. She'd been visibly upset, but it wasn't until we got back to the ranch with Brody distracted that she told me the detective on her case had been updating her, and told her they thought the guy was heading west. She didn't want to talk about it and ruin our day, and I got why, but we still talked a little about her worries. Even as she said it wasn't logical, the man would hunt her down, after all he'd gotten away scot-free. I understood the abstract scaring you, though.

Brody pulled both our attention away to announce dinner. Remi relaxed almost immediately and squeezed my hand before giving me a soft kiss. "Thank you for listening."

I assured her I'd always listen, but the kiss sure was an added bonus. It brought the response I'd hoped for, and she'd laughed her way into dinner.

Paige outdid herself with a nice spread, even though it was just the five of us. I couldn't complain that it was just us. I liked that the first time Remi had a chance to really sit down with my parents, it was without the added chaos of my siblings. At the moment, Remi sat on the porch with Paige, laughing as if they'd known each other forever. They'd bundled themselves under one of Paige's quilts, each with a glass of wine.

I loved the way Remi got along with my parents. Before we'd made it halfway through dinner, she'd been making wisecracks with my dad. They'd had each other cracking up, and Brody, who didn't understand all of it. The only problem I'd seen had been some sort of personal struggle in Remi. There were moments when her eyes held a sadness I couldn't place. I'd have to ask her later.

Dad approached the truck whose tailgate I perched on. The sun would start its descent soon, and I planned to be back on the porch with Remi for that. For now, I was happy to let Paige and Remi chat.

"Paige certainly likes Remi." Dad hopped onto the tailgate beside me. He might be about to turn fifty, but the years running the ranch in excellent shape. Some days I thought he was in better shape than I was. "I do, too."

"I noticed. You two were really cutting it up at dinner."

"I like her sense of humor. What can I say? We all have a smart-ass streak in us. She fits in well on that front."

"I know." I sighed, glancing back toward the porch. "She's great with Brody, too. He really likes her."

"Brody loves everybody, but he's definitely attached to her." Dad's hand clamped on my shoulder. "I'm glad you finally took a chance, son. It's been a long time since you even tried."

"Brody had to be my focus."

"Nah. It was before that." He scratched the back of his neck, squinting at the pasture where horses grazed. "For a while, I thought Paige and I announcing our plans to marry had something to do with it."

I laughed loudly enough to draw the attention of the women on the porch. Brody even ran around the side of the porch to the front to see what was going on. Considering how engrossed he'd been playing with the miniature version of the ranch earlier, I'd clearly made some noise. "Sorry, but that's nuts. It's definitely not the reason. We've always loved Paige, even before the divorce, and even more once we moved back home."

"I said I thought it for a while, not that I still believe it." Dad joined my chuckling. "I realized you stopped trying after Julia."

Once he pointed it out, it became crystal clear in my head. After the nightmare relationship with Kelsey in college, I'd had just two more somewhat serious girlfriends. Julia was the only girl I'd dated in Dominion Falls after I finished school.

We'd been pretty serious, but I still hadn't told her everything. I couldn't. Whether it was weak or just a defense mechanism, I'd never told her the truth.

She'd ended things when I'd been thinking of marriage. She told me it always felt like I'd been holding back. Plus, she'd received a job offer in New York. It was after she left that I took a break from dating. Then Rhodes got sick, and Brody came along. "Yeah. I guess you're right."

"I didn't care for her very much. She was always looking past the ridge."

"You think anyone who wants to leave Dominion Falls is ridiculous."

"Of course I do. Look at it." He gestured toward the distant mountains, then encompassed the entire valley in the sweep of his arm. "What more could you want?"

"You do know that not everyone agrees with that. Some people feel trapped by a small town and those mountains." I ducked under his sharp look. "I said some people, not me. Sheesh."

"Good boy."

I laughed, nudging his shoulder with my own. "Just because I was more interested in the hotel than the ranch doesn't mean I don't love it here. I do. With every fiber of my being. I'm just not big on farm life."

"You always complain about being compared to the portrait by your desk."

"It gets tedious sometimes. Thanks to Remi, I'm appreciating it more. She loves the history of this town. You know, she's read through a lot of the diaries."

"Not yet. She knows of their existence, though. I gave her a brief tour of our apartment, too. Let her sit on the couch." That wasn't all we did on that couch, but I wasn't about to tell him that. Especially since I planned to take her back there again and this time lock the doors. "She was like a kid in a candy store in there, and I didn't even show her how many of the clothes we still have. Gunner interrupted us."

"You'll have to make sure you give her the full tour sometime."

"I plan on it." Boy, did I. Silence fell between us again, comfortable as ever. I focused back on Paige. The familiar twinge hit my chest when I thought of how she'd accepted everything I'd told her of our past. "Dad."

"Yes, son?"

"I told her. Everything."

He took the news quietly at first. "Did you really?"

"Yes. All of it that was mine to tell."

His hand clapped my shoulder. "That's a first. You've never told anyone before. You and your siblings hardly talk about it anymore. Ever."

"I know. I wanted her to know. She's been through some things too. I thought maybe she'd understand a little. Or that it would help her understand my recent assholery. I didn't realize it would help me as much as it would help her. The burden feels lighter somehow."

"When you share your burdens, they become lighter. It's a fact we tried to tell you all, but some things you have to learn on your own." He squeezed my shoulder before pulling me into a one-armed hug. "I'm proud of you."

"Thanks, Dad."

"Does this mean we can expect to see Remi more often, and not just in passing when she takes on that cantankerous horse?"

"I sure as hell hope so." It might have only been a couple of months since we met, but I cared for her. Now that I'd shown her my worst pieces, I wanted her to see them all.

"Then let's join them, shall we?"

"Good idea."

"Oh, and son."

"Yeah, Dad?"

"Brody can spend the night over here tonight."

Chapter 45

Remington

My nerves were on high alert. The drive back to my place hadn't given me any reason to be quite this nervous. Conversation flowed easily, and he held my hand the whole way. The only indicator I had that something could happen had been when he said Brody was spending the night at his parents. I didn't remember any mention of that before we went over. Then there was the heated way Colt had scanned my body when he said it.

I shivered at the mere memory of it. *Down, girl. Jeez, when did you get so horny?*

Colt was in my living room picking out a movie while I got some snacks together. It wasn't like this was the first time we'd been alone. It was the first time since we'd reconciled, though. There existed every single possibility my brain, or libido, was jumping the gun here. For all I knew, Colt actually had always planned for Brody to spend the night at the ranch with no ulterior motive involved.

Even after our, whatever it was, not really an argument because there wasn't any talking. Even amid that spell of bad blood between us, I still dreamed of those nights we'd come so close in the past only to be interrupted by Gunner first, and Brody the second time.

The memory of his touch at the hotel, so soft and strong all at once. The insistent drive of his fingers pulling me closer to ecstasy than I knew I could get. Then there was the way he'd said my name when I'd gone down on him at his place. Every second of those memories had become the star of too many fantasies.

"Fuck, stop it," I whispered to myself. It wasn't enough. I was already so fucking turned on, and the man was in the next room. "It's just a damn movie."

The gods knew we hadn't discussed moving forward to anything intimate again since we'd reconnected. The way he'd been looking at me this past week, though. It was dates and gentle touches of affection, but there was a new level of connection there.

No, not connection. Intimacy.

Ever since he'd told me about his past, there'd been something deeper growing. I'd sensed the spark of it before everything went to hell. It was like the moment he opened himself up to me, the spark had returned as a roaring bonfire. I wouldn't mind moving forward in our relationship on a physical level, not that I ever had. But he'd trusted me with something deeply personal and painful, and I couldn't deny how much that affected my feelings toward him. That sort of trust didn't come easily to him, I knew.

"Superhero schlock or cheesy eighties movie schlock?" Cole's voice carried into the kitchen, dragging me away from my thoughts. Thankfully. I was spiraling and about to go jump him if I didn't get a grip on myself. Humor laced through his tone. "Remi? Hello?"

"Tough call." I shook off the last of those engrossing thoughts to come back to the matter at hand. The movie. I grabbed the tray of snacks and wine I'd put together to carry into the living room. "It really depends on what eighties movie you're talking about. Revenge of the Nerds? No. The Goonies? Always."

"What about Ghostbusters?"

"That works, too. I do like Slimer." I set the tray down on the coffee table, re-situating the crackers that had moved in transport.

"Sigourney Weaver and Rick Moranis are in this, not to mention the Ghostbusters themselves, and you like Slimer?"

"What can I say? I've always been a little weird." The moment I settled beside him, he draped his arm over my shoulders to pull me closer. I easily leaned into him. "Take it or leave it. I am what I am."

"I'll definitely take it." His thumb brushed along my arm as the movie started. I swear I felt every nerve come alive under the gentle touch. "My dad liked you a lot, and clearly so did Paige."

"They're really nice, which makes them easy to like." It wasn't a lie. We'd fallen into such an easy rapport in no time. It honestly made me homesick for something I hadn't had in over a decade with my parents. "I miss when my parents were like them."

"That's what it was."

"What?" I looked up at him, trying to figure out what that meant.

"There were moments even amid laughter that you looked sad." His brow furrowed as he studied me. "What did you mean, you miss when they were like them?"

"Growing up, my parents were actually a lot of fun. At least, that's how I remember them. Maybe it's rose-colored glasses, but we laughed a lot. Traveled a lot. I mean, nothing is perfect, and my dad and I were at loggerheads sometimes. Mom always said it was because we were so similar."

His hand rested on my knee, and this time he was the one holding space for me to talk.

"Overall, I had a pretty great childhood." I winced a little. "Sorry."

"You don't have to apologize for having a good childhood." He squeezed my knee. "What happened with your parents?"

"I had to go no contact."

He was silent for a minute. "I get that. But what happened with your parents to cause it?"

"I wish I knew what happened to them. For more than a decade, it's been like our belief systems were suddenly completely different. I still don't understand how we ended up with such vastly different viewpoints. They're the ones that raised me, so it should be the same. I went no contact five years ago and haven't talked to them since."

Realization dawned on his features. "You've only talked about Lexi since you got here. Never your parents or really any family."

"The pandemic broke us irrevocably. While I worked insane hours living through the horrors of it all, my parents were denying it was real. I caught it, a lot of us did, and ended up in the ICU. They never once checked on me. When I reached out to them before I got put on the respirator, when I could hardly speak because I couldn't breathe, they told me to stop being dramatic, that I was fine. Lexi stuck by me in full PPE, in my hospital room for several hours every day, even on her days off. She became my family."

He brushed his finger across the bridge of my nose. "That's where that scar came from. Wearing those masks."

"Yeah." I knew the spot was barely visible unless I was in the sun a lot, which I always stayed in the sun when I could. "Wearing an N95 for well over a year can do that to a girl. Lexi and I call them our twin battle scars."

"They kind of are." He moved closer, drawing my legs across his lap. "Sometimes our friends can become the best family. I'm sorry you felt like you had to leave Lexi and be so far from who you considered family."

"This was Lex's idea, really. There was plenty I could have done down there to avoid going back to work in the hospital, but after what happened, I shut down."

He tucked a stray lock of hair behind my ear. "Shut down?"

"I didn't leave my apartment for three months. Half the time I didn't let Lex in when she came knocking. It was almost like agoraphobia. Hell, maybe it was." I took a deep breath, exhaling it just as hard. "I couldn't even go to Disney. Or any of my usual activities. I had trapped myself in my apartment, watching life pass by out of my window."

"Doesn't sound much like you, at least not how I've known you."

"It wasn't. I got locked in what I think you called a fear spiral."

"I did. And that makes sense."

"Lex suggested a complete change of scenery." I smiled softly. "Her first recommendation was here, and she made it sound too good to pass up."

"Lexi's brilliant."

"Don't tell her that. It'll go straight to her head."

"I wouldn't dream of it."

We got one, Janine yelled on the TV, followed by the blaring alarm sound.

We both jumped at the interruption. I laughed, leaning against his shoulder. "Well, damn. We missed the whole start of the movie."

"At least we didn't miss your favorite character. That would've been tragic." Once again, his thumb trailed along my arm, raising goosebumps in its wake.

"Maybe." Right at that moment, neither the movie nor the snacks I'd prepared interested me.

"Maybe? I thought you picked this for Slimer." His words brushed across my forehead. The hand he'd set on my knee coasted toward my thigh, making grateful I'd returned to shorts after our ride. His fingers coasted across my skin in gentle circles that shouldn't have been enough to make me wet, but fuck, it did.

"I've also seen it about fifty times."

"What bearing did that have on your choice?"

"I don't care if I get distracted." Both of his hands grew still, which made me wonder if I'd regret the admission. The silence stretched for a few minutes, long enough for the characters to get on the elevator on the screen.

My breath caught when the teasing trail of his fingers ceased. The anticipation was already killing me, and he hadn't made a move. The wait was interminable. Then his palm flattened on my thigh, running up toward my hip, along my side until he reached my breast. His thumb ran over my pebbled nipple, a gentle touch that I felt through my thin shirt. I released the breath I'd been holding in anticipation and moaned softly.

"Remi."

"Hm?"

He abandoned the touch, leaving me to whimper softly until his hand encircled my neck. I didn't fight the suggestion of his thumb urging me to tilt my head back until I met his intense gaze. "Remington."

"Yes?"

"I want to take you to your bed to finish what we started weeks ago."

"Why so far?" I wrapped my hand around his wrist, but didn't pull his hand away.

"Because it'll be a damn sight more comfortable than this couch, and I think we're going to be at this for a while."

Laughter cleared some of the heady dizziness from my brain. "That's what I get for choosing aesthetics over comfort."

"We'll discuss that lapse in judgment another time." He leaned closer, his lips hovering right over mine. "Do you want me to take you to bed, or do you want to watch the movie?"

"Forget the damn movie. I'd rather have you."

Chapter 46

Colton

Remi sat on the edge of her bed, toeing off her shoes. Not once did she take her eyes off me as I stripped off my shirt. She bit her lower lip, her hips shifting. Her gaze raked over my torso so intently I swore it burned along my flesh, lighting a fire. If I didn't want to take my time and give her every bit as much pleasure as she'd given me last month, I'd be all over her in a second. There was one thing more important first.

I moved closer, noting that her legs opened as I drew close. Her fingers danced along my abs, tickling hints of heat as she lowered them to my waistband. I tilted her chin up once I was right in front of her. "Are you sure you want this?"

"Yes. With protection. I'm clean and on the pill, but I'd rather make sure all bases are covered." With a little pressure, her fingers tucked into my waistband, slipping along my flesh, but not pushing them down yet. "I've got some in the bathroom if you don't have any on you."

"Right after I met you, I bought some. I've carried them with me ever since." The pink that dotted her cheeks, coupled with her pleased smile, made my admission worth any potential embarrassment.

"Well. Don't I feel special?"

"You should. I haven't needed them in eight long fucking years."

"Eight years? Shit. No pressure there."

I grasped behind her knees to pull her firmly against me. The warmth of her rested right against my erection, drawing a low moan from my chest. "None at all."

"Fuck." She tugged on my neck. I captured her lips at the suggestion. My tongue swept across her lips until they opened, and I lost myself in her taste. She lowered us to the bed, my hands on her hips to keep her secure against me. I wanted to taste every inch of her, so I abandoned her mouth to explore.

I trailed my lips down her neck, licking and sucking as I moved. I paused at the little dip where her neck met her shoulder. She whimpered softly when I sucked lightly. I released her hips so my hands could explore as my mouth was.

When I reached her chest, I brushed my thumb over her peaked nipple again. Her body arched beneath me, begging for more. She added to her body's plea with a low moan. "Colton."

I tugged her shirt free of her waistband, lifting it above her breasts. She removed it completely for me. A thin, lacy bra that hid nothing stretched across her taut pink nipples. I cupped both breasts in my hands. "Look at those pretty little nipples."

She looked up at me with hooded eyes. She arched into my hands. "Colton, please."

I sucked a nipple into my mouth, letting my thumb trail over the other. Her breath hitched, her hips shifting, so she rubbed against my cock.

"Fuck." I gripped her hips to stop their motion. If she kept that up, I'd come in my jeans like a fucking middle schooler. "Eight years, Remington."

"I know." Her hands ghosted down my chest. "But I want you now."

"I want to enjoy you. If you keep doing that, there'll be nothing but a quick fuck."

"We could start with that." She pushed to sit, her lips brushing across my chin.

"Remington."

"There's a whole night ahead to take our time." Her legs wrapped around me, tugging me roughly against her. We both moaned at the impact. "If that's what you need, I'm dying to feel you inside me."

The faintest whisper of self-control held me back. "I want this to be good for you. You did it for me before."

Her eyes flickered to mine at the mention. She actually licked her lips at the reminder. There was no doubt she was going to do me in. "I remember."

"It's your turn."

"Screw that. You can make it up to me all night if you need to. Eight years is a long time to have only a hand for company." Warm fingers trailed along my waistband, popping the button open. She slid down my zipper painfully slow so I could feel every vibration from each tooth. "Fuck me, Colt. We can be sweet later."

Her hand dipped into my jeans, wrapping around my cock. An animalistic growl emerged at her touch. My body jerked, my cock growing impossibly harder. I clasped her wrist to pull her hand free. With my last shred of restraint, I spoke through gritted teeth. "Give me a minute to get the condom."

She actually pouted when I pulled her hand free. As I took a step back to remove my jeans, she scooted right out of her shorts. There wasn't a stitch of clothing underneath. Apparently I could get harder.

"Did you not wear any underwear today?"

A sexy smile curved her lips. "Do you like that I didn't?"

"I sure as shit love that." I pulled the condoms from my pocket, tossing them on the nightstand before I stripped out of my jeans as fast as possible. The damn things got stuck at my ankles, and it took a few minutes and Remi's giggle to realize I'd forgotten to remove my shoes. I leaned against the wall with one hand to tug off a shoe.

Her sexy hum coasted over me. "I like this view."

When her hands brushed over my ass, and her lips climbed my back, I shuddered. "Remington."

Her hand dipped lower, sliding between my thighs until she grabbed my balls. She was going to be the fucking end of me if I didn't get this done. I kicked the last shoe off along with the jeans. She released me as I spun to find her kneeling with her knees spread wide. Her eyes lowered to where my erection brushed her thigh.

Even though she tugged me toward the bed, I held back. I cupped between her thighs, running a finger through her cut. "You're so wet for me."

"I told you, I want to feel you inside me. Now." She moaned as I slid my finger deep inside. I withdrew only long enough to add another finger. Her tight cunt squeezed around me with her moan. Her head dropped back, and she made a beautiful strangled whimper when I hooked my fingers and pulled them back.

As she had the first time I'd touched her, she clung to me with a nearly brutal strength. Her nails dug into my shoulders as she whispered my name. I worked her in and out, pressing my thumb into her clit. If we were doing this fast, I was determined that she got some pleasure out of it.

Her body tensed. Those delicious sounds grew louder. I withdrew my fingers right as her thighs clenched. I trailed my fingers along her stomach up to brush along her nipple again. "You are so fucking gorgeous like this."

She clasped my hand in hers. Her eyes burned with intensity as she sucked her fingers into her mouth, tasting herself. My cock twitched at the reminder of how those lips had felt wrapped around it. Goddamn if she wasn't hot as hell. I'd knowns she was gorgeous, but she became a totally different animal in the bedroom. "Colton."

"Yes?"

"Fuck me now, please."

"Since you said please." I wasn't sure how much longer I could hold back, anyway. I tore open the wrapper. She tried to take the condom from me, but I shook my head. "If you do it, we'll be finished before we start."

Once again, a delicious pout formed on her lips. I leaned forward to suck her bottom lip into my mouth. "It's because you have me so goddamn turned on. Stop pouting."

"Then come take me." She lay back, spreading her legs to reveal her gorgeous, wet pussy. She almost did me in the rest of the way when she slipped her finger between her legs to rub her clit. Thank God I finally had the condom on.

I grabbed her thighs to pull her to the end of the bed. Her legs hooked around my waist, her finger still rubbing her clit. I slid in her slowly until I'd buried myself deep inside. Her back arched off the bed, a deep moan slipping free as she shifted her hips.

I managed a few slow strokes before she dug her heels in. "Colton. Please. Fuck me harder than that."

I hooked my arms under her thighs to lift her to a better position and thrust harder. A gasping moan erupted from her lips. Her hands fisted the bedding, but she kept begging for more. I drove into her harder, faster. A sound I'd never heard from my own lips roared out of me as I came.

With every pulse, I pumped slowly into her again. I nudged her fingers aside to rub her clit until she cried out. Her body sagged beneath me, a soft smile on her tantalizing lips. She kept her legs wrapped around my waist even after I released my hold on them.

Her hazel eyes met mine, her smile growing further. "That was a good start."

"Just a start? Wait, good?"

"Okay, a great start." She groaned when I withdrew. When I went to the bathroom to dispose of the condom and clean up, she rolled onto her belly to follow my progress. "Still a magnificent view."

I smirked in the mirror. "Glad you approve."

"Oh yes, very much. Now come back here. We said we'd be sweet later."

"Yes, ma'am."

Chapter 47

Remington

The warmth of Colt wrapped all around me. It was a delicious feeling to have him pressed against my back. At some point after our third round, we'd both dozed off. The sex had been incredible, more amazing than my fantasies. Having him sleep next to me was amazing as well. I don't know if it was exhaustion from our activity, or having him here, but in my brief foray to sleep there'd not been one nightmare.

By the hand trailing down my sternum, it was a good bet I wasn't the only one awake. My body was deliciously sore, but not enough to stop his fingers' progress toward my pussy. I was already wet just thinking about him touching me again. I bit my lip to cover the excited whimper in my throat.

His warm chuckle against my ear let me know he hadn't missed it. "I love the noises you make. It just gets better when I touch you here."

I gasped as his fingers coasted across my clit with just enough pressure to send a ripple of pleasure coursing through me. Against my better judgment, I rocked my hips against his touch. Something about this man made me ravenous. There was one little problem, though. I forced my hips still. My voice was husky when I found it. "Before you go too far."

"Yes?"

"We need more condoms." I'd applied the last one on the nightstand myself when we'd returned to bed after actually getting a snack. Despite my warning, his fingers continued to stroke along my pussy. "Colton."

"I'll get them in a little while. First." He gripped my hip, spinning me onto my back so fast I yelped. His lips closed over my nipple before I could wrap my brain around a protest I didn't really want to make. He sucked hard enough to send a whisper of pain on top of the pleasure, which he added to with a small bite.

Strangled whimpers caught in my throat as I arched toward him. I buried my fingers in his hair, clutching on as a jolt of warmth coursed through me. His tongue flicked across my nipple, and he moved to the other side, giving it the same treatment. Every nerve ending was aware of where our bodies connected, and where they didn't. It wasn't enough contact.

I didn't know what it was about this man that made the sex so fucking good. Maybe it was the fact I'd told him everything, and in turn he'd opened up to me. Or maybe it was just good genes. When his tongue flicked across my clit, I no longer cared.

My legs dropped wide open to give him better access. He took full advantage of my position, his fingers sliding into my already wet cunt. Each torturously slow movement of those long fingers sent ripples of pleasure through me.

"You taste so good." I'd never had a man talk to me like he did, much less tell me I tasted good. He reinforced the statement by replacing his fingers with his tongue. One hand planted on my abdomen when I bucked in response.

Everything else disappeared except those cool blue eyes staring right at me as he ate me out. It was hotter than I had ever imagined it could be. The intensity of his gaze ramped up the pleasure. My eyes fluttered closed as my muscles tensed in anticipation.

"Look at me." He paused only long enough to say it. I did as he said, staring down at him again. The hand on my abdomen slid down until his thumb reached my pussy. He pressed hard on my clit, and stars burst across my vision until I simply couldn't keep my eyes open anymore.

I cried out, my body bowing off the bed as I came again. He didn't give me time to breathe, capturing my mouth with his. His tongue thrust in so I could still taste myself on him. It made me moan, grasping at him for more.

He pressed his body firm into mine, peeling my hands from his back. When he pressed those into the bed, he let his lips coast along my throat. "Where are the condoms?"

"I can get them."

"Just tell me where."

"Bottom right drawer." I pouted when he lifted off me to retrieve them. The feel of skin against mine was something I already coveted. That could be trouble, because there was this thing called reality that would interrupt this pleasure fest far too soon.

I stared at the ceiling, attempting to memorize every sensation coursing through me in that moment. My body flushed, pussy still wet. The soreness from his impressive size filling me so often tonight.

"What are you thinking so hard about?" Colt dropped the full box of condoms on the nightstand before crawling toward me with an unopened condom in his hand.

"I'm trying to memorize this to keep it with me."

"You planning on forgoing the experience again?"

"God, no. I'd like to do this as often as we can, please." A bright, possibly goofy grin plastered itself across my face. I would have been embarrassed if he hadn't responded with one of his own. "It's just—I've never been like this with a man before."

He searched my eyes, a finger brushing a lock of hair off my forehead. "How so?"

"I told you to fuck me."

"I remember. It was hot as hell." His pupils dilated at the memory.

"I've never once been that bold." The minimal touch of his finger on my forehead wasn't enough, not even close. I slid my hand up his chest, his neck, then buried my fingers in his hair. He obliged me by leaning closer until we were once again skin to skin. "Nor have I gone three rounds and felt desperate for more. Shit, I've never gone three rounds. And it usually takes my vibrator to get the job done."

A wicked smirk creased his features. I could've sworn his eyes actually twinkled. "A vibrator? Really? Where?"

"Nuh-uh. Tonight it's going to be just us, because you're proving more than enough. Maybe next time I'll allow some vibrator play."

"Oh, you're cruel." His lips closed over mine, and he kissed me thoroughly. Our tongues danced together as we pulled each other closer. He nibbled down my neck, sucking that little dip at my shoulder that drove me crazy. "It's never been like this for me, either."

"You were pretty young. I doubt that."

His laughter brushed along my skin. I trailed my fingers along his back, memorizing every curve of muscle. "That's sort of making my point. I didn't care about their pleasure all that much. It was a means to an end."

He was fully on top of me now. The wrapper crinkled as he tore it open. I slid my leg up to wrap around his waist, eager to have him ever closer. "I can't say I'm not grateful for the change, whatever the reason."

"You're the first person I've ever told." His gaze held mine so intensely I swear my heart stuttered to a complete stop. "The first person I let in that deep."

My search for a response got lost in a moan as he thrust deep inside, filling me completely. God, it was like we were made to fit together. I would have acknowledged how cheesy that thought was, but he thrust deep again, and all thoughts scattered.

Our bodies found their rhythm easily, building to the crescendo that was inevitable. He grabbed my ass, lifting my hips for a better angle. I would've complained that the position lessened our skin to skin contact, but the angle made every thrust hit me in such a perfect way I was whimpering and begging in moments.

The tremors of pleasure hit moments before he cried out his own release. His body pressed into mine, rolling us to the side. I kissed him lazily, our intertwined bodies making no move to part. When he pulled out of the kiss, he wore the softest smile as he studied my features. I brushed my fingers along his cheek, wondering at the gravity of what he'd told me. "Am I really the first person you've ever told?"

"Yes. Maybe it's our shared delusional enlightenment, but I want to share all of me with you. Even the ugly and broken parts."

"There's nothing ugly about it." I smiled sadly. "Then it's delusional enlightenment for the win, because I haven't ever told anyone about my parents. Lex only knew because she was there for the phone call."

"Weren't you engaged?"

"I was." I lowered my gaze, a little embarrassed about this part. "He didn't know. I told him I lost them during covid and let him make his own assumptions from there."

"He thought they were dead."

"Yeah." I grimaced at the confession. It wasn't my proudest moment, but cutting parents out was still a hot-button topic, and it was easier to let people assume. "I never corrected him."

He pulled me close to kiss my forehead. "If it helps, I've done the same thing. Anyone who asks, I just say Darlene is gone and leave it at that."

"So you don't think I'm awful?"

"Not at all."

I released my relief in a gust of air. "Thank goodness."

"Remington." His forehead pressed to mine. "You're an amazing woman. Don't you doubt that for a second."

"Same goes for you, except you're a wonderful man, not a woman."

"Are you sure?"

"Pretty sure. You might need to prove it again."

"Gladly."

Chapter 48

Colton

It had been a long time since I had slept this deeply or this well. It wasn't a long enough rest because Remi and I had spent hours wrapped in each other last night, but daylight was here. I gave in to the drag of consciousness for only a minute. I rolled over to drag Remi back against me so I could fall asleep again, but my hand landed on an empty pillow.

I blinked away sleep as I sat. "Remi?"

No response came right away. I rubbed my eyes against the onslaught of daytime. I could have laid in bed all day and called in sick to work that night. It wasn't often I called myself in sick, but it would be worth it to spend the whole day with Remi.

First, I had to find her. I hopped out of bed and grabbed my boxers. "Remi?"

I padded to the bathroom to see if she was there. After a knock, I slid open the barn-style door. Nothing.

The minute I opened the bedroom door, the smell of breakfast hit me. She was cooking again? A quick scan of the living room showed no evidence of our midnight snack. She'd cleaned as well.

I found her standing over the griddle portion of her stove in her short little robe. If there were a god, there'd be nothing underneath. My cock stirred to life at the mere thought. Clearly, it didn't take much around this woman. Remi was singing along to the music playing from her Echo again. This time there was a little swaying dance with it. The soft fabric swayed, revealing occasional glimpses of her round ass.

I didn't want to startle her again, so I intentionally bumped into the door frame on my way into the kitchen. She glanced over her shoulder before looking back at the griddle. Then she froze. Turning slowly, her eyes raked over me from top to bottom, much as I'd done to her moments ago. Red seeped into her cheeks, and she shifted her legs before turning back to the griddle.

She cleared her throat. When she spoke, her voice was husky. "Good morning."

"Good morning to you, too." I wrapped my arms around her from behind. Her body pressed into mine easily, a soft sigh slipping from her gorgeous lips. She shifted so that the curve of her ass pressed into my cock. I had to bite back a groan. "You know you don't have to cook for me every time I stay over, whether intentional or not."

"Maybe this is all for me. You don't know." She glanced at the big plate already filled with a tower of French toast. "Okay, maybe not."

I kissed her neck. "I'm serious."

"I know. I have trouble sleeping more than a few hours at a time. Years of twelve-hour shifts got me used to only a few hours of sleep at a time. The sun was up, and so was I. You were sleeping pretty deeply, so I let you continue. Besides, I worked up an appetite last night."

"You and me both."

"I remember. I was there."

My hand slid under her robe. Soft skin met my fingertips. As I trailed my fingers down, I found my wish was granted. "Nothing underneath. Just as I'd hoped."

"Colton."

"I love it when you say my full name."

"The feeling's mutual. Now, stop. We have to eat."

"We will." I turned off the burners under the griddle.

She turned to face me, her arms wrapping around my neck. "I suppose that's fine. If you really aren't that hungry."

"Not really. I have a lot of lost time to make up for." I slid my hands to her thighs. She hopped as I lifted until her legs wrapped around my waist. The bedroom was way too far away. I wanted to taste her, devour her again. I didn't think I'd ever get enough.

I set her down on the table. She lay back with no encouragement. The robe slipped open, barely holding onto her breasts. I pushed it aside with no effort at all, taking care to graze my fingers across her nipples.

I pulled her back to sitting while I dropped to my knees in front of her. With one good tug, I got her to the end of the table. Her fingers buried in my hair when I brushed my lips across her thigh. Inch by inch I moved closer. Her legs spread wide for me, and I could see she was already wet before I got there.

I ran my tongue along her clit. She clamped down and tugged on my hair. The flash of pain had me tugging her even closer.

A phone started ringing, bringing us both to a screeching halt. I dropped my head onto her stomach with a low groan. "Damn it. That's me."

"Go. Answer. It might be about Brody. I'll finish breakfast, and we'll revisit this after."

"Promise?"

"Most definitely."

With that promise secured, I grabbed my phone off the coffee table where I had left it. It wasn't my parents, it was work. "Hello?"

"Mr. Mitchell. It's Carrie." My morning desk clerk's voice shook. "So sorry to bother you. I know you aren't due in until this afternoon."

No, I wasn't, and that was if I even went in. Then again, Remi was scheduled too. Maybe after work we could revisit the Mitchell apartment. Remi emerged from the kitchen with a stack of French toast and some plates. Her robe still hung open, and I couldn't drag my eyes away from her curves catching on the delicate fabric.

"Mr. Mitchell?"

"What? Oh. Right. Sorry. It's fine, Carrie. What's going on?"

"It's the Petersons, sir. They're demanding to speak with you. They say they were promised free meals and room service, and a hundred each for the casino because they're VIPs." Her muffled voice was barely audible, as if she were cupping the receiver. "I tried to explain we don't offer any of those services, and they're making a scene in the restaurant."

"Damn it. I knew they'd be trouble." When they'd checked in, they'd had a certain attitude about them. "I'll be there in about five minutes."

Remi's brow pursed. She tucked her robe back around herself. "Is something wrong?"

"Clients acting disgruntled over imagined promises, and making a scene about it." I crossed the room to pull her tight against me. "I've got to go deal with it, but then I'll be right back."

"You say that, but once you cross that threshold, you'll be wrapped up in business the rest of the day. I won't see you again until I report for my shift."

"No. Nope." I brushed my nose with hers. "I don't think that'll happen."

"Why not?"

I brushed my lips across hers. "You made a promise. You said we'd finish what we started."

"I did, didn't I?"

"You did, and I intend to see we keep that promise."

"Bully for me."

Chapter 49

Remington

I t was time to hit the brakes. My basket was absolutely full. I might have a lot of shelf space to fill in that upstairs room, I had plenty of time to do so. Now that I'd found the world's most incredible used bookstore right in the middle of New Town in a totally inconspicuous and small strip mall, I could come wander for more whenever I wanted.

With four rooms that overflowed with shelves and so many books that some were stacked on the floor. Some books were new, but most were for resale. They must have been building inventory for years upon years. I wondered if one of Jane's family made this place. She'd love it, except for the chaotic nature of the way the books were put away.

I had no clue how they'd fit such a vast store into what appeared to be a small space. Among the treasures, I'd found books I hadn't read in years that had a nostalgic quality to them. I'd even found some vintage first-run

Disney books from the thirties in their collectibles section, and reasonably priced enough that I grabbed them all.

I'd already stored four full baskets with the front desk, and my fifth was nearly overflowing. Before I returned, I would get these home to see where I stood on shelf space. I'd already spent two hours here, but I could imagine spending an entire day and still not seeing everything it offered.

My phone buzzed in my purse. I fumbled with the basket before setting it on the floor. I didn't bother looking at the caller ID, afraid they'd hang up. "Hello?"

"Remi."

I stopped before I picked up the basket again. I thought I recognized the voice, but that didn't seem right. "Gunner?"

"Yeah."

"Okay. What can I do for you? Is something wrong?"

"Sort of. Colt asked me to call. He's tied up at the ranch. West got a cow, and it's in labor."

I twitched my lips against a laugh. "I thought West promised not to take in any other animals until his hand was healed. And how did Colt get roped into helping with the birth? He hates that part most of all."

"I might've said I was working."

"Gunner Lucas Mitchell."

His laughter carried through the line. "What?"

"You're terrible. I should hang up on you right now. As it is, you know I'm going to tell on you to Colt." That was it. At some point I was definitely going to need to use the revenge penises on this man.

"I know you will. That's fine. I'm still not going over there."

"Why did you call me again?"

"Right. Colt wanted me to tell you what I told him because he couldn't call, and ask you to go pick up Brody and take him to the ranch tonight instead of home."

The Brody thing made sense. "Can't he tell me when I get there?"

"I think he wanted to make sure all bases were covered. He already made me tell Prairie first."

"Oh, did Darlene text?"

"You know, then."

"I do."

"Interesting. No, she didn't text this time. I got an update from my friend at the FBI. Darlene wasn't wrong. There's been some incidents that indicate he's heading our way."

"Is Colt spiraling?" I needed to get out of here if he was. I could come back at any time.

"Nope. I think the cow in labor is a great distraction." The humor returned to his tone. "But seriously, he sounded pretty okay when I told him. Angry, sure, but not spiraling."

"I'd still feel better if you checked on him if I have to wait until Brody's day camp is done."

"I'm not going to help with a cow in labor, Remi. Forget it." He hung up on me.

"Bastard." I sent a text to Colt, and another to West, just to be sure everything was okay on their end before grabbing my basket. I had an hour and a half before I could pick up Brody from day camp for Colt.

Fortunately, right in the middle of the main room of the store, there was a small café. The menu was simple, but everything offered was farm to table. The only thing not cooked on site was baked goods, which all came from How Sweet. Nova really had a lock on most of the baked goods in this town. The only other place with some sweets of its own was Turner's in Old Town. I wondered how she had time to breathe, much less hang out with us.

I dropped my full basket on the counter, offering an apologetic grimace to the clerk. "Do you mind holding these as well while I grab some food? The minute I walked out here, my stomach started rumbling. I blame the bacon."

"Try working across the room from it all day." The young man with classic Scottish looks grinned. His name tag read 'Gill'. "I can work up your bill for you while you eat. Then you don't have to wait for me to scan everything when you're done. You'll be all ready to check out and leave."

"You can do that? That would be amazing, actually."

"Sure can. Aspen set it up for us so we can recall orders with a scan of a bar code. I've actually been adding each basket to your order while you explored."

"Well, thank you so much. I didn't know you could make my life that much easier." I pushed the basked across the counter toward him. "Although you probably shouldn't have told me. It makes it more difficult to think about leaving."

"You still have to get them home. We don't offer delivery for orders this large." He leaned in, grinning slyly. "But if you're looking for a specific book and you order less than ten, we make deliveries all evening."

"You're trying to kill my savings account, aren't you?"

"I'd never admit it if I were."

I laughed my way to the café counter. Everything sounded delicious, but I settled on the Mediterranean sandwich and a carrot mango smoothie. I'd try a latte with a dessert.

My phone pinged. Colt had already texted back. He reassured me he was hanging in there, and his anger was more at Gunner at the moment. I chuckled, responding quickly that I didn't blame him one bit. I glanced around the café for a place to sit as I stashed my phone away.

The seating area was warm and comfortable. Every single chair appeared so plush you could sink into it and nap, or read for hours. There were no hard café chairs encouraging you to make quick work of your lunch.

Across the room, I spotted a familiar face. Prairie sat on the edge of one of the plush chairs with her computer open, her phone beside it, and a stack of papers on the other side. The woman's normally cheerful face was strained as she riffled through papers before checking her phone.

"Prairie? Everything okay?"

"Oh. Hi." She brushed some loose strands of hair out of her face. The strain eased into a warm smile. "Sorry I didn't see you sooner. I'm pulling my hair out here. There's been a scandal with the headliner I planned for Founder's Day, and his agent is forcing him to bow out. I need a replacement for them. Then, one of our acts for the county fair canceled, but is trying to convince me to let them do Founder's Day. I could give them the headliner spot, but they aren't big enough, and I'm not rewarding bad behavior. I have to fill their slot and figure out how to tell them to piss off eloquently."

As always, Prairie had run through her troubles at the speed of light. I smiled sympathetically. "If anyone can do it, it's you. You're the epitome of kill them with kindness."

"Some days I truly wish I could."

"Don't we all? Although I'm not as good at it as you are."

"That honestly surprises me, given your previous career, and your current one. Customer service at its worst. At the bar, it's all the drunks. At the hospital, it's demanding hotel service instead of quality care." Prairie sank into her comfortable chair. "You're welcome to join me. I won't bite. I might curse a bit, but I won't bite."

"Cursing I can handle. Honestly, I've been bitten before, too. You aren't far off on the customer service at its worst." I settled into the seat opposite her so I wouldn't interfere with her paperwork when my food came.

Even though she slouched in a comfortable position, Prairie's eyes kept darting back and forth between the papers and her computer. "I don't think I've ever seen Colt so happy."

The subject change almost gave me whiplash. "I'm sorry?"

"Sorry. My brain. It makes connections you wouldn't believe. I'm serious, though." Her blue eyes focused on me intently. "It's great to see. You've been good for him. Brody was when he came along, but after that Colt fell into a bit of a rut. He was a stick in the mud, honestly."

My lips twitched against the laughter bubbling up. "I don't think he was a total stick in the mud. He and Brody have quite the adventures together, from what I hear."

"What you hear? Didn't I hear he dragged you to the cabin?"

A few days ago, Colt had suggested a hike instead of going to the swimming hole. I didn't realize he meant a hike up through the foothills and into the mountains to a cabin set in an old section of the mines. This part of the mines had been closed years ago, and all tunnels sealed off. Colt's grandfather had built a cabin to use for hunting. It was a long hike, and the lack of seating was bad, but the view of Old Town had been amazing. "Um. Yeah, he did."

"He knows you're a city girl, and he dragged you to that decrepit old building?"

"You're one to talk." A male voice startled us both. Aspen stood over Prairie, his nose wrinkled before he smoothed it out to sip his coffee. "You might have been raised here, but you're no country girl. Can't even ski or hunt."

"Wasn't raised here." Prairie was the curtest I'd ever heard her. There was a flash of anger shown in her furrowed brow before she smoothed it right back into her typical bright smile. The transformation was startling. "Did you make a special trip to insult me, when I know for a fact you complained the *entire* time you were elk hunting off the res with Briggs, Gunner, and Oakes?"

"Whoever told you that lied. You're the spoiled princess here."

"Maybe I'll get you a tiara, all pretty sparkly and pink. Princess." She batted her eyelashes, wiggling her fingers at him. "Now be gone before someone drops a house on you."

It was like a tennis match between the two, and I was saved from the sparring by my food. When Aspen walked away, still grumbling under his breath, I turned my focus on Prairie. She'd returned to her task as though absolutely nothing had happened.

The familiar pleasant demeanor she seemed to always keep stayed right in place, all innocence and smiles. There was something else there, though. Every time I saw those two together, they sniped at each other. I'd think they liked each other if I still believed the childhood lie that boys only pick on you because they like you.

Prairie twirled her pen around in her fingers rapid-fire, her full attention on her computer. Based on everything Colt had told me, I knew there was more to this woman than her cheery demeanor. I wouldn't tell her what he'd told me. It was her story to tell, much as my story had been mine to tell. Colt's story unfortunately intertwined with hers.

She might appear the pretty, happy, mindless optimist, but she was clearly highly intelligent and good with people. Based on the lineup I'd seen for the county fair main stage, she'd charmed several big names to come to this little valley.

I gasped so loudly several heads turned our way.

Prairie's blue eyes widened, staring at me. "Are you okay?"

"It was you." I dropped my volume in hopes everyone would ignore the rest of our conversation. I'd bet my stack of books she didn't want everyone else knowing.

"What was me?"

"The revenge penises."

Her lips curved in the most devious smirk I'd seen on anyone. "I don't know why you'd think that. I'm a delicate princess."

My snort was loud enough to draw attention to our table again. I coughed to cover the sound and moved to the chair right next to her. Even though I was starving, I had to know the truth before I could eat. I all but whispered, "Did you revenge pene Aspen?"

"All over his precious home gym, and his damned man cave."

"Why?"

"Because he's an ass every time he sees me. When he insulted my ability to get some talented acts for Founder's Day, I thought it was time to employ some rainbow phallic revenge."

"It is the best kind."

Chapter 50

Colton

Remi and Brody sat huddled together in his treehouse, having what appeared to be a deep conversation. I'd never seen Brody so serious, and Remi listened intently to every word he said. I loved seeing how well they got along, especially considering how much time I'd been spending with Remi lately.

Every spare minute of time we could get alone, I wanted her in my arms. I don't think I'd ever been this insatiable for a woman. Not even with my last serious girlfriend, and I'd been eight years younger with a lot less responsibility then.

Now there was Remi, and I had an entire hotel and its staff, and of course my priority had always been, and would remain, Brody. But Remi had moved into a top spot right beside Brody for me. Every minute she was near, listening, supporting me.

I tried to do the same for her, especially when she kept getting calls from the detective. She'd expressed how much she just wanted to forget it had happened and be left alone. That thought process concerned me, and based on what she told me, it bothered Lexi, too. I wondered how much it was or wasn't my place to urge her to get help. I wanted it to be my place, but would she agree?

We seriously had to have a talk about where this was heading. I was prepared to say I was in it forever if she'd have me. That didn't mean she was in the same place. Ever since my dickhead move weeks ago, we'd been exceedingly honest with each other. That could be why I was afraid to address the elephant in the room. Would she tell me it was too soon to tell her I loved her? Would she tell me I was just delusional and not delusionally enlightened?

What was more, I didn't want Brody hurt in all of this. He adored Remi and had pulled her into our lives before I was prepared to pull her the rest of the way. Still, we were cautious. Remi never spent the night at my house, even though I'd spent several at her place. With it being the height of summer, Brody was spending a lot of time sleeping over at both family and friend's homes. With my work schedule, it wasn't unusual for that to happen, which eased my guilt over it.

Whenever she was around him, Remi was all about Brody, to the point of almost ignoring me sometimes. I could see why she'd chosen pediatrics when she'd been a nurse. She was a fucking natural with him. I couldn't count the number of times I'd found them like this every time they were together. Sometimes the discussion was as light as talking about Disney. Other times, it was as serious a conversation as a six-year-old could have.

Gunner's news about Bryce had thrown me for a loop, but the distraction of a cow birth and Remi arriving right after helped me get through that. Fortunately, Darlene had stopped texting me, and I'd seen no sign of her for the past two weeks. I didn't know whether to be worried or relieved about it. Gunner assured me that while there were hints of Bryce appearing in neighboring states, there'd been no sign of Darlene since her last visit. I knew he'd been watching, but he couldn't be everywhere all the time. Especially not when he liked to have a life outside of work.

I went inside to get the last dish for dinner, ready to call them out of the treehouse. When I got back outside, they were already climbing the steps to the deck. "What were the two of you up to this time?"

"Nothing." Brody hopped into his chair.

"We were discussing our favorite songs." Remi settled into the chair across from Brody. "Brody has some strong opinions about what makes good music. We were sharing my earbuds to listen to different songs."

"I didn't know you cared so much about music, Brody." As soon as I got settled in my seat, Remi's hand found mine to give it a squeeze. I squeezed it back before grabbing the tray with the chicken on it. "I made you chicken nuggets, but there's a leg, too."

Brody snatched the leg, leaving the nuggets behind.

Remi gasped loudly. "What, you'd take the leg from me? I thought we were friends."

Brody giggled, biting into the chicken leg. "Barb-cue."

"Complete sentence, please." I never corrected the cute misspoken words like barb-cue, cala-pitter, and elfanant, but I took exception to his not asking for something the correct way. Demanding with one word was plain rude.

"Barb-cue sauce, please." Brody's whole body moved with his swinging legs. It was a wonder he'd asked for sauce seeing as he was already half done with his chicken.

"Corn?"

"Cob corn." Brody's eyes shone with eagerness when I picked up a cob with the tongs. "My favorite. Dad makes it special."

"Is that so?" Remi used the decades-old tool I'd found at the thrift store that held the pat of butter to spread on the corn, with a salt shaker on the other side.

"I don't know how special it is. It's a trick I learned from a friend in college. Some milk and sugar into the boiling water. It makes them sweeter and juicier, I think."

"Sweeter and juicier is always best." Her plump pink lips curved into a smirk. Her hazel eyes shifted toward green, something I'd noticed happened when she was turned on. God, I wanted to kiss her when she looked at me like that.

"That's what I think." I cleared my voice when my voice cracked.

Brody giggled, his mouth full of corn. "You sound funny."

"Yes. Well, anyway. You know the fair starts in a couple of days."

Remi wiped her lips delicately, removing the shine of butter, but not my attention from them as she spoke. "I know. I saw Prairie at Once Upon a Book the other day, fretting over an act that reneged at the last minute."

"She must have been thrilled."

"Oh, yes. Pleased as punch. Her mood only got better when Aspen showed up and needled her. What is it with those two?"

"Oil and vinegar. I don't know any real reason."

Brody's brow furrowed as he looked between us. "Dat's weird."

"What is?" Just like that, Remi's attention went back to Brody.

"What you guys said."

"Pleased as punch? Oil and vinegar?" Her warm laughter made me smile as much as it did my son. "They're phrases called idioms."

"Still weird."

"I suppose they are. See, idioms are parts of bigger phrases. If you don't know where they come from, they're harder to understand." She pondered for a moment. "Would you rather we didn't use them?"

"They don't make sense."

"I'll take that as a yes." Remi nodded my way. "I think we can avoid idioms when Brody is around, can't we? We might have to think about it."

"I can try, but they come so naturally." I wasn't used to having to think about what I said, but I'd give it a shot. "We got off topic."

"True. You mentioned the fair?" She reached for the bowl of green beans. "It starts this Saturday, doesn't it?"

"It does. I thought we'd go opening night." I didn't miss the way Remi paused, glancing my way before resuming her task. While we'd gone on several so-called dates with Brody present, we hadn't so much as held hands during them. The three of us at the fair together felt much more like a family activity. "All of us together."

Brody's mouth was shiny with butter, and several remnants of kernels stuck to his cheeks. "Remi can come, too? Yay! You want to come, Remi? Can you come? We can ride the Ferris wheel. It goes so high up, up, up." He lifted his hand higher with each up.

Remi's brow furrowed, but her mouth twitched. The battle raged for only a moment before a smile broke across her features. Her eyes sparkled with amusement. "First of all, Brody. You've got a little something right here." She pointed to her own cheek.

Brody swiped a napkin across his entire face, somehow missing almost every scrap of corn and bit of butter. "Are you gonna come to the fair?"

"If you and your dad don't mind my tagging along, I'd be really happy to have someone to go to the fair with." She covered the side of her mouth I sat on when she spoke again in an exaggerated whisper. "Are you sure we want him to come with us?"

I could clearly see the finger she pointed my way, and the not-so-subtle gesture of her head in my direction. I'd have been insulted if I weren't so amused, as was Brody. He was giggling loudly, clasping his hands over his mouth. "And just what is wrong with my attendance at this event?"

"Word on the street is that you're a stick in the mud. Oh, sorry, Brody. A stick in the mud means he's boring."

"I am *not* boring." I had a strong feeling just who told her that. "Prairie only says that because of—reasons."

Remi caught my hesitation to say why, but never broke her smile. "Then I suppose if it's fine with Brody that you come, it's fine with me, too."

"Yeah, Dad. You wanna come?"

"I thought I was the one who brought the whole thing up."

Chapter 51

Colton

The fairgrounds teemed with people. Considering it was the opening night of the fair, it wasn't unexpected, but made navigating through to get to everything Brody wanted to see and do a challenge. Of the three of us, I seemed to be the only one concerned by it. My two companions were carefree as could be. Remi and Brody kept nudging each other and pointing this way and that. She'd even picked him up so he could see better over the crowd.

Remi insisted on paying for ride tickets. She dismissed my protest, pointing out I'd paid for our entrance and she wanted to do her part. The look she gave me was so stern, I'd backed off quickly. I definitely didn't want to get into a fight at the ticket booth. Or at all, really.

Brody bounced around like a wild child, indecision and sugar mixing until we were being dragged every which way. He wanted to ride a ride, but he also wanted to try some deep-fried something or other. No, he wanted to ride the Ferris wheel with Remi, or the swings with both of us. Or he wanted to see the animals in the 4H building. No, definitely fried something.

Remi guided us both off to the side after about an hour of this, tucking us in between two food stands. She kneeled in front of Brody, poking him in the stomach. "I think we need to ride the rides first. There are some rides that could make you sick because they move fast or spin a lot and can upset your tummy. You don't want any food in there, you could vomit and ruin the whole fair for you."

"I know I don't," I added. Thank goodness Remi had this talk with him. I had a feeling he'd do just about anything she asked of him. He wasn't the only one who felt that way. Every time she looked at me a certain way, I was ready to hand over anything she wanted just to keep that look on her face.

Through his wrinkled nose, Brody giggled. "Ew. Vomit."

"Yeah. Ew, vomit." She took his hand before rising to her feet. After a glance around the area, she pointed back the way we'd come. "Why don't we start with the swings, and then maybe the tilt-a-whirl? Once we know if those bother you, we can talk about doing some others."

"Okay." He hop-stepped, clutching both my and Remi's hands. His legs swung wildly forward with each step before he finished it with a hop. He'd wait for us to get a step ahead and do the same. If he'd been any heavier, I'd worry about him taking Remi's arm out of its socket. She didn't seem the least bit fazed, though. "Swings, swings, swings. Afterward, can we try some of those fluffy Oreos?"

"Deep-fried Oreos *after* rides." I tried to sound stern, but I was too busy laughing to appear anywhere near tough.

"I'll make a deal with you. We'll save the Ferris wheel for last. It's best ridden when it's nice and dark. You'll be able to eat before because it isn't fast, and it doesn't spin you around, so you're not as likely to get sick." She had as much laughter in her voice as I did. The look she cast me was a little exasperation, the rest, total adoration.

Brody, as expected, was in complete agreement with whatever Remi said. We found the swing ride and got in line. Then we were penned into a sort of cattle chute, so I took Remi's hand in mine, pulling her close. Brody continued to dance and move in front of us. The sounds of the carnival were sufficient for him to find some sort of random rhythm.

I tucked Remi close and kissed her temple. "You have him wrapped around your little finger. You know that, right?"

"I'm aware. I also know that with great power comes great responsibility."

"It's good you know that." I nudged her ear with my nose. Her head tilted just enough that I could brush a kiss along her neck. "Because Brody isn't the only one wrapped around your finger."

"That's a dangerous admission, sir. As much as I'll be careful wielding my power with the impressionable young Brody, you may not be spared from my full wickedness."

"That's exactly what I'm hoping for."

Her smile curved into a delectable smirk as she turned to face me. Her body pressed into mine, our lips barely an inch apart. "Also good to know."

"Are you gonna kiss?" Brody stared up at us, all signs of his wiggly dance gone. Hands set on his hips and his brow knit together, he narrowed his eyes at us. Crap. Would this whole thing be a problem for him?

"What if we were?" Remi turned her full attention to Brody once again. I didn't miss that her hand still lingered in mine. Or that it made my heart do a weird stutter in a way I didn't think I'd ever noticed before.

"Kissing's gross. Kaia tried to kiss me on the swings last week."

"Wait, what?" I did a double take to stare at Brody. Remi's fingers touched my chin, gently pushing it closed. That was enough to get my brain in motion again. "Did you just say Kaia tried to kiss you?"

Brody was already over the whole discussion. He moved forward when the line did, resuming his chaotic dance.

Remi chuckled beside me. "That's the age. The girls want to kiss their princes; the boys want to race frogs or some nonsense. Well, sometimes. Gender roles are so very nineteenth century, after all."

"Keely didn't mention anything about it." Brody had just spent the night over there a few days ago, and I'd heard nothing about any of this.

"It's likely she didn't know either. Unless he'd done something like hit her, it was just another day on the playground." She squeezed my hand gently. "Don't look so worried. He still thinks it's gross. You don't have to panic so much for a few more years."

"He's just growing up so fast. I swear all I did was blink, and there is, six years old."

"The joy and curse of being a parent. You get to watch them grow up, but you also have to watch them grow up."

I squeezed her hip, pulling her back against my side. "You do know that made no sense."

"If it didn't make sense, you wouldn't have told me so. You'd have asked what I meant." She bumped my hip with hers, then stepped forward to take Brody's hand as it came to be our turn. She helped him onto a swing, bringing the bar down and clipping the chain between his legs to the bar. The easy cheer she'd had all day descended into a calm seriousness. "Now that you're in here, there's to be no wiggling or dancing. We're going up really high, and the last thing we want is a fall."

Brody immediately stopped his wiggling. His brows knit together as he leaned forward to look at the ground. "Could I really fall?"

"If you're not careful, buddy." I checked the chain between his legs to make sure it looked secure. I trusted Remi, but this was a first for Brody. Last year he'd been too young for any but the smallest of the rides, or at least I'd played it off that way. This year he'd been begging for weeks for bigger rides. And I couldn't hide the fact that he was taller than the minimum height line any longer. "Hold on and don't dance around. I'll be in the swing behind you."

"Where will you be, Remi?" He leaned around me to find her. I'd have been insulted, but I couldn't blame him. He was a goner for her, and so was I. The smile she bestowed on my kid was everything. It was more than the look she gave me in the mornings I was lucky enough to wake up beside her.

"Right here in the swing next to you." She already had it claimed and was waving people away from the swing behind Brody for me.

"Okay. You can go, Dad. I'll be good."

"Well, alright then." I did my best to keep my face neutral, but grimaced as soon as he was out of sight. He really was growing up too fast some days.

Remi reached out to squeeze my hand. She leaned as close as she could while still clinging to her claimed swing. "He'll be fine. And he still needs you."

"I know, I know." I settled into the seat. The chairs were so much smaller than I remembered. Then again, I hadn't been in them since I was probably fifteen and Dad and Paige insisted we try to enjoy some of the childhood things we'd missed.

Within minutes of the ride starting, Brody was cheering loudly. He kept his promise not to dance, but he spread his arms and legs out like a starfish, yelling right into the wind hitting his face. Remi laughed so hard, tears slipped down her cheeks.

It only took another look at Brody for me to join her. It meant the world to me to give him a real and full childhood like this.

Remi caught my eye and tossed a wink my way before turning around to mirror Brody. Arms and legs spread wide, she yelled into the wind.

I didn't have as much space to move as they did, but I joined in the revelry with them. This was turning out to be the best fair ever.

Chapter 52

Remington

The discordant music of the fairgrounds might be brutal to my ears, it still couldn't mess with my good mood. Chaotic energy spurred Brody on with every step, as it had all day long. The day full of fun and sugar was spurring him on ever more. I knew it was getting close to his bedtime, but he wasn't showing any signs of slowing down.

In fact, he was currently dancing circles around Colt at the funnel cake stand. I had sincere doubts that adding more sugar to the equation would do anything to help. It was a special night, though, and I had a strong feeling Colt was too tired to argue anymore. I couldn't blame him, I felt the same. Funny how Brody didn't seem tired, but I was pretty sure Colt and I would crash hard the second we got to a bed.

They returned with two plates. Brody's dancing had stopped as he concentrated hard on not spilling his funnel cake. He had it at eye level, watching for any movement. Colt's free hand immediately laced with mine, stirring up those damn butterflies again. All day, every single look he'd tossed me, every time he took my hand, they'd been there. I was a goner for this man, through and through. I hoped he felt the same.

I gathered Brody close while we steered through the crowd to some picnic tables to eat. Brody dove in without hesitation, devouring his funnel cake. Colt and I were slower in our nibbling. I was over-sweetened, which was saying a lot considering I thought sugar was a food group on its own. Fair food was heavy, though.

With powdered sugar all over his face and an empty plate in front of him, Brody grinned at me. "Ferris wheel?"

"I did say we could go on the Ferris wheel after eating, but are you sure you're done eating? After the Ferris wheel, it's time to head home. Are you sure you're done? Completely?" I gestured broadly to the long line of food stands. "Because there's plenty you haven't tried."

"Apple roll!"

Colt's brows furrowed. "Huh? Caramel apple?"

"No. Apple roll." Brody pointed off down the line of stands. "Apple. Roll. Dad, you know."

"I think he means the caramel apple cinnamon roll." I did my best to keep my laughter in check when Colt's face paled, then looked a little green.

"More sugar. Goody." He rubbed his hand over his face. "I'll get it."

"I can go."

"No, no. I need to walk off some of the sugar we've gorged ourselves on if I'm going to have anymore." He leaned down before he walked away. "I'm never getting him to sleep tonight."

"I'll help. It's partially my fault, after all."

"Partially?"

I smacked his arm, sticking my tongue out as he walked away laughing.

Brody swung his legs back over the seat. "Let's go look at the duck game!"

"No, wait. We should wait for your dad." He took off before I'd finished my objection. I ran after Brody, trying to monitor his path through the crowd. The kid was fast, but I kept up enough to catch him right at the edge of the booth. "Don't run off like that, Brody."

He ignored me, scanning the ducks floating past. After he examined the prizes hanging above, he pointed. "Can we play? I want an elfanent."

"I think we should go back to wait for your dad. He's going to wonder where we went." Even as I said it, I pulled out my phone to text Colt, so he'd know where we were. The last thing I wanted to do was worry him. "And you're not supposed to run off without one of us close. You know that. It's too easy to get lost in a crowd like this."

"Yeah. Yea. Can we play?"

"Fine." I fished a ten out of my bra to hand off to the vendor. "Two runs, please."

"You've got it." The vendor turned his full attention to Brody as he told him how to play.

I kept one hand on Brody's shoulder, scanning the crowd for Colt's return. Given how tall he was, I expected to see him easily enough once he got close. My phone pinged with a message from Colt saying the line was crazy-long and asking me to keep an eye on Brody. I assured him I would, turning my attention back in time to see the vendor handing Brody the very elephant stuffie he'd pointed at.

"Look, Remi! I'm gonna call him El-um." He pursed his lips, his whole face scrunching in thought. "Elmar!"

"That's a great name. Now let's get back to the table."

"What about ring toss?" Brody waved toward it. "They gots a snake. Or the fishies. You get a real fish if you win."

I sighed, but nodded. "Fine. Let me text your dad."

Brody swung back and forth with Elmar clutched tight to his chest while I texted Colt to tell him we'd be heading toward the ring toss and fish bowl game. I had a strong feeling Colt wouldn't care for a fish on top of the kitten they were likely getting, but we weren't likely to win, anyway.

"Look, Remi!" Brody pointed to a balloon. It rose and sank over the waves of people seemingly on its own. When it bobbed out of the crowd, I saw it was untethered. I thought maybe it was losing helium, but then saw the broken plastic weight tied to all the balloons' strings. It looked like it was barely hanging on, which meant the balloon would fly away soon enough. "Can I get it?"

"Leave it. I'll get you a fresh one when we leave."

"But look, it's lost. Someone lost it, they're probably sad. I'll get it."

"Brody! What did I say?" I raced after him again. The balloon had already drifted out of sight. I glimpsed Brody running between two carts before he was gone. After I'd pushed through the crowd to where he'd gone through, I stepped between the game booths into the darkness.

The suddenness of the darkness after the lights of the midway left me temporarily blind. I closed my eyes hoping to get them to adjust faster. "Brody. Where are you?"

"Right here. I caught it. Look."

When I opened my eyes, my vision had adjusted to the dark enough to spot the pale coloring of the balloon. "There you are. Brody. I told you not to—"

His scream tore through my heart. I swear it stopped beating when the scream cut off abruptly. "Brody? *Brody!*"

I tore across the stretch of grass between the midway and the tree line. The balloon hovered right in front of the trees, wobbling a moment before rising into the air. "No, no, no. Brody? Brody, please, no hiding."

The woods were right there. He wouldn't have gone in there. He couldn't have. I couldn't hear anything but the fair. "Brody? Please tell me you didn't stumble on a snake. I hate snakes."

I tentatively stepped into the underbrush, pushing aside branches of bushes and tall grass. A few feet in, I tripped on something and hit the ground hard. "Oof. Brody? Talk to me, please."

My brain, jostled by the fall, finally emerged out of its panic enough for me to remember I had a flashlight on my phone. With it on, I scanned the area. "Brody? Where are you?"

The bright light landed on a pair of shoes, but they were far too big to be Brody's. My heart caught in my throat as I lifted the light along the form.

The face that confronted me had stepped right out of my nightmares. Detective Wilder's warnings raced through my head, but it was too late. I choked on my scream when it lodged in my throat. "No. How?"

The lined face furrowed as he looked me over from head to feet. "What to do with you?"

I cast my flashlight across the area. My heart stuttered to a stop when I spotted Brody on the ground nearby. His new stuffed toy, Elmar, had a stand across it that looked chillingly like blood. All of my fear from seeing the face from my nightmares fled. Brody was in trouble.

I rushed toward him without hesitation. I never made it.

Pain exploded through my head; stars burst across my vision before the world went completely black.

Chapter 53

Colton

Caramel dripped along my knuckles even though I held the container by the very edges, so close to the edge, I thought the whole thing would break and fall to the ground. I hoped Remi had some more of those towel tablets she'd brought. My hands needed cleaning in the worst way.

The crowd hadn't thinned at all, so finding the duck game took several minutes. Neither Remi nor Brody was there. Her last text said they'd probably try the ring toss or the goldfish game. I hoped it was the ring toss. I didn't need a goldfish in the house.

I edged through the crowd, doing everything in my power to keep from getting caramel on everyone I passed. The crowd in front of the ring toss was light. It wasn't surprising. It was one of the hardest games to win. Very few people proved willing to try the game. Unfortunately, Remi and Brody weren't there either. Where could they have gone?

I searched the surrounding crowd, and down several game booths to see if I spotted either of them. They were nowhere to be found.

My phone. I needed to check to see if she'd texted another location while I was getting this monstrosity of a snack. The last thing I wanted to do was fight the crowds back to the picnic tables. Honestly, I was sick of carrying the snack. Clearly, Brody didn't want it too badly.

I dropped the plate at the end of the ring toss stand. Ignoring the dirty look from the barker, I used the very tips of my fingers to drag the phone from my back pocket. Remi owed me a bath after this. A shared bath, if I had my way.

One touch of the power button lit my screen enough to show me there were no messages. That didn't make sense. Remi wouldn't go anywhere with Brody and not tell me. I spun in a circle, trying desperately to find them in the crowd.

Worry crept along through my brain like the itching of spiders crawling. My heart raced double time. It would be impossible to find them in a crowd this size with no info. I was tall enough to see somewhat over the crowd, but it didn't help me a bit in a place so packed.

The lights of the Ferris wheel blinked behind the games opposite where I stood. Maybe he'd convinced her, or dragged her, there. He'd been talking about it nonstop for days, ever since Remi had mentioned it at dinner. He'd been talking about it for days, and brought it up a lot during our time here today. That had to be it.

I abandoned the cinnamon roll to push my way through the crowd. With sticky fingers, I hit Remi's name in my contacts to call her. I could barely hear the ringing over the crowd, but it rang and rang until it reached voicemail. "Remi? Where are you? I thought you were playing games with Brody. I can't find you. Call me. Please."

My course through the crowd was anything but subtle this time. The worry was morphing into panic. The curses I got for my efforts did not even bother me. I had to find them. Something was wrong. It had to be. Remi would've reached out for anything. Even a run to the bathroom. I knew she would.

I stumbled into the clearing in front of the Ferris wheel, scanning the line wildly. There were plenty of familiar faces, but not the ones I was searching for. As each car rolled around, I searched for them. I listened for Brody's laughter and calling me silly because I was worried. The wheel made a complete turn, and my heart froze. They weren't there either.

"Remi? Brody?"

"Colt?" A hand landed on my shoulder. I spun to find Aspen's concerned face staring back at me. His brow pursed. "What's going on?"

"I...they...where?"

Nova was beside Aspen, her delicate features creased with worry. She grasped my arms gently. "Breathe, Colt. What's wrong? What happened?"

"I can't find them. I went to get the fucking cinnamon roll, and they're gone. Gone. Where could they have gone? Where are they? *Remi! Brody!*" My words tumbled over each other on their way out. The outright panic I'd been holding back crawled along my skin like the fiery fingers of hell. This was hell. My heart stuttered to a stop. "Where's my son?"

"I'm sure they're here." Nova ran her hand along my back, the other hand supporting my shoulder so I didn't slump to the ground.

My vision tunneled so tight I could only see her white sneakers. Buzzing filled my ears over the cacophony of the fair. My lungs tightened until I couldn't get a deep breath in.

Nova's warm voice remained calm. "Breathe, Colt. In and out. Slow down. Aspen is calling Gunner. He'll get everyone together, and we'll all search. They can't have gone too far. Brody probably dragged Remi on some grand adventure. He always likes a good adventure."

"He's been nonstop." I took a deeper breath. My vision widened a little. It made sense. All night he'd been going a hundred miles a second. We'd had trouble keeping him reined in with two of us, and Remi was on her own with him. "Maybe Remi didn't have time to text."

"Exactly. She's going to feel horrible that she worried you so much." Nova straightened my shirt when I stood back up. She offered a nod. "There you are. See? Here comes the cavalry. We'll find them. No need to panic yet."

Sure enough, all our friends were moving through the crowd like a wave. Even Trudy from Turner's and Margo the librarian were with them. I wondered where Wick was. Maybe one of his dogs could help.

Gunner pulled me aside. "What happened?"

"Brody. He wanted one of those caramel apple nightmares. I offered to go get them so maybe Remi could sit. I guess Brody didn't let her. She texted and said he'd dragged her to the duck game. She sent me this picture."

Gunner wrinkled his nose when he took my phone. "Sticky."

"Caramel. He won an elephant. And she says they were going to the ring toss next. He hasn't sat still all night, so I wasn't surprised. The line was long, so it took a while to get the food. When I came back, they were gone. I can't find them, Gunner."

"Did you try to call?"

"Voice mail."

"Okay. I want you to go back where she said they'd be. She's probably going to steer him back that way as quickly as she can. In the meantime, I'll get everyone to spread out and search." Gunner set his hands on my shoulders to bring my focus back to him. "Keep calling her. I'm sure they're on the fairgrounds somewhere."

"Okay. Yeah. I'll keep trying." I stared at my phone in my hands. It didn't seem like enough.

"Go back to where you were supposed to meet her." He spun me around and shoved.

I stumbled a few steps before getting my bearings. The ducks and the ring toss. Go back there, that's what I needed to do. Gunner shouted some instructions behind me. I did as he'd told me to and jogged back to the midway.

There wasn't a person I passed I didn't check their face. I hit redial again and again, trying to reach her. I didn't even bother leaving voicemails after the first three. "Where are you, Remington?"

Chapter 54

Colton

Somewhere along the line, Gunner set in motion the clearing of the fairgrounds of anyone not involved in the search. The midway sat devoid of almost every person who had swarmed it earlier. Moorely told me when she'd been assigned to sit with me they had sheriffs guarding all the exits watching for them.

I sat on the ground, head in my hands, the other clutching my phone. I hit Remi's name again, desperate to have her answer. My hand shook as I drew the phone to my ear again. The line rang and rang until it ended once again at her voicemail.

She wouldn't do this. She wouldn't ignore me. She wouldn't just disappear with my son.

But where was she? Where was he? What the fuck happened?

I threw my phone across the grass, where it thumped against the booth across from me.

Aspen scooped my phone off the ground. Without a word, he plopped onto the ground in front of me.

"Is it your turn to babysit?"

"If you must know, yes." Aspen twirled the phone between his fingers. His nose wrinkled, and he held the phone out by his fingertips. "Gross."

I didn't bother to respond, hitting my head against the ring toss booth behind me. Large spotlights wheeled past, being turned to face the dark strip of grass behind the midway.

Aspen tugged a cloth from his back pocket and used it to wipe down my phone. "What the hell is all over this?"

I raised my hands, revealing my sticky fingers. It was entirely possible my hair was sticking up at odd angles thanks to the caramel-covered fingers I'd been raking through it. "Caramel."

"It's been two hours. Why haven't you washed your hands?"

"Gunner told me to stay where we were supposed to meet." I resumed banging my head back against the ring toss. It was clearly pointless for me to stay here, but I had no clue what to do next. Tears burned behind my eyes. "You were all so sure they were here."

"They probably are." He tapped the screen, holding the phone to his ear. When he clearly got the same result, he pulled out his own phone and tapped in Remi's number.

"You think she's ignoring my calls on purpose?" My sharp tone made him jump. The implications of that suggestion ripped at my worry and turned it into something else I couldn't name. To think Remi was ignoring me or doing so while having my son.

"No. I don't think that."

"Good. She wouldn't."

"I know. It was worth a shot to call her from my phone if she lost her phone or it got stolen. Remi and I never exchanged contact info, so my number would likely come across as unknown." He lobbed the phone back to me. "Keep trying."

The spotlights clicked on one by one down the line, flooding the area with light. Voices called back and forth behind me. Remi and Brody's names were both shouted from every direction. They had to be right here. It was a mistake. Maybe they had trouble. Maybe one of them got hurt, and they went to the hospital too fast to call.

It had been two hours. She would have called by now. Someone would have. Her emergency contact might have been Lex, but Lex would know to call me. I dialed Remi's number again, my heart lodged in my throat. "Please. Pick up, pick up, pick up. Please. Come on, Remi. Please."

She didn't pick up, but a shout sounded close by from the search party. "I thought I saw something. In there."

Aspen and I both flew to our feet. I rushed between the two booths and into the wide stretch of grass beyond. People scoured the area, searching every nook and cranny. Flashlights shone into the woods at the edge of the fairgrounds.

Another shout sounded, and several flashlights bounced through the woods. Gunner raced into the trees on the trail of a flashlight. "We need a medic!"

The world tilted. A medic. Someone was hurt. Someone was.

Aspen grabbed my arm tight. "Easy. Wait for him to tell us what's going on."

"To hell with that." I raced toward the trees, making a straightforward path on the trail Gunner left behind. "What is it? Is he okay?"

Gunner stopped me in my tracks about five yards from where several flashlights shone onto one spot. "Don't go any further. We don't know what's happened, and I don't need you messing up the scene more than the medics will."

Scene. The word made my stomach drop. I barely blinked when the EMTs pushed past me. "Scene. Scene? Gunner. Is he—oh, God."

"It's not him. It's Remi." The strain in his voice was doing little to soothe my nerves. If it was Remi, then where was Brody? Why did she need a medic? What the fuck happened? Gunner gave me a shake. "We're going to keep searching the area for Brody, but we need a more organized search now so we don't lose any trail that might be left. I've asked Seth to help with the tracking. He's bringing Oakes. Wick is getting his best search and rescue dogs together."

Seth Turner and Oakes Longfeather were two of the best trackers in the county. If they still needed to search,, "He's not with her."

"No. The stuffed elephant in the picture is near her, but he isn't there. It's possible he got scared and ran off when she got hurt and wound up lost."

"You also told me they were probably lost in the crowd at the fair." Crunching leaves drew my attention to the approaching EMTs. Remi was out cold on the litter. Her skin, normally full of color from her tan and life from just being her, was pale in the patchy light from the flashlights. A dark stain ran down the side of her face to her shirt, where it spread wider.

The world spun again. The ground rushed up to meet me. At the last minute, someone caught me, settling me down easier than I was about to land. Briggs' face swam into view, a weak attempt at a grin on it. "I never knew you to be squeamish at the sight of blood."

I glared at my brother. "Got hurt? That doesn't look like she just fell. If she looks like that, what happened to my son?"

"We're going to find out, but not if I'm stuck dealing with you. Let me do my job, Colt. Go back to the midway. You know what, go with Remi. I'll have an officer there anyway to question her when she wakes. He'll be able to keep you posted on the search." Gunner nodded to Briggs. "Get him out of here, please."

Briggs grabbed me before I could lunge at my brother. Between him and Aspen, I got dragged all the way back to the midway. Every fiber of my being wanted to run back to wherever Gunner was. Briggs and Aspen would easily overpower me, as proven by the way they dragged me to the picnic tables where I'd sat with Remi and Brody just hours before.

They dropped me into a seat, but didn't go far. Lights flashed red and white across Aspen's face. "Do you want to go with her?"

I stared at the ambulance where they were just getting Remi onto a stretcher. My heart wrenched seeing her like that, but she had people taking care of her. We didn't know where Brody was. "I want my fucking son. I'm not leaving until they find him."

"Fine. Briggs, keep him here. I'm going to talk to Moorely and Nova. One of them will go with her and keep us posted on how she's doing." He didn't wait for an agreement from me or Briggs before walking away.

Briggs didn't move an inch, not letting his focus waver for one second. The man body-checked people for a living. I didn't stand a chance of making it past him.

Prairie settled onto the bench beside me. She didn't offer any platitudes, thankfully. Instead, she laced her fingers with mine and rested her head against my shoulder. The simple gesture grounded me as nothing else could have in that moment.

Seth and Oakes passed by with a small group of fellow hunters and trackers. Several of Wick's search and rescue dogs went by a few minutes later. I would sit here all night if I had to.

There had to be some answers about what happened. To where Brody was.

I didn't know how long I sat there, but Prairie dozed on my shoulder. Dad and Paige had shown up with the EmpowHer League and a bunch of food for those helping with the search, and those waiting for news like us.

The sun was just coloring the sky when Keely approached from the parking lot, still in her black scrubs. There still wasn't any news from the search, and Keely's expression was grim. I didn't think I could take any more bad news. I straightened to get away, but Prairie was still lying on me.

Briggs roused at Keely's approach and kicked Prairie's shoe to get her awake. Dad walked over from the food table and put a hand on my shoulder.

I opened my mouth, but no words came out.

Dad nodded to Keely. "How's Remington?"

"She's stable. The surgery went well."

The word 'surgery' came as a punch to the gut so much that I physically flinched. My throat was dry as I tried to speak for the first time in hours. "Surgery?"

"Yes." She exhaled slowly. "Dr. Young said she had damage to one of her kidneys from the attack. It appeared to be a stab wound. He's shared all the information with the officers stationed at the hospital."

My hand shot to my chest, my old scar twinging at the words. Dad's hand tightened on my shoulder. Someone stabbed her? And it sounded serious. "I thought...her head."

"Yes, there was a head wound as well. She's going to be concussed when she wakes." She turned when someone came racing out of the brush.

Gunner jogged up to us, but his focus remained on me. For one heart-stopping minute, I thought he had horrible news about Brody. Instead, his gaze flickered to where mine still sat over my scar. "I just heard. She was stabbed?"

I met my brother's eyes before looking away. If Remi had been attacked so violently, what did that mean for Brody?

Chapter 55

Remington

It was happening again. The worst part of nursing. I couldn't escape, not even in sleep. Those damn alarms and call bells ringing through my brain.

This wasn't a call bell. It wasn't an alarm. What was it? Consciousness tugged me closer. No, not a call bell. Not an alarm. The beat was steady, strong. The sound of a heart monitor. Those rarely invaded my dreams.

I shifted to get more comfortable. Aching pain stretched through my body, causing a whimper. The low hum of familiar voices reached me over the monitor. Moorely and Nova. I wasn't a nurse anymore, so why was I hearing a heart monitor? Why did I hurt so much?

I cracked an eye open to figure out what was going on. The familiar sight of a hospital room met my gaze. A whiteboard scribbled with information across from my bed, and an IV pole beside me. The smell of those blasted purple wipes. An oxygen sensor was clamped to my finger.

It wasn't a dream, and I wasn't a nurse any longer. I was a patient.

Why was I the patient again?

My brain scrambled to figure out the last thing I remembered. The fair. I'd been at the fair. With Colt. Brody. Brody.

Everything came back in a rush. My heart rate picked up as I scrambled over the details. Brody ran off. I caught up to him, but the scream, his scream. I found him, but also saw—oh, shit.

"It was *him*." I clambered to sitting, ignoring the screaming pain in my body. My breathing escaped in short bursts. I looked around the room wildly. The IV tugged on my hand, but I didn't care. I needed to go. Brody was in trouble. We had to find him. I tried to scramble out of bed. No, no. Fuck, I had to hide. But we had to find Brody. I fought against the hands that gripped my shoulder until the pain in my side made me double over. "No. I have to go. It was him. It was him. Brody. Where's Brody?"

Moorely's face swam into focus. Her hands pressed on mine where I gripped the footboard. She crouched below me, holding tight. "Remi. Relax, please. You're going to hurt yourself."

"It was him. How?" My body trembled in a combined response to my pain and panic. "Why? Why Brody? Oh, God, Brody. I have to call Wilder. I have to go."

"Remi, please." Nova smoothed a hand over my back. "Lie back down."

"Where's my girl?" A familiar voice shouted before Lexi rushed into the room. "Oh my God, Rems. Look at you."

I clasped her arms before she could embrace me. "It was him, Lex. How did he find me? Why would he?"

Lex's brow furrowed. "Who, Rem?"

"Him. It was." My head spun, and I sank to my rump, grabbing the footboard.

Lex glanced between the other two women in the room. "Do you know what she's talking about?"

"No idea. She just woke up screaming it." Nova continued to rub my back. "Remi. You're not making much sense. Oh, geez. You're bleeding."

"I popped a stitch. It's nothing." I'd felt it happen and didn't care. "Lex. It was him. I thought Wilder was nuts, but he's here."

"Who? Wilder? Sweetie, you're not making any sense." Lex smoothed down my hair before cupping my cheeks. "Who?"

Movement at the door caught my attention. Gunner walked in and watched me curiously. Behind him, Colt hovered in the doorway. Colt wasn't looking at me, or anyone really. He stared blankly across the room.

Gunner kept his full attention on me. "Yes, Remi? Who was it?"

"The man that attacked me in Florida. I don't know his real name. I don't know how he found me, or why. Why would he hurt—oh, shit. Is Brody okay? Please tell me he's okay. I tried to get to him, I did."

"Shhh." Lex pulled me against her when I broke down in tears.

"Brody's missing," Moorely said quietly. "We haven't been able to find him."

"No. No." My knuckles turned white as I grasped the footboard. "Brody."

No wonder Colt couldn't look at me. This was all my fault. I didn't blame him one bit. I'd hate me, too. Maybe I already did.

"What happened, Remi? I'm going to need a statement." Gunner drew closer to the bed.

"She just woke up, Guns and Roses." Lex moved between me and him. "She just learned Brody is missing. Give her a minute, for pete's sake."

"They don't have a minute." My voice shook badly. It was a wonder anyone could understand me. My mind raced over what had happened, trying to remember whatever details I could. "They have to find Brody. He's what matters. Not me."

"Of course you matter." Lexi spun to face me, her brow furrowed. "Don't say that."

"Brody was all over the place. We'd plied him with plenty of sugar, which didn't help. Colt went to get one final dessert before we went on the Ferris wheel. Brody almost got away from me." My voice cracked. Lex set her hands on mine. I took a shaky breath. "I caught up with him at the duck game."

Gunner brushed Lexi aside gently. "You texted Colt and told him where you were."

"Of course. I didn't want him to worry." I released the footboard only to twist my fingers in my gown. Hoping to find him, I searched every second of the time we were separated from Colt. "He won an elephant. I sent Colt a picture."

"We have it."

"He named it Elmar. I told Colt we were going to the ring toss, or maybe the goldfish game. While I was texting him, Brody spotted a stray balloon.

The weight had broken and was barely holding on. He was worried someone had lost it."

"Back to the elephant." Gunner's tone was gentle, which surprised me. He had his phone out, likely recording me. "We found it in the woods near you with blood on it. Was it your blood?"

"No." A strangled wail came from the doorway. Tears slipped from my cheeks, and I had to close my eyes. I couldn't bring myself to look at Colt. "He chased after the balloon. I tried to catch up with him again. He'd gone behind the stands, and the change in lighting left me blind for a minute. After catching the balloon, he called out to tell me. He was so happy, just like always. I'd just spotted the balloon when he screamed."

The words poured out faster and faster, the pace of my heart increasing enough that my nurse-brain was concerned for the person who was panicking. Lexi pried my hand free of the gown before pulling it into hers. She rubbed my cold hand between her warm ones. "Breathe, Remington. Breathe."

"I tried to get to him, but it was so dark. When I reached the woods, I found the balloon, but it had lost the weight and rose into the sky. I ran into the woods, worried he'd stumbled on a snake. It wasn't until I was half lost and had tripped that I thought about the flashlight on my phone. When I turned it on, I saw his shoes first. Not Brody's the man's."

"They were still admitting him in the ER when things went sideways." Lexi spoke for me when my body jerked. "We never found out who he was. He disappeared that night, and the hospital didn't care to pursue it further, even though two people died, a nurse and a tech. Remi was pretty severely injured, too. With no evidence or clues, the police mostly gave up, except for Detective Wilder, who has continued to pursue the case. He said that a man matching Remi's description was suspected in crimes outside of Florida."

My hand tried to curl in hers, but she kept it flat between hers. I closed my eyes against the onslaught of panic, trying to breathe deeply against the rising trembling of my limbs. "It wasn't much of a description. It was dark."

"If there's a description, I'd like it. I'll need this detective's information."

"Of course." Lexi rubbed my hand between hers again. "Breathe, Rems."

"He said something to me when he saw me." I still didn't understand that part. If he were here and didn't recognize me, what was the point? Why Brody? Was it a sick coincidence? "He didn't seem to recognize me. I don't understand."

"What did he say, Remi?" Gunner leaned against the foot of the bed, his phone hovering close to me. "Did he say something about you or Brody?"

"He said, 'What am I going to do with you?'. That was it." I took a shaky breath. There wasn't much left to tell. "I saw Brody and the blood on his elephant. I tried to get to him, and that's all I remember."

"That's it?" Gunner frowned. "You were stabbed. You don't remember that?"

"No. I think he hit me." I raised my hand to my head. "There was pain, and that was it."

"That would explain the lack of defensive wounds. So you don't know his real name. What about images? Was there CCTV?" Gunner's attention focused on Lexi now.

"There was. Nothing definitive enough to call it a clear picture. I think they got one good image when he was coming into the ER, but after that he was hidden under a hat and hoodie. We've never seen it. There's only Rem's description that I'm aware of." Lex pulled me closer. "The administrators wanted nothing more than to hush up the whole incident. Once he escaped and went off the radar, they figured they were in the clear. They said he was from the mental health facility, and that was that. Like it was all we needed to know. Except he walked in off the street, he wasn't brought in from a facility."

The anger in her tone eased some of my panic. She was still furious for me. An idea came to me, a friend we'd made on the security team a while before the incident had happened. "What about Logan? Did he have access?"

"He did. I don't know if he still does, or if he's willing to risk firing to get it, but I'll ask him. Are you okay?" Lexi bent to meet my eyes.

"Why are you here?" I didn't know why I had asked.

"Sisters, remember? Where else would I be? Left my shift early and everything. The minute Nova texted, I was out of the door." She kissed my forehead. "I'm going to text Logan. Guns and Roses? Are you coming?"

Gunner tapped his phone to end the recording. He rolled his eyes. "Would you stop that? Let's go. You can give me all the information you have, and the contact for your detective."

"He got in trouble for pushing the matter," Lexi's voice faded as they went into the hall. I didn't know that. That could be why I hadn't heard from him in a couple of weeks.

I sank back onto the bed. Every ache and pain reasserted itself. Nova still stood beside Colt, but he wasn't doing anything. Not even crying. He just continued to stare at the wall as he had been since he got here.

Moorely squeezed my hand gently once I got settled back on the pillow. "Are you hungry? You've been asleep forever."

"Yes, thank you." I couldn't stop staring at Colt, even though the haunted look in his eyes gutted me. Every bit of anger he might feel, I probably earned it. Maybe he'd feel better if he could let it out.

Moorely pulled Nova away with her, leaving just me and Colt in the room.

"I'm sorry," I whispered.

He jolted, his gaze flickering back to me. "Why?"

"I didn't keep a good enough eye on him. The man was...hell, I don't know why he went for Brody. I'm so sorry. I don't blame you for hating me."

"I don't." He stood at the foot of the bed, his whole body sagging. "I don't hate you."

"You're terrified."

He nodded. His jaw ticked with tension before growing lax again.

"Have you slept at all?"

"No."

"Come here." I patted the bed. He could hate me later, but there was nowhere else in the room even slightly comfortable.

"You're injured."

"I don't care." I scooted to the side with the slightest wince as pain came from the place where I'd been stabbed. The spot of blood wasn't too big, so I'd probably only popped one stitch.

Colt sank onto the bed next to me, staring at his hands.

"All the way." I pulled him down beside me. Fully clothed, he turned to me, his head settling on my shoulder. He was way too tall for the bed, but curled one leg over mine, the other dangling off the side of the bed. I brushed my fingers through his hair. "They'll find him. He's going to be okay."

"What if they don't?"

"They will. I have to believe it. For you. You have had enough pain for five lifetimes. You won't get more. He'll be found."

"You don't know that."

"I don't, but I believe it. With all my heart."

Chapter 56

Remington

I don't know how much time passed. I'd intermittently dozed off as well. Anesthesia always clung to me like a wet blanket for a good twenty-four hours. It figured I would doze when I so wanted to be awake.

If I were to wager a guess, Colt would be sore as hell when he woke. His position didn't look the least bit comfortable, although I didn't mind his weight on me as it was. It might be the last time I felt it. Now that he'd actually slept, he might be of a clearer mind and have enough energy to be angry with me.

All I knew was I wanted to get out of here. I felt like I needed to be out there helping with the search. Maybe it was my guilt talking, but it didn't matter. I had to comb the entire valley, I'd do it. God willing, they hadn't left town, but there was no guarantee.

Lex popped her head into the room. She nodded when I put my finger to my lips and crept to the bedside. "Logan was home from work already, which I expected. He's going to check for us when he gets back to work. When I told him what happened, he was happy to help. Wilder said he'd been taken off the case and the Orlando PD dismissed the FBI from their part of the case, insisting it wasn't related. Gunner's checking with them anyway to see if they released the video, or to get a copy of the drawing from your recollections."

"Hopefully they're more cooperative with him than they were with us, but it doesn't sound like it if they tried to pull out of the FBI investigation. Can they do that?"

"Gunner said they have to be invited. He's inviting them himself."

I set my hand on hers. "Can you get me out of here?"

"Rems. You just had surgery last night. I know nurses make the worst patients, but this is extreme, even for you."

"She's right." Colt's tired voice made me jump. "You have to heal."

"No. I have to help. I'm going crazy here." Rather than suffer whatever glare Lexi was giving me, I set my hand in Colt's hair. "I thought you were asleep."

"I was. Woke up a little while ago." He didn't move to get away from me like I thought he would. The only movement was in pulling his phone from his pocket. "No messages."

"The dogs lost the trail on Tanner Road." Lex took the chair beside the bed. "They checked with old man Cox, and he said no one drove by all night, and you know he's anal about anyone driving by late at night because the lights shine in his house. No one tried to drive through the res either."

I had no idea what any of that meant. "Huh?"

"It doesn't look like anyone left town between when Colt realized you were missing and they started the search. The only other option out of the valley is the road north, but it's closed after damage during the melt this year." She shrugged. "That means he's likely here somewhere. Unfortunately, it's a big valley. Small town, big valley."

"There are lots of places to hide in the hills. Abandoned mines and cabins, as well as cabins only used for hunting that haven't been opened for the season yet." Colt pushed to sitting. His hand rubbed the back of his neck. "I need to go back out there."

"I need to help, too." The only thing that kept me from moving was Colt's pinning stare. "Really. I'm fine enough. It's easy enough to make a pressure dressing out of a bit of packing and an abdominal binder. I won't overdo it, but I can't lie here helpless. I've done that before, and all I got for my trouble was some scars and PTSD. No resolution. I can't let that happen again."

Lex sighed heavily, pushing to her feet. "I'll talk to them, but you know it'll probably mean AMA papers."

"I'll sign them. Just get me some clothes and the papers. I'm ready." Without waiting for either of them to agree, I hit the button to stop my IV.

"You're not going to listen to me, are you?"

"Nope." I picked the corner of the Tegaderm up.

"Then let me do that before you bleed all over the place." Lexi reached across to set her hand over mine. "I'll get some gauze and we'll remove it. Moorely is getting you some clothes already since they cut you out of yours."

"Fine. Just get it done." I waited until she left to speak to the man eying me in silence. He still sat beside me on the bed, though I couldn't imagine why. "You don't have to stay here. I'll be fine. Once I'm out, I'll help however I can. I'll stay out of your hair, I promise."

His brows knit together. He shifted so that he faced me fully. "What the hell is that supposed to mean?"

"I told you—I don't blame you if you're angry with me. I sort of hate myself right now, anyway. You have too much on your plate to be worried about me being around to remind you of how I lost him."

"Remington. You didn't lose him."

"But I did."

"You tried to get him. He was." His words choked off. It was another minute before he caught back up with his sentence. "Wild as anything. With the two of us together, we hardly kept up with him."

I brushed some tears from his cheeks with my thumbs. When he leaned forward, I touched my forehead to his. For several minutes we just sat there like that. His hands cupped my elbows, but he didn't push me away. I took a shaky breath. "We'll get out there and we'll find him. One way or another, we're going to find him."

He gripped my arms tighter. "You should rest. You've been through an ordeal."

"And he's going through one now. I was resting after surgery. It was medically induced, but I was resting. I have to help. I can't sit around and do nothing. Not this time. I want to help. We need to bring Brody home."

"I don't know where to begin."

"Then we'll find out what everyone else is doing and join in the search. That's where we'll start." My chin wobbled. "I wish he'd taken me. I don't understand why this happened. If he didn't remember me, why take the child I was with?"

I couldn't bring myself to suggest he was just looking for any child to steal. That was the most horrible thought. If he were a random predator, we were less likely to find him.

"Did you sleep at all?"

"Yeah." He cleared his throat. "Thank you. I needed it."

"I know. Now that you're rested, you'll be better able to think clearly. If you want to go on ahead and get started, I'll have Lex bring me to wherever everything is being handled."

"No, we'll go together."

It filled me with some comfort to know he wanted to go together. Perhaps he didn't hate me, or maybe he would wait until after we found him. "I still can't believe you want anything to do with me."

"You didn't do this."

"I know. In my head, anyway." When he took my hand in his, I clasped my other hand over the top. "It's not your fault either."

"How much do you believe it's not your fault?"

"About three percent."

"Same."

Chapter 57

Colton

Everything around me was so muffled, I barely knew if anyone was talking directly to me. The only time it seemed like I could focus was when Remi guided me. She was wounded, badly enough that she'd had surgery, but I was the one being treated like an injured sparrow.

At least she'd stopped apologizing or asking why I wasn't mad at her. In all honesty, I didn't have the space to be angry. It wasn't like she deserved any of my anger. She didn't do this.

Remi donned one of the fluorescent vests with little more than a wince. She carried another one over to me. "Here you go. We've been told to join West and Aspen at their search grid."

"Right." I slid the vest on, but didn't move. The rumble of ATVs carried through the valley. They hit all the checkpoints for news.

Her hand slipped into mine, and she pulled me toward a truck loaded with people to head out to join or relieve others searching. Before I could hop in, my phone pinged. I checked it hoping it was something about Brody. Instead, Darlene's name stared at me. Every bit of me tensed until my head spun. The plastic edges of the phone cut into my hand from my grip.

Remi slid back off the tailgate, waving them on and shouting we'd get another ride. She approached slowly, setting her hand gently on my arm. Her voice soothed me like a cooling balm. "What is it? Is it something about Brody? Did they reach out to you?"

I shook my head vehemently, thrusting the phone in her face.

"Oh. Okay." She pinched the phone delicately between her fingers. After she'd read the screen, she lifted her gaze to mine. "Go on, open it."

That was the last thing I wanted to do. I didn't need to deal with her when I was searching for my son. He was the only thing that mattered. But what if?

"What if she knows something?" Remi pegged my biggest fear of opening the message. Darlene sure as shit hadn't protected us. What if she'd done something with him? Is that why she showed up again? Did she tell Bryce about him? But it couldn't have been Bryce, Remi named him as the man that attacked her. She set her hand on mine, bringing me back into focus. "Do you want me to do it?"

"Please."

"Okay. Just a minute." She pulled out her own phone, sending a text before prying my phone out of my grip. Without asking, she pressed my thumb to the screen to unlock it. Her lips thinned as she studied the text. She shook her head slightly. "I don't think she knows anything. She mentions your stepfather, I think. The whole thing is pretty vague."

"What does it say?"

"She says that he reached out and knows where she's at." She set her hand on my arm, moving closer until she was right against me. "Another one just came through. She says she's worried about him coming after all of you and to watch out for everyone. There's nothing specific to Brody here."

"Is she the one doing this?"

"We'll tell your brother. He'll send someone to look into it."

Gunner ran up right after she'd mentioned him. It must have been him she texted. He didn't look at me, but focused on Remi. "What is it?"

Remi handed off my phone. "She doesn't specifically mention Brody here, but Colt's worried she's involved. That maybe she showed up out of the blue because he's reached out to her before this." She'd put more into my words than I'd given her. She'd read me like a book, because every bit was right. All of my worries and fears laid out before me.

Gunner's eyes darkened as he read the texts. I could almost feel the mirror of my anger vibrating off of him. "Did she tell you where she was staying?"

It took a second for his words to sink in, and several more for my brain to snag on the fact he was talking to me. I searched my memories for all conversations and text messages. "No. Not specifically, but I'm pretty sure she was in Pueblo. She wouldn't have stayed here in town."

"No, she wouldn't have. I'll call over to Pueblo and issue a BOLO for her, and check on the one we put out for Brody. We'll get answers, Colt." He handed my phone back to me. "Don't block her this time. We'll see if she talks herself into a corner when you don't respond. She was never good at keeping her trap shut."

Remi slipped the phone back out of my hands, tapping the screen a few times.

"Remi. I said, don't block her," Gunner snarled.

She blinked at his rebuke, and ensuing glare. "I only muted the conversation. If he isn't blocking her, he doesn't need to hear her constantly texting."

His glare softened. He set a hand on her shoulder, nodding. "You're right. Thanks. Keep an eye on him?"

"Not a child." I couldn't even work up the energy to sound as annoyed as I normally would.

"No, but your brain is going in a million different directions." Remi slipped her hand in mine to pull me toward another truck. "Let's go to our search grid. You'll feel better if you're doing something."

"I doubt that."

She didn't argue with me. She didn't offer words of comfort. In fact, she agreed with me. "You're probably right, but you'll go crazy if you just sit here, so we're moving."

"Thank you."

Her movements were stilted when she climbed into the truck. I didn't miss her wince of the strain in her tone when she brushed off my thanks. "You're not the only one who needs to keep busy."

"Are you sure you're up to this?" I settled in beside her.

"Yes." She avoided my gaze for her answer. "Lex told me there's a huge group of townies that are in on the search. Someone from the Mitchell clan is organizing volunteers and assigning shifts."

"Sounds about right. It's a decades-old tradition."

We hit a bump that jostled everyone in the truck bed. Remi whimpered before she pressed her hand to her side.

"You shouldn't have checked out of the hospital."

"Shut up." With her teeth gritted, she took several deep breaths in through her nose, expelling them loudly out her mouth.

"Remington."

"Hush, please." She closed her eyes. Once the strain eased in her features, she finally looked at me. She offered a crooked grin, probably an attempt to distract me. "I'm getting enough of a lecture for this from Lex later. You know why I have to do this, so don't you join in."

"Fine. I think our search area will be punishment for you." It would be better to follow her lead. She was doing her best to keep me both distracted and in decent spirits. That was the sort of person she was. I pointed toward the west. I'd noticed that the truck ran over the foothills toward the base of the closest mountain peak, where old boarded-up mines could be seen against the rocks. "It looks like we're climbing."

She lifted her gaze to follow my finger. The squeal of the truck brakes didn't cover her low groan. "You're not funny."

"I'm not trying to be. This is our stop." I hopped out of the truck. Before she could protest, I scooped her into my arms to get her out of the truck. Once her feet were on the ground, I waved toward a trail. "This leads to the original Daugherty mines. That's where our grid base is, I'm guessing. There's electricity there since the town offers tours."

"Let's do this, then." She straightened her shoulders and vest. The half-smile returned. I didn't miss that the smile didn't bring a sparkle to her eyes like it usually did. She might have been trying, but it wasn't any easier for her than it was for me. "We've got a long way to climb."

"If you're not up for it, you can stay at the base."

"I thought I told you to shut up."

Chapter 58

Remington

We'd been going for several hours, climbing and searching. We were well up the mountain and had passed many old mine entrances. My side was killing me. I wasn't about to complain, because there were things more important.

Colt's voice echoed from inside the open mine we'd just found. Someone had taken the boards off. Gut instinct told me it wouldn't be this easy, but I wasn't about to stop him from trying. He had to be doing something, just like I did. It would take a very firm hand to get him to stop, even when they called us down to avoid the danger of such searches at night.

Colt emerged, shaking his head. His hair stuck up in every direction. The dark circles had returned under his eyes as though he hadn't slept at all earlier. He looked like hell. I imagined I didn't look much better. He ran his fingers through his hair. "Nothing. It looks like some kids were using it to party in."

"That's safe." I shielded my eyes to look up the mountain. Thankfully, there were plenty of old trails crisscrossing their way up the mountain, so we weren't trying to scale actual rock face. The sun shone brightly overhead, even on its approach to the peaks of the mountain. We had only a few more hours left to search before it got too dark to be safe.

Colt's grunt could have been an agreement with my comment or something else. It was hard to say. His eyes trailed the path we'd already climbed, then looked up. "Let's keep moving."

"Good idea."

He looked me up and down. A frown darkened his features more. "Are you okay?"

"I'm fine. Let's move." We weren't stopping now, even if I wasn't *exactly* fine. I'd manage well enough until we couldn't search any longer and hitched a ride back to base on one of the all-terrain vehicles. I wish we could have used one for the climb.

We made our way along the trail. Colt stayed in the lead to warn me about any pitfalls in the trail, for which I was grateful. One misstep and I could pop another stitch or just stretch the still tender area. I wouldn't abandon Colt when he needed support.

The other teams' calls for Brody echoed through the area. Every once in a while I spotted other teams moving at the same pace as us. Being somewhere in the middle of all the teams, and both too wrung out to shout, we'd come to a silent conclusion to let them handle that.

The boards used to seal the next few mines completely covered them with no signs of disturbance. There'd be no chance that Brody could be in them.

The steady beat of a helicopter propeller drew closer, then passed right overhead toward the north. Throughout the day, the chopper had been circling, looking for any signs of them. The occasional catch of static on the walkie clipped on Colt's jeans never led to anything but someone changing out with a fresh searcher.

My feet slid out from under me on some loose rock. I flailed my arms to steady myself. Colt's firm hand grasped my elbow tight. As soon as I was steady, he pulled me back onto the trail. As hard as I tried to stop it, a squeak of pain escaped my control. I exhaled some of the pain. "Fuck."

"You should go back down."

"Not without you."

"Go down, Remington. Before you're seriously hurt."

"I already was." I pressed hard into the wound for a moment. "We're supposed to stay a team. I'm not leaving you."

"You aren't doing me much good in pain like that, now are you?"

I clenched my jaw against the sharp retort I wanted to make. Honestly, I was surprised he'd bitten his tongue for this long. There was no way I'd successfully hidden my struggle from him, even in his distracted state. None of that mattered right then; only Brody did. "We aren't moving any slower than the other groups. Look, they're on the same level as us. You aren't staying up here alone in the state you're in. I won't let you. If you go into an open mine without someone there, you could get seriously hurt. I'll let myself bleed out before I leave you alone."

He didn't bother checking the status of the other groups. For a minute, his eyes flashed with anger. It was only a minute. His features fell as if I'd kicked his puppy. All the anger melted along with his stance. He fell back onto the rocks. "Sorry. I know you're doing your best."

"You don't need to apologize. You aren't wrong. I shouldn't be up here. I just couldn't sit down there all nice and safe while you're out here searching. Sitting still would kill me almost as much as it would you. It's killing me that he's not here." Tears tried to flood my eyes, but I forced them back. He didn't need my tears.

"You really care about him."

"Of course I do. He's amazing, just like his dad."

He extended his hand toward me. I took it, letting him pull me into him. With his face buried in my shoulder, he held me tight enough to make me smart.

I wasn't about to complain this time. He needed to do this. I hadn't yet seen him cry. That isn't to say he hadn't last night, but today he'd been dry-eyed. I wrapped my arm around him in return as he shook with tears, trying to soothe him without losing hold of my sorrow.

"We have to find him."

"Yes, we do. Are you ready to go again?" When he lifted his head, I wiped the tears from his cheeks. I let my forehead press against his. "Take a few more minutes. I need to check to see if I'm bleeding badly and replace the pressure dressing. Then we'll get moving again."

He nodded his agreement. His gaze drifted down the mountain. "Brody isn't here."

"I know we haven't found him yet."

"No, I don't think we'll find him by checking the mines."

"Do you want to try somewhere else?" I peeled open the binder to check my wound. In a bit of good news, there wasn't any blood soaked through to the binder, and the outer section of gauze didn't have any blood, either. As long as I wasn't bleeding internally, then I was doing pretty well. Pain notwithstanding. I palpated along my abdomen, relieved that it still felt soft. So far, no sign of internal bleeding. I'd take that win. At least I hadn't screwed up too badly coming along for this unexpected mountain climb.

"I don't know where to start."

"Nobody does. That's why they're following directions. There are people all over the valley searching, and the helicopters have been by just about every hour." I peeled the gauze from my skin, tenderly checking the line of stitches. They were a little red, but outside of the popped stitch, they all seemed intact.

"Are you okay?"

"It looks like it. Just having pain, but I see nothing alarming." The blood on the gauze appeared to have come from the area of the lost stitch if the ooze of serosanguinous drainage was any indication. I packed the used gauze into a bio bag and grabbed some new to re-pack the wound. "Do you want to go back down?"

"No. There's a few hours left before we lose sunlight. Maybe there'll be news before then."

"I sure hope so." Once the binder was back in place, I got to my feet. I'd added a lot more gauze to increase the pressure. Thanks to that, the area didn't ache as much. "Shall we?"

"Let's go." Colt's long strides guided us along several more paths along the rock face. When we got to a spot with a big step up, he reached out to haul me up.

We kept on like that for another hour and a half, with the sun drawing ever closer to the mountain peaks. I couldn't deny that desperation clawed at my belly. Wasn't it a rule that the first twenty-four hours were the most important in the search for a missing child? Or was it forty-eight? Either way, it felt like letting the sun go down with no news was a horrible sign.

Colt's increasingly frantic movements in his search hinted he felt the same.

My phone dinged. Colt froze, staring at me with wide eyes.

"It's probably them telling us to come down before it gets too dark to make it down safely." I didn't think it wise to mention that sort of announcement was likely to come over the walkies. This was more direct. And from Gunner. I read the text with my heart sinking. "Get on the walkie and call for a ride. Your brother wants us to come down. Immediately."

"Why?"

"He says they found something."

Chapter 59

Colton

We couldn't get down the hill to the closest checkpoint fast enough for a ride. Several times along the way, Remi told me to go on ahead of her, but I wanted to make sure she got down safely as well. Besides, she was helping keep me sane.

Barely sane, but sane. Her warmth, support, and caring. How much she loved Brody. It helped calm something in me as well.

Even so, my heart was in my throat. If Gunner had been specific about what they'd found, it would have been good news. If he'd said anything more than to get down the hill, it would be good news.

He'd only said they'd found 'something'. It didn't bode well. I'd thought I knew what having my heart broken was like before, but I could feel it shattering now.

Remi kept her hand in mine the entire time, even when suggesting I go on ahead. To her credit, she was trying to rush every bit as much as I was. I couldn't tell if it was tension, fear, or pain that lined her features. It was probably a mix of all three.

It took too long, but also no time at all, to hit the checkpoint. Thankfully, there was already a vehicle there waiting for us. I helped Remi climb into the 4 seater UTV and tossed her a helmet before jumping in myself. Ryker didn't waste any time, throwing it into gear and heading down the mountain to the base. There were a couple of times Remi yelped when we hit a bump. I'd have checked, but we were going too fast for me to safely turn to see her.

We finally landed at base, and all three of us rocked forward at the sudden stop.

Remi thanked Ryker and handed him the helmets back before sliding her hand into mine. She spotted Gunner at the same time I did and gave my hand a squeeze. "Let's go."

Gunner stood rigid at the far edge of the impromptu camp. His hands clasped behind his back with his gaze on the town instead of the trail. A lifetime with my brother told me everything I needed to know. I stopped so short, Remi nearly landed on her ass with how hard she got jerked backward.

"What the hell?" Remi's words stopped when she met my gaze. Her delicate fingers touched my jaw. "Colton. You don't know anything yet."

"I know my brother. He doesn't have good news."

She stepped in front of me, clasping both my hands. For several moments she let me stand there staring at him. She drew my hands to her chest, her thumbs rubbing soothing paths along the back of them. "Would you like me to talk to him first?"

"No. I need to hear it. Just give me a minute."

"Take them all." She didn't move one iota. Her gaze stayed locked on mine while she continued to hold my hands in hers. She didn't push or cajole while I waffled on whether I could make my feet move.

"We should go."

"We will when you're ready. You aren't ready yet." Her small hands were warm in mine and held on with a firm strength that was the opposite of their delicate appearance. "Take a minute. Take ten. You're allowed to take what time you need."

I closed my eyes with her permission. My head dropped, and hers pressed against it. Another touch to remind me she was there to support me.

Her hands released mine only to clasp my cheeks. My breath was shaky as I inhaled. "I don't want to know if it's bad. I want to keep hoping."

"That's fair. I'll offer again. Do you want me to go talk to him first?" Her thumbs trailed the same soothing paths on my cheeks they had on my hands. I hadn't realized I'd shed any tears until she did.

"No."

"Alright." She didn't move until I wrapped my hands around her wrists to move them. At that point, she stepped back. When my eyes opened, I found her encouraging smile. "Are you ready now?"

"No."

"Shall we go anyway?"

"We have to."

Her hand laced with mine again as she stepped beside me to clear my path. Even though I remained still for several seconds, she waited quietly.

I finally put one foot in front of the other until we were right behind my twin. "Gunner."

He turned to face us, his face creased with lines I hadn't noticed yesterday. Is that what I looked like now? Rather than face me, he turned his attention to Remi. "Thanks for bringing him down for me."

"Still not a child."

"Maybe you shouldn't dawdle," Remi suggested quietly. "It's best to get things out in the open quickly, or they'll fester until he's in too big of a panic to hear your words."

"Do I have to tell you I'm not a child, too?" I narrowed my eyes at Remi. She didn't balk at my anger.

"Of course you aren't. You *are* burying your panic, though. So am I, and despite being an ass, I'm convinced your brother is, too."

Gunner shrugged. "I am what I am."

"Some things you don't have to be proud of," she muttered.

"You're right, Remi. Colt, you should probably sit down."

"Maybe you should just tell me." I held on tight to Remi's hand, despite my momentary annoyance with her. "Rip off the fucking Band-Aid."

"We found a car."

My heart pounded loudly in my ears before he could finish. I could barely make out what he said next. Only a few words reached my consciousness.

"Blood—back seat—rental."

The world spun. Pain jolted through me until my teeth clacked when my ass hit the ground.

"Colton." Remi's voice came from so far away, she might as well have been at the bottom of a mine shaft. "Colton Lee Mitchell, look at me."

Warm hands clasped my cheeks. Even when she moved my head this way and that, I couldn't see her through the pinpricks of light my eyes were letting in. It was like I was in a bubble, and everything was far away.

"Thanks." She was muttering quietly to someone about shock and a panic attack. Or hell, she might have been yelling for all I knew.

Blood. There'd been blood in a car. Remi had seen his blood on the stuffed toy, the same toy Gunner said they found with blood on it. Someone hurt Brody. He'd bled enough that they'd found some in the backseat of a car. Where had the car been?

Where was Brody?

I screamed it at Gunner, but there wasn't a response. My mouth moved to scream again, but I couldn't make it work.

Something cool touched my forehead, and the rocky ground pressed into my back.

"Where is he? Is he—was he—"

"There wasn't a body," Remi soothed. She was a little closer now, her voice more easily discernible from the buzzing racket in my ears. "Are you able to listen now?"

"I was."

"You weren't." Remi lifted my head a little. Water touched my lips. I let it trickle in and swallowed. "That's it. Drink a little more. You're still pale."

"Here." Lexi's voice popped in. Where'd she been all this time? "Nova had some."

"Leave it to the queen of sweets to have diabetes." Remi touched my chin. "Open."

I obediently opened my mouth. She placed something on my tongue. Sickly sweet, and chalky. Like a sweet antacid tablet. My nose wrinkled at the taste. The flavor was enough to shock me back to the present. Remi and Lexi were both staring at me, with Gunner right behind. My head lay in Remi's lap, my legs raised up to rest on a chair.

Remi closed her hand over my mouth when I went to spit out the tablet. "No, you don't. Finish it. You haven't eaten enough, and your sugar dropped. I'm surprised you were still standing. I think shock made the adrenaline give way to the hypoglycemia."

"Huh?" It came out more like a muffled snurf with her hand still clamped over my mouth.

"Just finish the tab. You'll feel better."

Chapter 60

Remington

All this time Colt had been worried about everyone but himself. Or maybe he was punishing himself. Lord knew I had the same inclination, whether a conscious thought or not. I'd encouraged Colt to sleep, but didn't think about making him eat. Not even before we started climbing the damn mountain for hours on end. When was the last time he'd eaten? For that matter, when was the last time I'd eaten? Damn it. Why didn't I think of even grabbing some protein bars, something. "Stupid."

"Stop that." Lexi remained beside me, helping clean up the supplies we'd used. She left the glucometer in place so we could check his sugar again once he'd had a minute. "He's not the only one worried sick. You're not just worried. You're also gravely injured. It's easy to miss things in times of personal stress."

"Good thing I'm no longer a nurse if I didn't catch this earlier."

"I thought I told you to stop that."

"She's right." Colt's voice croaked when he spoke, but color had returned to his cheeks. He'd been so pale right before he fell. My heart had completely stopped a minute before my brain kicked in.

Gunner returned from the table with a plate full of food. "Will this work?"

The plate had a sandwich, a protein granola bar, and some fruit. It appeared Gunner had learned a trick or two being around Nova. "That's great. Colt, you need to eat. We addressed the sugar, but I don't know when you ate last, and you need protein and healthy sugar to get you back on an even keel."

Colt pushed his way to sitting, dropping his legs from the chair Gunner had put them on when I was barking orders. He stared at the plate for a minute before taking it. When he took a large bite of the sandwich, I was satisfied that he was going to listen. His subsequent rapid bites told me the first one reminded him he was hungry.

Gunner tapped my shoulder, crooking his finger as he took a few steps away. Lexi gave me a nod and a gentle push to follow him. "Go ahead. I'll be right here keeping an eye on him."

"Not a child," Colt muttered around his sandwich.

I couldn't help myself, I leaned in to kiss his temple. "We're all aware. Eat. I'll be right back."

He took my hand and squeezed, his eyes drifting to Gunner.

"I'll be right back. Promise. I'll tell you whatever he says. You need to sit and eat." I rose when he released my hand. I brushed the dust from my pants as I followed Gunner. "What is it?"

"I need to get back to the scene." He didn't take his eyes off his brother. The genuine concern and pain on full display was such a rare sight, it was the first time I really thought he and Colt looked entirely alike. "I hate to leave him like this, especially since I don't think he heard a word I said."

"Lex and I will tell him. You need to do your job. We'll take care of him as best we can. He won't be fine until Brody's found. Maybe not even then." I eyeballed Colt, pleased to see he'd finished the sandwich completely now. He downed the juice Lexi handed him. The tight worry for him released its squeeze on my heart. "I'll keep you posted."

"I'm glad you were here and realized what was happening so quickly. You must have been an excellent nurse."

"I was." I went back to Colt's side without another word. Gunner made his goodbyes brief before he mounted the horse he'd left tied at the trailhead.

Colt moved to get up, but we held him down. He let out a groan of frustration. "Where's he going? I have questions."

"I'm sure you do. We'll tell you what they know. It isn't much, but you passed out before you really heard any of it." Lexi tapped the button on the blood pressure cuff still on his wrist. "Once we're positive you're back up to snuff, we'll tell you everything."

He plucked a grape from the plate. "I didn't know I was hungry."

"You've had plenty on your mind. I didn't think to feed you, only to see you slept." I grunted when Lexi slapped my arm. "What? I didn't say it?"

"You were thinking it. You're not stupid." She turned Colt's wrist to show me the cuff.

The blood pressure read 118/75. Another tight twist of my heart released. "Your blood pressure is back to normal. Let's check your sugar, and then we can talk. How's your ass?"

"Don't you already know?" Lexi clapped her hand over her mouth the second she finished. Her eyes grew wide. "Fuck. That was inappropriate for the situation. I'm not in a nurse's station."

A spark of humor lit in Colt's eyes before the haunted look returned. I brushed my hand along his cheek again, and he leaned into the touch. "I meant you hit the ground pretty hard. You're going to be sore, that's expected. Are you having any acute pain in the area? If you are, you might need X-rays to check your coccyx."

"She's worried you broke your butt. She likes it too much for that to happen." This time Lex didn't apologize for her outburst. I sighed and shook my head at her.

"Nurses have dark humor. We make jokes at the most inopportune times. It's how we cope with the regular stresses of the job. Especially in the ER."

"You said 'we'." Colt didn't respond to my question about his pain. His hand caught mine before I could pull away. I hadn't even caught it, so how had he? It was still a natural reflex for me to say 'we'. "Not 'they'."

"He's right." Lexi's dimple emerged. She poked Cole's finger to check his sugar. "You know what they say: once a nurse, always a nurse."

"Still not going back." I glared at her disbelieving hum. "Now isn't the time for this discussion. There are more important matters at hand than my career choices."

"Distraction is always helpful, even when it seems like the wrong time."
She held up the glucometer, releasing another band of panic from my heart.
"Ninety-seven. Much better. Your color looks better, too. I think you're up
to snuff now."

"Thanks for the help, Lexi." He winced a little as he shifted positions.

"What's your pain level?"

"Passable." He readjusted his legs with another wince.

"That's not the correct way to answer." I quieted when he took my
hand again.

"If you're done fussing, I'd like to stop hearing the same three words
over and over in my head on a loop."

"Three words?" When Lexi carried the glucometer away, I moved
closer to sit beside him. "What three words are you hearing?"

"Blood. Backseat. Rental."

"That's all you heard? No wonder you passed out."

"Yeah, it is."

"Okay. I'll tell you what Gunner told us if you promise to stay with me
while I go over it."

He tugged me closer, holding on to my hand like a lifeline. "I will."

"Those three words make it sound so much worse. Then again, your
mind is going to make everything worse. Now promise you'll stick with me."

"I promise. Just tell me."

"Okay. They found an abandoned car on the back roads. Gunner
mentioned a place called Trapper Village?"

"Out near Moorely and Aspen's land. A little farther north and slightly
west. There used to be several old trappers who lived there for years until
they all died out."

"Ah. That makes sense." I'd noticed that a lot of things around here
were named for logical reasons like that. "Anyway, the car was a rental.
There was a small amount of blood in the backseat, but not enough to make
them think the injury was severe. They aren't even sure it's Brody's yet, but
given the circumstances, it is an assumption."

His hold on my hand grew tighter, and he folded me into his arms.
"There's no sign of him, then? Nothing at all?"

"Not yet. Gunner said they were moving the search north tomorrow
after the discovery." I lifted my gaze so that I could continue to monitor his
reactions. "There's also the possibility they switched cars, or this is a

distraction. Gunner said they aren't taking down any of the roadblocks until he's found."

His eyes closed. Though he paled a bit, his grip on my hand remained strong. "What about your picture? Did it come?"

"We're still waiting for it. Logan's at work, but he hasn't had time to do any digging. Gunner's going through bureaucratic red tape at work to get the image and the sketch they made of his defining features, but that always takes time. Even in these situations, apparently."

"How am I going to make it through the night knowing he's out there scared and alone?"

I leaned back into him, taking a shuddering breath. "One minute at a time. It might be the longest night ever, but it will pass. Once it does, we'll start again at first light."

Chapter 61

Remington

After Lex and Nova dropped us off at my place, I'd made Colt eat again. She'd insisted she would stay at Nova's even though I had a perfectly good guest room. Honestly, I appreciated the time for Colt to decompress. And for me. I needed to eat. I needed to breathe. And I needed to cry. All the same things Colt did.

Colt wasn't in any way able to handle going to his own house. Aspen brought some of his clothes over for him so he wouldn't have to step foot in the house until he was ready. Honestly, I didn't know which would be worse; to go home and see everything knowing he's missing, or to not go at all not knowing how he actually was. Did it feel like giving up not to go home? He hadn't fought a lick when I'd suggested my place.

I was probably overthinking everything. Which wasn't surprising. Colt wasn't the only one overly tired and underfed. I'd gotten some food down myself. With that added bit of strength, I convinced Colt to get some sleep. It took hours, but he finally dozed off when I turned on some white noise and sat with him a while.

The only thing I wanted to do was make this as easy on him as I could. It would never be easy, but perhaps if I helped take care of him, he would have the energy to keep going. At least for now, he'd slept and eaten. Two very important elements in maintaining not just energy, but hope.

Once he was finally asleep, I dealt with my surgical site. I cleaned and re-bandaged it. Another quick exam confirmed there still wasn't any sign of internal bleeding. I slipped back into the bedroom. Colt might be sleeping, but he wasn't sleeping calmly. He had tossed and turned so much that he tangled himself in my sheets.

With as much effort and strength as my injury allowed, I worked on extricating his legs from the cocoon of cotton. I tossed the sheets back over him before I climbed in next to him.

Even in sleep, the worry that lined his brow all day remained. I tried to smooth it down with my fingers. I gently ran them along the line until it eased some. He reached out, tugging me close so suddenly I squeaked in surprise and pain.

I closed my eyes, taking deep breaths until the flash of pain subsided. Once it settled enough, I checked on him again. My accidental complaint hadn't woken him, thank goodness.

His head rested on my thigh, arms still wrapped around my waist. I didn't have the heart to move him, even to get more comfortable in search of sleep. For the first time since we'd left the mountain, he was calm, still, and the worried crease of his brow was gone. I couldn't do anything to disturb that.

I could at least convince myself it was fine, knowing that years of night shifts, followed by these weeks of working late evenings at the hotel, made it difficult for me to sleep at night anyway. It wouldn't be a problem to stay up a little longer, as long as I could get comfortable.

I tucked a pillow behind my back before turning on the TV, muted with closed captions. While he slept, I absentmindedly ran my fingers through his hair. My phone stayed tucked into my side on vibrate in case any news came through. I wanted to make sure that anytime there was news, he'd know.

Lex texted after a while to check on us. A fellow night shift nurse like me, she'd been more exhausted from being up for the search than now. I wondered when she'd last slept. When I asked, she deflected my question with humor. In other words, she hadn't slept. At all.

I asked her how Violet was doing and was told she was having a great time at her friends, and to stop worrying. Muttering under my breath, I told her to catch forty before I came over with my handy sledgehammer to ensure she did. After her promise of retaliatory treatment, I put the phone back aside.

Colt's even breaths were comforting enough for me to doze in and out for a couple of hours. When I woke again, the streaming service was asking if I wanted to continue watching. I clicked yes, leaning back again.

At my movement, Colt stirred. He pressed up until his arms were straight and twisted to squint at the TV.

"You should go back to sleep. There's been no word yet."

"We should get up and start looking."

"It's three AM."

"So?"

"So, it's dark as hell out there." I smoothed down his hair. "What luck would we have in the pitch dark?"

He sagged back onto the bed. "I need to be doing something."

"You are. You're resting so you will be strong enough to search at first light, and all day." I took the momentary respite from his hold to slide down into a lying position beside him. "I know it doesn't seem like enough."

"You're not sleeping." He couldn't figure out what to do with his hands. They twitched together, then pressed into the bed before he rubbed his face.

"Night shifter. It takes only one night, one event, to flip my clock." I resumed running my fingers through his hair. It seemed to calm him more than my words could. "Besides, I need some attention on my phone in case we get any word. I don't want to miss a text or call."

"Neither do I."

"You won't, because I'll tell you. I promise."

He rolled to his side, and I mirrored him so we faced each other. I took his fidgeting hands into my own, not surprised to find them cold. His eyes closed when I pulled his hands close to me. "I'm surprised I slept at all. I thought for sure there'd be nightmares."

"You were fighting them, holding onto me like a drowning man with a life preserver."

"I was. You were. You are." Tears shimmered in his eyes when he fixed them on me. "I don't know what I'd do if he were gone."

"I know, but he isn't. Not yet. We're going to find him."

"You can't promise that."

"No, you're right. I can't." I scooted closer. "But I won't give up on him, or you. As of now, he's not gone; he's only missing. Missing things can be found. They're found all the time. You'll take this one step at a time."

"Remington." That was all he got out before he broke down again.

I pulled him gently toward me, and he didn't make me wait for it. He held on tight again, his head buried against my shoulder as he wept. Tears burned my eyes as well. I tried to raise my eyes to the ceiling to stop them, but it didn't work like it usually did. It wasn't my turn to lose it. Colt came first. Every step of the way.

A tear slipped down my cheek anyway. I curled into his hold, no longer trying to stall my own tears. I don't know how long we lay there crying, or even who stopped first. All I knew is he settled once they did. His breathing slowed, nearing sleep again.

I rested my chin on his head while I traced my fingers up and down his back. His breathing evened out. Relieved, I let my eyes close. Maybe together we'd be able to catch forty winks. Or at least twenty each.

I hoped to God we had positive news before that happened. I settled into Colt, heavy waves of sleep tugging me down with it.

When my eyes fluttered open some time later, Colt was no longer wrapped around me. Panic momentarily gripped my heart, but his hand settled on my stomach. I released the breath I'd gulped. "Why aren't you asleep?"

"I slept. A little. I didn't mean to wake you."

"It's fine. I shouldn't have been sleeping. I'm supposed to be keeping an eye on you."

He gingerly lifted my hand in his. "You've been taking care of me. I'm not the only one who needed sleep."

I spread my fingers and watched as our hands folded together easily. "You should worry about yourself, not me."

"Ditto." He sank down next to me, his arm sliding under my shoulders. "This night is never ending."

"It will end, and we'll start again in the morning." I tilted my head toward him, meeting his halfway. Our fingers remained laced together. "He's a strong little boy. He'll be okay."

He shifted to kiss my temple. "Thank you."

My phone buzzed on the bed behind me, making us both jump. Colt sat bolt upright, staring at it. "What? What is it?"

"I don't know yet. Let me check. It's probably just Lex checking on you again." It was Lex, but she wasn't checking on us. I stared at the message on my lock screen for a long minute, the blood draining from my face. It buzzed again, and a third time, but thankfully my lock screen didn't show pictures.

"Remington. What is it? What's wrong?"

"I. Sorry. She said she has the pictures." My hand shook too much to unlock the phone.

His hand closed over mine, holding it steady. "Remington?"

"It's been months. It shouldn't be this hard." I exhaled long and hard, willing away the roiling of my stomach. My fear wasn't what was important. Brody was. "Okay. Here we go."

My phone buzzed again before I could open it. Colt jumped at the sound.

"She says she's taking the pictures to Gunner for us." I took one more deep, bracing breath and unlocked the phone. The moment the picture popped into the chat window, an involuntary shudder went through me. There were two pictures. The moderately clear picture of his face, and a blurry zoom in on the tattoo on his forearm, the one detail not released to the public.

My hand convulsed around the phone. A lump of fear lodged in my throat.

"Remi. I need to see."

I swallowed against the lump of fear in my throat and nodded. The man wasn't here in this room, it was just a picture. I turned the phone toward Colt.

The primal yell he gave startled me so badly I tumbled out of bed. I hit the ground with a grunt of pain. I'd lost my phone in the fall somewhere. When I looked up, Colt had it, glaring at the screen. "What the hell?"

He shoved the phone toward me before pulling it back to stare at it. "This is the guy that took him? Are you absolutely sure?"

"Yes. I'll never forget that face, or the tattoo." I struggled to my feet, taking in his wild eyes. Tension coursed through his body as he scrambled out of the bed. I thought for sure he was about to throw my phone. "Colton? What is it? You're scaring me."

"That's my fucking stepfather. Bryce."

Chapter 62

Colton

"I'm sorry. What?" Remi had paled when she'd seen the pictures, and now she was white as a sheet. "No, no, no. That can't be. How could it? He was in Florida."

"It's him, Remington." Fear climbed up my throat until I unleashed another yell.

Remi's icy hands settled on my chest, drawing my attention back to her. Tears shimmered in her eyes, but not one of them escaped. She brushed her fingers through my hair, over my ears. "I believe you. Let's get you dressed. I imagine Gunner will come here as fast as his cruiser will allow."

I noticed her hands trembling when she grabbed my pants from the chair in the corner. It wasn't until she reached for my hand I realized I still gripped her phone in mine. At least I hadn't thrown it across the room.

This wasn't real. It couldn't be happening. It was all a horrible nightmare. That's all it was. All it could be. It wasn't possible.

My breathing picked up as my vision blurred and became disjointed. Everything did.

Shaking hands guided me to sit, pressing my pants into my hands. "Get dressed."

If Bryce had Brody, he was in the worst danger imaginable. If Darlene had anything to do with him getting his hands on my son, I'd kill her myself. For that matter, I was going to kill him. I was going to find him and kill him with my bare hands if I had to for everything he'd put us through and kept putting us through.

"Colton."

Where would he be? He'd want to be close to exact as much pain as possible on us. He loved that part of it. It would be even better for him to watch us lose our minds over Brody being missing. To see our panic and fear. The last time he'd seen us had been in court, and we'd not shown any of the panic and fear he'd craved.

"Colton, please. Look at me. Come back from wherever you are." Her hands were still like ice when she set them on my cheeks. It was enough to startle me back to the present. To her room. In her house. Where she'd been taking care of me, injured as she was. A weak smile crossed her lips. "There you are. You need to get dressed. Lex said they're speeding down Tanner Road. They'll be here in minutes."

I realized my pants were in my hands. When had they gotten there again? Where had her phone gone?

"Pants on." She disappeared through the door.

I shoved my feet through the legs and hopped into the pants. There was no point in bothering with a shirt right then. I stormed into the living room. Remi was nowhere to be seen.

"Socks and shoes are by the couch." Remi called from the pantry. After some clattering, she emerged with a percolator, which she put on the stove. "You won't be going anywhere unless you're fully dressed. That is, if you even have somewhere to go."

Did he have somewhere to go? Bryce hadn't ever lived in this area, so where the hell would he go? There were so many places to hide in the mountains. We'd discussed that at length. How could he have known about half of them? Based on what Remi told me, as of a couple weeks ago he'd been on the move, not in this state.

"Socks. Shoes."

Right. Socks and shoes were at the couch. I had to stop staring at Remi working in the kitchen. My socks and shoes were put on, as ordered. I stalked into the kitchen, where she arranged mugs as if any of us would want to drink coffee when there was action to be taken. "Bryce never lived here. How the hell would he know enough about the area to hide?"

"Especially if he was in Florida as little as eight months ago, and Missouri two months ago. And why? That explains why he'd target Brody, especially seeing as he didn't seem to recognize me even if I sure as shit recognized him." A cup rattled, skittering across the counter before crashing on the floor. The crash startled through my spiraling brain. "Damn it."

I reached across the counter to take her hand in mine. She was still ice cold. The sudden dose of clarity brought the realization that the monster of my past was also the monster of hers. "He's really the one that attacked you?"

"Yes." Her voice was small. She stared at where the mug had crashed. I squeezed her hand, which she returned. "I should clean that up."

"I'll get it."

"No, it's fine. It's—" Tires squealed to a stop outside. "Damn. That must be them. Coffee's almost done. Why don't you meet them?"

I didn't need to be told twice. I rushed to the door to meet them. Remi took the light pollution guidelines seriously, so the front yard was pitch black beyond the squares of light from the living room window.

Two car doors slammed, and the gate creaked open. Fast footsteps raced past me into the house. I didn't care about them as much as I did about the steady, heavy footfalls coming up the walk. As soon as he was close enough, we immediately clasped each other in a hug.

"The fucking bastard," Gunner mumbled. His hold tightened even more.

"Complete shit."

We held each other for several minutes, our hold getting tighter and tighter. The horrors we'd faced flashed through my mind on a continuous loop. I knew they were for Gunner as well. How could they not be?

The clatter of a spoon broke through our tight hold. Slowly, we each pulled back. We spoke at the same time.

"We need a plan."

"I'm going to kill him."

His hand fell heavy on my shoulder. "I really don't want to arrest the best of us."

"Self-defense."

"Premeditation if you're already talking about it."

He was right, and I knew it. It didn't matter. I wouldn't let this slide. I would find my son, and he would pay. "If I need to, it's going to happen."

"Let me find him and deal with him."

Anger flared against the camaraderie we'd just shared. "Really? Justice that moves at the speed of molasses? Jails that don't keep true criminals in."

"Colt."

"Have you even received the pictures from Orlando, or are you still dealing with the red tape? I don't have *time* to wait for you to find him. He could *die*."

"Colton. I said we'd find him, and we will."

"Colton." Remi's voice eased some of the red from my vision. Her soft hand circled my forearm, dragging my gaze to hers. Her hazel eyes still shimmered with tears. "Why don't you come inside? We'll all fortify ourselves with some food and discuss our next steps."

"We'll be right in." I set my hand on hers, giving it a reassuring squeeze.

She stood on tiptoe to speak low in my ear. "Remember, he's scared, too. We all are."

I leaned down to brush my lips across hers. "Thank you. We'll be right in."

After a nod, she slipped back toward the house.

I took a step closer to my brother. "Have you told West or Prairie?"

"Not yet. Nobody wants to be woken at three-thirty in the morning to hear news like this. It's bad enough you were. It can hold until daylight."

On that, I couldn't argue with his point. I spun on my heel to head back inside. In the five minutes we'd been outside, Remi and Lexi had laid out a small spread of breakfast pastries and had bacon and eggs cooking. "What are you doing?"

Remi arched a brow. "It's called cooking."

"Remington."

"I said fortify. That requires real sustenance. And sweets, because these past few days have been utter shit and we've earned it."

Chapter 63

Remington

L exi set the last dish in the dishwasher with barely a clink. Once she shut and started it, she turned to face me. "Can you tell me?"

She didn't have to explain what she meant. I knew exactly what she wanted to know. The Mitchell twins had been squirrelly about the reasons they were so freaked out about the picture. Based on her question, I'd say Gunner hadn't told her a damn thing.

They hadn't once said aloud over the course of our breakfast that it was their stepfather. It would confuse most of the town when it came down to it, but it wasn't my place to tell. It wasn't my story, and I had to leave it up to them.

I shook my head with a regretful grimace. "Not any more than you already know."

"I know why you're freaked out. I was there with you through it all." Lex pulled me into a tight hug. "You're in a blinding panic."

There was no point in denying it. I was. It wasn't just because of what happened to me, either. It's what happened to them, and what could happen to Brody.

"Something tells me this guy didn't follow you across the country."

"Why would he? They never caught him, and I got no justice for what he did. Neither did Casey nor Cyndi, nor their families." That's what had been bothering me since his appearance. I knew it was weird then. Now that I knew the truth behind it, a solid lump had lodged itself in my throat. I prayed to whatever gods existed to keep Broy from the sort of pain and torture Colt and his family had faced. "We need to get Brody away from that man."

"Right. Then you *do* know."

I didn't like the implications of her tone, like she was insulted I knew when she didn't. I had a damn good idea of where that came from. Why she was so mad I knew about Colt and Gunner than she did on this matter. Before she'd moved to Florida and met me, Gunner had been her best friend. And now she knew he hadn't told her this. I shoved her back, narrowing my eyes. "I also know that Mitchell genes are fucking strong."

"Shut up." Lexi's face flushed at my implication. She cast a wild glance at the door, as if I'd been overheard.

"Sorry. That was uncalled for." I let my head droop. "Colt told me in confidence, and it isn't my story to tell. Just like it's my place to tell anyone here about Violet."

"It's exhausting to keep this secret."

"I know. You always pretended we were roommates when Gigi visited. I can't believe you haven't even told her." I took Lexi's hands in mine. "It's not my place. For either of you."

"Thank you."

"No problem." I pulled her back into a tight hug, even though it made my side smart. "We have bigger fish to fry, anyway. Love and support you, no matter what. You know that, right?"

"I do. You're the best."

"What are sisters for?" Shouts from the next room caused us both to turn.

"I'm so glad they're handling this like grown men." Lex's tense features didn't match the casual dry humor in her tone. "Do we need to separate them?"

"Probably would be best. I know Colt was yelling at him outside about the pace of Gunner's legal path being way too slow."

"Can't blame him for that. If it were my kid that had been kidnapped, I'd be crawling over every rock and boulder to find them."

"Exactly."

Lexi shivered next to me. "I just can't imagine. Poor Colt. I'd die."

"He is dying. That's how he's feeling, anyway." I squeezed her hand. "Let's go separate them. Colt's going to want to head to the new search grid immediately now that the sun is rising. I'm not letting him go by himself."

"Do you have everything you need to take care of yourself?" She set a hand over my surgical site. "I've got some hydrocodone if you need it."

"Makes me itch, and would put me to sleep with as little as I've gotten."

"Heard that. Let's go." Lexi pushed through the swinging door to the living room. She used her nickname for Gunner to get his attention. "Roses has to take me back to my car. I'm picking up Nova, and we'll be going to where they're setting up the new base."

Gunner's lip curled at the nickname. She'd told me once she'd made it up to annoy him, using the band name Guns N Roses to play off his name, usually just shortening it to Roses. He'd, in turn, used her last name of Oleander against her by calling her poison. "Not in the mood."

"Come on, Roses. Let's go before this brotherly love wakes the neighbors."

Colt stood rigid, jaw clenched as he stared down his brother.

Gunner urged Lexi toward the door. "In a minute, Poison."

"Just get the fuck out of here. I have to go search for my kid, not stand around with my thumb up my ass." Colt took a step toward his brother. "I won't give him even a second more with that maniac if I can help it. You know fucking why."

Lexi tugged on Gunner's arm when he went for Colt. "Let's go."

I wrapped my hand around Colt's bicep. There was no way it would pull his attention from his brother, and I didn't have the strength to hold him back. I hoped just my touch would keep Colt from attacking. "Gunner, please."

"Yeah, yeah." Gunner stormed for the door. He paused at the threshold for several long seconds. "Don't let him do anything stupid, Remi."

"I'll do my best."

Lexi blew a kiss as she closed the door.

The second the door shut, the tension drained from Colt like air from a balloon. He dropped into the chair he'd been sitting in before the argument. "It's all hurry up and wait for him. It's like every second doesn't fucking count when it does."

I held steady when he punched his own thighs in frustration. "Colton."

"Don't defend him."

"He knows every second counts." I didn't balk when he glared at me. "It's true, and you know it. You're the one that told me he's the one that dragged you out and got all three of you to safety? That tells me he's more than aware of the danger here, and how tight our timetable is. He's the sheriff. He has to follow the law."

"It's not his kid. He doesn't even fucking know what it's like."

"Doesn't he?"

"Remington."

I settled on the arm of the chair, drawing him close. Relief flooded me when the tension left his shoulders again. I brushed my fingers through his hair. "He knows what it is to love someone completely. Three someone's, actually. Maybe he can't hold a relationship, but his love for his family is absolute."

He turned his fists over, opening his hands to stare at them. "Stop making good points."

"Anything you need." I rubbed his back to let him stew in his own juices for a few minutes. He leaned against me, wrapping a hand around my calf. Satisfied he was calmer, I let out a small sigh. "You should finish getting dressed. We'll head toward the new base for the search. Lex said she'd send me a ping as soon as she gets the info. We might as well head that way since we're already awake and moving."

"Right." He might have agreed, but he didn't move.

"Colton." I let him tug me into his lap.

He held me for several minutes. "Are you feeling up to this?"

"Honestly?"

"Please."

"I'm sore as hell, but you know I can't sit here."

He released a shuddering breath. "You fell. Are you sure you're okay?"

"There's no bleeding, I'm just sore. I'm fine." I kissed his forehead. "Let's go. I'm going to be fine. Brody is what's important. You can yell at me for doing too much after we find him."

"Right." He stood, setting me gently on my feet.

When he disappeared into the bedroom, I went into the pantry to gather supplies. I grabbed protein bars, dried fruit, and a few electrolyte drink packets to mix into our water. Then I filled two water bladders, mixing the electrolytes into one of them.

When I went to lift the full bladder, Colt took it from me, and the other one too. He stashed one into the bag of snacks and put the other into the backpack with the opening for the drinking hose. I stepped forward. "I have another backpack for the other water bladder."

"You can't carry it."

"I can."

"Fine. I won't let you. You're not healed." He slung the second bag over his shoulder. "Let's get moving."

The ride to the site went by in silence. Several times I considered trying to initiate some sort of conversation, but everything that ran through my head felt forced. Besides, Colt was a million miles away. He remained distracted throughout the instructions barked through a megaphone. I had to get our assignment, the boxed lunch and dinner, and lead him up the road to the flag checkpoint where we were supposed to start our climb over the foothills.

"Are you ready to go?"

"Hm? Right. Yeah." Colt tugged the bag higher on his shoulder, staring at the foothills before us.

"What's going through your head? You're a million miles away, and not like you have been."

He lowered his gaze to meet mine. "It's bothering the shit out of me."

I waited a minute for him to continue. When he didn't, I prompted, "What is?"

"Why in hell would he stay here? He never lived her. He's never even been here. He'd know Pueblo better."

"You don't think they're here?"

"I honestly don't know."

"Your brother's convinced no one left town before they set up the roadblocks. At least not on the main roads if he didn't dump the car until the next day."

"Why do you say that?"

I gestured behind us. "Because everyone was searching, and they didn't find that car until the day after he went missing, and in the evening at that. It makes it seem like he's still here. Maybe he hid Brody, then dumped the car?"

"Yeah. But why?"

"I haven't the foggiest idea." I tugged on his hand. "Let's get moving. You can think while we walk."

He finally obliged and moved with me.

For hours we searched along the area assigned to us. Little to no conversation happened between us. He remained wrapped up in his head, distracted from everything except searching, which he did diligently.

When we stopped for a brief lunch of snacks and some of the electrolyte water, the silence continued. I didn't think it would be smart to interrupt his wandering thoughts. Maybe he'd figure out the puzzle eventually.

My voice grew hoarse, but I couldn't stop yelling for Brody. Voices echoed through the valley, calling for him as well. We had to find him somehow. I had to believe we would. Soon.

We made it to the base of the mountain before we stopped again for dinner. The sun crept ever closer to the peaks overhead once again. We were going to have to live through another night at this rate. The very idea of another night with him out there terrified me. I could only imagine what Colt was feeling.

Lexi texted to ask how we were. I told her we were going a little further before flagging down one of the off-road vehicles running through regularly.

"What do you say? Another hour? Lexi wants to know."

He stared up at the mountain. It was as if he didn't even hear me. Maybe he didn't. His brow furrowed, and he sat straighter.

"Colton?"

"He never lived here."

"I know." I didn't know where he was going with this. Or why he was stuck on this one point. "We should get moving. We have to keep looking."

"But she was born and raised here." He flew to his feet. "We need a vehicle."

"Where are we going?"

"To find my son."

Chapter 64

Colton

R emi didn't make a peep while we headed to the flag that was the checkpoint for the off-road vehicles. I didn't realize how fast I'd been walking until we stopped. Remi's breath heaved in and out of her in great gusts. "What. Are. We. Doing?" Each word punctuated by a gasp for air. She clutched her side and bent over to catch her breath. Damn, had I really been walking that fast?

"We're going to borrow the ride of whoever comes next?"

"To find your brother?" She lifted her gaze to mind. "And tell him what's going on?"

I shielded my eyes to check where the sun hung over the mountain peak. We had maybe an hour of daylight left. The last thing I wanted to do was waste time finding Gunner, explaining what I'd figured, and waiting for him to decide. One that would lead to our having to leave Brody with that monster for another night. "No."

Her hand circled my forearm. I didn't want to look at her and see her doubts and fears. I was too busy struggling with my own. My one singular focus had to be Brody. I had to get to him.

She pulled gently on my arm until I finally looked at her. The crease in her brow could have been concern or anger. I couldn't tell because she stood right in my shadow where I couldn't see her expressive eyes. "I promised him I wouldn't let you do anything stupid."

"You said you'd try. You can try, but then I'll have to leave you here."

"You're insane if you think I'm letting you do anything on your own!" Blinding panic raised her voice a couple of octaves. It was enough to drag my gaze from the road to her.

"I have to do this."

Her hand clenched my arm when the buzz of a motor sounded over the hills, getting louder each second. "Let me text them where we're going. Then we can go."

"Fine." I flagged down the approaching four-seater. Thankfully, Aspen was inside. That would make it easier to get the vehicle. "I need your ride. You can wait here for the next one."

Aspen's brow furrowed. "I can take you where you need to go."

"Just give me the damn ride."

"Aspen." Remi stepped in front of me to stop my charge. "Please. It's important."

I braced my hand on the frame of the vehicle. "I don't have time to argue. Get the fuck out."

"Okay, okay." Aspen hopped out, stepping aside. "Your brother's going to ask."

I glanced at him, glaring hard. "Tell my brother to use his fucking brain and he'll know where I'm going."

Remi rushed to the passenger side when I revved the engine. She called an apology to Aspen as she climbed in. The second her ass hit the seat, I took off. She yelped and spun in her seat to look behind us. "Colt! Damn it. That was my phone. How am I supposed to tell them where we are now?"

I tore over the hills as fast as the vehicle would take me. Remi scrambled for a helmet when we launched over a hill. Several checkpoints went by in a blur on our journey north. She braced one hand against the dash, the other gripping her side. When we passed the final checkpoint, I kept heading north.

"Where are we going?" Remi's shout barely made it over the wind and the engine. "And I need your phone to tell Lexi where we're going."

"Darlene grew up on a small plot of land west of the creek at the base of the mountain. Before the divorce, Dad used to joke she was from the wrong side of the creek. No electricity, no running water. It was pretty much a shithole."

"Can we slow down? These bumps are killing me."

I slowed the ATV the slightest bit. Hurting her in any way wasn't intentional. I actually hated that I had. But I had to get to that cabin. I had to get to Brody. "For years her family just built onto an old trapper's cabin."

"Wouldn't your brother have already thought of this place if that's where Darlene grew up? Maybe he had already checked in when he saw the picture. We could ask him." Desperation kept her pitch high. Her hand curled around the roll bar when we flew over another bump. She paled a bit, but didn't ask me to slow down again.

"Darlene's family moved out when her dad got a job in Old Town that paid well enough for them to move. She was a teenager. All she talked about was how much she hated the place."

"How would he know about it? If she hated it so much?"

"She talked about it all the fucking time. Talking about the horrible home she grew up in. The irony was completely lost on her."

"So?"

"She hated even more that her dad kept it and went back to it when he got old. We never met him before the divorce, and he was dead by the time we came back. She never forgot where it was. Get her drunk or high and she'd tell you."

"Colton." She jerked forward at my sudden stop. Her body froze now that the vehicle was at a stop. When she spoke again, her voice shook. "He was armed."

"With a knife." I climbed out of the vehicle, facing the woods to the west. They were already dark in the low light of sunset.

She climbed out with a few grunts and walked slowly around the vehicle. It took her a minute, but she stopped in front of me. She set her hand on my chest. "Wait."

"Remington. I need to."

"Give me your phone."

"I don't have it." I'd noticed hours ago, but had said nothing because she had hers. With everything that had happened the night before and the rush we were in to get out searching, I'd left it on the charger in her living room.

The color drained from her face. "My phone flew out of my hand when you took off. Are you saying we're out here, potentially with a murdering maniac, with no way to contact anyone? At all?"

"Stay here by the ATV."

"Oh, no. You are *not* going in there by yourself." She gestured wildly to the woods on the other side of the creek.

"It's fine. I'll be fine."

"No." She braced her hands against me when I took a couple of steps. Her feet slid along the grass when her strength gave out. "Your righteous anger isn't enough for this, Colt. Please, please. Think about this."

I stared over her head into the dark woods on the other side of the creek. They swayed in the light breeze that seemed to always carry through the valley.

"Please. Listen to me for a minute."

"No. I have to do this." I pulled her closer with her elbows. "Stay here."

"Not on your life."

"If he's in there and I walk away, I'll never forgive myself."

"Colt."

"You're not changing my mind."

Tears sparkled in her eyes, but her jaw set in a stubborn line. "What good are you to Brody dead?"

"Take the ATV. Go back. Stop getting in my way."

"No."

"I have to do this."

"Have you thought about *why* he did this?" Her hands rested on my chest with the lightest pressure. She wasn't trying to stop me physically. It was her words that were meant for that. "Why would he take your son? He doesn't know him. You and your siblings are what he knows. You're what landed him in prison. Your medical records. Your testimony."

My heart stuttered to a stop. My throat went dry.

"Think about it."

"You're saying it's me he wants."

"Yes."

"Good. Then let's give him what he wants."

Chapter 65

Remington

This was a horrible, no-good, very bad, absolutely terrible idea. We were on a high-speed collision course with no way out. Not one I could see. It wasn't like I could drag Colt along and force him back to base camp. I didn't have the strength to do that in good health, and the rough trip through the valley had taken its toll on my injury.

Colt practically vibrated with nervous energy. It was shocking he hadn't already gone ahead and left me behind. It was also remarkable that he hadn't passed out from the rush of adrenaline spiking his blood pressure.

I had to bring him back into focus before he went off half-cocked any more than he already had. "What's the plan?"

He finally dragged his attention back to me. "Plan?"

"You aren't planning on going in there blind, are you? Do you even know where the place is? Or do you just know the general area? Do you know what the place looks like? If it's even still standing?"

"I have a good idea of where it is."

That wasn't reassuring in the least. "And?"

"I don't know if it's still standing, alright? I've never gone there."

Still not making me feel any better. "Okay. What are we facing? I'm assuming there are places to hide from view since the trees look pretty dense out there. What are you planning to do? Are you just going to burst in and pray he doesn't have a gun?"

"Well, yeah." The nervous, angry energy ebbed under my questions. Maybe I was finally getting through to him. Maybe he'd even back off the whole idea. "You were stabbed. He has a knife."

"That doesn't mean he doesn't have a gun!"

"Then why didn't he use it?"

"Because he was smart enough not to use it near a crowd of fairgoers."

"I'm not going back for help. If he's in there, I just can't, Remi."

"Even though it would be the smartest thing we could do right now?"

He brushed me aside and strode toward the creek. I had to run to keep up with his long strides, and it wasn't like my legs were short. I scrambled to get ahead of him, setting my hands on his chest again. Thankfully, it made him stop. "Remington."

A lump formed in my throat at the desperate plea in his tone. Nothing I said was going to change his mind, and that terrified me. "Please. I have a bad feeling about this."

"Then stay here."

"Fuck that!"

That stunned him enough to blink down at me.

"I still say we need a plan. A real one."

"We'll figure it out as we go."

"No." I poked him in the chest with my finger. "Listen to me, goddamn it."

His jaw ticked, but he said nothing else.

"I'm moderately smaller than you, seeing as you and Gunner are giants. When we get there, maybe I should try to see inside, if there's a good way to do that?"

"I need to get to Brody." He pushed against me again.

"Brody needs you not to get yourself killed." My voice cracked under the strain of holding him back. "Colton. Think about Brody. What would he do if he lost you?"

His eye twitched, and he looked off into the woods.

"I'll go with you. We'll go together, but slowly. That way we can see the situation before he sees us. God willing, and the creek don't rise." Not to mention, going slower gave us a better chance of Gunner showing up. If Gunner remembered what Colt did. Aspen knew what direction we were heading. Hopefully, it would spark his memory.

"Fine. Now stop blocking me."

Despite his supposed agreement, he wasn't slow all the way down the slope to the creek. It was dry enough that we hopped across with no problem. I grabbed his hand when we got into the woods. "Hold on."

"Remi, stop!"

"Shush. Listen. The ATV wasn't exactly quiet, especially with you racing at top speed. What if he already knows we're here? Hell, he might be watching us instead of the other way around." My gut clenched at the idea. This was stupid, stupid, stupid.

"I know. I'm hoping he does. If you're right, and he doesn't even care about Brody, then you can get him while I deal with the asshole."

"I don't like that plan any better. None of these plans are any good. This is a terrible idea all around."

"*Remi.* Either shut up and help me, or go back to the ATV and get help. I'm not leaving these woods without Brody."

Everything about this was horrible, but I couldn't live with myself if I let him go in there by himself. "Shutting up."

The deeper into the woods we got, the slower we moved. Every crack of a branch or rustle of a bush made my stomach twist tighter. Every shadowy place had the potential of having this nightmare come to life hiding within.

It was the worst version of a nightmare I'd ever seen. Because it was real.

I clung to Colt's shirt and let him lead the way. I didn't believe he knew where he was going, even though he moved as if he did. He'd stop sometimes for several minutes. After he'd looked around and mumbled to himself, we'd go again.

"Do you know where it is?" I whispered, desperately hoping nobody was listening. The loud crack of a branch up in the trees made me jump with a squeak. There was a huge rustle as a large limb went through the trees, hitting the ground with a thump. "What was that?"

Colt squeezed my hand, removing it from his shirt. "The wind is picking up. Old branches break off."

I hadn't really thought that man was in a tree pushing branches down to smash us. Not really. My heart rate refused to slow. "You didn't answer. Do you know where it is?"

"I'm pretty sure we're close. We should get there before it gets completely dark."

"That's reassuring." He moved again before I could say anything else. At this point, there was no going back. I'd never find my way out of these woods without help now, not with how dark it was already. For that matter, how was anyone going to find us?

I turned back the way I thought we'd come, seeing no sign of a path or clear direction of where to go. My lungs tightened, the air thinned until I felt lightheaded. I reached for Colt, but my hand swiped empty air. When I spun around, he was gone.

"Fuck. Fuck. Fuck. Colt? Where are you?" The wind rustling through the branches overhead, and the creak of trees swaying was louder than my whisper. Had he even heard me? I didn't dare yell.

I was completely turned around now. Which way had we been going? I spun in a circle, getting dizzy with a blooming headache. I had to latch onto something before I lost my mind.

We'd been going mostly uphill; I knew that much. If I went against gravity, maybe I'd find him. Step by step, I crept through the trees, occasionally hissing Colt's name. He couldn't have gotten that far ahead of me. Then again, I'd wasted time figuring out which way to head, and was moving at a snail's pace now.

When I rounded a large tree trunk, a spark of light caught my eye. I blinked a few times to be sure I wasn't imagining it.

No. Not my imagination. A faint flicker of light lay somewhere ahead of me. I moved closer, scanning the darkness around me for any sign of Colt or his stepfather.

"Colt?"

A hand clamped over me. Fear seized me. I screamed into the hand, fighting against the man pinning me tight against him. I kicked and scratched anything I could reach.

"Remington. It's me."

I stilled, my nails still digging into his arm.

"I was trying to keep you quiet, but you just made a racket. Hopefully, he didn't hear it over the wind." He withdrew his hand from my mouth. "It's dead ahead."

"If you want to keep me quiet, don't pounce on me like that. I thought you were him." I crouched beside him, willing my eyes to adjust better to the darkness. A house of sorts grew out of the darkness. It was a mishmash of a building, rooms added as necessary with no rhyme or reason, much like Cole had said.

Moreso, some rooms had collapsed with time and weather. The light I'd seen flickered against a wall visible between two misaligned boards. The whole thing looked like it would collapse if the wind blew the right way.

"I've got a bad feeling about this."

Chapter 66

Colton

The surrounding woods were quiet, save for the wind making the trees sway above us. Remi's nails dug into my knee. I could feel her trembling. Now that my eyes had adjusted to the dark, I noted the beads of sweat on her forehead. She was terrified.

I put my hand on top of hers, hoping to calm her. If she freaked out, we'd have trouble for sure. I just wanted to go take a peek and see what we were up against. "Stay here. I'll be back in a few minutes."

"What? No." She pulled on my hand with surprising strength. "Are you nuts?"

"Stop asking me that."

"That place looks like it could fall in if you blew on it. He's probably not in there. The light is a trick to draw us out."

"We won't know that until we look, will we?" Her constant objections were driving me up a wall. I didn't have time to think and plan like she wanted. I had to get my son. He was probably right there, and she was keeping me from him. If only she'd stayed at the ATV, I might be done with this whole thing already.

"Then let me go." She said it with confidence, but her hand still shook.

"Not a chance." It was one thing to risk my neck.

"I've got at least a fifty-pound advantage over you." She half rose. "Should we go around back? He'll probably keep an eye on the front."

"Good idea." I pulled on her hand, leading her through the woods. With the wind blowing like it was, I wasn't as careful as I'd been on our way here. She kept slowing me down, pulling us down in a panic every few seconds. How did she expect to check the place out if she was too scared to walk through the woods?

With the constant pausing, it took us almost ten minutes to get around back. It seemed silly and foolish at this point. Maybe I was wrong about the whole thing.

Remi's features hardened as she crept toward the edge of the woods where she'd cross into the clearing. We hadn't even discussed what we were going to do, and she was heading out.

I grabbed her ankle right before she put a hand out. "I thought you wanted a plan. Now you're going off half-cocked?"

"Yeah, well, I'm taking a lesson from your rulebook." She kicked off my hand, crawling into the clearing before I could grab her again.

It was one thing when I was the one taking the chances. This wasn't even her fight. Or maybe it was. Bryce had hurt her, too. Destroyed her own life in his own way.

My heart rate kicked up as Remi moved across the clearing toward the house. Sweat broke across my forehead. I wanted to call her back. She needed protected as much as Brody. How stupid could I have been?

I moved to the edge of the woods so I could run out at the first sign of danger. My vision blurred when she set her foot on the floor of a half-fallen room.

She edged forward so slowly; I had to suppress the urge to yell at her to move faster so she could get out of there. If she insisted on doing this, she needed to get in and out so she'd be out of danger. I'd get Brody. She didn't need to risk herself anymore. I never should've let her do it in the first place. I should have left her with Aspen.

Her leg inched forward, and she balanced on the ball of her foot. Her upper body moved back and forth as if she were trying to find a safe path.

She finally took another step, and in the next thirty seconds slid her body into a small opening between some boards. That was it. She was gone from view. Now I had no clue what was going on. Now I had two people in danger, two people near him.

I pressed my hand into the rough trunk of the pine next to me, trying desperately to bring the feeling back to my hands. If anything happened, I had to be ready to run. If I weren't afraid it would make too much noise, I would have jogged in place to get my blood flowing.

Movement near where Remi had disappeared sent a gust of relief from my lungs. She crept back out as slowly as she'd entered. After a few steps, she looked into the woods where I was. She gave a thumbs-up. With her next step, a loud crack sounded. Time stopped, then moved in slow motion. Her eyes widened as her feet dropped, then her legs, then her body. Her scream echoed through the woods until everything went silent. Including my own heart.

My heartbeat came roaring back with a vengeance, pounding in my chest, my neck, my ears, my head. Fuck, fuck, fuck. Was she okay?

A large figure burst out of the front door. He turned his head this way and that, peering into the woods. He looked right at me, but didn't make any moves. His eyes probably hadn't adjusted yet. I crouched to be out of sight when his vision did return.

How was I going to get to Remi? Or Brody? Even from where I was, I could see the glint of steel in his hand. The question was, was it a knife? Or a gun?

Bryce prowled around the clearing, continuing to scan the tree line as he went. He paused when he got to where Remi had gained access to the house. The spot where she'd fallen through drew his attention. *Fuck.*

He stopped on the edge of the floor, peering down. "That you, Colton?"

I had no idea if she was okay, and if she'd be able to hide if she was. A moment later, it didn't matter. He clicked on a flashlight and shone it into the hole in the floor.

A cold chuckle that immediately brought back a flood of memories shivered along my spine. My breath caught, and I had to close my eyes against the flood of torment. I couldn't help them if I crashed out now.

"Well, well. What do we have here? What are you doing out in the woods, girly?"

My eyes snapped open. The flashlight caught on the weapon in his hand.

A gun.

And he was pointing it into the hole.

Red flashed in my vision. Heat raced through my body. I took off without thinking, charging right for Bryce. The weapon swung toward me, and I dove, catching him around the waist and tackling him to the ground. The gun went off. Remi screamed again.

The impact of the landing rolled me right over Bryce. I kept the momentum and rolled back onto my feet.

Bryce's cold chuckle cut through the darkness. His flashlight had rolled away, lending no help in the darkness as it shone into the woods. "Somebody learned to fight better."

"Necessity taught me. I swore you'd never do this again."

The solid thump of a footstep on a board sent another wave of panic through me. He was going for Remi, or maybe Brody. His cold voice cut through the night. "I got stuck in prison for ten years because of you brats."

"You almost killed me. And considering what you did to Prairie, the death penalty wouldn't have been enough." I headed back toward the house, hoping my eyes readjusted quickly.

Another footstep.

Silence.

I took several more steps toward the light I still saw shimmering in the house.

Remi's shaking voice barely made it out of the hole in the floor. "Please. Don't. Please."

If Remi distracted him, I could get Brody out. How could I leave her to fend him off when she didn't even want to be here? I'd dragged her into this mess kicking and screaming.

"Colt! Get Brody! *Go now.*" Remi's yell cut off in a strangled gasp.

I raced around to the front of the house. When I burst through the door, I searched around for him. A small form curled on the floor under a table. "Brody."

Brody whimpered when I touched him. "No."

"Brody, it's me." I picked him up, rushing toward the door. If I could hide him in the woods, maybe I could come back for Remi.

The crash of wood stopped me in my tracks. "I wouldn't if I were you."

I turned slowly to find him dragging Remi out of a trapdoor. Her face was red, eyes bloodshot as she grasped at the arm that held her in a chokehold. His other hand had the gun pointed right at her head.

"Put the boy back."

"Not a fucking chance." I pulled Brody tighter to me. He trembled in my arms. Weak little whimpers slipped through his cracked lips. I looked back at Remi.

She had both hands on his arm, trying to pull it from her neck. Her lips were turning blue. Her mouth moved silently for a minute before she rasped, "Go."

"Do you think I'm kidding?" He pointed the gun downward and fired. Remi couldn't scream, but her face contorted in pain. Her hands left his arm. I couldn't see where they'd gone because all of my attention was on Bryce.

"Let them go." My voice cracked at the thought of leaving Brody. I had to make sure he was safe, that Remi was safe. In the end, that's what mattered. I was a full-grown man, not the child he'd nearly killed anymore. If I could get them to safety, I knew I'd be able to figure a way out. "They've got nothing to do with this. It's me you want. It would be a bonus if Gunner were here, I bet. You'll have to settle for me, though."

His grip on Remi had loosened enough that her lips were no longer blue. Her face was pale; her eyes glassy. Worry blossomed in my chest. Would she be able to get him out?

"Remington." Calling her name brought her focus to me. "You take him home."

Tears shimmered in her eyes. She shook her head weakly. I didn't know why she was saying no, but I couldn't think of any other way. This wasn't her battle to fight.

"Do we have a deal, Bryce? Let them go." I put my full attention on my stepfather. "You can have me. Isn't that what you came for?"

"It's tempting." He let Remi go, and she collapsed to the floor. "But how will the boy go anywhere without her?"

I finally pulled my gaze from him to Remi, and the red spreading across the surrounding floorboards. "Remington?"

Chapter 67

Remington

There was way too much blood. I might be swimming in it. Was I? No. I needed to focus.

It was way too much blood. My whole body grew weaker with each second. Every ounce of blood that seeped, or gushed, out was like one more second further from this life. I'd put pressure on the wound immediately, but it made no difference. What I needed was a tourniquet.

If it wasn't too late even for that.

The floorboards shook with Colt's running steps. He dropped to the floor in front of me. The knees of his jeans soaked up my blood. Brody lay curled in his arms. "Remington. Remington, look at me. Please."

I studied Brody's dry, cracked lips. The dark circles under his eyes. The shallow breathing. He looked so tiny compared to two days ago. "He's dehydrated. Get him to safety."

"You're going to take him. You can. You will." Colt's voice was firm even as my living nightmare chuckled above us. "What do you need?"

"I'm getting too weak to hold any pressure." My vision wavered as he set Brody down next to me. Pain shot through me when Colt pressed both of his hands firmly against mine. The pitiful whimper that broke free was the best I could do, even though my brain screamed at the pain of it. "Take him."

"What do you need?" Colt clipped his words. "Tell me. Remington!"

"Tourniquet." The world spun and tilted on its axis. "Might be too late."

"No. It's not. You're getting out of here. This is my fault. All my fault. You have to get out of here."

"Brody. He needs you."

He pressed his lips to my forehead. "Tourniquet. What can I use?"

My skin felt clammy. Cold. My heartbeat fluttered in my chest. "Oh. There it is."

"Remington?"

"Hypovolemic. Shock." I was wondering when it would hit. The pressure of Colt's hand disappeared, and a rush of blood welled under my hands.

"This is fun, watching you try to save them both. What if I shot him, too? Who would you choose?" Bryce's voice moved as he strolled around the room casually.

"He's in severe dehydration." My voice didn't carry the ferocity roaring through my brain. Wait. Where was I going with that? Lights flickered in my vision. "Oh, dear."

Fabric tore right by my ear. The room bounced around and then tipped over. No, wait. That was me that fell over. I closed my eyes, letting out a shaky breath. Sleep. I could sleep.

It sounded so nice, sleep. My limbs were jelly anyway. It wouldn't hurt.

Pain ripped me from the darkness. Colt leaned over me, tugging on something. His knee pressed into the wound while he tied his torn shirt around my leg along with a stick. He started twisting the stick. I whimpered as each twist brought it tighter and tighter.

Then, I couldn't feel my leg anymore. Well, at least it didn't hurt.

"Remington." Colt's fingers brushed along my cheek.

I tried to say hi, but a strange noise broke free instead.

"Please. Talk to me."

"Shock. Pretty lights." I tried to wrap my brain around a coherent thought. Something was going on. Something was wrong.

Bryce walked past my narrow field of vision. Oh, right. We were going to die.

"Is the tourniquet tight enough?" Colt's voice drew me back to him.

"Yup." The 'p' popped loudly in the room.

"Let's get you up. You have to get Brody out of here."

I snorted. That wouldn't happen. I couldn't walk, much less carry a six-year-old through unfamiliar woods. "You funny."

"I'm not trying to be. Look at me." His icy blue eyes swam into focus. They shimmered in the candlelight as droplets of flickering flame slipped down his cheeks. He clutched my hand to his chest. "Please. You can't do this."

"I'm in shock. Lost too much blood. Can't feel my leg." Look at me. Three whole sentences. Maybe my brain would work again. I'd probably lose my leg if I didn't lose my life. Cool.

"Okay, that's enough theatrics. I told you they weren't going anywhere. Now, Colt. You can pick one. Which will it be? Of course, neither of them will get very far in their condition, now will they?" Bryce stopped his pacing. "Make your choice."

"Go to hell." Colt cupped my cheeks. "Remington."

"It's too late."

"As soon as you can, get him out of here."

"Colton. Don't be stupid."

"I love you, Remington. I'm sorry I didn't say it sooner." He kissed my forehead before pulling Brody close. Colt glared at Bryce over Brody's head before he leaned in to whisper in his son's ear. When he'd finished, he settled Brody against my side. "I'm not playing your games, Bryce. They've got nothing to do with this."

Bryce's lips twisted into a sinister smile as he raised his gun, pointing it in our direction.

Colt moved away, circling away from us, his focus on his stepfather. Bryce kept the gun trained on Brody and me. I couldn't tell which of us would take the hit. "You move, and I fire."

Cole stopped where he was, about ninety degrees from Brody and me. It was a split-second. A moment when his eyes flicked toward us, and that was it. He took off toward Bryce. The gun fired. Colt tackled Bryce, and they were tussling. The gun skidded across the floor.

I'd felt no fresh pain from the discharge. Panicked, I looked over Brody and saw no sign of injury on him. I turned back to the fight raging just feet from us. Colt scrambled for the bun, but Bryce pulled him back.

A punch landed on Colt's nose, and blood spurted from the injury. Colt retaliated with a brutal punch to Bryce's eye that stunned him enough for Colt to run for the gun again. All too quickly, Bryce recovered enough to tackle Colt. They broke through the wall, rolling over and over in the grass.

The crack of gunfire echoed through the woods. The rolling battle of men slowed, then came to a stop.

I tried to move, to force myself to stand, but my limbs were too weak. "Colton? *Colton.*"

Gunner's voice echoed mine. "*Colton.*"

Chapter 68

Colton

A high-pitched ringing filled my ears. The decrepit cabin swam in and out of focus. I tried to clear the iron taste from my mouth, but it was hopeless. Blood trickled down the back of my throat. My nose throbbed with my heartbeat. I couldn't tell if there was any movement in the house. Were they okay? I thought I heard something over the ringing in my ears, but it sounded so far away.

The gun had fired awfully close.

Too close.

Shit. Had it hit me?

I shoved Bryce. He didn't fight back. He lay limp like a deadweight. With a great heave, I pushed him off of me. He flopped back on the ground, eyes wide open to the sky.

A dark, round spot under his chin had a little blood trickling from it. A few inches the other way, and that would have been me.

Dead.

The bastard was dead.

I couldn't be happy about it now. I had to see if Brody was okay. And Remi. Was she alive? Fuck. "*Remington.*"

I scrambled to my feet. Before I got two steps, something rammed into me. I fought against them, shoving them off and flying to my feet in a defensive stance. Gunner held up his hands in surrender. His lips moved as though he was speaking, but the high-pitched whine kept me from hearing a word.

I tugged on my ears, then rubbed my finger in one of them. Nothing.

I turned from Gunner to the house. My heart stopped when I saw Brody and Remi lying on the floor so still. She was paler than pale. His sweet little face was mottled, his hands almost blue. I rushed through the hole Bryce and I had made in the wall to their side.

Remi's eyes fluttered open. Her lips moved as she said something. I shook my head, pointing to my ears. I tried to clear away the ringing again, even hitting the damn things.

"Dead." Gunner's voice finally won over the ringing in my left ear.

"Remington." I pulled her and Brody close. "We have to get them help. She's lost a lot of blood. So much blood. Too much blood. God, Remington. I'm so sorry."

"Shhh. Shh." She tapped her fingers against my cheek.

"And Brody, he hasn't woken up at all. They need help."

"I've radioed for help. Chopper will be here in ten. We'll get Remi and Brody to the hospital as soon as it gets here." Gunner crouched beside me. "This was fucking stupid, Colt."

"Colton." Remi's voice had faded to barely a whisper. I almost didn't hear it. She blinked slowly at me. Brody curled against her, and she curled against me. "I love you, too. But he's right. This was stupid."

"I know it was." I kissed her forehead. Her eyes slipped closed then, and stayed that way. My heart seized. "They need to get here faster."

"They're coming."

"The second she fell through the floor, I realized how stupid it was. Until then, I only cared about getting Brody back. Then I realized it would kill me to lose her, too."

Gunner clapped his hand on my shoulder. He cleared his throat, sniffling. "We all could have lost you, too. If that gun had fired a few inches the other way, it could've been you. You were so fucking lucky."

"I know." The lump in my throat made it tough to swallow. As much as I'd threatened it. As much as I'd wished it. The reality was, I'd killed a man. A horrible, evil man, but I'd killed him. Dead. "I killed him, Gunner."

If I hadn't been holding so tight to Remi and Brody, my hands would be shaking. Gunner hung his head. "Yes, you did. It's not an easy thing to live with."

The thumping beat of a helicopter grew louder. Gunner stood and fired a flare into the air. From there, it was a blur of blinding lights and movement. They took Remi and Brody far too soon. I wasn't ready to let them go and trust someone else to care for them. I tried to go with them, but there wasn't room with both of them.

My eyes remained glued to the basket stretcher being lifted to the chopper. They'd fit both Remi and Brody in it at the same time. Then, they were in the helicopter, and it was gone. Back south toward the hospital.

When the chopper disappeared from view, a new sound penetrated the clearing. The rumble of ATVs, and I thought I heard the puttering rumble and jarring chatter of chainsaws hitting trees. The sharp crack of multiple trees falling followed. "Chainsaws?"

"You didn't think I came alone, did you? That's a team clearing a path for us. We'll leave by off-road so we can get you to your son and Remi."

"Thanks. The conservation committee is going to make you plant a ton of trees after this."

"Worth it. I think I'll have them level this shithole while they're here. Lowder is in that group. He's always happy to destroy things."

I didn't care if they tore it down, burned it down, or whatever. As long as I never had to think about or look at this damn place again. My gaze returned to the clearing where Bryce's body still lay. "And him?"

"He'll go to the morgue, then I'll send him to Pueblo for burial. I don't want his body on these lands. This is our place." Gunner's friendship with Oakes on the res was coming through. I didn't blame him, though. Much like the house, I wanted nothing to do with that evil man ever again.

The headlights of several ATVs bobbed into view. One by one, trees closer to us fell out into the woods. The path was wide enough for two ATVs. The first vehicle that came into the clearing made a jarring stop. Four figures poured from the vehicle and raced toward us.

Without hesitation, our entire family came together in a powerful hug. When Prairie sobbed into my shoulder, I broke right along with her. We clung to each other for I don't know how long. When the tears finally slowed, Dad and Paige fussed over me, then Gunner, and then me again. Prairie leaned against Gunner, wiping at her tears.

"It's over, Prairie." Gunner hugged her against him. "The bastard is gone."

She nodded, her eyes closing as she leaned into him.

"I need to go." I hated to leave them with everything so fresh. With so much for us to talk about. There was something more important. Two something's. "Brody. Remi."

"They need you. We won't be far behind, son." Dad clasped my cheeks, tears in his eyes as he took me in. He clapped the back of my neck and pulled me into another tight hug. "Once they're okay, I hope this finally brings you peace."

"Thanks, Dad. I'll see you at the hospital." I ran to a vehicle that didn't have the sheriff's logo on it and revved the engine before heading back down the mountain. The trip seemed to take forever, but I finally saw the lights of the hospital on the other side of New Town. I spurred the engine faster, and with flatter ground I fairly flew the rest of the way.

At the ER, Keely came to get me, taking me directly to Brody's bay. I leaned down to kiss his head, eyeing the IV in his arm. "Is he going to be okay?"

"He should be. We're rapidly infusing him with fluids and electrolytes to get him back to normal levels. After that, it's a matter of observation." She frowned and touched right above my nose. "You need medical attention, too."

"Later."

"Fine. But I'm holding you to that."

"Are there signs of any other..." The word caught in my throat. My stomach roiled even thinking about it. What little food I had in my stomach threatened to reappear. I ran my finger along his forehead. "Any other trauma?"

"There are some bruises on his face and a laceration on his head. As soon as he's more stable, he'll be scanned to check for broken bones." She studied me. "That isn't the trauma you meant, is it?"

"It was a vile, sick man that took him."

"I'll let the doctor know, and we'll get the exam done."

"Thank you." I bent down and pressed my forehead to his. "My strong boy. I'm so glad you're going to be okay."

For several minutes I remained there, just reveling in having him back. Safe. Well, he'd be safe soon.

Keely cleared her throat. "I sent a note to the doctor. He's on his way. Do you want to go see Remi while that exam is done?"

"Yes." I kissed Brody's forehead. "I'll be right back, buddy. I'm going to check on Remi."

Keely offered me a weak smile when I headed toward her. "Kids are remarkably resilient. He'll bounce back quickly, I think."

"What about Remington?"

"Her case is a lot more serious. She lost a lot of blood. The tourniquet likely saved her life but may have put her leg at risk." Keely grabbed me when I swayed. "Easy. Let's sit you down."

"No. No. I have to see her. Just give me a minute." I braced my arm against the wall.

"Of course."

"I might have cost her a leg?"

"You saved her life. Focus on that."

Chapter 69

Remington

A warm hand held mine. Gentle murmuring bounced through my head without finding form. Where was I? My addled brain struggled to remember what had happened. I couldn't remember what the last thing I remembered was.

There was something I needed to do. Or something wrong. Who was talking? What were they saying?

A knock on the door brought my brain into focus.

"She isn't awake yet?" Colt's voice was strained, scratchy. Had he slept at all? Colt. Brody. I wanted to scream and ask what had happened, but my body hadn't caught up with my brain yet. Then, he eased my mind without having to ask. "Brody was hoping to visit."

Thank goodness Brody was alright. My last memories were becoming clearer, and Brody had been unconscious and dehydrated.

"Come on in." Lex's voice was soft. She shouldn't still be here. There were things she needed to take care of. "Hey there, Brody. Come on over here. I know Remi would love to see you if she woke up."

"Can I touch her?" Brody's small voice was close to my side now.

"Go right on ahead. Maybe it will help her come back to us, knowing that you're okay." Lexi squeezed my arm. "She's doing so much better now. Nice and strong. As for you, young man. I'm surprised you're still here. I thought they'd discharge you today."

"They wanted another night of observation. I don't mind at all. I'd like to know he's doing well. Although it's been hard to be in two places at once." Colt remained on my left. His fingers trailed along my hairline.

"She'd understand. Brody is your priority."

"She is too." His hand settled on the top of my head. "I know she'd understand, but I feel like I should be here, too. I'm the reason she's here. Brody, don't climb into the bed."

Sure enough, the small hand that gripped mine had pulled on it. The tug of my blanket showed me he'd half succeeded. I wanted to tell them it was fine, that I liked having him there. My eyes and voice were really taking too long to obey my commands.

Lexi's warm laugh eased my worry that they'd deny Brody the chance. I was just so glad he was okay. It was nice to have him nearby. "It's fine if he goes up. Just be careful. I'm sure her right side is still tender, and we don't want to jostle her leg too badly."

Brody climbed up the bed until he tucked into my shoulder. He released a happy sigh. "Wake up, Remi."

My voice still wouldn't allow me to respond. I wondered if I was making any muscle movements at all. If I were, they'd surely comment on it.

I took a mental inventory of my injuries and pain. The spot on my side where I'd been stabbed at the fair had reduced to a dull ache, even with Brody curled against it. His small hand patted my sternum. He was singing so low I wasn't sure the others heard him over their conversation. It was the same two words on repeat in a singsong whisper. "Wake up. Wake up. Wake up."

Weirdly, my left leg hurt. A lot. That didn't seem possible. Between the blood loss and the tourniquet, I couldn't imagine my leg had made it. Which meant that I was likely experiencing phantom pain.

Even though I knew it in my mind, I swore I could still feel the ache throbbing in the ankle I'd twisted or sprained falling through the floor. My thigh burned as if it were on fire. It was probably right where they'd had to make the incision to cut it off. Before I'd lost consciousness, I'd known my leg was most likely gone, if I lived at all.

At least I'd lived.

Finally, after what seemed like hours, my arm responded to my order to move. Slower than molasses uphill in January, it crossed over to set my hand on Brody's.

"She moved. Remington?" Colt leaned close enough to touch his forehead to mine. Instantly, my body relaxed, remembering how it felt with him close. "Are you awake?"

I managed a hum of assent. My eyes fluttered open to find him right where I thought he'd be. His eyes filled with so much emotion, my brain didn't have the energy to pick them apart and dissect them. I attempted to smile, and it felt shaky. At least I hoped it was a smile instead of a grimace. "Hey."

"Thank goodness." Lexi squeezed my leg. "You've been out for three days. Dr. Young was concerned about an infection hiding in there. They took a blood culture yesterday."

I ignored them both to turn my attention to the young boy whose hand I held. He appeared fully recovered, and full of life again. "Hi, Brody."

"Hi!" Brody pushed his hand against his dad's cheek to move him out of the way. He wrapped his arms around my neck in a brutally tight hug. I couldn't complain. I was too happy to see him doing so well. "Daddy was so worried, he's been crying lots. I thought boys weren't supposed to cry."

Everyone in the room laughed at that. I ruffled Brody's hair. "Gender norms are such a lie. It's fine if boys cry, and it makes them better people to show their emotions. And girls can play sports and hunt, all those things that are supposed to be boy things."

"That's good, 'cuz he's been crying *so* much. Me too." He settled back in against my side. "Are you gonna be all better now?"

"It would seem so. I think we'll both have some things to adjust to, though." I stared at the ceiling as I took another mental inventory now that I was fully awake. Those phantom pains still plagued me. "It's so strange. I mean, I'd heard of it, but knowing these things mentally differs from experiencing them in the flesh."

"What's strange?" Colt pulled my hand against his chest. He held on for dear life, running his other hand along my arm. He probably didn't realize how tightly he was holding on. I didn't care. It was nice to feel something again.

"My leg. I can still feel it." At his furrowed brow, I turned to Lexi. "It's the strangest thing. I swear I can still feel the ankle I sprained when I fell through the floor. I didn't know phantom limbs could do that."

"Sweetie." Lexi smiled softly. "Your leg is still there."

"What?" I tried hard to piece together my last memories of being in that house. I could see Colt tightening the tourniquet until I couldn't feel my leg. Brody's small body, made even smaller by the dehydration, curled into mine. The sheer amount of blood I'd lost. "I thought for sure it was gone."

Colt lowered my hand to my leg and pressed it down for me. "It's right there. They saved it. They said it was close, but they got it. I'm so glad. I'd hate to think that I was the reason you lost—"

"Hey. Hey." I clasped his hand as hard as he'd held mine minutes ago. "None of that."

"It's because of me."

"No. You weren't the reason. Even if I had lost it. He was." Tears filled my eyes until he was nothing but a blur. "You saved my life by stopping that bleeding."

"You're just saying that because you still have your leg."

"Am not. I was thinking it before my body caught up with my brain and woke me up. At least I'm alive. Thank goodness we all are."

"I wouldn't argue with her, or she'll get angry." Lexi bent over the bed. "Hey, Brody. Do you want to come with me to get Remi something to drink? Maybe even a little something to eat? Just a little so we can see how she tolerates it."

"Can we get her ice cream?" Brody perked up at the idea. "Hey. Can we get *me* some ice cream, too?"

"You bet. You've earned it." She helped him off the bed before leaning over to kiss my forehead. "I'm glad you're alive. Now stop scaring the chiz out of me."

"I'm glad I'm alive, too." I squeezed her hand before looking at Brody. "I don't know what this hospital has, but my favorite is strawberry ice cream."

"Me too!" He hopped his way to the door. "Come on, Lexi."

"I guess we're going. We'll be back soon. Be careful with her, Colt."

"Like she's made of glass." Colt didn't let go of my hand where it lay on my leg. His other rested on my head, his thumb brushing along my temple.

"Don't go too far. She doesn't need to be spoiled." She yelped when Brody tugged her hard out of the room.

"Yes, you do." His eyes shimmered. Unlike back at the house, none of them fell. I remembered the drops of fire on his cheeks from the candlelight. "How could you think I'd leave you and take Brody?"

"How could you think I could have carried him out of there?" My voice shook as much as my hand when I reached out to touch his cheek. "Thank you for doing everything in your power to save me. To save him."

"I'm just glad you're still with us in one piece."

"It can't really still be there. I can't believe it." I pulled aside the blanket to take in my leg. They had bandaged it and propped it on a pillow. "I thought it was a goner."

"Dr. Cross is one of the best surgeons for veins and things. Just ask her. She's more than happy to tell anyone who does."

I chuckled softly. "Veins and things?"

"Yeah."

"Cardiovascular surgeon?"

He shrugged, with a playful lift at the corner of his lips. "That's what I said."

My laughter burst free, and I smacked his arm. "You're a putz."

"Yeah, but you love me." He flushed when the words came out of his mouth. "I mean. No, I'm sorry. I shouldn't have said that."

"But I do. I told you so."

He searched my eyes for a long time. "I didn't think you'd remember."

"I'm surprised I remember as much as I do. Come here." I patted the bed beside me in the spot where Brody had lain.

"I don't want to hurt you."

"That's why I said come over here, not sit there." I squeezed his hand. "I don't want you towering over me with sad puppy-dog eyes. Put down the side of the bed so you can get closer."

He glanced down at where our hands remained clasped together. With some reluctance, he released my hand, then did as I asked. With a little instruction on how to get the arm of the bed down, he pulled the chair right up close. Once again, he folded my hand into both of his. He kissed the back of mine gently.

"That was a terrible time to tell me." I smiled at his guilty grimace. "It almost felt like a goodbye. Although I wasn't sure who you were convinced was going to die."

"Me." He took a ragged breath. "I led you into that nightmare. It's all my fault."

"Shh. I already told you it isn't. It's his." I wanted nothing more than to pull him closer, but he was too far away and I was too weak. "You were focused on Brody. That's what you're supposed to do. It's part of why I love you."

His gaze lifted to mine, watery and intense. He rushed up so fast, I gasped. Even though he'd caught me off guard, I welcomed the kiss. My entire body relaxed under the familiar sensation. After a moment he slowed, and then eased away. His eyes focused on mine. "Sorry."

"Never apologize for kissing me."

"Just hearing you say it means so much." He brushed a kiss across my lips gently. "I love you, too."

"It's still shit timing of us, isn't it? All this love and nothing we can do about it."

Finally, he laughed softly. "That can wait. What matters is that you're alright. The second you fell through that floor, I realized what a mistake I'd made. How much it would kill me to lose you, too. I should have made you stay at the vehicle."

"Made me? Pfft. I'd like to see you try."

His brow rose as he looked pointedly at my leg. "You couldn't stop a fly right now."

"Fair." I sighed heavily, looking at the leg for a long minute. A new realization struck me. "Well, crap."

"What?"

"It looks like I moved out of Gigi's too soon. I won't be able to get around my place with a leg like this." I gestured emphatically at the wounded limb. "I'm helpless."

"First, you're not helpless. Second, about that getting around thing."

"What?"

"Well. Brody sort of insisted that we have to take care of you."

"Brody insisted, hm?"

"Honestly?" His lips curved into an adorably sheepish grin.

"Yes."

"He did. I just didn't argue with him. At all."

Chapter 70

Colton

I hefted the large casserole dish in front of me. The smell of the food Gigi had sent was divine. She'd offered it for our party on the strictest demand that she come by to see Remi the next day. I knew Remi wouldn't mind the visit, so I'd agreed.

Of course, I would have agreed to anything to get this dish as part of our dinner. I left my car in front of the house, where I technically wasn't supposed to park, so I could carry it inside. I didn't plan on staying long; I had somewhere important to be.

The door to Remi's quaint house flew open before I could knock. There was no one in my line of sight, so I peeked over the edge of the casserole dish I held to find out who'd opened it. It was no surprise to find Brody beaming at me. "Did you bring her?"

"No, son. Not yet." I rearranged my hold on the dish to ruffle his hair on my way through the door. Streamers covered so much of the living room ceiling I could hardly see any of the drywall. Over the table in the dining area hung a huge 'Welcome Home' banner. "I brought Gigi's famous chicken and dumpling casserole to be thrown in the oven."

"Oh my goddess, she's an absolute angel." Lexi grabbed the dish right out of my hands, lifting the foil to peek inside. "I haven't had this in ages."

"Maybe you should visit more often." I nudged her shoulder before scooping up Brody. He laughed as I lifted him high enough to bat the streamers. Laughter and music spilled from the kitchen. "What's going on in there?"

"Nova, Moorely, and Prairie are having a pre-party warmup." Lexi led me into the kitchen. "While Nova is baking, of course."

"I could have done this all at the bakery, but half the fun of baking for family is being with said family. Although we are missing a very important part of this celebration." Nova scooped chocolate batter into a cupcake pan. "When is Remi getting out of there again?"

"I'm going to pick her up now. I just stopped by to drop off the casserole. Where are the guys?" I glanced at Brody. "Did you scare them off?"

"Moorely did. She yelled like this." Brody shaped his fingers into claws and bared his teeth. He added in a snarl for good measure.

"I did *not*. I told them to leave is all." Moorely's cheeks darkened. "They were in the way, and Briggs was being so annoying and intentionally getting in my way. I told them to get out of here and get some more supplies before I cut them with the butcher knife I was using to cut fruit."

"What you're saying is Brody wasn't too far off?" I smirked at her huff of annoyance. "And why, may I ask, were you cutting fruit with a butcher knife?"

"I just told you. Briggs was being annoying."

"That's the third time this summer Briggs has been in town. That's a new record."

"Don't remind me." Moorely's blush deepened as she punched at the dough in front of her. She spun it and punched it again. "The jerk disappeared for five fricking years and now we can't get rid of the jerk."

"Mo, stop! My dough." Nova pushed her away from the dough she'd been abusing. She adjusted it carefully, patting it for good measure. "I told you to use a gentle touch. We don't want this dough tough. We want flakey. Flakey."

"Sorry. You know I suck at baking." Moorely wiped her hands on a towel. "Anyway, they should be back any minute. We'll have this place ready and decorated for her by the time you get back from the hospital."

"It's already pretty decorated. What else is there going to be to do?"

"Don't you worry about it." Lexi urged me out of the kitchen. She scooped Brody right out of my arms. "You've got nothing to worry about here. We'll take care of everything."

"Fine, fine." I held up my hands in surrender, backing the rest of the way out of the kitchen. "I'm going, I'm going. We'll be back in thirty minutes, maybe forty-five. I'll let you know if we'll be any later."

"Remember." Brody pointed a finger at me, his face pursed into a stern frown. "No telling. It's a secret."

"I promise."

Over the week and a half Remi had been in the hospital, every one of our friends had rallied around to make everything easier on her, Brody, and me. They'd also taken it upon themselves to get Brody and me settled in at Remi's, which we planned to occupy during her recovery. Maybe longer if things went well.

She'd tried to insist it was too much to ask, uprooting Brody from his home. The thing was, it was Brody's idea. Honestly, I think part of it was still being afraid because the first time he'd seen Bryce had been in his bedroom window.

After we'd completed the move and had a better timeline of when Remi would be home, Brody had the brilliant idea to give her a surprise welcome home party. Prairie and Nova were there when he suggested it, and that was the end of any protest I could've made. They were too into the idea to be stopped. Clearly, they'd had fun with the decorating. It was going to take forever to clean up the mess.

For Remi, it was worth it.

Remi had months of physical therapy ahead of her, and possibly more surgery if the bullet fragment they'd had to leave in caused problems. Lexi told me that during her operation she'd died on the table a couple of times. Between the blood loss, shock, and trauma, it was beyond lucky that she'd lived.

As it was, her ribs were still healing from the CPR, and her leg was in pain. I doubted she'd last long at this epic party her friends had planned. She'd be far too tired to enjoy it, but would likely force it for Brody's sake.

I think all of them were determined to let Remi and Brody both know they weren't alone, and wouldn't be alone. It was sweet of them, if overwhelming.

As for us, and our healing, I'd already scheduled therapy appointments for Brody and myself to deal with the trauma of the past few weeks. As resilient as kids might be, I also knew too well how much trauma at a young age could affect a person. My siblings and I all had our own idiosyncrasies from ours. This whole thing had brought mine back up in spades, and probably theirs, too. I couldn't tell them to help themselves, but I could help Brody and me. And Remi, if she'd let me. Lexi told me privately during the past week that Remi had never sought therapy after what had happened to her in Orlando. She might be more resistant to getting some help, but I'd support her either way.

At the hospital, I peeked into the room to find Remi already in a wheelchair. Her right leg bobbed rapidly, hard enough to make the chair click with each bump. I was pretty sure she was biting her nails, but she whipped them away from her mouth as soon as she saw me. She offered a timid smile. "Hey."

"Are you ready to go home?"

"Honestly?"

"Please."

"I don't know. I'm eager to get the hell out of here, but..." Her gaze drifted toward the mountains beyond her window.

"It's scary to go out there again."

"Yeah. I know it's in my head. I know he's dead. But it's a lot."

I crouched in front of the chair, setting my hand on her good leg. "It is a lot. That's for sure. Honestly, Brody is still sleeping with me. Speaking of, if we share a bed, expect that."

A flush spread across her cheeks. The timid smile relaxed. The tension she carried settled just a little bit. "I told you, neither of you needs to stay with me. You have your own mess to deal with. Brody went through a lot, too."

"That's why we need each other." I pursed my lips. "Besides, Gunner already took it upon himself to build you a ramp into the house."

"He did what?" Her brows pinched adorably close together. It took some effort not to smooth it out with my fingers, or with a kiss. "Is he any good at carpentry, or should I be concerned for my safety?"

"I hate to admit it, but he's shockingly good at it. Most of the modifications to his house were done by him." I shrugged. "He enjoys being sheriff. Carpentry is his escape. He can really take his aggression out safely with a hammer."

"Maybe he's onto something. I wouldn't mind busting a few things sometimes."

"If you tell him that, I'll bet he'd oblige." I took her hands in mine. "We've discussed this at length. We're staying at your house to help you out. Not only did Brody insist, but I honestly think he's afraid to go back to his own room at our house right now. Just because we're doing this doesn't mean I expect it to be permanent or for anything to happen, especially with you still healing. This is all at your pace. We both have some things we need to deal with mentally."

"Are you calling us mental?"

"A little bit." I pinched my fingers close, then spread them wider. "Or maybe a lot?"

She used her own fingers to push them about an inch apart. "Somewhere in the middle."

"That's fair."

"Lexi's going to hassle me about going to therapy again after this."

"Don't be mad, but I think she's right. I'm going to start next week. So is Brody."

"No more delusional enlightenment?"

"Oh no. We'll always have that."

Chapter 71

Remington

The unexpected party took a lot out of me. I felt infinitely grateful not only for the party and the friends who organized everything, but I was exhausted. Brody was too, if the way he dozed in the chair with his head on the picnic table was any indication.

Thankfully, the party seemed to be winding down. Almost everyone was in the backyard sitting by the firepit. I'd come outside with them, but I was too tired to put much effort into partaking in the conversation. Colt eyed me, then Brody. He leaned close. "Let's get you to bed."

"Take care of Brody first. That will give me time to say my thanks and good nights."

"Are you sure?"

I squeezed his hand, dredging up a tired smile. "Take care of your son. I'm not really going anywhere right now without help."

"I mean, you could. You're capable of more than you think you are."

"Flattery will get you nowhere, tired as I am."

He chuckled low, brushing his lips across mine in a gentle kiss. "I'll be back in a few."

"Okay." It was kind of embarrassing how content I was knowing he and Brody would be around for a few weeks at least. I'd dreaded the idea of being on my own and trying to manage. I also hadn't treasured the idea of going back to Gigi's. One could only lean on someone's kindness for so long.

"Hey, girlie." Lexi plopped into the seat Colt had abandoned. "You look ready to crash."

"I very much am. I'm surprised I haven't already fallen asleep." It took some effort to suppress a yawn. "Colt's coming back for me soon. Listen."

"Don't lecture me. I'm the one who's supposed to be lecturing you."

I leaned closer to keep our conversation as quiet as possible, even though everyone else was engaged in their own conversations. "You've been here far too long. Weeks. You should go home. Violet needs you."

"Violet is having the time of her life sharing her vacation with Rylee and her family. If I go home now, I'll ruin it for her. They just got to Disney a couple of days ago." Tears shimmered in her eyes. "I'm going home in two days. I want to make sure you're settled in, and then I'll be joining Violet at Disney. First, I need a vacation from this, and then I need to look for another job. I've been gone too long to believe it's still there."

"I mean, there *is* still a nursing shortage." My snort made me wince when my ribs smarted. "Oh. Ow."

"On that note. Hey, guys? Remi's going to crash soon." Lex got everyone's attention. "Let's say our goodnights."

"You don't have to leave. I could sleep through a hurricane at this point. Please stay and keep Lex company." I got to my feet. It wasn't like I was entirely helpless, but it hurt to stand for too long.

Briggs and Aspen were the first to reach me. Both shook their heads, and Briggs gently pushed me back down. "You take it easy. When I come back for Founders' Day, I expect to see you recovered."

"That's almost three months away. I'd better be." My laughter came easily. I'd only met Briggs a few times since he lived in Chicago playing professional hockey, but I'd liked him instantly. It seemed everyone did, even Moorely despite her claims to find him annoying.

"Agreed. So don't overdo it. Follow your PT." He pointed at me. His good-natured grin countered the stern furrow of his brow. "A good trainer means everything for injury recovery."

I gave him a mock salute. "Yes, sir. I'm glad we got to meet this summer, but after that mini-lecture, maybe I'm glad your training season is starting soon."

"Oh, ouch." He clasped his hand over his heart.

"Drama queen." Aspen pushed him back toward the fire. "Get some rest, Remi. Sorry if my sister's idea of a good time caused you any distress."

"I loved the party; I'm just too tired to love it for too long. In a few weeks, I'll be up for more. You go on having fun, though."

"Will do." He jogged back to his friend's side, where the pair immediately started joking around.

The planners of this great party were next to come up to say good night. I took each of their hands, grinning at them. "Lex told me this was a great town, but not what incredible friends I'd find here. Thanks for arranging this for me."

Nova waved me off. "I like any excuse to try a new recipe."

"Chocolate chili with blackberry frosting was amazing. I'd add it to the roster."

"The bailey's custard filling really took it to the next level."

"I agree wholeheartedly. That filling was amazing." I turned to Moorely. "And your decorations were over the top extreme. I *loved* them."

"See, Lexi? I told you she'd love them." Moorely winked at me. "Or she just loves that she isn't the one that's going to be cleaning it up."

"Maybe a little of both." It was true. I was glad I wouldn't have to clean up the craziness that had become my living room. "At least something good came out of my injury. The excuse not to clean up after the party."

"Well, that and Colt staying here." Moorely winked. "Get some rest. We'll be by tomorrow to clean up. This time, it'll just be the girls, I promise."

"Thanks, it's much appreciated. I've only got a couple of days left with Lex." I was grateful for the darkness to hide my blush at the mention of Colt staying at my house. It was a few more minutes of goodbyes with them before Gunner approached.

He gave me a grin so similar to his brother's, I couldn't help but return it. It seemed so strange to think that at our first meeting I hadn't liked Gunner one bit. He'd grown on me and shown a different side to himself when not in a place he felt he had to flaunt his handsomeness. "West and

Prairie said you needed rest more than you needed goodbyes. We'll all come by in a couple of days as a family to say what needs said."

"They could have said goodbye. I'm not that tired."

"Yes, you are." Colt's hands settled on my shoulders. "We'll head out to the ranch in a couple of days for a big family dinner. You can tell them yourself you weren't tired if you prove me wrong and stay up longer than five minutes after you lie down."

"Well, that's just not fair. You know I won't last." I tilted my head back to look at him. I offered a small smile. "It proves nothing. That doesn't mean they can't say goodbye."

Colt kissed my forehead gently. His thumb brushed along my jawline. "The party wore you out. You've got circles under your eyes."

"He's right. You look terrible." Gunner's grin returned to the familiar, annoying, wicked one. "Just awful, really."

"Shut your mouth, you jerk." Lexi pushed him backward, still laughing. "Only I'm allowed to say such horribly honest things to her. Get out of here."

Both Colt and I laughed at the tussle that ensued between the two of them. Colt turned my chair around before I could protest, wheeling me toward the door. "Those two are quite a pair. Gunner won't admit it, but he misses her. They were best friends throughout high school and beyond. He was mad when she moved out of state."

"Is that when his catting around got so bad? Lex never hinted that it was bad, only that he preferred to date tourists occasionally."

"Now that you mention it, yeah. I think it was. She kept him in line." He stopped the wheelchair beside my bed. "I think we were all surprised they never got together. Even more surprised when she announced she was moving to Florida."

"I'm sure she had her reasons." In fact, I knew she did. I hadn't ever suspected the true reason until coming here myself. It was Lexi's choice to keep whatever she wanted to herself. "If it helps, she's done well for herself in Florida. I know she misses home, though."

"Maybe she'll come back one day." He helped me over to the bed when my leg wobbled on standing. "Not tired?"

"Shut up." I eased onto the bed slowly. The moment I did, the aches in my body made themselves known. "Now I hurt."

"I should have made you come in earlier."

"Made me?"

"Asked you with strong intention?"

"Better." I chuckled softly. "Fine. I'm tired. You go enjoy the rest of the party. I'm going to sleep. After I take some medicine."

"Lexi can enjoy the rest of the party. I've had enough." He got my pills and a glass of water from the bathroom. "Here you go. This is everything the doctor ordered."

"Ugh. I hate pain medication." I tossed back the pills with a sip of water. While he fussed about the room, asked where my pajamas were and got everything ready so I could sleep, a rising sense of worry tangled my stomach in knots. I hadn't been alone for more than a couple of minutes since the attack. "Will you stay?"

"I planned on staying. That's why Brody and I are here."

"I mean in here." I swallowed against the lump of panic when he paused. "No, sorry. I know you need to be with Brody."

"Remington." He took my hands in his. "Brody is right next door. I was just surprised you asked."

"Brody needs you, too. I'm being selfish."

"Remi. Listen."

"Daddy? Remi?" Brody stood in the doorway, rubbing his eyes. "Can I stay in here?"

Colt sat on the bed next to me, holding out his arms to his son. "Bad dream again, buddy?"

"No. I just wanna stay here." Brody climbed up next to Colt, but then curled up near me. "Don't want Remi lonely."

"Of course you can stay." I couldn't have said anything else, as cute as he was being, and how sweet it was that he was worried about me. "Maybe we'll stay here, and your daddy could stay in the other room."

Colt actually stuck out his lip in the most pitiful pout at my suggestion. Brody nodded sleepily. "Yeah. Night, Daddy."

I chuckled, winking at Colt. "You heard him."

"You're not serious?"

"Of course I'm not."

Chapter 72

Colton

In a month's time, Remi made significant progress. She was already walking with a cane. The physical therapy, and her adherence to it, had done wonders. I had to admit, this month at her place had been pretty damn great. After a couple of days of figuring out a rhythm, especially considering Remi's injuries, we fell into an easy routine. I returned to work, and there'd been a slew of help to check on Brody and Remi when I did.

I knew she was eager to return to work as well, but physically she wasn't ready. It turned out Remi wasn't very good at being patient. She was restless, but found things to do to keep her occupied most of the time. It helped that she and Brody had become really close. As much as I'd loved seeing them together before all of this, it was even better now.

It was going to be tough on Brody when it was time to leave. Hell, it would kill me. I didn't miss our house in the settlement at all. Remi's place was homey, especially after we replaced the uncomfortable sofa with something we could enjoy.

Then there was the matter of the kittens, who only knew this house, and were pretty deeply bonded at this point. I didn't know how we'd separate them if it came down to that. We were going to have to sit down and have a talk soon. I know Brody and I didn't want to leave, but it was Remi's house and her decision.

Brody started therapy, and so did I. Remi finally agreed she'd start as well once her physical therapy lightened up. I didn't blame her. The physical therapy sessions took a lot out of her. Determined as she was to improve, she'd had to receive scoldings from her PT for pushing too hard. So, being physically exhausted from her physical dealings was one thing. Adding in therapy would also take a lot out of her, if my sessions were any indication.

I'd just left one, in fact. My brain throbbed with some of my thoughts, but I expected that after the past few sessions. There was a lot to unpack with the renewed feelings from the past that I thought I'd already dealt with.

I'd made peace with the detective's determination that Darlene wasn't involved in what Bryce had been up to. That didn't mean I wanted anything to do with her, but I was learning to relegate my feelings to matters of the past. Thankfully, the text messages had stopped when everything went to hell. That's what she'd always been good at—disappearing in times of trouble. It was weirdly comforting to know that some things stayed consistent.

I pulled my car into Remi's driveway, way back behind her house. The distance was tough for Remi when she had to go somewhere. At least the walkway was covered and protected from storms. As I walked past the small stable, the first strains of music hit my ear. The closer I got to the back door, the louder they got. Remi and Brody's voices both carried loudly over the artist. They were having a great time, from the sound of it. I slowed my pace and eased to the back door to peek into the kitchen.

Brody danced and spun around the room, singing loudly and off-key into a wooden spoon. Remi's moves were more subtle, more confined to a small area. Her voice hit every note perfectly, unless she interrupted herself with a laugh over a dance move Brody pulled. When he got close, she took his extended hand and let him spin around her.

I pushed open the door when she spotted me. "Did you guys decide to have a party without me? That's not very nice."

"Daddy, go!" Brody rushed forward to push on my legs. "We're not ready."

"Ready for what?" I clasped his wrists, looking to Remi for help. "What's going on?"

Remi turned the volume down on the virtual assistant until she didn't have to yell. "Brody. It's okay. If he wants to help us, he can."

Brody turned his back to me, bracing his feet to push against me. "But it's for him."

"Brody." Remi's voice took on a warm sing-song effect. "I bet he'd enjoy helping make the cake with us. Besides, we can give him the tough job of frosting it."

"Cake?" I scooped Brody into my arms, resting him against my hip. "What's the occasion?"

"Remi wants us to stay!" Brody bounced in my arms, but then clapped his hands over his mouth. His eyes widened comically. "Oh, no."

A blush swept up Remi's neck to her cheeks. "Well, we were going to discuss it over dinner, but since Brody spilled the beans."

"Remington? Are you sure?" I moved closer. Hope bloomed brightly in my chest, and I knew it spread to my face with a wide smile I couldn't contain. "I mean, I've had the best time living here, but I want you to be sure. We've only known each other for a few months. I'd understand if you weren't ready."

"When you've been through intense experiences, it sort of speeds up the bonding process. Besides, Brody and I have been having fun this past month. And since you come as part of the deal, I guess that means you can stay, too." Her lips twitched in a feeble attempt to hide her smile.

"Honestly? I was dreading the day we were supposed to leave." Kissing her temple, I pulled her to my other side. "I'm in."

"Are you sure? You have a house of your own."

"I've been trying to encourage Prairie to move in and out of the apartment building. She can save money on rent, since the mortgage is less than what she's paying. If she agrees. She said something about me being a loser that never put in a pool."

"Loser? That doesn't sound like her. Stick in the mud? That I can see." She leaned into me with a warm smile. "And that tells me you were thinking about staying here too, if you were already making plans."

"Apparently so were you and Brody." I set Brody on the counter, placing one hand on either side of him. With his wiggling and grinning, it was hard to keep a somewhat stern expression in place. "Are you sure you're ready to stay here?"

"Uh-huh. And that's not all." He clapped his hands and let them rain down like fireworks. "Remi, tell him."

Remi's brows twitched, and she grimaced. "Let's just say Brody is convincing enough. West and Brody together could get state secrets out of the leader of North Korea."

Unease settled in my gut. I had a feeling I knew where this was going. "What did they convince you to do?"

"Well. There's a foster horse that can't be with the others on the ranch yet, and West's solitary pens are already being used. Since we have the old barn by the garage and a small paddock, I said he could keep her here." Remi flashed her teeth in a hesitant smile. "But I'm not exactly ready to take care of her by myself yet."

"Oh, I see. You don't want me to move in because you want me to move in. You want us to stay so I can care for West's rescue."

"No, that's just an added bonus." Her smile softened. "I want you to stay because I love you, and Brody, and I've loved this month. Having you take care of the horse is cake."

"Cake! Let's finish making it." Brody smooshed my face in his hands before I could kiss Remi. "You aren't good at baking. Listen to Remi."

"Yes, sir," I mumbled through my smooshed cheeks. When he tried to scramble down, I let him so I could pull Remi closer. "Well, if it's because you love me, then I definitely want to stay here. This last month has been really great."

"Agreed. So we're doing this?"

"We are."

"Delusional enlightenment will make it possible?"

"No. Just love."

Her smile broadened. "That's even better."

"I love you, Remington."

"I love you, too, Colton."

"Me too!" White powder rained down on us. Brody stood on the kitchen island, fistfuls of flour in each hand. "Let's make the cake!"

Remi laughed harder than I'd seen in a while, brushing flour from my cheeks. "He's going to be a handful, isn't he?"

"Always."

"Then let's get this cake made so we can settle down this evening and appreciate this momentous occasion." She turned, but before she could get far, I pulled her back. Her body easily pressed against mine. "Yes?"

"I look forward to tonight, but first." I leaned in to press a kiss to her lips. They softened under mine as her body relaxed into me. Her fingers fisted in my shirt, but she withdrew first.

"I love you. Let's finish that thought later."

"Later? But what about—"

"That's our other celebration. Physical therapy is down to twice a week, and I've been cleared for more activity, as long as I'm careful." She brushed her lips across mine.

"Are you sure you're ready?" I kept my eyes focused on hers in hopes she'd know I meant more than physically.

"Yes. Now let's get moving before we get dusted with flour again."

"One more thing." With her body already flush against mine, I couldn't resist the urge to pull her into another kiss. "I love you."

"I love you, too."

Epilogue

Remington

"Dad. Stop. Geez." Brody led his horse to the mounting steps. "I'm not five anymore."

"I know, I know. You tell me all the time." Colt's brows turned down, and I swear he full-on pouted over Brody's refusal of help. He checked and tightened all the straps on the horse.

"I know how to saddle my horse." Brody almost whined in his exasperation. "Uncle West showed me ages ago."

I had to bite my cheeks to keep my grin hidden. At just over eight-years-old, Brody seemed to be tumbling into his tweens far too quickly for either of us. He still had absolutely beautiful moments of pure sweetness, but boy howdy he did not like to be babied. I couldn't believe that a couple of years ago they'd moved in just to help me after Colt's stepfather had nearly killed me and Brody. Once here, they'd never left.

It had been two years of ups and downs, figuring out this situation of living as a family. On the days I missed my solitude, I'd go for a ride, or hole up in the library-slash-office upstairs for a while. It was never long. I missed my family too much.

My family. I didn't think I'd say it again once I cut my blood family out of my life. But first was Lexi, and now the family I'd found here in Dominion Falls. Moving here might have been a response to trauma, but it ended up being the best decision of my life.

The horse we'd taken in for West two years ago had become a permanent resident. We'd then added to it with one each for both Colt and Brody. I still worked at the hotel because I actually loved the job and the people. But after a year of therapy, I'd gone back to nursing part time on the pediatric unit at George Young Memorial. There was buzz about them adding a full pediatric wing and ER in the next few years. The Director of Nursing had asked if I'd be interested in managing it, or at least helping train the staff. I was still deciding that. The timing would be important, because I had some big plans coming along.

Today was our second anniversary of living together. Colt had something planned that involved a ride through the valley. I was barely keeping a lid on my secret that I had for him and Brody. I'd learned long ago that I couldn't tell Brody a secret and not have it shared, and this time I wanted to keep it close to the vest.

Colt turned his attention to me. "Are you ready?"

"I am, I think. You still haven't told me what we're doing." I happily accepted his help into the saddle, if only because I knew he'd slip in a kiss. He didn't disappoint.

"You'll see." Colt led his horse to the gate, opening it for Brody and me to pass through. "Let's get a move on so you can stop pestering me."

I glanced at Brody, who shrugged before letting his horse lope out of the paddock. For a split second, I could have sworn he and Colt shared a secretive grin. The whole thing happened too fast for me to be sure.

We rode for almost an hour. I'd figured out pretty quickly where our final destination would be. It was our favorite spot on his family's ranch, where there was a swimming hole. He and Gunner had even built a dock out into the water to jump off into the deepest portions. Whenever the weather was warm enough, it was the first place we'd go.

As soon as we got there, Brody hopped down. He'd already taken his shirt off and was hopping on one foot to remove his shoe when both Colt and I said, "Wait a minute."

Brody let out the biggest sigh, adding an eye roll to his implication of our apparently egregious behavior. "I just want to swim."

"And you will. First, we're going to have our picnic." Colt gave Brody a pointed look.

"Right. Right. Okay." Brody grabbed the basked and trudged to the little gazebo set up near the dock.

"Oh, the teen years are going to be so much fun." Colt rubbed the back of his neck. "Shall we join the grumpy one for lunch?"

"Definitely. I'm *starving*." For the first time that day, I could've added. I didn't, but I could have. I laced my fingers with his as we headed to the gazebo where Brody already had most of our lunch laid out. "This looks amazing."

"Okay. I'll see you guys later. I'm gonna swim."

"Wait a minute." I set my hand on my hip. "I thought this was a day for us?"

"Dad wants to be gross, so I'm out."

"Wait a minute." I let out a sigh when Brody groaned and rolled his eyes. He meant Colt wanted to show affection, but it was important for us all to be there. "I want you here, please. I've got something important I wanted to talk to you both about."

"You have news?" Colt held me close, searching my eyes. "But I had something I wanted to talk about today, too. That's the point of this."

"Then we can kill two birds with one stone. Come on, Brody. Join us. I promise we won't be gross until you're gone."

"I doubt that." Brody trudged back, plopping onto the bench. "So, what is it?"

"It's an inauspicious start, but fine. I wanted to—"

"I'd like to go first. And I wanted Brody here, so thank you for insisting." Colt gave a small nod to Brody.

As much as I wanted to tell them my news, Colt looked too excited for me to argue. To that matter, Brody was doing his best, but he couldn't hide his own smile. "Fine. You can go first."

"Thank you." He took my hands in his before dropping to his knee. My heart leaped into my throat, cutting off any reaction I could have made.

"Remington Sage Collier, Brody and I have loved having you come into our lives. You've made our lives fuller, happier."

"And funner." Brody grinned. "You let us have food fights and suggest trips to Disney."

I let loose my laughter, winking at Brody. "I thought you didn't want part of this."

"Eh. As long as I'm here and all."

Colt cleared his throat. "Excuse me, I was saying something."

"Right. Of course." I nodded to him. "Go on."

"He wants to know if you'll marry him. Us. Make it official and stuff."

"Brody!"

Laughter bubbled free. Brody's input truly lightened the whole situation. "Well, Brody. Who do I answer?"

"Me. Of course." Brody lifted his chin with a grin.

"What about him?" I nudged my head toward Colt. Colt groaned, his head resting on the back of my hands.

"He can hear it, I guess."

"Right. Before I answer, there's something I have to tell you both." Colt's hands tightened around mine, his head lifting. There was concern darkening his eyes. "Relax. I didn't say no. I wanted to tell you something first, and then we can decide."

"What?" Colt searched my eyes.

"Brody is going to be a big brother."

Colt flew to his feet, hope making his eyes dance. "Really?"

Brody jumped onto the bench at the same time. "I am?"

"Yes, really." I yelped when Colt grabbed me around the waist and spun me around. The second my feet touched the ground, Brody nearly tackled me. "Oof. I guess you're okay with having a little brother or sister, then?"

"Yeah!"

I looked up at Colt, one arm still around his neck while my other kept Brody close. "What do you think?"

"I think you've made us both happier than we could have imagined."

"Then my answer is yes. I'd like to make this official and stuff."

Brody cheered and whooped.

Colt pulled me close. "I love you, Remington."

"And I love you, Colton."

The End

Coming in 2026:

Sweet Sunset Serenade

Novalee June Young's Story

About the Author

Sarah Cass weaves heartfelt stories with heat, mystery, and magic. A nurse by day and author by passion, she balances life with her husband, four kids (counting her daughter-in-law), and six rescue cats. Her creative spirit extends beyond writing— she crochets, knits, makes jewelry, and bookmarks, all while binge-watching *Grey's Anatomy*, *Star Trek*, and *Friends* on repeat. Sarah has published novels across multiple genres, including:

- *The Dominion Falls Series* – a spicy historical western mystery with 10 novels, 2 novellas, and more on the way.
- *Holidays in Lake Point* – sweet, small-town contemporary love stories with interwoven characters.
- *The Tribe Series* – an urban fantasy/paranormal romance full of shifters, secrets, and supernatural suspense.

Raised between Buffalo, NY and Ontario, she's lived in six states and currently resides in Florida—with dreams of Colorado skies. Her upcoming series, *Dark Sky Valley*, revisits the Dominion Falls world 150 years later in a modern spicy western romance full of action and desire.

Her stories reflect her author tagline: **"Labyrinths of the Heart, Nightmares of the Soul."**

www.ingramcontent.com/pod-product-compliance
Lightning Source LLC
Chambersburg PA
CBHW030541020726
47494CB00005B/1446